Praise for Vaughn R. Demont's
Lightning Rod

"An amazing book—inventive in its magic, gritty in its urban setting, winning and funny in its very likable hero...a mixture of adventure, comedy, and deep emotion...stays with you long after you've read it."
~ *Rachel Pollack, World Fantasy Award winner*

"...the intensity and adrenaline of the opening stayed with me...funny...emotionally wrenching... Did I enjoy *Lightning Rod*? That's a yes."
~ *Dear Author*

"Here there are entertaining set pieces, genuinely thoughtful ideas and some great characters...a self consciously smart book."
~ *Reviews by Jessewave*

"Vaughn R. Demont has created an absorbing and enjoyable fantasy with an unexpected finale."
~ *Literary Nymphs Reviews*

Look for these titles by
Vaughn R. Demont

Now Available:

House of Stone

Broken Mirrors
Coyote's Creed
Lightning Rod
Community Service

Lightning Rod

Vaughn R. Demont

SAMHAIN

PUBLISHING

Samhain Publishing, Ltd.
11821 Mason Montgomery Road, 4B
Cincinnati, OH 45249
www.samhainpublishing.com

Lightning Rod
Copyright © 2013 by Vaughn R. Demont
Print ISBN: 978-1-61921-414-9
Digital ISBN: 978-1-61921-084-4

Editing by Anne Scott
Cover by Angela Waters

First Samhain Publishing, Ltd. electronic publication: October 2012
First Samhain Publishing, Ltd. print publication: December 2013

Acknowledgments

My most heartfelt thanks and gratitude go first to my amazing editor, Anne Scott, who I believe is the only person to have read this manuscript more than I have. My deepest appreciation also goes out to my steadfast beta readers Pam, Dave, Kim, Scott G., Chris H., Nicky, Debra, Harmony, Mike W., and ID Locke, but most especially to Chris S. Thanks for sticking with me. Thanks to Dr. Curtin for telling me it was wrong. Thanks also to Tool, Rise Against, and Muse, for without their music James would just be another guy on the street. And finally, my eternal gratitude to my readers, things are only just getting started.

Dedication

For Rachel Pollack, who helped me chase the dream.

Part I

Abdication

Chapter One

May

I have two modes reserved for post-sex. Conversational and scared rabbit.

When Heath finished with a grunt and an almost laugh of relief mixed with bliss, I let him fall asleep and focused my eyes on the bedroom door until his breathing grew rhythmic and I could hear the rough snerk of a snore.

Scared rabbit.

He was quiet this time, every other time he's vocal. I'm not exhausted, another change. Usually I'm out, drained by the time he's finished, but tonight I can't sleep. I'm wide awake, aware, and I don't want to spend the next couple hours in his arms while I wait to fade out.

There's a definite art to slipping out of bed. I have to move slowly, keep my muscles flexed, use the nightstand to support myself and prevent any excess noise. You would think that the most efficient method would be feet first, but it's not. Eventually you have to literally move your arse (sorry, ass) and that causes a lot of creaking unless it's a really nice mattress, and we don't have one of those. So it's face-first for me.

I use my hands to ease myself down and forward, trying not to squirm at the dusty, dingy feel of the floor, until I'm able to swing my right leg over and touch the cold hardwood. After that it's a simple matter of getting my other leg over, standing up, stepping lightly, and retrieving my clothes from the pile near the door.

As I stop in the doorway, the frame littered with red markings Heath painted when we first moved in, I look back at the bed, seeing him sleeping there, a few inches taller than I, brown hair shorn close to his skull. He took most of the blankets in his sleep, but I can handle it, since the mid-May weather is keeping the flat warm.

Apartment. Not flat. Apartment. He's talked to you about this.

The apartment is a shoebox, to put it lightly. The main room consists of a small table with two chairs next to a window that could only be opened with a brick. There's also a combination sink/stove with a few Tupperware containers in a stack next to it, all of them holding dry goods. Heath says if I gave him more we'd be living in a condo in Allora by now, but I don't know what else I can do. I'm living on ramen, I quit smoking, I even started hopping turnstiles to save on subway tokens. I don't know what else I can shave back.

I exit the apartment as softly and carefully as I can, leave the door unlocked behind me because I can hardly redo the chain from the other side. Once out the door, I trot down the dimly lit hallway to the communal bathroom at the end of it, still naked, my T-shirt, hoodie, jeans and underwear bundled under one arm and my beat-up Chuck Taylors, the socks stuffed deep in my shoes and probably stiff from sweat, under the other. My St. Jude medallion is around my neck. I don't take that off. He lost his St. Anthony medal. I'm not allowed to think that's ironic or funny. I haven't been to Mass since we met. Heath's been playing around with atheism, but I think he's more comfortable with just hating God. Sometimes I envy him for that.

I just wish things could be like they were in the beginning.

Once in the bathroom, I close the door behind me, pull the chain attached to the dangling light bulb overhead, and set to getting dressed. The floor is dirty, cream-colored tile, the toilet's seat is barely attached, there's a sink with a cracked mirror over it and a shower stall with plenty of mold inside.

After getting dressed, I look in the mirror, smooth out my hair and brush back some stringy red locks. Irish red, that's the shade he calls it, it's one of his little jokes, the other being that I see dead people due to the white streak in my bangs. I don't. I also don't have an accent. Well, I do occasionally, but it's more Oxford than Dublin. I only slip into it by accident and he's never really liked when I—

What's wrong with my face?

That...

That can't be me.

But the guy in the mirror, his right eye is nearly closed, puffy, the skin mottled with dark colors, his lips are fat, cracked, teeth stained with dried blood.

I mean, he's... But he's never...

Not *that* hard...

It was just a stupid fight, and it was my fault anyway. I mean, I snuck one of his smokes (one of the ones he rolls himself) but I was having a rough day but I *knew* they were his and I should've bought my own but my legs were sore and...

And I just shouldn't have pissed him off. I know he has a temper and he can get a little...

I stare into the mirror, meet my dirty green eyes, see the bruises on my cheek visible under the dusting of stubble. I look at my forearms, weak and lanky, at the dark finger-shaped marks there.

"I don't want to be here anymore."

If I run, though, he'll...

But if I don't come back, he can't. He'll be mad, but he's always angry about money, and if I'm gone he won't be spending as much.

I slip back into the room, stepping slow and easy. He's still asleep, but I'm trembling. I'd wake him up if I slid back into bed, and he might be mad, he might...

My eyes adjust quickly to the dark room, the only light indirect from streetlamps. I need something to protect myself, if he...

Keep it together. Just get something sharp.

The silverware would be too noisy, that would wake him up. He has a small blade though, for opening the post, I mean the mail. It's on the counter, half of a broken set of scissors, something he picked up before we met. It's junk, so he won't miss it. I slip it into the large front pocket of my hoodie.

If I'm going to do this, I have to go.

Now.

I pull up my hood and leave the flat, walking as slow as I can down the hallway toward the stairs, prefacing every step with a silent prayer, my thumb and index finger gently rubbing my medallion. No creaks. First part's over. The walls are yellowed, chipped paint, trash on the steps. It's a slum just barely inside the Benedict on 82ⁿᵈ and M. We're on the fourth floor, I mean fifth. Walk-up. Cheaper than the dorms.

Dad will understand, right? Shit, I'm going to have to tell him. I doubt he'll start quoting Leviticus, he's not as Catholic as Mom is. Still, should I call?

No, no, get out of the building first, that's the priority. Heath could wake up at any moment and notice I'm gone. Get some distance.

I descend the stairs, picking up speed with every flight until I leap the last six steps, the landing echoing in the ground-floor lobby, but I'm out the door before I have time to wince. I'm sore, hot, aching, but not tired. It's a cool May night, but my hoodie is stained with sweat. I reach the 80ᵗʰ and R station, my palms slapping the top of the turnstile as I vault over. There's a train pulling in, the Blue Line, heading for all points west.

Oh fuck, what am I doing? I can get back before he's noticed I'm gone, right?

What if someone saw me jump over? I'll get picked up and they'll call the flat and he'll know and I'll have to explain and there'll be a fine and we can't afford a fine—he'll get so pissed...

I get on the train, take a seat in the corner, away from the few scattered people here and there. I probably stink. I haven't washed these clothes in a while. I thrust my hands into the hoodie's pocket, mostly so people won't see me wringing them together over the broken scissor.

As the train pulls away from the station, I swear I see him there on the platform—a chill runs through my hands—but when I check again, it's empty. It's a sign, that's what it is. I'll just ride to the next station, get off, go home, and if he's awake, I'll say I went for a little walk because it was a nice night, or something like that. That's okay, right? Yeah, he shouldn't be too mad.

The train jostles slightly on the tracks, enough to make me brace against the wall, and see the sleeve of my hoodie and a metal glint in the frayed threads of the cuff. Something's tangled in there. I pull it free slowly, delicately. It's a chain, silver, a small medallion attached to...

"Fuck, fuck, fuck."

St. Anthony of Padua. Patron saint of missing things. His medallion, he was so pissed when he lost it, even though he never goes to Mass and...

And it was stuck on my clothes and...

I can't go home now.

No one pays me much mind, but I keep my hood pulled forward, my gaze cast toward the floor. Every time the train makes a stop I tense, knowing I should check the doors to see if he's there, but if he does get on, he'll see me if I look up, so hell with that. What am I going to do?

What am I going to do?

This is how it goes for several more stops, until I feel a hand nudge my shoulder, a male voice telling me we've reached the end of the line. It's not him, but when I look up the man has already moved down the aisle toward the door. I only see the back of his head, but his hair looks dyed, badly, in brown, black, blond and gray. I want to ask him where we are, but a glance out the window answers the question.

Victory Station.

It's a hub for the United Transit Authority, or UTA, as well as the bus station, built under Victory Tower, tallest building in the state. If I'm going to carry this all the way, this is the place to do it. I can buy a bus ticket going, well, anywhere but here.

It takes an hour of wandering around to work up the nerve to get in queue for the ticket booth. I keep my eyes on my feet, shuffling forward when I see the feet in front of me move. Before long I'm in front of the window, the woman behind the glass taking a look at me and immediately casting her eyes downward. I start to speak, patting my jeans for my wallet as I see the small sticker on the window reading *Identification Required for All Ticket Purchases.* Would they take my student ID? Would they...

I took the wrong jeans. My wallet's back at the apartment.

Wordlessly, I exit the queue and head toward the array of chairs in the waiting area. I can feel my throat tightening, panic creeping across my skin.

Just give it up. Time to go home and take my licks and hope it won't be too bad. Maybe things will be different if he knows I'm willing to leave. Maybe he'll treat me better. I walk to the bank of pay phones and realize that I'm still without money, and I doubt he'd take a collect call from me.

I do see a familiar face, or at least hairstyle. The man from the train is seated on the floor under the pay phones, dressed in jeans and a T-shirt. I take a deep breath and walk over to him.

"Hey, you got any quarters?" On closer examination I can see that his face is bruised, some dried blood in his eyebrow, but he doesn't seem all that concerned about it.

"Just used my last one, honestly. Nine-one-one's a free call, though. What, you get mugged?" I look away, closing my eyes, my throat feeling tight again. Damn it, don't start the waterworks, he'll hate you if you do. No one likes a crybaby. I hear him speak up. "You okay?"

After a few seconds, I shake my head, sniffling again.

He pats the floor next to him, trying to put me at ease with a smile. "Getting mugged happens, man. It sucks, I know. Been rolled a few times myself." He actually laughs. What's with this guy? "Bit of advice? Never count the day's take before you skim off the local gang's cut. You'll end up with your ass kicked and out two hundred bucks."

Great, he's a criminal. I don't see many options, though. I've been wandering around the station for an hour, Heath must've noticed that I'm gone by now. I sit on Bad Dyejob's right and pull my hood forward more. "That what happened to you?"

"Nah, this was my dad. Don't get me wrong, it's not like this is a regular thing. My brother, every time I see him he hits me, seems like." He shrugs. "I don't know, maybe he's got a pituitary problem or something, whatever kind of hormone imbalance fucks people up in the head."

Am I overreacting? Am I making a mistake? I mean, this guy is... I turn toward him. "So this happens a lot."

"Mugging, or getting smacked around? I don't know, in this city..." He reaches toward me. Fuck, I'm gonna get mugged. All I can do is wince before he touches me.

"Oh damn." He pauses a second, taking his hand away. "Listen, I didn't mean to make light of anything. I mean, if your dad is hitting you, then you need to—"

"My father doesn't hit me." Dad is a good man, and other than chasing women, God wouldn't have any problems with him. "My brothers don't either. My family isn't like yours."

And he laughs, what the hell is so funny about that?

"I hope not. I wouldn't wish my family on anyone. My mom's snapped, or she's about to, my grandfather's got a crazy ex with serious boundary issues. One half-brother belongs in jail and the other will someday be devoured by pubic lice, and hell, I'll probably end up a third-rate con artist." He smiles at me again, but this one's more sincere.

"You'll say all that to someone you don't know?"

"Stranger's confessional. We'll tell anyone anything if we think we'll never see them again."

I whisper under my breath. "There's only one person I never want to see again."

"What was that?" He leans toward me with a wink. "It was a crack about my hair, wasn't it? It's okay, think of it as a life lesson to never get drunk with a chick who thinks you'll look hot with highlights and streaks."

I don't answer, and he looks under my hood. He takes stock of the bruises and marks on my face. His voice softens. "Listen, uh, I'm sorry if I'm cracking jokes. Just what I do, you know? Be straight with me, you okay?"

What did he call it? Stranger's confessional. I wish it could be one of those things where it wouldn't be real until I admitted it, but I still feel the heat in my skin, the blurs in my vision from my swollen eye. It happened, whether I admit it or not. I look down at the floor, and I shake my head to answer him.

"You don't have to tell me any details, it's all right. Besides, uh..." I'm guessing he wasn't expecting this when he dropped into Victory Station to probably pick pockets or smuggle cocaine. "So you're leaving...her? Him?"

I can feel the tears coming. Damn it. "Him." I take a few breaths, try to keep it together. "I just... I looked in the mirror and saw..." I touch my face briefly. What am I doing? "God, I was so stupid. He's gonna be so pissed, he's—"

"Hey." He places his hand awkwardly on my forearm. "You're doing the right thing here. It's the brave thing."

Yeah, right.

"I can't go anywhere. I don't have any money, I just came here because..." My face feels wet. "I just ran out, I grabbed some clothes and ran. Everything is back there, I don't have ID, I can't get a ticket and..."

Dyejob doesn't laugh though. A few people do look but keep walking. He reaches into his pocket and takes something out.

"What's that?"

He fans out five cards at me. "Your bus ticket, or well, it will be once I find a couple fish." He looks at the passing crowd, and I notice that his eyes are golden brown, closer to golden. "I work this right I can get you bus fare to Idaho if you want in fifteen minutes."

"But what if you lose?"

He stifles a laugh as he pats my forearm gently. "You're adorable." He shows me three cards, a queen and two aces, before he starts shuffling. "I don't lose, okay? It's not pride, I know how to work the cards. More than that, I know how to work the mark. It's all about distraction, that's why we all talk and rhyme and chat up the crowd. If I can get you to take your eyes off the cards for a second, I've won." He flips the cards over, showing the same queen, but two different aces.

"How'd you..."

"Magic." He grins big, and I'll admit it's slightly infectious. He prattles on for a bit more, but I'm having trouble buying it.

"They don't know it's obvious that you're cheating?"

He laughs, good-naturedly. "Man, everyone knows I'm cheating, doesn't stop them from thinking they can beat the game anyway." He sighs, looking over at the crowd. "God, pride is a lucrative sin. Greed too. Even if they're on to you, there're ways around it. You play it straight to throw them off or you do a turnover or pull a drop..."

He stares off into space for a moment.

"Um..." I wave a hand in front of his face.

"Sorry, I uh...I just realized that I have to get out of here." He holds up his hand. "Do you know anyone in the Capital?"

"My father, well, kind of close to there, he's in the Mews." A nice suburb for the upper class.

"All right." He reaches into his pocket and takes out a bus ticket, putting it in my hand. "This is what you're going to do, okay? You get on the bus, ride it to the Capital, and when you get off, look for a black guy with bleach-blond hair wearing a motorcycle jacket. His name is Bank, tell him the cracker had to give you his exit." His fingers push my chin up, my eyes lock with his. "What are you telling him?"

"The cracker had to give me his exit?" Oh God, am I agreeing to be a drug mule? "I can't take your ticket, though—"

"Yeah, you can. Think you need a getaway more than I do."

"No, they check identification, and I don't have mine, and—"

"Relax." He takes his ID out of his wallet. "Just show the driver this when he checks the new passengers. I bought the ticket with that one, and I can always get another."

He gives it to me, and it looks a little fake, and the photo, well... "I don't really look like this."

He exhales hard, biting his lip. "I'd hate to say this, man, but right now? You don't really look like anybody." He pats my arm again, that's as far as he's willing to go. Am I the intimidating one in this exchange? "Listen, it's awful that this happened to you, but right now, as bad as this sounds, it actually works in your favor."

What? "How?"

"No one's going to pry, or ask twice. Yeah, you don't look like the picture, but given your condition, they're going to give that minefield a wide berth and let you slide. And if anyone asks from now until you get home to your dad, your name is the one on the ID, okay? Hey." He makes me look at him, and his eyes are sincere. He probably practices that, but it's working. "Hard part's over. You're going to be all right."

For better or worse, I believe him. I nod once. "Thank you. You're saving my life, you're my hero."

"Don't mention it."

"I don't even know your name."

He chuckles. "Well, seeing as I'm kinda smuggling you north, just call me a coyote. Only, y'know, without the extortion and shit." He stands, and helps me up. "Your bus is over that way, might as well get in line."

Oh my God, I'm getting out of here. I'm going to get away, all thanks to the kindness of strangers. Everything can be okay. This can really be over. I want to cry, but I'm not ashamed to this time. I hug Dyejob, my coyote, as hard as I can. He returns it, patting my back gently. After a few seconds I start across the lobby to the departure gates.

I glance back at him, and he waves, still smiling, his voice echoing across the distance. "Hey, you never told me your name either."

"It's..." I look down at the ID before smiling back at him. "James Black."

Chapter Two

The driver doesn't even ask to see my ID. One glance at my face and he punches the ticket and heads back to the front of the bus. The only seat I can find is in the back, next to the tiny bathroom door. I curl up on the bench, little visible through the window thanks to the tinting and late hour.

When the bus starts moving, I finally let myself breathe easily. I'll have to leave school a while, but considering my grades suck and that I've skipped classes a while now, I doubt my parents will take issue. Dad will be pissed, but hopefully he'll understand. Mom will get a call, no doubt. Would she fly back here for this? Mom and Dad are currently on their third separation, because divorce is a mortal sin, and have been living in separate countries off and on since four months before I was born. I lived with her, switching between Oxford and Allora until I was twelve (hence the occasional accent slippage) when I was shipped back across the pond permanently for prep school. Dad was adamant about me being home for Christmas.

My brothers (I have six, all older) will remember this incident when they're adding grist to the holiday rumor mill, but the bruises on my face will be mercifully edited out, more for their reputations than mine.

Thom, my youngest older brother, will likely track down Heath and beat the shit out of him, and in the process wreck his own career. I won't let him do that, I don't want him blaming me for anything, Thom and I are on thin enough ice as it is.

The bus is relatively silent, the overhead lights turned off once we're onto the main streets. Conversation is muffled, a few coughs, the occasional sneeze. No one's looked at me twice. I gently rub my St. Jude medallion. Sometimes your hopeless case gets picked, right? Dad said not to take it the wrong way when he gave it to me. It had gotten him through college when he never thought he'd graduate.

The bus comes to a stop. I can make out an intersection ahead. Red light, I guess. I return my attention to the scant passing people heading home from bars. The driver announces we'll be crossing over the North Bridge in about ten minutes, and then it's express service to the Capital. We'll be arriving close to four in the morning. I put my hands in my pockets, my fingers feeling cold all of a sudden.

I hear words spoken as someone sits next to me, nothing I can quite make out though. I don't make eye contact, I only see a white jacket in the periphery, and even that's a blur.

"I knew I forgot to lock the fucking door."

Oh God, no.

"So I ask around a little, and a guy sleeping in front of the building tells me he saw you tearing ass toward the Blue Line." I don't remember anyone sleeping in front of the building when I left. The bums took to the alleys after that one man froze to death last winter.

If I don't look at Heath, it won't be him. As long as he doesn't see my face, I can act like I don't know what he's talking about, that maybe he's got the wrong guy.

"So I ask myself where you'd go. What would be the stupidest decision you could make to follow an impressive string of bad decisions?" He leans into my vision, his stark gray eyes boring into mine. His voice not rising, but gaining intensity. "A *thirty-dollar* cab ride later, I get to the station just in time to see you hop on this bus. *Seventy* dollars later, I'm chasing this bus with a ticket so I can fucking get on, and what do I find? You. Where'd you get the money for this, Miles?" His hand grips my chin roughly. "You been trying shit behind my back?" I have no idea what he's talking about, but I don't want to sell out my coyote.

He shoves me against the window, my shoulder pressing hard into the glass. I shut my eyes hard, trembling, biting back the tears. They only make him madder. I don't expect anyone to do anything. Heath's told me that no one cares; I've never seen evidence to the contrary. We're all children of man, that's what he always says before he starts in on me.

"I am sick of cleaning up after you. When are you going to get it in your head, huh? Trust me, Miles, you are not getting off light this time. Next stop, we're going home. Copacetic?" He snaps a finger in front of my eyes. "Copacetic?"

I bite my lower lip hard. I nod once.

"What was that?"

"Copacetic."

"Good." He lets go of my face, grumbling. "Fucking hell. Why do you have to be so melodramatic? It's embarrassing. I'm on a goddamned bus at two in the morning when I could be home asleep, worrying about finals. If I flunk out it's on you."

I doubt he'd pass anyway, I've been doing his homework. I don't think he even knows what classes he's taking anymore. I don't say a word, though. I don't want to risk making this worse. I'm already in the midst of a monumental fuckup, why push it further?

"How'd you get the ticket, Miles?"

I don't answer. I keep looking down, hoping I can ride this out. He waves something in my face. My wallet. I reach for it but he snatches it away.

"Everything's in here, not that there was ever much. You're not smart enough to stash money, so how'd you get on this bus without ID? You tell them some lame story? Cry a bit?"

I keep my mouth shut.

"Miles." He punctuates it with a light shove.

"I'm sorry."

Fuck, that slipped out.

"You're *sorry*?"

A chill washes over me, dread weighting my hands. "I'm gonna be sick." I start nudging him aside, trying to get to the small bathroom. "I'm gonna be sick. I'm gonna be sick. I'm gonna be—"

"Jesus, fine." He lets me by, pushing me hard toward the bathroom, my shoulder hitting the frame. It stings, but I get inside, lock the door. I hear a knock a second later. "Don't try to hole up in there, we're going home after I have a chat with the driver."

There's some muffled muttering outside, but I can't make it out. He's right, I can't hide in here. Eventually they'll drag me out and they'll make me leave with him.

The space is tiny, triangular in shape, small marker tags all over the limited signage. The seat is cracked, the chemicals under the bowl sloshing, the smell pervasive, the room rocking with the motions of the bus. There's a window, tiny, covered with a thick metal screen, probably for ventilation.

I wipe my face with my sleeve, cursing myself. I finger my medallion, feeling Heath's St. Anthony medal next to it. Maybe that's how he found me. It'd be nice if it worked in reverse, if the right novenas could make you unfindable. Maybe I could ask St. Jude for that, but I think I used up my luck just getting on the bus.

Besides, I doubt patron saints would lift a finger for—

I'm thrown hard into the wall as I hear a loud crash and crunch outside. Screaming soon follows as I open the door. Passengers frantically clutch their seats, but I don't see Heath. I jump across the aisle. We're on the North Bridge, but the angle's weird. The walkway is literally right outside my window.

The screaming intensifies as the bus starts to pitch forward. I can't see ahead with the writhing mass of people, but out the window the sidewalk sinks away at an angle and...

Oh fuck oh fuck oh fuck, we're going over we're going over we're—

The screams grow deafening in free fall, the barest of seconds before we hit the river. A figure in white wades through the crowd back toward me, rage in his eyes even as the bus starts to take on water through broken windows. The driver is slumped against the spiderwebbed windshield, a smear of red on the glass.

All that matters is that Heath is coming. I panic, yank the scissor out of my jacket, and hold the blade the way I've seen in horror movies.

"Stay away from me!" There are tears streaming now. He's going to be so mad. "Just stay away!"

Heath doesn't stop. "What the *fuck* are you doing with that?" His voice carries over the screaming, the slowly filling cabin and resultant pandemonium not fazing him. "Give it here."

He reaches out his hand, and a choked cry escapes me— fear, rage, I don't know—but I swipe at his hand, the blade slashing easily through his palm and spraying the seat backs with crimson as he bends over, wincing, covering his hand and screaming in agony.

Oh God, he'll kill me now. I can't apologize for this. He won't eventually tire and go to sleep and maybe have it be better in the morning. I can't kill him though, I don't want to go to hell, and I'm sure that the decision one way or the other's going to be made once the bus is fully claimed by the river.

I look down at the scissor blade, and then at the window to my left, then at the blade again. It won't work, but damn it, I don't want to sit and wait patiently.

I don't want to be here anymore.

"Damn it, Miles, no!"

I funnel my fear into my voice as I stab at the glass with the shear, desperate, no time for saints or prayers. Only time for me. "*Break!*"

The tinted glass wobbles a second before crackling, shattering. The force of the water knocks me hard against the bathroom door, the screaming devolving into screeches and guttural noises. The blade is still hooked by my finger, and I point it toward the window as I strain to push forward. The water pounds against my chest, making it hard to breathe, but the air is fast becoming a rare commodity, the panic drawing it away in huge gulps. When I look down the aisle, I can see that Heath is caught in the throng, his violent swings finding little purchase in disrupting everyone's aimless adrenaline-fueled attempts to escape.

This is it.

I inhale deep and hard, and dunk my head under the water, struggling to get my body through the open window, suction fighting to get me back inside.

My arms feel heavy. Legs are trembling. My mouth opens, bubbles dribble out.

A split-second image of old cartoons. Bubbles popping at the surface with cries for help trapped inside.

Keep moving, keep moving. I can't get this close and fail. I won't let myself. If Heath couldn't take me then I won't let the North River do the job for him.

God damn it, *I will not die.*

Chest is burning. Freezing, Eyes closed now. Just kicking, kicking, kicking. Am I moving upward? Lungs are sheathed in fire. Only the river can extinguish—

I hear cars, loud honks, unmuffled by the water. My mouth opens to air, my lungs greedily drawing it in. Far above is the moon in a clear, open sky, nearly full. It's the most beautiful thing I've ever seen.

I made it. I'm alive.

I get my bearings and head for safety.

I feel dead, my lungs reminding me that taking up smoking was a bad idea. I slip under the surface a few times, but emerge coughing and sputtering, the current carrying me downriver as I steadily progress toward shore.

The docks are high, no ladders, I don't even know where I am, but I would guess between Allora and Destry Bay. I manage to make it to a pylon and cling to it, my limbs wanting to fall off. I slip the scissor blade back into my hoodie pocket, an action that nearly puts me under again. I just breathe, concentrate on keeping my grip. There's a yacht moored at this dock, its lights on, but I'm too exhausted to shout over the music coming from it.

And maybe I've lost it, but I swear I hear the chorus to "Come Sail Away".

"Help." My voice is small, muted, breathy. My muscles are far past the Jell-O phase. I look up toward the yacht, the name *Argo* in simple black letters. I strain my chest to put pressure on my diaphragm, project. "Help!"

"Someone down there?" The voice is male, vaguely bored, but I've got someone's attention, the music's turned down.

"Help." I cough and spit out river water. "I'm down here. Help, please."

"Shit." The music is turned off. I think I'm being left to die when a ladder is thrown over the side, fifteen feet away. A flashlight is shone down on me as the man speaks again. "Get to the ladder, my associate will pull you up."

I push off from the pylon, reduced to a dog paddle now. I can make it, I can do this. My legs awaken with pain, cramping hard, my arms spasm, my head dropping below the surface.

I lunge forward, my grasp finding the bottom rung of the ladder. Slowly I pull myself up, breaking the surface again and catching my breath. Everything feels numb or sore. I don't know how I hold on as the ladder ascends quickly. Hands pull me over the side and onto the deck. I promptly turn on my side and vomit what feels like half the North River.

"Get him a blanket. I don't want someone dying on my boat on my first night off in ages."

Three voices reply to him, all deep and intimidating. "Yes, sir."

"Of course, sir."

"Right away, sir."

I'm rolled onto my back, where I can see a man kneeling over me, maybe five-six, black hair cut stylishly short, his skin pale, eyes a steely gray, an aquiline nose, and a look of general disinterest. He's dressed in a suit, black on black on black. "All right, let's sit you up."

His hands are cold as they prop me against the railing. It's so hard to stay awake, but I'm afraid to fall asleep. "Thank you."

27

"You should feel lucky, I only take appointments on my night off in very special circumstances." A blanket is wrapped around me seconds later. I don't even know if I have the energy to shiver. He looks up at another man, very broad in stature, and tall enough that I don't see his head. "Thank you, that will be all for now."

No reply is given, but the tall one clomps out of sight. The man in the suit turns his attention back to me. "I give up, who are you? My brother put you up to this? I won this boat from him fair, free and clear."

I remember what Dyejob told me, and I'm not in the Capital yet.

"James Black." I struggle to take out the ID I was given, and the man plucks it from my hand, inspecting it.

"This is a terrible fake ID." He holds up the picture to my face. "Let me guess, you went bar-hopping even though you're underage, got in a fight, and they tossed you in the drink. Am I close?"

We can go with that, it's better than the truth. "How'd you know—"

He flashes a million-dollar smile. "I know everything." He leans in closer. "Especially that you're lying." He stands up and takes out a smartphone, tapping at the screen. "You see, Fate only delivers two kinds of people to me who are ready to die. Usurpers and sorcerers."

I start pushing myself along the railing toward the bow, trying to put some distance between me and him. "I'm not ready to die."

"No one ever is." He looks up from his phone. "Besides, you're supposed to be dead when I get there. And you're certainly not supposed to come to me." He easily closes the distance between us. "And the funny thing is, you're on my list, but you're not." A smile, but it's somehow not reassuring. "James Black, who doesn't exist, is on my list. Miles Canmore, who just vomited on my deck, isn't. And yet, here you are, Miles. Or, well, I suppose James now. Big night for you."

I blink, press my thumb to my wrist, causing him to chuckle.

"Relax, you're alive as far as I can tell, and telling is one of my fortes." He pulls over a deck chair and takes a seat, peering at me. "But now I find myself in a unique position. Most would just kill you outright, save themselves the future trouble."

"I don't understand. Who are you?"

"I'd rather ask you that question, honestly, but seeing as you made yourself my guest for the evening..." He slips his hand into his jacket, produces a business card, and hands it to me. It's high quality, but I can't tell much else about it. The text says a name at first, David something, but the letters waver and fade, and then show five letters.

Hades.

My heart climbs up my throat. "You're..."

"A god. Not your god, *a* god, but I'd like to think I'm just as organized."

"But that's not possible."

He flashes that smile again. "Of course it is, I have an excellent support staff." Hades raises a hand. "I know what you meant. Since I answered your question, you'll answer one of mine. Would you count what I've done for you as a favor?"

I look at him confusedly. "I don't understand."

"Pulling you out of the river, would you consider that a favor owed to me?"

"I...I guess so?" I pull the blanket around me tighter. "Are you going to kill me?"

"I don't kill people. I don't often spare them either. Regardless, if you owe me a favor, it would be in my best interests to keep you alive so you can pay me back. I hate debts owed to me. Nothing more offensive than an unbalanced ledger." He offers his hand, helping me to my feet as he gets up. "I suppose I should be taking you somewhere."

"Can I go home?"

He laughs. "Allow me to reiterate. You're forgotten. There's no home for you to go to. I would suggest you keep to your adopted alias."

"But how can... What about a..."

He places his hands on my shoulders. "I'm not expecting you to understand any of this, much less accept it, but little can be done to change the facts. I don't even know how to explain how things work when one of you comes along. For now, they will see you to be as you claimed: James Black."

"Who's they?"

"The humans, James, who else?" Hades steps back and taps at his phone, making a call. "Kerry? Bring the car around, I need to drop someone off, and call the Impecunious, let him know I'm on my way." He glances over me again. "Should I tell him to have coffee ready?"

This is where I break down. This is where the night finally snaps the final straw. A few hours ago I was thinking about leaving Heath. Now people are dead, Heath is dead, I nearly drowned, I'm forgotten, whatever that means, and the god of the underworld is claiming I owe him a favor. And apparently he's taking me out for coffee.

I just sob.

"Huh." He turns off his phone. "And here I was convinced you'd rage and rave." He whistles softly. "Mr. Cerberus, take our guest down to the car, get him a fresh blanket."

The large man returns and glowers down at me.

His skin is pitch-black, head bald, eyes a dull red, teeth white and sharp. His other two heads—one on either side—look just the same.

"What is this?"

"Sniveling trash."

"He Ra'keth?" The third head spits the last word at me.

Hades chuckles. "If he were, you'd be dead. Behave. If I can be patient, so will you." All three heads grumble as I'm scooped up with ease, its powerful arms holding me in place as I tremble in shock.

"Stop staring."

"It's rude."

The center head grins widely. "I hear Keth blood tastes of nectar."

I'm carried down the gangplank toward a small parking lot where a limo awaits. The interior is all in black leather, bordered with bench seats and interrupted on the right by a minibar. I'm shoved inside by the three-headed man, who grumbles under his breath, throwing a dry blanket at me seconds later.

Hades, or at least the man who claims to be him, joins me after that, sitting in the backseat. He and I are alone.

"Can you tell me if Heath—"

"Sorry, I can't share information about others." The limo goes into motion, and he gestures to the rack of bottles. "Think you've earned a drink. Don't worry, it's all from the land of the living." He rolls his eyes as he leans over and pours himself a tall glass of whiskey. "That one thing was invented for *one* story, and I'm stuck with it because Seph and I have marital issues." He waves his hand. "Neither here nor there, though."

"What can you tell me?"

"You got me on my night off, so less than normal but more than usual." He takes a sip of his whiskey.

"Why are you helping me, if you are who you say you are?"

He flashes another high-beam smile. "Simple, you owe me. Someday I'll call in your debt. We have, as it's called, a verbal contract. Much cleaner than hacking up our arms and swapping blood, wouldn't you say?"

"Where are we going?" I look out the windows and see that we're heading east, toward Beckettsville. "Hell?"

"Hell isn't my jurisdiction. We're going to 69th and K. Need to have someone keep an eye on you for a little while." I tense, and he sighs. "It's more for your protection than anything else. I'd prefer no one knew where you were. Then again, it's not like you can contact anyone."

"What if I just—"

He holds up a hand to stop me. "You are forgotten. Your family won't know you. Not my fault, that rule was put in place by the Recluse. You don't like it, you can take it up with him."

"Who?" Having a drink is sounding like a better idea by the moment.

"You'll find out eventually, your kind always does."

"My *kind?*"

"You're an Anu'keth." He smiles. "It means..."

The words escape my mouth before I'm even aware I'm saying them. "Usurper to the Throne."

Chapter Three

I wake up some time later, the limo still in motion.

"You dozed off." Hades takes another pull off his drink. "Not surprising, considering the night you've had."

Through the tinted windows I can see a neighborhood in urban renewal, the remaining graffiti above street level. There's a wide variety of tags, though I don't recognize the writers. We must be in Beckettsville.

"How long was—"

"Just a few minutes."

I look over the rack of bottles and find an expensive brand of bottled water in the minifridge. After choosing it, I fidget with the bottle.

"Something wrong with that, James?"

"Could..." I look down at the floor. "Could you open the window?"

"Which one?" He arches a brow, suspicious.

"Any of them. Please. It's just the tinted windows, I'm having trouble seeing outside and..." My breathing gets a little more ragged.

"All right."

He opens the moonroof, and the sky is far above. Everything's already settling. I drink the water slowly, looking upward the whole time. "Thank you."

I put the water bottle on the rack with the liquors, the shelf lined with a mirror that gives my reflection. I'm bruised, my eye swollen, my lips still fat.

"Why is this happening to me?"

"Were you actually asking, or was that just a general lament? Fate plans things oddly, none of it makes sense at first usually, but..." He sighs wistfully, looking out the window. "Should've known there was a reason I finally got a night off."

"Is that why you were listening to Styx?"

His eyes dart to mine, his face going cold. "Are you certain I was listening to Styx? Are you an expert on Styx?"

"I heard 'Come Sail Away', that's one of their biggest—"

"You didn't answer me. Are you an expert on Styx?"

"Well, no, but—"

"No further questions." He looks back out the window, a self-satisfied smirk crossing his face.

"Huh? It's not like we're in court—"

"Oh look, we're here." He pushes a button in the roof console. "Kerry, park somewhere handy, I'll only be a moment."

Hades waits for the limo to come to a stop, and the door is opened by a tall, svelte woman dressed in a black chauffeur's uniform, her hair long and blood red, stylishly tangled, her skin pale, eyes coal black, a pair of long knives at her sides. Hades gets out first, nodding curtly. She smiles in reply, revealing jagged teeth.

I swallow hard as I exit the limo, my eyes locked on the woman. Hades laughs. "Relax. Though if you want to stay on her good side? On the day I come for you, don't run."

He motions grandly to the building we're parked in front of, a squat three-floor walk-up affair built out of faded red brick with the entrance on the corner. Through the windows I see the first floor contains a diner, the setup a traditional long counter with scuffed chrome borders and stools in front, the seats of the stools and booths that are along the windows covered with a faded yellow leather usually found in a shitty Buick from the seventies. It's understandably closed, but Hades bangs on the door regardless.

A silver-scaled face emerges from the pass-through, training golden eyes on us, long whiskers dangling from his snout, a bit of thick gray smoke trailing up from his nostrils. I see long dagger teeth bare for a moment, then the face vanishes.

"Wh-what was that?" I take a step back, gently bumping into the woman, Kerry. I squeak softly before stepping back forward.

"A pain in my ass." He bangs on the door again. No one comes to answer. He takes out his smartphone and holds it toward the window. "I am bringing up the number for Argentus the Opulent." A few seconds go by. Nothing. "I am pressing *Call*." He holds the phone to his ear. "It is now ringing. I wonder what time it is in Munich?" A few more seconds. "Argentus! Yes, it has been a while. Oh, I just wanted to tell you a little story about the Impecunious..."

The door is yanked open loudly, held by...

I've played a certain game before, back in high school. Heath had me stop after I got into college, since only geeks and nerds and the otherwise unlayable play it. I wasn't expecting this.

Regardless, I'm sure that the dragon now staring at me won't take it too kindly that I'm snickering because he's shorter than me. And I'm five-eight. I shouldn't be laughing though, he's got two claw and bite attacks per round plus a breath weapon with God knows how many damage dice.

The dragon looks at Hades while I collapse in fits of giggling onto the sidewalk. "So what is this, then?" His voice takes me by surprise, mostly in that it's accentless, like the presenters for the nightly news. This only pushes my laughter further into the realm of hysterics. "Because it's looking like the saddest start to a practical-joking career ever."

Hades gently taps his phone with his free hand, the screen showing no call in progress. The dragon takes a step back, looks up toward the sky and mutters something I don't catch. The god smiles genially.

"By the river, you're easy." He slips his phone back inside his coat. I feel Hades's eyes on me. "Get up, you're making a terrible first impression."

The dragon sighs, not helping me as I find my feet. "So again, what's this?"

Hades gestures to me. "Your new responsibility. He needs a place to stay, a way to means, and protection. You can offer all three."

The dragon chuckles, practiced-sounding, but true. "The hell I will! I got zombos wandering the alleys, Georgies sniffing around the neighborhood, two sidhe on the Renewal Committee trying to push me out *and* a damned union that wrangled dental for people who work for tips."

The woman steps forward, baring teeth. "You are addressing a *god*."

The dragon snorts. "He's not *my* god."

Hades appears unfazed. "Tell me, Dave, what's the size of your hoard?"

I blink. "His name's Dave?" I have to fight to not start laughing again, or at least not be convinced this is a dream. Dragons are named Gorbash or Bahamut or Smaug; they are not named Dave.

The dragon ignores my comment. I should probably be grateful for that.

"I'd rather not say."

Hades *hmm*s in mock contemplation. "And why is it that size?"

"You know why."

"And who advised you *not* to make that particular investment?"

The dragon grumbles. "You know who did."

"And when you did it anyway, who did you call when it fell through?"

The dragon growls but doesn't meet the god's eyes.

"Exactly, Dave. I'm calling in that favor."

Dave looks at me, then at Hades in shock. "You're calling in a *dragon's* favor? For him?"

Hades nods curtly. "Indeed. An Anu'keth's favor is worth more." He looks between the two of us. "Gentlemen." The god returns to the limo despite both the dragon and me calling for some explanation. The woman, Kerry, doesn't answer either.

Even when I run over to knock on the window to the backseat, she drives off regardless.

I turn to face the dragon, his short arms folded as he looks at me crossly. "The medals, who are they for?"

I look at him oddly before I realize what he's referring to. "Oh, uh, St. Anthony and St. Jude."

"Good. I have issues with St. George." He taps a footclaw on the sidewalk slowly. Behind him I see a long scaly tail keeping time in the same fashion. "You know how to wash dishes?"

I nod once.

"You smoke?"

I shake my head. "I quit."

"Might as well start again, I'll need you to get mine. There's a place down the block, don't stare at the guy's head. I get two cartons of Virginia Slims, and you don't tell nobody I smoke the chick sticks." He looks me over again, my face particularly. "So what happened to you?"

I avert my eyes. "I ran away from home."

"Uh-huh. Not my business. Won't happen here, though. What do I call you?"

"My name's..."

He holds up a hand quickly. "First rule, never ask anyone's name, or tell anyone yours. Never know when the Recluse might be watching. Ask what to call them." He tics his head, motioning for me to follow him inside, and I can now see a set of tiny wings hugged closely to his back. Shortly after we're both in the diner, he closes the door and locks up.

"That's the second time I've heard that said. What's the Recluse?"

"That's what we call him. No one's seen the Recluse, not in almost seventy years. No one who's lived to tell about it, at least."

"But...what is he?"

"He's the Ra'keth. And a Sorcerer King can do some scary things with names, so I don't go handing mine out, and neither should you."

More to learn about it would seem, but right now I don't care about that. I just want to be somewhere safe. I want to go home.

"Okay, you can call me James. James Black. I guess I call you Dave, then?"

"Hold on, this ain't a done deal yet." He *hrm*s, still tapping his footclaw. "What's your opinion on the Gryphons' secondary this year? Should we sign another strong safety, or would a middle linebacker be a better choice?"

My jaw drops slightly. "Uh...I don't really follow football." I've gotten used to calling the *real* football soccer. My mother will be quite irate.

Dave exhales hard. "Well, at least you knew what I was talking about." His eyes narrow at me. "Favorite AC/DC album?"

I do my best not to get a deer-in-the-headlights expression. Dad's into jazz, my brothers prefer various American rock bands, and Mom would never dream of listening to anything Australian. I'm mostly into indie because it's cheap to buy. "How can I pick a favorite? That's not even possible."

A second passes, and the dragon grins, big and toothy. "Now *that's* an answer I can get behind." I follow him through the diner, past the kitchen, into a long narrow hallway, lit by a couple of hanging bulbs and a lamp above an exit door. The walls are marked with scratches and gouges. The hall is just barely wide enough for Dave to travel down it, his scales dully grating against the sides. He bypasses the exit, proceeds to a set of stairs, and motions for me to go ahead of him. "This'll take me a couple minutes."

I manage to squeeze by and head to the first floor (er, second), only to find that after emerging from the stairwell there's no ceiling to separate this level from the third floor. Instead there's a massive open space, the roof having a huge skylight, though the area is still relatively dark. The floor is hardwood, heavily marked by his claws, the room largely unfurnished, though I can see a huge array of posters along the walls. A Wurlitzer jukebox provides some illumination at the far wall, next to a large freezer. On a table next to the jukebox I see something important, and I cross to it, my steps echoing in the vast room.

I reach the phone, its buttons large and damaged, but I still get a dial tone when I pick up the receiver. The numbers are punched out quickly as I turn my head back to the stairwell, cupping my hand over my mouth and the receiver to prevent echo.

After eight rings, I finally hear his voice, tired, worn, introduced with a hard smoker's cough. "Hello?" A second passes. "Do you have any idea what time it is?"

"Dad, it's me." I swallow hard. "I wanted to let you know I'm okay. I don't know if they called you yet. I'm sorry I had to leave school but Heath was... God, I'm sorry, I just want to come home. Can I? I'll do whatever you want, I don't want to be here anymore."

"Hold on, hold on." I hear the click of the brass lamp my oldest brother, John, got him for his fiftieth birthday. "Who is this?"

"It's..." I look toward the stairwell, and Dave hasn't made it up yet. "It's Miles, Dad."

"I think you've got the wrong number, I don't have a son named Miles." I'm too shocked to respond. "Listen, it sounds like you're in trouble, whoever you are, so let me give you a number to call, in case your dad doesn't answer or can't help you out." After a few seconds of silence he tells me a string of numbers that I don't recognize. "I'm sure it'll turn out all right. Good luck to you."

I try to tell him that it's not the wrong number, but his tone, so casual, not a hint of dishonesty... "You're not joking, are you?"

I hear a soft chuckle. "Trust me, I've got six boys. I'd be a terrible father if I forgot I had another one. I'll let you go so you can call your dad." I hear a click, and then the steady pulse of a busy signal.

"Wish you hadn't done that." Dave steps into view.

I hang up the receiver, feeling numb. "Am I in trouble?"

"Just seems like you've been through enough tonight. You're beat up, you smell like the river, you're dropped off by Hades of all people, wouldn't have recommended making that call."

I look down at the phone. "He said he only had six sons."

"As far as he knows, he does. You crossed over, Black, you're one of them now, one of the Keth. They aren't on the loom of Fate. Bad trade-off, if you ask me. Sure, I'd love to make my own destiny, but I'm not about to give up everyone I ever knew for it. Granted, it's the Recluse who added on that last bit." He beckons with a claw. "C'mon, I'll show you where you can sleep for now. It's not much, but I wasn't expecting company. I might as well stay up, get ready to open a bit early."

He leads me to a large wooden tub, empty, before motioning to the room at large. "Used to need more space to sleep, but this works for me now. Shouldn't be too bad. I sleep like a hatchling in this thing. We'll figure something out for you later."

"I'm sorry I'm putting you out like this." He stops me by raising a hand.

"Well, Hades is a crafty bastard. He was doing me a favor, actually, which he'll no doubt take advantage of later. I couldn't have refused you sanctuary if I wanted to. You're Keth, I'm a dragon. Dragons guard the Keth. That's what we were created for." He smirks, showing teeth. "Granted, you could've done better, but I'm the only local. Most of the family's still in the old country."

"The Keth?"

"No, the other dragons."

"No, I mean, what are the Keth?"

"Sorcerers, Black, sorcerers. Y'know, magic?" He wiggles his claws in the air, but I blink.

"Magic is real?" He gives me a look, and yes, the fact that I was dropped off at a diner by the god of the underworld and that I'm talking to a dragon does click after saying that. "How do I know I'm not crazy?"

"Simple, world's not ending. That's always a good sign that a sorcerer's gone fully 'round the bend." He fishes a windup alarm clock out of the tub and carefully turns it off before tossing it to me. "Set it for noon, you'll start after the lunch rush, the girls can show you the ropes."

Not knowing what else to do, I obey. "Are you saying I'm a sorcerer?"

He shakes his head. "Nah, right now you're a dishwasher working under the table. In a few years though, who knows? Just, uh, don't start slinging spells around me, okay? Gives me a bitch of a headache." Dave taps the side of the tub. "Might as well get some sleep."

I climb in, the tub pretty much a bowl with limited gouges and scratches, the contour providing more comfort than anything. "So, what'd you mean, when you said you used to need more space?"

The dragon grumbles, and before heading to the stairwell, he shakes a clawed finger at me. "Best advice I can give? Never take a stock tip from a fucking Coyote."

Part II

Exile

Chapter Four

May—Two years later

The night had barely begun and already the world was coming to an end. A flight of dragons had been spotted, all with scales red like burnished metal, a horde of zombies emerged from the local cemetery, goblins set up in the network of tunnels beneath the city were preparing to attack, and a cult of dark ritualists sought to raise a cannibal god that possessed a name that could not be spelled by mortals.

And I, the noble sorcerer, was tasked with stopping it all.

At present my foe was the leader of the aforementioned cult, who was dressed in dark robes and oversized golden unholy symbols.

I'd surprised him, managing to sneak into his temple through means I didn't quite understand, but the opportunity to end it all quickly was before me.

I have to choose the perfect spell. This is my only shot.

The initiative is mine to exploit.

"Okay..."

The leader is less than fifty yards away, the altar about ten feet behind him.

I could strike him with magical energy, nah. Maybe...

I've got it. It would take a bit out of me, but...

I roll several specialized cubes in my hand and drop them with a sense of finality.

"Okay. I'm going with a fireball centered on the altar. The blast radius should take care of the ritual materials and do a hefty bit of damage to the high priest." I cast my eyes downward, calculate the numbers in my head. "Fuck. Uh..." I look to a set of yellow slitted eyes peeking over the screen, boring into mine. "Twelve?"

I should've gone with magic missile.

"Well, Black, it doesn't go well for you. But the flight of dragons crashes through the roof and kills the cultists and saves you."

I perk a brow. "The *red* dragons?"

"You have a problem with that?"

"They're red dragons. They wouldn't save me."

The voice behind the screen gets a bit huffy. "And why is that?"

"They're red dragons. They're evil."

A silver-scaled snout pokes over the top of the screen, a plume of smoke issuing from his nostrils with a snort. "Now that's just racist. I've got two cousins who're reds that donate to Greenpeace." The silver dragon gets out from behind the screen, throwing his hands up in defeat. "I don't get why you do this, it's all so inaccurate."

I follow after him, leaving the table and my eighth-level elven wizard Radcliffe to the whims of Fate for now. "Because it's nice to pretend I'm a sorcerer who actually knows what he's doing?"

The dragon gives me a dubious glance, and I sigh. "Okay, less incompetent. I'm used to running bards." I yawn heavily, looking at the clock, seeing that it's past five. "We've got to open, don't we?"

Dave nods and motions to the stairwell. "Go ahead and lay out the condiments, unlock the side door for the girls, start the coffee and..." I start down the stairs, but hear him call after me. "And go pick up a carton of Slims!"

Once I reach the kitchen, I step into the freezer and dip into Dave's stash. It's located in an "empty" box of Virginia Slims, each pack usually having a couple twenties in it, enough to swing his next carton at least. I never take more than I need. Dragons *know*. Once the money's in my pocket, I close my eyes and take a deep breath.

Two years and I can do one spell. One. Uno. A notch above zilch, and I cribbed it. I first cast it while I was drunk.

"My mind is *focused*, my heart is steady."

Saying *focused* always feels a bit weird, like I'm mucking up the pronunciation.

But damned if it doesn't work wonders.

The weariness of the night fades off, my senses sharpen and hone. It's the magical equivalent of a double espresso without the bothersome crash. According to Dave I'll figure out more, something about the magic awakening as I gain experience with it. I start the coffee, wipe down the counter, go through the rest of my morning routine. The shift's long, but it's easy to put my brain in a drawer and while the time away.

"Are you guys open?" The voice is muffled, coming from the front door. I turn to see a white guy in his twenties wearing jeans, a Tenacious D T-shirt, and quite possibly the worst dye job I've ever seen. The hair is black, too black to be natural, roots visible, varied colors underneath so he likely dyes a *lot*. His thin groomed beard is dyed black as well, a couple blond hairs sticking through. I'm sure he had eyes of some color or another but the hair grabbed my attention. I just stare for a few seconds until he starts banging on the door to break me from my reverie.

Oh yeah, hard to have the diner be open when I forget to unlock the door.

I open up and let him in. "Sorry about that. Sit wherever you want." As he walks by me, I see a scar on his brow, and that his eyes are golden, definitely not human. Damn it. Still though, the diner's run by a dragon so I can hardly deny service based on lack of humanity. He looks a little familiar but in the two years since I started living here I've seen all sorts of weird shit so it's tough to nail down anything specific.

"Can I get you anything?" I return behind the counter, and he's taken a seat in front, drumming his fingers lightly.

"Don't suppose I could talk to your supervisor?" His voice is easy, smooth, and his grin has plenty of teeth, white and straight and perfect, like a TV news anchor just back from the dentist. Oh, that's why he's familiar. Only one kind of supernatural comes across that smarmy.

I give him a dubious look. "What, you don't like my service already?"

"Oh no, it's not that at all." Again, that perfect smile. "Just have an opportunity to discuss with—"

I lean in close. "Sorry. My boss has made it an issue not to take stock tips from Coyotes." His eyes go wide and I have a little smirk of my own. "Perhaps you should dress the part next time and consider a hat for that lame-ass bottle job." I fish my order pad out of my pocket. "Now what can I get you?"

"God damn it, someone beat me here already?" He almost growls, smacking the counter in irritation. "Here I thought I'd lined up an easy score. Dragons are just...easy as a cop show's subtext, you know?" He fumes a few seconds more, but regains his composure and focuses on me. "But obviously there's someone here far more worthy of my attention." He flashes a high-beam smile. "Have we met? I'd hate to think my reputation precedes me."

"You look vaguely familiar, but I think I'd remember that hair. If you're not going to order anything, I'm going to have to ask you to leave." To my credit I give him four seconds. "All right, get out of here."

"Decaf. Cup of decaf." I wait to see if he'll order food, but no, he appears intent on legal loitering. I pour the joe for him and push over a small basket of creamers and sugar. He takes it, adds plenty of sugar. "So, you bit or dead?"

"Not a were, and it's dawn. Do you start all your conversations this way?" Weres tend to avoid the diner as a dragon runs it. Vampires are creepy as hell and lousy tippers.

"Just the people I find interesting."

"You ask all the people you find interesting if they're bit or dead?"

"Touché. How about I read your fortune instead?" He quickly produces a thick deck of large cards from his jeans. Tarot cards. He sets to shuffling them like a Vegas dealer.

"No thanks. I don't buy into destinies." Since I apparently don't have one anymore.

"C'mon, I'll even let you draw one for free. It'll be fun."

"Wanna bet?"

This time his smile's more natural. "On a tarot reading? What're the terms?"

"I don't even know how you'd do something like that." I get three teacups from behind the counter and put one of the packets of creamer underneath one. The Coyote snickers softly.

"You sure about this?" He starts moving them about the counter with remarkable speed and grace. "Okay, what're we playing for? How about...if you win..."

"You tip me for the coffee. Fifty bucks. And then you go."

He doesn't break his stride. "And if *I* win, you let me talk to your boss uninterrupted for ten minutes."

"Deal."

He sweeps his hands over the three cups with a flourish. "Okay, where's the creamer?"

I chuckle at him. "A guy once told me that everyone knows that monte players are cheating, but they think they can beat it anyway." I move around the counter toward him, and he keeps his face placid. "So the question usually isn't 'which cup' or 'which card', but rather 'where did he stash it', you know?" I run my fingers along his side, and he shivers slightly. "If you were smart, you'd hide it maybe here..." I move my finger just above his waistband, pointing at his groin, almost touching. "Or here for some lame creamer pun." I keep my eyes locked with his as I lift up the center cup with my free hand. "Or maybe you're just not that smart."

I glance to the counter to see the small cup of creamer revealed and look back at him with a grin. "I'll take my fifty bucks now."

The Coyote grins back even wider, starting to unzip his fly. "Move your hand down there a few inches and I'll make it a hundred."

"Ugh." I yank my hand away.

"What in fresh hell..." Two voices to my right, near the door, say it in unison. Shit, I forgot to unlock the side door.

The first voice belongs to Sharon, meaning that her sister Monica would be the other. Sharon has her bleached-blonde hair tied back in a tight braid, her face showing her entrance into her thirties with crow's feet marking her deep-brown eyes. Her skin looks tanned, but that's just her natural complexion, much to her sister's envy. She's already wearing her smock and name tag, her gold cross around her neck. She will also be peeved that I made her use bad language.

"Need any help there, Jimmy?" Monica's tone does not imply this is a serious offer. She's still in her twenties, her dirty-blonde hair perpetually under a baseball cap to duck the hairnet rule, her skin is paler than her sister's, but they have the same eyes. Monica prefers casual dress, tight T-shirts with bright designs and hip-hugger jeans. Monica brings in better tips, much to the chagrin of her sister. Monica could also care less about her language.

Time to think fast.

"His zipper's stuck. And he's leaving. Right now." I chuckle slightly to him. "Uh, little help?"

"Yeah, uh, it's like he said." He slips off the stool and digs a dingy bill out of his pocket, putting it on the counter. Inspection reveals it to be a five.

I tap his shoulder and glance obviously at the bill. "Excuse me? I think you're short."

He shrugs nervously. "I'll owe you?"

Sharon sighs and looks to her sister. "Mon, make sure everything's prepped and clock me in." She glares at the Coyote and me while Monica heads into the kitchen where the time sheets are located. "We don't tolerate that sort of behavior in here."

"Sorry, Sharon." I nudge him toward the door. "I'll make sure he gets a cab. It's not like there are any dishes yet."

Once we're outside, the Coyote whistles sharply at a passing taxi and waits for it to return. "So how'd you know what I am?"

"My boss has been cheated before. He gave me a primer on spotting you guys. Eyes are always a dead giveaway."

"Yeah but, you shouldn't be able to see..." He inspects me a second. "Oh. I know what you are. Only one kind of human's able to see us." He leans in close. "You're a sorcerer." He bows elegantly then. "You can call me Spencer. Remember it, because I'm the one who's going to trick you." The Coyote turns to get in the cab.

"Spencer? Watch your head."

"What? Why—" He then bangs his temple against the doorframe, misjudging his approach. "Fuck... Ow."

"You gonna live?"

He closes the door and gives a Grunstadt address to the driver before waving me off. "Yeah, yeah, copacetic." The cab pulls away, and I stop dead.

I hate that word.

"Jimmy, you okay?" I look over and see Monica peeking her head out at me. "You look like you're going to be sick. You're not, are you? I'm not up for dishes, not today."

God, is it Wednesday already? The local classic-rock station tends to stack its rotation with AC/DC on Wednesdays. It starts simply enough with Dave tapping his feet. But by the third hour he'll be singing along, and I've learned in the past two years that dragons are three things: intelligent, loyal and tone-deaf. The station takes requests, but when you request that they play less AC/DC it only encourages them to play more.

As I make my way back into the diner, Monica needs to help me out. The memories bubble up to the surface. I know I have to ride it out, but...

God damn it, why did he have to say *that* word?

"Dave?" I stumble into the kitchen, lean over the sink. "I'm not feeling too—"

The water around me is freezing, sounds of shouting and screeching not muffled, more amplified. Hands reach out of the black, thin and skeletal, digging into my skin, tearing, slicing, pain blossoming everywhere.

Fingers clamp around my neck, pry my mouth open to force the water into my lungs. My body seizes, agony ripping through.

A face emerges from the black, angry gray eyes meeting mine.

I open my eyes with a shout, thrashing on my futon, the blanket making tearing sounds as I fight my way free. I tumble onto the floor, my eyes finding the skylight. I focus on it, steady my breathing, rub my hands together quickly to warm them up as they're cold. The sun is high overhead, obscured at the moment by a cloud. My clock shows that it's nearly noon.

I've never felt this drained, like I could still sleep for a week, but I'm not checking back into that nightmare. I make my way down to the diner, keeping my steps careful on the stairs.

When I enter the kitchen, Monica is working on the dishes, grumbling, as dishwashers don't pull tips. Seeing me, she tries to push down her frustration. "You okay?"

I rub my temples slowly. "I don't know what happened, I just felt dizzy for a second and then..." I look at the clock to reconfirm the time. "I'm sorry, I didn't know I'd be out that long."

Monica gives a look to Dave. "You're working him too hard and too much. We need to bring on someone else."

Dave shrugs. "Fine, put the *Help Wanted* sign out before you take your break." He bends his neck at a disturbing angle, though anyone else would just see him actually turning around. "How 'bout you, Black? You need a little bit?" He waves off Monica, who clocks out for her break, digging the sign off a shelf before leaving the kitchen. Once she's out the door, he snorts a plume of smoke. "What the hell were you doing, Black?"

"Huh?"

"You're not Ra'keth, kid, you can't go slinging spells like that without wearing yourself out *fast*. And stop casting that damned wake-up spell, it's probably meant to be a stopgap only." He turns back to the grill, cursing softly as he shunts a burnt patty off to the trash. "Sharon needs help out front, just man the register until Monica gets back."

"I wasn't casting anything—"

"Bad enough you were talking in your sleep, now you're casting too? Chattering about man and children and shit... I've been chomping Tylenol for a solid hour thanks to you."

I nod once. "Sorry, Dave."

He looks upward, muttering what I've discerned is a religious expletive, though I still don't understand it. "Black, don't apologize to me, just don't burn yourself out." He tics his head toward the pass-through. "Now get out there."

I obey, head out front where the lunch rush is in full swing. Sharon's thankful for the help, and I'm extra thankful, as Dave's started singing bars from "Back in Black". Sharon gives me a cup of coffee for while I'm handling the register.

"Jimmy, could you get the guy at the end of the counter? I've got pickups for three and four."

I take a sip of my coffee and promptly drop it after seeing who's at the end of the counter. He's a few inches taller than me and about a year older, short black hair, well-tanned skin, deep-brown eyes, almost onyx in color, wearing a navy-blue jacket left unzipped. His eyes meet mine and I stop dead, staring. A few people applaud mockingly as I quickly sweep up the broken cup and wipe up the coffee before Sharon or I can trip on it.

Dave pokes his head through the pass-through. "What the hell, Black?" His eyes follow my gaze to the end of the counter. "Who's that?"

My voice is one of disbelief, of hope. "That's my brother."

Chapter Five

For the past two years, since that night, I've slipped away every now and then to call my family, hoping that one of them would recognize my voice. I could handle John, my oldest brother, telling me he was on the Do Not Call list and promptly hanging up. John was always a dick.

It stung a little when Mark, my exact middle brother (three older than him, three younger, me included) told me I had the wrong number. I had memories of watching Oxford United take on Swindon Town with him. But I pushed through it.

It knocked me down for a week when Mom had no idea who I was.

To think I looked forward to college to get away from them. That I was grateful to get out of family holidays because I didn't want to come clean about Heath.

And now the one brother I couldn't call is standing in front of me. It can't be coincidence. Of all the diners in all the world, that's how the line goes, right? I walk over to him.

"Hi."

He nods, sits on the stool. "Coffee, please? No decaf." He grins. "And, no offense, but could she bring it over?"

I quickly fetch the coffee, my face red. I set it in front of him and stand there a few moments until he looks at me. "This is all right, thanks."

I swallow hard and force a smile. "Can I get you a menu or..."

"Yeah, sure. What's good here?"

I work in the kitchen. I should know this. "Uh..."

"Fries are always crisp, and I can recommend the patty melt." Sharon comes to my rescue, though she looks at me oddly.

Thom nods again, sipping from his coffee. "Sounds decent, I'll go with that. Fries first if they're ready."

Sharon takes the order and puts it on the wheel, leaving me standing there. Thom peers at me.

"Okay, any reason you're staring?" He catches me looking at my feet. "Listen, I don't mind guys who go that way, but I don't, so..."

I blink. "Oh God, no." 'Cause, well, ew. "It's not that, it's just uh... You look familiar." I take a breath. "Have we met before?"

Thom studies me. "Not that I can remember." His eyes narrow. "We didn't meet at the *office* before, did we?"

"Huh?"

Sharon places a platter of fries before him. "He's asking if he ever busted you, Jimmy." She returns to the other customers and gives me a look to imply I should get back to them too, but I can't pass this up.

"You're a cop? I thought you were going for pre-law."

Thom blinks at me now. "How'd you know... Wait, wait, wait..." A big smile crosses his face, the one I remember. "Were you in the pledge class behind mine?" Right, Thom had been in a fraternity.

So I lie. "That must be it. I heard that story about the marshmallow."

He fakes an indignant look but still laughs. "You can't prove anything. So... Shit, I can't quite place your name."

"Jimmy!" Sharon motions to the register and the line of people building at it.

"Damn, listen, I gotta get back to work, so..."

"No problem. This place is on my patrol. Jimmy?"

I shake my head. "I prefer James. I'm not twelve." I grit my teeth, looking at the register. "I'll be right back over. Wouldn't mind catching up."

He shrugs. "I'll be here."

For the next few minutes I am the wind. My body buzzes with adrenaline. I see Thom's lunch get passed to him, and I struggle to work the line that never seems to end. It's as if suddenly every person in the City wants to pay with exact change or needs the no-personal-checks-ever policy explained to them in detail.

The last person in line is Thom. He hands me the check and starts digging for his wallet, but I hold up my hand. "Forget it, on the house."

"You sure?"

"What?" Dave pokes his head through the pass-through. "Everyone pays, Black."

"Dave, c'mon." I look at him pleadingly and whisper soft enough that only he'd hear it. "He's my brother."

"Black, I don't care if he's the earthly manifestation of the Dragon God himself, he pays. *Everyone* pays." He snorts another plume of smoke, and I grumble, looking back to Thom.

"Okay, with tax it comes out to four-forty, Officer."

Dave growls, "What the hell are you doing, Black? Cops don't pay."

I put away the check, and confusedly, Thom looks beyond me to Dave and shakes his head. "Okay, then..."

"You gotta go already?" I probably sound desperate. I can't ask if his phone number's still the same, or any of the other questions I'd want to ask him. Instead of being his brother, I have to keep up the charade of being his "brother".

"I'll be around. Kinda curious how someone from our frat ends up, well, here. No offense meant, just uh..." He grins. "Yeah, I'll talk to you later, James. Stay out of trouble."

And my brother leaves.

Monica returns a minute later, and it's back to the kitchen after bussing the tables. I'm grateful for that. It's a little too real out there right now.

"He didn't remember me." I start on a tall stack I brought in. "Of my whole family, he's the one I thought would... I mean, we were close, you know? Christ, I practically did try to pledge for his frat until I met…" I stop myself. I'm not going to say Heath's name aloud. Let it stay down there in the deep, cold and dark where it belongs.

"How many times do I have to tell you, Black? No one from your old life is going to remember you, because as far as Fate's concerned, your old life never existed. If your father didn't remember having you for a son, you think your brothers will remember you? You think your old friends will? That's the price you pay. One of them, at least." Dave takes a moment to light a fresh cigarette. "At least you're safe here, right?"

I mutter while drying a dish.

"What was that?"

"I don't know if it's worth it, that's all."

He's stopped paying attention to the grill, his yellow eyes on me.

"Don't get me wrong. I'm grateful, but other than you, I've got nothing. Just one friend, crash space and a dead-end job. I can't live like this."

The dragon turns toward me, worry on his face. "What are you going to do?"

I've thought about this before. "Maybe today was a sign. Hades told me my family wouldn't remember me. He said, *That rule was put in place by the Recluse. You don't like it, take it up with him.* So that's what I'm going to do."

Dave replies, fear in his hushed voice. "Black, that's insane. You think you can find the Recluse? Every mythic in the City's been looking for him for years. The Fae couldn't find him with their best trackers. I hear he took their Crown Prince for their trouble. The vamps sent a hunt after him, and for their insolence they lost a whole line. There were *three* dragons in this City once and now there's just me."

"Dave, how much of that is actually true? You've told me that the Recluse is the reason we have a new tax code."

He snorts a plume of smoke. "Is there any other explanation?"

"Yeah. It's called an election year." I sigh and look out the pass-through a second. "I can't hide here for the rest of my life. Maybe this Recluse has some answers, you know? It's not like I'm going to try to kill him. Would you rather I spent the next twenty years having to see my brother every day, knowing I could maybe help him remember me but was too scared to try?"

"You mean what you said?" His tone is still small, meek. I'm getting that Dave is younger than he lets on. "About me being your friend?"

"Yeah, that so hard to believe?"

He snorts and turns his attention back to the grill, fetching the new orders. "You're Keth, Black. Dragons protect the Keth, but that's all we are to you, just the..." He shows teeth. "*Things that keep you safe, guard your shit.*" Dave chances a smile. "A Keth certainly wouldn't talk about football with one of my kind. So you hopefully get why I wouldn't want you to go."

"Yeah, I get it." I turn my attention back to the sink. "I won't take too long, few days at the most. Think I've built up some vacation time, you know?"

He doesn't answer, not with words. But after a few minutes, I see him nod to no one in particular. I work until the end of my shift, and then prepare, because that's what you do before heading out on a quest. It's not like I'm heading out into the wilderness. At least I hope I'm not.

Food isn't an issue, I've got money and I'm in the City. Unless I go deep into the slums of the Benedict there should be a store every few blocks. I pack the shear, the last bit of my old life besides my medals, for protection, a beat-up Zippo I bought off Sharon when she tried to quit the fifth time, a compass from a dollar store, and extra clothes to go with the rest of my thrift-store-chic wardrobe.

Dave is pacing the hallway downstairs. I change my clothes—blue jeans, white T-shirt, black Chucks, and a gray-fleece, hooded jacket that's two sizes too big—and grab my knapsack, heading down to meet him.

"Well, this is it." I look past him toward the side door. "Zombos out already?"

"Just...wait a little." He holds his clawed hand toward me and opens it, revealing a silver scale about the length of my thumb. "Take it."

Gingerly, I pick it up, the scale feeling metallic, but light. As he takes his arm away, I see a gap in his scales under his arm. "Dave, what did you do?"

"You ever need me, you break that. I'll know where you are. In the meantime, I don't know, keep it for luck or something. I just get the feeling I'm not going to see you again, Black."

"Dave, I'll come back, don't worry. God knows you need a dishwasher, and I'm the only one on staff who can tolerate your singing." I clap him on the shoulder. "I'll be okay. I'm a sorcerer, what could happen?" Thinking better of it, I hold up a hand. "Don't answer that."

What I need is information, even the barest hint of a lead, and there's really only one place to go for that. "I don't suppose you could recommend a good tavern?"

"You're going drinking?" After a second he nods in comprehension. "I get you. Well, there's the Palace, but you'd stick out, and even I know that Keth aren't welcome there. Your best bet is going under the bridge." He gives me an intersection, which is in South Beckettsville, nowhere near the river or the bay. He extends his hand, and I take it, shaking it once. "You come back alive, Black. I'd be the laughingstock of my clan if I let a Keth die on my watch." Dave backs away from the door. "Already called you a cab. Just don't tell the girls I paid for it. Don't want them thinking they can get free rides off me."

With some trepidation, I head into the alley and to the street where the taxi is waiting. The driver looks human enough, but her ears have a slight point, eyes a soft autumnal orange, face smooth, perfect. Magazine-cover material, definitely. She even has the bored and distant look perfected. "Where you headed?"

I give her the intersection as I get into the cab, toss my knapsack on the seat. "Could you take a route that doesn't go by 82nd and M?"

Her reflection shows intrigue in the rearview. "Ducking work?"

"It's where I used to live."

The reflection smirks. "Ducking rent."

"It's where my ex..."

"Ah, ducking exes is something I'm familiar with. Yours sleep around too?" The taxi pulls into what little traffic there is this time of the afternoon, so the going's quick.

"No, he uh..." It's best not to get into it. I've had my stranger's confessional. "He drowned."

The mirth drains from her reflection at that point, and the cab continues on in silence.

"Listen, uh, I'm kinda starving, could we hit someplace first?"

"Didn't I pick you up at a diner?"

"Yeah, but I work there, so..."

A smile returns to the face in the rearview. "Yeah, I get it. I really only know places out in the Benedict, just where I get my coffee."

I lean toward the glass. "Coffee is exactly what I need. Is it any good where you get it?"

Now there's a grin. "Best you'll ever have. There's even fresh Danish every morning and afternoon."

"You've sold me." I slip a five into the pay slot. "Let's go."

The cab takes a turn and instead of south, we're now going east, into the Benedict, basically the industrial slum of the City. It's named for St. Benedict of Nursia, who you do novenas to if you want protection from witchcraft and gallstones. Too bad he doesn't cover unemployment. (That would be St. Cajetan.)

"So, you mind if I ask a personal question?" Her voice breaks my momentary reverie.

"Is it about my ex?"

Her reflection shakes its head quickly. "No, no. Just curious if you're bit or twin."

I blink. "Huh?"

"Well, you're going to Under the Bridge, and the vanillas don't go down there. It's a commoner bar, you know?"

"Wait, the bar is called Under the Bridge?"

"Yep, and the sun's up so you're not a leech, so, you bit or twin?"

"Neither?"

I see her hand move downward from the steering wheel. "You a hunter?" Shit, I know what that gesture implies.

"I'm looking for my brother." The cityscape turns more run-down with each passing building as we move east. "Well, I found him, it's just that he doesn't remember me."

I know what *bit* means, played enough D&D for that. *Twin*, I have no clue about, but I don't want to seem oblivious. *Vanilla*, I guess means regular human. And I don't want anyone to think I'm hunting, especially if it might get violent.

"Oh." Her hand moves back to the steering wheel. "Sorry, didn't mean to pry." The ride continues on a bit longer before she breaks the silence. "If you're going to Under the Bridge, you might want to change a few things, though."

"Like what?"

"Your clothes, for starters. They'll either kick you out or maybe kill you if they think you're a hunter, and the three hunters I've seen dressed like they raided a Dumpster. No offense, but you smell like a vat of grease that hasn't showered in three days. If the cab ride wasn't already paid for I wouldn't have picked you up."

We're in the Benedict now, mostly shuttered factories, barren overgrown lots, bleak storefronts that are boarded up, tenements that look more like places to squat than anything else. Few tags on the brick buildings, the ones there are just simple sprays. The real writers don't come out here. Hell, nobody comes out here. Weird place for a coffee shop.

She parks in front of a large closed-down factory where a couple of other cars are parked. Before switching off the engine, she looks at me. "Stay in here and don't panic if I suddenly disappear. I'll be back in a couple minutes." I get a pleasant and sincere smile before she exits the car.

I can see the sky outside but it's starting to feel a little cramped, so I'm sure she won't mind if I stretch my legs. After shouldering my knapsack, I get out and lean against the car while I count clouds in the late-May sky. Maybe when I get a little more money, I can look into therapy.

I glance into the driver's seat, mostly from boredom. The meter isn't turned on. Nice of her, I guess, but she did say that Dave paid for the ride, so I'll have to thank him for that. The passenger seat is flecked though, and if I were paranoid I'd swear it looked like...

Blood.

Okay, deep breaths. This doesn't mean anything. I mean, I was okay with coming out here. I was the one who said I was hungry, and she suggested...

This place is not a coffee shop. This is a place where informants get whacked.

I open the driver's side door, no keys, of course. The flecks on the seat are still wet. Shit, shit, shit. I can see a laminated card on the floor, and when I pick it up, it's the cab driver's ID.

And the cab driver's name is Ronaldo Chavez.

Damn it, I knew she was too attractive to be driving a cab.

"Fuck." I scramble backward out of the car and collide with someone. I hear a click a second later, something hard and metallic pressed to the back of my head.

"Two years. You think we didn't know about you, Keth?" Her voice has lost its niceness. Cold. All business.

"What makes you think I'm...whatever that is?" Feign ignorance, maybe I'll get out of this alive.

"You're not bit, not twin, not a leech, and a *dragon*, one of the stingiest creatures in creation, paid your fare. Don't take a knocker and an abacus to figure out."

"Listen, whatever it is that I did, I'm sorry." I raise my hands slowly.

"You haven't done a thing, *yet*." Her hand presses down on my shoulder, nudging me to my knees. I comply, feeling tears start to well up. "It's nothing personal, you seem like a nice kid, but you're Keth, and sorcerers don't stay nice. I'll make it quick. And for what it's worth, I'm sorry."

I don't want to be here anymore.

I close my eyes, I take a deep breath.

When I open them, the world is black, inky, the sky above me is lightless, no sun or ceiling, just water. Endless dark water. Where the *fuck* am I?

I fight the urge to leap into the air and start kicking. If I lose it, I'll drown. I have to stay calm. I get to my feet. My lungs start to burn, my eyes squinting to keep out the water, a dark-red haze in the distance and a growing roar accompanying it. My name is amidst the peals of hatred.

The Fae is a statue in the dark, holding the gun, pointing at where my head should be. The hammer is halfway home, her finger squeezed. Her face is passive, eyes somber. Right now, though, I couldn't give a shit if she feels guilty. I run away from her, away from the approaching bloody dawn.

My mouth bursts open as the sidewalk tears into my shoes, the dirt frozen in place, sharp like thousands of tiny blades. The water rushes into my lungs, the shock sending me headlong as the world starts again, the crash of the pistol behind me, I can't tell how far. I pick myself up and keep running, north, west, east, south, I don't know, just *away*.

My eyes lock on the sky as I wheeze, trying to keep my sprint from slowing to a jog. I'm not drowning, I'm not drowning, I can breathe, I can—

I hear the pistol crack again, and I break right into a vacant lot, the grass tall here, yellowed and dead, loud and rustling. I concentrate and suck air into my lungs, the world going black again as I collide into a wall made of grass, the blades becoming literal as they tear through my shirt and sleeves. I lean back into the trampled area, the sky growing red, the sound around me growing louder, angrier. I chance a look behind me and see ethereal crimson figures rushing toward me, talons materializing from their hands, their eyes sickly green, vaporous maws screaming my name. My *real* name.

The shriek that issues from me echoes theirs as the world returns, but I can't stop screaming, even as I see her emerge from behind a nearby building, finding me. My body feels beaten, bruised, drained, and to run forward would be into a bullet, and in the other place, it would be into the maw of the nightmare.

Panicking, I dive into the grass to the right, obscuring me from her for a few seconds while I dig through my knapsack for the scissor blade. Pulling it free, I grasp it in my hand, tightly. When I get back up, she's in front of me, the gun leveled at my head.

I won't be able to bring the shear up in time. I can accept the bullet, or take my chances with the frozen hell on the other side of time.

I hold my breath, bring the shear up as fast as I can as I pass between worlds.

The screech as the blade slices through the crimson haze is deafening, my head throbbing as I push through, around the time-stopped statue of the girl, through the trampled grass and out to the street. Errant blades slice cleanly through my jeans, drawing blood that hangs motionless in the air as I push forward toward the street, the half-shear before me like the tip of a lance. The haze parts for me until I reach pavement, my breath sputtering as I break right down the street, time returning with another crack of her pistol. The shear drips with a black ichor as I keep running, my gait altered by the cuts to my legs, my jeans stained with my blood as the shredded fabric clings to the wounds.

My sight locks on a building a block ahead of me, the only one at the intersection. I breath in huge gulps, the world flashing between darkest night and afternoon sun as I gain a few steps but feel like my insides are being chewed away every time I jump through the barrier.

The building is three floors, a storefront making up the first floor, the windows not boarded up, the architecture classic or

Victorian. I could give a shit what it's called. All I know is that someone might be there. Someone who could help me.

I reach the steps of the building, exhausted, my body ignoring adrenaline now. Turning to face the intersection, I see her approach, her face still cold, but more annoyed than sad now. Apparently my will to live has stripped her moment of any mercy.

She raises the gun, she won't miss. I don't have anything left. Will it hurt?

The gun goes off, but I don't feel a thing.

A wall of ice is now in front of her, a dark spot inside surrounded by a spiderweb of cracks.

"Did you enjoy that, miss?" The voice is male, adult, vestiges of a London accent. When I look up, I see a man over six feet, lanky, wearing black slacks, a warm red turtleneck, his auburn hair long, tied back neatly, wire-rimmed glasses with small lenses, pale complexion. He strides past me, down the steps, toward the wall where the girl is on the other side, standing still in shock and fear. "That was but a syllable."

The man holds up a hand when she starts to respond.

"No, no, I wasn't finished. Ice is fascinating, don't you find? Most elements, when frozen, compress, but water expands. It can take whatever shape you desire. Ice can be a wonderful teaching tool, would you care for a lesson?"

He steps toward the wall, and I hear him say...something, but I don't understand it. Her feet are suddenly encased in ice, though, and she drops the gun, raising her hands. "Please, I meant no—"

"Miss, I care little for what you mean." He runs his hand over the wall, and it goes clear as glass. Up above the sky starts to darken, thunder rumbling in the distance. "Much like with snowflakes, every kind of ice is unique, each with its own name. Did you know that?" The wall suddenly vanishes, and he kicks away the gun, which skids across suddenly frozen pavement toward a sewer grate. "Blood is mostly water, you know. Freezes nicely, I hear. Would you like to know *that* name?"

She quivers in terror as he steps closer.

"No?"

She viciously shakes her head.

"I see." He waves his hand, and the ice keeping her trapped shatters, her legs intact and unharmed. He leans in close to her. "Then *fuck off.*"

The woman with the orange eyes and pointed ears turns quickly and dashes away as the sky grows more turbulent overhead, lightning racing visibly across the sky. The man does an about-face and walks toward me. I want to be afraid, but I'm too exhausted to feel much of anything.

He kneels in front of me and inspects the half-scissor in my hand, his golden catlike irises meeting mine. "Are you here to kill me?"

I weakly shake my head.

He smiles and helps me to my feet. "Then I'd best get you inside."

"Who was she?" It takes so much effort to speak.

"Half-blood. Half-Fae. Doesn't matter though. Nearly everything will want to kill you, my young Keth."

I swallow hard, since I haven't had a good track record with people who figure out that I'm a sorcerer. "What makes you think I'm one of them?"

He laughs, opening the door to the shop, his face losing its earlier intensity. "Because, my dear boy, it takes one to know one."

Chapter Six

I'm seated in a plush, deep-blue overstuffed chair, my feet up on an ottoman. A couple of full-length mirrors are directly in front of me on a raised platform. The air is warm, comfortable, no dust hanging in the air.

Behind me are the front windows, the walls exposed brick with landscape paintings filling every gap, interrupted by a stairwell cordoned off by a velvet rope, and then a large shelf against the far eastern wall, filled with hats. To my far right is a display case with ties and other accessories, a classic brass cash register sits at the end of the counter.

The man went upstairs shortly after setting me in the chair, and I'm too exhausted to get up and follow him. I don't even know where I am, outside of being in the Benedict. All I know is that a lady who was kind of nice was actually trying to kill me.

And most especially I never want to hold my breath again. I don't know how I did what I did, but it fucking terrifies me.

I hear steps on the stairs, and the man returns, carrying two saucers with teacups, steam rising off them. He crosses the room and offers me one. "I didn't know how you took it, so I went with one lump and honey."

Meekly, I take the saucer and cup and blow off the steam. Lemon tea. It's good. "Thank you."

"Only proper." He sits on the dais in front of the mirrors.

"I mean for before. Outside."

Smiling, he shrugs. "Least I could do. It's been some time since I had company that wasn't hostile, even longer since that company was pleasant to look at. I'm grateful for the chance to converse."

I hide my confusion with a sip of my tea. "I don't get it, it's a bad neighborhood but there are people around." I gesture to the clothing racks. "You don't get business?"

"Not in some time. I doubt the locals could afford my work, and my home is nigh impossible to find." He motions to the shop. "This is merely a hobby. A man needs something to keep him occupied lest he go cracked in the head."

"So, who are you? I mean..." I remember the rule. "What should I call you?"

With that, he sets his cup and saucer next to him on the dais and peers at me. "An honest question, but I suppose that depends on the answer you seek. You ask what you should call me, which might be wholly different than what others might call me. And then of course there's what I call myself, but I doubt you've earned that. Which of these would you prefer?"

I tilt my head, studying his golden eyes that dance the line between exotic and unsettling. "You're not a cat, are you?"

He shows real surprise. "Beg pardon?"

"Just flashes of T. S. Eliot there." Mom teaches literature. "You know, 'The Naming of Cats'?" He still stares at me in disbelief. "There's the name their family gives them, the name the other cats call them, and the name that—"

"I'm familiar, I'm just pleased that you know that. Good to see that Keth are still well read. No, I'm not a cat. But with my Mark, I'm not surprised you think so." He can see my confusion, and continues. "Magic marks us as different from other humans, and unlike the mythics who can live amongst the blissfully ignorant, our Marks make us visible to all." He reaches forward, running a finger along my white streak of hair.

So *that's* how everyone can tell...

"I would suppose your magic skews toward death?"

I blink at his statement. "Why would you think that? What, white hair means necromancer?"

"I'm afraid I don't know that term. Marks are marks, nothing more. Perhaps there is some rhyme or reason to them, but none of us have ever been able to discern it. My pet theory is that it's a reflection of the Keth's soul, but I wouldn't want to monopolize the conversation. Besides, I've yet to answer your question. Why do I think that? Simply put, I felt it. Magic of that order sends out powerful ripples. I'm surprised you're not dead, honestly." He leans back, drinking more of his tea. "So what shall I call you, young Keth? I could come up with a name or two, though I warn they wouldn't be appropriate for polite conversation."

"James." I say quickly. "I prefer James."

His smile grows wider. "And that is not the name you call yourself. I would suspect it's forgotten to all but you, yes?"

No. No it's not. Those...things on the other side, they weren't calling for James. They were calling for Miles. "That's actually why I'm out here. I don't want to be forgotten."

He stands and turns to face the two mirrors, leaving me to watch his reflections. Eerily, the reflection on the left begins speaking while the one on the right remains quiet. "To not be forgotten, now *that* is a worthwhile pursuit." The right reflection then speaks. "Unless you prefer the warm blanket of anonymity."

The left. "To craft a legend, to be known in this world and the next!"

The right. "To be safe. Comfortable. Able to pursue your own desires!"

Left. "To be respected by even the gods themselves!"

Right. "To forsake destiny and walk the path of your choosing!"

Left. "To be feared!"

Right. "To be free!"

Both of them then speak in unison as he turns to face me and joins them. "To be the Ra'keth."

Weird reflections, odd speech, feline disposition, just a bit off... "So...you're a Cheshire cat?"

He laughs, the same as when he brought me inside, and points at me good-naturedly. "I like you. Most I've met think I'm insane."

"I think it's more that you haven't talked to anyone in..." I look around at the spotless shop. "How long have you been in here? Why haven't you left?"

He motions out the windows. "You saw the gathering storm?"

I nod.

"Not my doing. There are many that I've angered over the course of my life. When I leave my home, they can find me, and tend to make quite a show of it as you saw." He sits back down. "As for how long it's been..." He shrugs indifferently. "I'm getting away from the topic. And shame on you for letting me be so tangential. You were saying you have issues with being forgotten?"

"My family doesn't remember me. I thought I could handle it, but I saw my brother today and..." I look at the floor. "I can't deal with that. Someone told me that the Recluse set that rule, and if I didn't like it—"

"So you're looking to kill him." His tone turns deadly serious. "I tell you now, James, no one will end the reign of the Recluse but me. He has done his share of damage to my life as well. It is because of him that I am trapped in this prison, that all manner of gods call for my blood. Whatever reasons you believe you have, mine are tenfold yours."

I blink. "I, uh, was more thinking I could ask him how I could help my family remember me again. I don't want to kill anyone." Enough people are dead in my life. "So, you know who the Recluse is?"

"No one to be trifled with. Someday his time will come, and I will be there. Until then, I will bide my time." He gets up again and looks down at me in the chair. "How long have you been Keth?"

I shrug. "I don't really know. Maybe two years? I didn't figure out a spell until a year ago."

"Your...traveling?"

I shake my head. "No, that just started today. I learned a stupid little spell, just something to help me wake up in the morning."

He sighs with visible relief. "A good thing. Mucking about with the veil between worlds always brings ill tidings. Who knows what you might bring back with you if you keep hopping about?"

"Like...what?" I think back to the vaporous *things* that were over there, the black ichor on the blade when I came back.

He tilts his head at me, his expression reminding me of an addled kitten. "Didn't I say 'who knows'? If I knew, I wouldn't ask, I'd simply tell you, but I don't, so I can't. I suppose I could make use of a simile to illustrate the point, but analogies can be dangerous since the world is like a sandcastle. Regardless, I suggest you learn caution regarding your workings."

"Well, could you teach me then?" Be a sorcerer's apprentice. I keep myself from images of hacking walking broomsticks to death. "At least how to control what I can do so I don't blow myself up from talking in my sleep?"

He leans toward me. "And if I say no, what then?"

"Uh, I'd ask again and say please as well?"

That earns another laugh, and he shakes his head slowly. "I'm afraid I can't just take on a student."

"Why not?" I motion to the otherwise empty room. "It's not like you're doing anything."

He sighs. "I've never taken one. I would have no idea where to start."

"Maybe with ice?" He darts me a look, and I raise my hand in surrender. "Hey, you said outside it was an excellent teaching tool."

He stares at me incredulously. "Yes, to teach trespassers to fuck off. It took me *years* to perfect what I did out there. Besides, I'm well aware how tenuous my grip on reality is becoming. I could end up teaching you all the wrong things and you'll end up slashing Fate in twain whilst conjuring your tea and biscuits."

A moment passes. "What if I said pretty please?" He's looking out the window, not responding. "What about please with a cherry on top?"

He grumbles softly. "Curse you, now I'm in the mood for biscuits." He holds his saucer in front of him and murmurs more words that I don't understand, and the empty teacup disappears in a flash of blue light, several biscuits (cookies, rather) appearing in its place. He promptly begins to eat one.

"How did you do that?"

He perks a brow at me in disbelief. "Magic, how else?" A second passes. "It had one name, I changed it to another. What was once a pocket of air outside my window became a block of ice, which became stone, which became a teacup, which became biscuits." He shrugs again, indifferently. "Simple."

I stare at the cookies on the plate. "Those were originally air? How..."

His finger taps my nose. "Magic, dear boy. Magic." He leans back a moment, contemplating. "I want books."

I blink, trying to keep up. "Um, okay?"

He sets down the plate of cookies and helps me to my feet. I can stand, but I'm wobbly. "I can conjure anything I desire, James, but if I want to conjure a book, it can only be one I've read before, and a man can only leaf through so many penny dreadfuls for the fortieth time before he goes mad. Bring me books, *any* books, and our agreement will be copacetic."

I freeze. "What did you say?"

"Hm? I'd like books."

I take a deep breath. "You said copa..." Trembling, I look at my feet.

"It means quite satisfactory, at least I believe it still does. I'm hardly one to give a vocabulary lesson."

"Could you not use it? I..." I look away. I could swear I feel freezing water lapping at my ankles. "I just don't like that word."

He shrugs. "Fair enough, though I'll restrict you from using a word I find equally detestable."

"That being?"

He leans forward, eyes meeting mine, brimming with intensity. "*Putting.* It is an abhorrent word that puts on airs of sounding like pudding, but instead of sweetness it brings naught but bitterness to one's palate. We are agreed, then?"

Okay... Well, at least the imminent panic attack goes away. I have to be grateful to him for that, no matter how crazy it is to hate the word *putting.*

I nod in assent. "So no preference on books? Just go into a used book store and load up?" I stumble, my knees wanting to buckle, but he grabs me, holding me up, his grip gentle. Tension rises, more my fault than his. Our eyes meet a second before I quickly glance away. *For God's sake, James, you just met this guy.*

"I had a customer some time ago, back when I allowed them in. He was raving about a book. Perhaps you could find similar works. I can't remember the author. The title had the word *falcon* in it, though."

"*The Maltese Falcon?*" Thom loves those books, I'm pretty sure they're why he became a cop.

"I believe that was it, yes." He looks hopeful now. "You could find them?"

"Shouldn't be a problem. I can get a bunch of those, probably." I look toward the window. "One question though. How do I get back here, if no one's supposed to be able to—"

"Right, right..." His lips then press hard against mine, his breathing warm as it flows into my mouth, his tongue slipping in gingerly afterward. It only lasts a few seconds, but I feel limp as he pulls back. Wow. "That should be that, then. Off you go." He helps me toward the door and opens it, nudging me across the threshold. "By the by, you may call me Cale."

And he shuts the door behind me.

Chapter Seven

July

I hate magic.

I hate invocation, evocation, divination, alteration and transmutation.

But more than anything?

"I hate conjuration." I place another clean plate on the stack, the breakfast rush not too bad today. I actually have time to yawn.

Dave doesn't say anything, he just lets me go when I start off.

"I thought it was going to be cool, you know? But it *sucks*. All of those books I read when I was a kid, all those games I played, you just say a couple words or wave a damned wand and poof, there's a five-course meal." I scrub harder, Sabbath coming on to the radio to give my frustration a soundtrack. "Five *courses*. I can't even conjure a plate of French fries. And why? Because somewhere along the way someone decided that magic had to be complicated."

Dave, again, doesn't respond. He reaches for a clean plate and assembles the meal, puts it in the pass-through. "Order up!"

"Christ, you'd think French fries would be simple, right? Just use the name and bam! But no, there's a fu—" I stop myself. Sharon's on shift today, and I catch a glance from her. "Fudging infinite variety of French fries, and each one has a specific name."

It's funny. She, like everyone else who's not magical or mythical, doesn't hear me talking about the complex mechanics of manipulating reality, but the profanities come through loud and clear.

"So not only do I have to specify I want fries, but the specific type of potato, the cut, the amount of crispiness, salt, temperature..." I grumble, start on another plate. "I mean, at that point, the amount of effort and energy you're expending, you might as well drop by McDonald's."

That earns a glare from Dave.

"Or, here, if you want *quality* fries." I grin but it doesn't work.

"Stop getting down on yourself, Black, you just started."

"Dave, I've been studying with Cale five hours a day every day, and going over all of the notes he gives me another two or three hours a night. For six weeks."

"Well, what about Friday night? You conjured up that Jell-O mold. That's progress, right?"

I sigh. "It was supposed to be a shoe."

"Oh." He shrugs. "Well, didn't taste bad, at least." A few seconds pass before he speaks again. "Listen, if you want to do this full time, we can work something out. I can bring someone else on..."

"For what you pay me? Unlikely. Besides, washing dishes is normal. If I mess it up, a plate ends up a bit spotty instead of an oak tree suddenly transmuting into a monolith of Swiss cheese that's prone to spontaneous combustion." When I look over at Dave he's staring at me, and I snicker nervously. "Cale's been oddly specific in his cautionary tales."

"I've been meaning to ask about that. You sure it's okay to be learning from someone who seems a little..." He says a word I don't recognize, probably draconic, but he twirls a claw pointed at his head to give me context.

"As opposed to who? Besides, he's not as bad now. I bring him books, he gets actual social interaction. He's not as..." I remember last Thursday, when he was having an impassioned argument with his cup of tea when I arrived. "Well, he still is a little, I guess."

There's no response, not from Dave, but I see Monica standing at the pass-through, grinning. "Jimmy, you got a boyfriend?"

"What? No!" I turn my attention back to the dishes. "He's just a guy I'm studying with, that's all. Nothing more." So what if I've replayed that kiss a couple of times? It's the only kiss I've gotten in the last two years. Besides, I was exhausted and he'd saved my life and I didn't get any warning.

And it's not like I kissed him back!

"Yeah, sure. *Studying.* I used to *study* with guys in high school *all* the time. By the way, if you want to be convincing, Jimmy, you shouldn't blush when you say that." She chuckles, picks up the order and heads off to serve.

I return to my work. "I might be staying a little later tonight, since it's summer." Zombies don't shamble the streets until after dusk. I don't know what I'm going to do this winter for getting over to Cale's.

"Actually..."

"What?" I turn to face him.

"I need you to run over to Allora and drop off yesterday's deposit since *someone* gave me a splitting headache with all their half-assed casting." I get a hard glare. Dave wasn't kidding when he said that dragons are sensitive to magic.

"Isn't that Sharon's job?"

"It is, but if she does it today then *someone* won't learn anything. Besides, she's got something at her kid's school." Sharon has a five-year-old daughter, Tessa. She loves ponies and thinks my hair is pretty. Dave grins toothily. "And I figured you want to get paid this week."

"Fine. I'll do it. You realize the second I learn how to conjure twenty-dollar bills..." I think about it. "Well, my brother will probably arrest me for counterfeiting. Plus I'd probably cause a financial collapse or something." I grumble again. "I'm starting to see why all the wizards are so cynical in books."

I spend the rest of the workday on autopilot, which isn't that hard in the kitchen. The new girl, Annette, will be coming on after I leave. Nineteen, pretty, Mediterranean complexion, taking a year off to save up for tuition. I think she has green eyes, but I've only met her a couple of times. She seems nice enough.

Cale will be wondering why I'm late, so I'll probably have to stop at a bookstore and grab him some more Raymond Chandler. He's gotten into the hard-boiled fiction. It's too bad he doesn't have a movie projector. He'd probably love to see *Casablanca*, but the latest advance of technology I've seen at Cale's is a Victrola still in showroom condition, and his vinyl selection sucks.

When I get on the train, yesterday's deposit is in a locked envelope in my knapsack, which is secure and safe right next to me. The Blue Line goes to the Benedict and to Victory Station, so I don't worry about making any transfers.

I'm keeping casual, no shady types on the train, just a woman sitting across from me, older, an executive in an expensive-looking pantsuit, gray hair tightly tied back in a bun. I've only had to do this a couple times, but it's pretty easy to drop it off in a night slot or toss it at a teller. The bank does all the work, really, it's just taking up time.

Should've showered before I left, given that the woman across from me is looking at me with slight revulsion. I probably smell like a vat of grease, but screw it, I'm grateful to be off my feet.

I do my best to look friendly to the woman, the "tip me" smile as Monica calls it. Don't want her freaking out. All I get back is a derisive glare. Bitch.

So instead, I think about French fries. Maybe I can stop at that one place in Grunstadt. Heath took me there in the beginning, but the fries were good enough that I won't hold that against them. The place even had a chalkboard to tell customers that the fries that day were made from russet potatoes from a farm just outside of Boise, Idaho. They came in a soda cup, curled, crispy, almost hot enough to burn your tongue.

Damn, I can practically *smell* them and—

And in my hand is a large white soda cup, filled to overflowing with French fries, just like I remember. *Exactly* as I remember.

Cale said he could only conjure books that he'd read before. Is it the same with everything else?

Gingerly, I take one and bite it, and my God it's perfect. No Jell-O here.

However, a chunk of the seat next to me is now missing. Also, I feel like I just ran three miles. Fuck, McDonald's is still looking like the better alternative.

And now I'm thankful that the vanillas don't see things like this, though I move my knapsack to cover the hole I've made in the seat. Nothing says people won't notice that, and I'd rather they didn't until I'm off the train.

We're going under Victory Tower now, into the station. The train comes to a stop, and I disembark and promptly dry heave into the nearest waste bin while the executive lady walks by, snorting in disgust. How the hell does Cale do this? Maybe magic's like a muscle or something. Anyway, it doesn't matter now. I've got to get the deposit to the bank and—

Wait, where's my knapsack?

I turn to stare at the train as the bell tolls, my knapsack still on the seat, in clear view, as the doors start to slide closed.

"Fuck!" Panicking, I hold my breath and nearly scream as the time-frozen Victory Station phases in.

It's not dark here, the station brilliantly lit with green balefire, the floor scored with craters, the tracks replaced with rivers of black ichor, silver fire, cloudy mists, a thick red liquid, all of them teeming with flailing people.

I can see the train on the silver river, the door frozen open, the executive woman standing between me and it. "Miles Canmore."

Fuck the deposit. I'll work it off. I open my mouth and suck in...

Acrid air. The frozen station remains as I cough and hack, my nose burning with the smell of brimstone.

A bony finger wags gently at me. "Now now, let's not be rude, Miles."

"I don't even know you!" I circle to my left, but she simply pivots to keep facing me.

She laughs cruelly. "No. You don't know me, not anymore. Not since you left my daughter's tapestry. Would you like to leave this place, Miles?"

I swallow hard and lift my arm to my mouth, squinting my eyes to keep them from aching. "Yes!"

"Then I want one simple thing. I want the life of the god-killer. You will slay the Ra'keth."

How can I kill the Sorcerer King when I don't even know who it is?

She steps toward me, slowly, foreboding following with her. "I believe that is a fair bargain for your life. After all, you weren't supposed to leave that bus. Now be a good boy, Miles, and do as I say."

The way she says my name, it sounds the way that Heath would...

Right before he'd...

And I was so afraid to fight back, even though I could feel the punch deep inside me, yearning, screaming, raging to get out.

"No."

I don't want to be here anymore.

She laughs suddenly, incredulously. "*No?*"

All I wanted was for him to feel everything he'd done to me, all of the fear, anger, helplessness, the shame, the aches from cowering in a corner for the better part of a day knowing what would happen if he found something out of place. I wanted him to know what it felt like to be a conduit for his rage, to steel myself and let him fuck me because I knew it would avoid another fight, keep him from taking it out on someone else, how low and worthless and *useless* I felt whenever he...

How it would happen again and again, without warning, without reason, like lightning strikes from a vindictive god...

I owed him pain.

I extend my hand toward her. "My name is *James Black*." An arc of argent electricity lances from my fingers, slamming into her body and sending her with great speed into a support pillar ten feet away where she crumples into a heap. I step toward her. "And I am *no one's* fucking lightning rod."

I get onto the train, leaving her behind as the world becomes normal again. Collapsing onto the seat, I find my knapsack with the deposit envelope still inside, as well as the cup of fries still next to it. I feel woozy, my nose runny, wiping it only stains my shirtsleeve red.

"What the fuck did I just do?"

"You hit a goddess in the face with lightning, James." I jump out of my seat and find Hades sitting across the car from me as it lurches into motion, starting the run out to the Benedict.

"How'd you know—"

"I know everything." He sighs audibly. "You couldn't have done it somewhere other than the arrival lounge? Thirty score souls were traumatized by your display. Tartarus has been rampant with stories of the Lightning Rod for four days." He motions to me. "You're going to ask who the Lightning Rod is. It's you. You'll then ask how it could have been four days, since you were only there a few minutes, and only gone from this side for less than a second. Simple, time flows differently, it's been four days in Tartarus. Time moves slower in the land of the living, especially nowadays, which is ironic if you think about it." I'm about to speak again, but he rolls his eyes to interrupt me. "I. Know. Everything."

"That answers that, I guess." I lean back against the window. "So, I'm in trouble, I take it?"

The god smirks. "Gee, you think?"

"Why—"

"Why would a goddess attack you like that? Fate hates nothing more than a sorcerer." I don't bother asking how he knew. I think that's obvious by now. "She can't see you."

I shake my head. "No, that's not right. She followed me when I was moving."

Hades rolls his eyes. "Of course she can see you, she can't *see* you, and she's supposed to *see* everyone. Just like you don't know her anymore. Keth are off the loom of Fate, so why would you know who the Fates are? The only reason you aren't being hunted down as we speak is because this occurred in *my* domain. The blind fury with the abhorred shears will not be slitting the thin-spun life without my say-so if it's happening on my turf. Furthermore, I'd appreciate it if you'd limit your jaunts into my realm. The only Keth that are supposed to be wandering Tartarus are the ones I've collected."

"You mean, I haven't been stopping time?"

"Of course not. Like it or not, your awakening as Keth is linked to the deaths of over thirty people. I'm not saying their blood is on your hands, but you claimed your thread from the river of death, which I pulled you from. Therefore, I suppose it's easy for you to slip the veil between the living and dead." He watches me stare blankly ahead in horror. "James, nothing's changed. You're alive, you're Anu'keth, and most importantly, you owe me."

I swallow hard. "Uh...does this mean I'm a necromancer?"

Hades scoffs. "By the river, James, this isn't a damned game. Do you know what it means to be Anu'keth? You have one purpose and one purpose only: kill the Ra'keth and take the throne."

"Could I ask you a question?"

He stares at me coldly. "Yes, you have to do it."

"That wasn't what I was asking." This takes him by surprise, and he motions with his hand for me to speak. "She said the Ra'keth was a god-killer, do you know anything about that?"

Hades puts on a poker face. "I can't comment on that."

"Can't or won't?"

He smiles slightly. "Yes."

"Fine. Then why are you helping me? I mean, it can't just be 'protecting your investment'."

"You think I have an ulterior motive?"

I look at him plainly. "You're a lawyer, aren't you?"

That earns a million-dollar smile. "I can take that deposit. I'm the bank the dragon trusts his money with." He holds out his hand, and I dig through the knapsack and hand the envelope to him. He tucks it inside his jacket and produces a cigarette from thin air, lighting it.

Even after two years I still have a craving for nicotine. I stay strong though. "It's not a good name."

"Hm?" He exhales a plume of smoke. "What was that?"

"The Lightning Rod, it's not a good name. I said I wasn't one."

Chuckling, he stubs out the cigarette on his finger. "Keth rarely get to choose their names. You should feel fortunate your story started before your legend did. Imagine if you were named for what happened in the river." He sees me visibly shudder, and he points at me gently. "You're going to be an interesting one, James Black."

"Is that why you're helping me?"

He laughs, shaking his head. "I'm not helping you, I'm protecting my investment, just like you said. I'll be honest, kid, you're a means to an end. Still though, two years and you can only manage three spells? Maybe I should've found another Keth."

"Fuck you."

"Oh, he's insulted." Hades produces a quarter and flips it at me. "Here, use that to call someone who gives a shit." The train reaches one of the stops on the way out to the Benedict, and he gets up, heading to the door, and flashes his high-beam smile. "Now I've got to get going. Much more important things to do. If you ever need legal assistance, you let me know."

I throw the quarter back at him. "Sure. Fine. Whatever. And phone calls are fifty cents anyway." Asshole. He catches the coin deftly and pockets it, never losing that smile as he departs. Dick.

The train leaves the station shortly afterward and continues its ride out to points east. My nosebleed has thankfully stopped, but I'm still woozy. Apparently I can bring up other things from my memories than French fries.

I don't know what came out of me, what composed that lightning, but it was terrible, powerful, and despite how drained I am now, at the time it felt limitless. And to tap it, to let myself feel those memories that I'd been pushing back for two years, to make them into...

It felt *good* to be the one giving out the pain for a change.

To be like Heath.

And that scares the shit out of me.

Chapter Eight

After the 90th and V station, I get to Cale's the way I do every day: wandering blindly.

The way he put it, you can't find him if you're looking for him. I discovered his shop only because I was fleeing for my life. Now, if I'm calm enough, I can follow whatever kind of charm he laid to help find my way back.

Calm is the tricky part, and the day I've had takes me an extra hour to get there. The worst part is that the haze of his enchantment lifts the moment I get to his building, and I feel like an idiot for forgetting yet again that he's at 106th and R street. I've tried writing it down, but something always happens, like the pen running dry, the paper gets lost, or wet, or goes through the laundry. I gave up after the fourth week.

"Hello?" The bell rings as I come inside. The shop is empty of life, but everything's been cleaned, so I know he's at least been downstairs today. I'm not to cross the velvet rope to the stairs without his permission, and I haven't earned that yet.

Outside the day is fading quickly. Not much time to study if I want to get home before the zombies are out.

"Cale?" I don't want to burn time waiting for his crazy ass to come downstairs. "You here?"

I hear footsteps not long afterward, and he descends to the shop, carrying a book, his finger sandwiched between the pages to mark his place. He's wearing a blue silk shirt today along with his black slacks and shoes, no tie. "I suspected you chose to skip your lessons for the day." He studies me a moment. "Is something amiss? You look out of sorts."

Stepping over the velvet rope, he crosses to me, inspecting closely. His fingers trail lightly over my cheek, under my eyes, his voice stern. "James, what have you been doing?"

Great, another interrogation. Whatever. I turn away from him and step toward the door. "I don't need this."

"You're leaving already?"

I grit my teeth. "I have to get going before dark, I'm running late as it is."

"Then why come out here at all?"

I turn toward him. "You know, I'm starting to ask myself the same thing. I'm learning more out there than I am in here." I'm getting woozy again. Uppity fucking asshole wasting my damned time.

He blinks once. "Well, there's no need to shout about it."

"I'm not shouting!" I put my hand on the doorknob, my knees buckling. "Oh fuck…"

The floor comes up to meet me shortly before everything goes black.

I don't know how much time passes, but thankfully, I'm not tied to anything.

There's a painting in my view, a street in a city, a café on the right, the indication of a river on the left, all in black swashes of paint, strange brushstrokes in the sky. I don't know if it was supposed to be famous, but it seemed familiar.

I'm in a bed, down mattress, wide enough for me to spread my arms and not touch the edges. The sheets are smooth, off-white, a thick blanket on top of me.

The rest of the room is sparsely furnished, a large area rug on the floor, an older pattern of wallpaper that reminds me of my grandparents' manor in England. There's a high-backed leather chair next to the bed, facing it at an angle, a copy of *The Big Sleep* on the night table. Light is provided by a pair of sconces on opposing walls.

The door opens and Cale enters, unamused but not angry. "This, my young Keth, is *precisely* why we do not draw on our souls when we work our will." He sits in the chair and huffs.

"This is also why I've been asking you to study conjuration and transmutation, so that the impact on you would be minimal. Instead, you stumble into my shop appearing to have nearly killed yourself with magic, start raving from soul-sickness and promptly lose consciousness." Muttering, he conjures a saucer and cup of tea, the book on the night table vanishing. "I didn't get to finish that, I'll have you know. Marlowe had just gotten into a gunfight with Canino. Now I'll never know how it turned out."

I take the tea and sip it. "Sorry. Do you want me to tell you how it—"

"Don't you *dare*." A soft smile cracks through his façade.

I work my back up to sit against the headboard, and he gives me aid. "I was doing what with my soul, now?"

"Have you ever heard the phrase that energy cannot be created nor destroyed? Magic works on the same principle. We cannot simply create things from thin air." He pauses a second. "Well, I *could*, but I would require a significant volume of thin air. Regardless, the power to work your will must come from somewhere. Transmutation takes some getting used to, as it can induce nausea, I've found, when first perfecting it. But it's far preferable to the alternative."

That would explain why conjuring French fries made me react like it did.

"So that's why I'm so tired?" Like I could sleep for a week.

"That, and maybe I have been running you a bit ragged over the last month."

"Six weeks."

He looks up, lips moving as he counts silently. "Are you certain? It hasn't felt that long. Now that you're in a better state, are you willing to talk about what you did to drain yourself to this point?"

No.

"I'm sorry I yelled at you."

He waves a hand. "Forgiven, forgotten. Without the soul the mind goes quite cracked. You'll be a bit moody for the next few days though. Your dragon friend may understand, but I can't say the same for other people you work with."

Oh right, work.

"What time is it?" Maybe I can still make it to the station, or hail a cab or something.

"Half past midnight."

Zombies will be out in full force. I'm here until morning.

"I would think the news that someone's soul is drained would be more off-putting." He gestures to my tea, and grudgingly I sip more of it. "And shame on you for making me say that detestable word." God, he can't even say it in a hyphenated fashion?

"Never really thought about it. I mean, I'm kind of lapsed as far as church goes. I can't even remember when I last went to confession, much less took Communion. Know my patron saints, at least." Heath openly mocked me whenever I mentioned going. Near the end I was conditioned enough to know going would put him in a hitting mood. "Will it get better? My soul, that is."

"Indeed, in a few days. Plenty of time to research the alternatives." He stretches in his chair, yawning.

The moment starts to get awkward, considering he's tired and I don't see any other beds. I glance at the painting on the wall. "Who did that?"

"Hm?" He looks over to the canvas and smiles to himself. "That would be mine."

"You did that?" I study it more intently. "So, what is it?"

"A small café next to the Seine at midday."

"You've been to Paris?"

He shakes his head. "Never." He yawns again. "No, I scried the image in my sanctum and held the viewing open while I painted the scene. All of the paintings downstairs were done in much the same way. You see, simply because I am confined to this place does not mean I cannot see the world outside. Unfortunately I cannot conjure anything I see, since it will only be what it is, an image. But at least it proves a marvelous way to pass the time."

His eyes look heavy. Damn it.

"Do you have a couch or something? I don't want to take your bed."

"I'm afraid not. You've never shared a bed before?"

I look away. I haven't since...

He laughs lightly. "James, unless you prefer the company of men you have little to worry about with me." I shimmy quickly over to the far side of the bed as he sits on the edge, leaning over to remove his shoes. A few seconds pass, and I hear an amused *hmph* from him before he continues. "I had suspected. Well, you still have little to worry about. It's been so long since I shared my bed with a man that I've forgotten what all of the fuss is about."

"What about when you kissed me, when we first met?"

He looks over his shoulder while he unbuttons his shirt. "That was a charm so you could find your way here and continue under my tutelage. I must thank you for that."

I arch a brow. "The kiss?"

"The tutelage. I had no idea how close to cracked I was fast becoming. Having someone to talk with has helped put me back on an even keel." He shrugs off his shirt, and I can see his back, his build thin, but lithe, his skin marked with numerous symbols, all of them curvy script and wholly illegible, but aesthetically pleasing to the eye, toned in a warm and soothing blue. "Though I will admit the kiss was enjoyable as well."

"Well, thanks for teaching me. Probably haven't been the best student." I take my normal position on a double bed, namely the edge. Takes a bit of balance, but I've got a lot of practice. I face away from him toward the wall, but I look over my shoulder when I hear a short zipping sound. "Cale? Just how much are you undressing?"

"Hm?" He's wearing, uh, nothing, and I only catch a glimpse before he slips under the covers but, well... Wow. "You have nothing to worry about. I'll be the perfect gentleman."

"The perfect gentleman wouldn't have shed all of his clothes."

"The perfect gentleman wouldn't allow his tailored clothes to be wrinkled." He narrows his eyes at me playfully. "Unlike someone."

I, thankfully, am still dressed. "These aren't tailored. I bought them at a thrift store." I shrug. "I'm poor."

"Is there a reason you're all the way over there?"

"What, going to say you won't bite unless I ask nicely?"

"More that I'm worried you'll fall off sometime during the night. That can't possibly be comfortable." He tilts his head at me. "Are you perhaps masochistic?"

"I'm suffering through this conversation, aren't I?" I look back at the wall. "I just don't want to take up too much space, that's all."

There's a long pause. "I'm intruding on something."

"Huh?"

"Is that why you seem skittish? I would guess there is someone else. When you're not in a mood, you are rather thoughtful, easy to talk to, and you're pleasing to the eye."

"You're asking me if I have a boyfriend?"

"I am."

"Why?"

Another amused *hmph.* "I have my reasons."

"That's an easy question. I did. He's dead."

"I'm..." I don't have to look over my shoulder to see that he's searching for the right words. "I'm sorry."

"I'm not." A second passes. "And I don't want to talk about it. I just want to sleep, all right?"

"Yes." I hear him exhale softly. "Yes, of course." He murmurs a word, and the room goes dark. There aren't any windows, no skylights. I can already feel panic setting in.

"Cale?" I try to keep my voice steady, but fear is tingeing it.

"What's wrong?"

I swallow hard, my face burning in shame. "Could you turn a light back on?"

"Hm? Oh, I don't have electric lights. Those are a pair of spells."

I start to curl into a ball, clenching my eyes shut. "Could you put one of them back on then?" Now panic is working in. I can feel the darkness around me. I can see the woman from earlier today in my mind, her bony hand reaching toward my face.

"I'll do one better, repeat after me. Slowly." He says some strange syllables, making me repeat them one at a time. The third is the most difficult, as I have no idea what a soft *k* is, but it ends up more like a flow of breath than a sound. "Good, now, look toward the wall and say them all in succession."

I don't know if I can remember. It's so damned dark in here. I can't see anything. It's cold, is it cold? Did I slip into Tartarus? Oh God, oh fuck, I'm scared, I'm so scared...

"James." I feel a warm hand on my shoulder, but I still practically jump out of the bed. I can feel tears flowing freely down my face. He's going to hate me now. No one likes a crybaby, that's what Heath always says. I was so stupid to think I could do this...

"James." I feel his arms circle me slowly. "Shhhh... You're safe." The words are whispered sweetly in my ear. "Just concentrate, push everything from your mind, remember the light that was there before on the wall, let the name come to you. I know you can."

Right now I can't remember anything other than the water rushing through the broken window, water around me, above me, below me, inescapable. I can feel myself shaking from the cold of the river. If I open my mouth, it'll flow into my lungs and I'll never get out.

"James Black, you are safe here."

The name cuts through the din in my mind, granting me clarity. All too quickly I'm reminded of what my name really is, that I can't hide from it, but it lasts long enough to remember an image from when I was young, the name of the memory slipping past my lips.

The room is gently lit with hundreds of tiny lights, taking up a corner and forming a vaguely triangular shape. The first Christmas after Mom and Dad split up for the last time, Dad got an apartment. Nice enough, but sullen. He got the tree for me. I was nuts about the tree lighting in Victory Square back then. That was the first year he wasn't able to take me, but he'd tried his best to recreate it. I was too young to appreciate the effort.

"Feeling better, James?" I become aware that Cale's still holding me, but I don't shimmy out of his grasp just yet. I'm more concentrating on the fact that the room isn't submerged and it's okay to breathe. "You gave me a bit of a fright there."

I reach up to wipe my eyes clear. "Sorry."

"I would suppose it's nothing you'd want to discuss." He doesn't give me time to answer. "I can respect a want for privacy. It would be hypocritical not to, considering."

I'll admit I smile slightly at that.

"Sorry I didn't do it right." I motion to the lights. "I know I was supposed to just make the light on the wall."

"I would hardly expect perfection the first time an apprentice attempts a working. I'm more pleased that the lights are bright and cheerful and that my wall isn't on fire." Sighing softly, he looks over at the wall. "A shame about that sconce, though."

In the dim light I can see that the glass of the lamp is heavily perforated now. I wouldn't be surprised if the number of lights matches the number of holes. "Sorry. Again."

"It's easily fixed. Normally light is acceptable to draw from one's soul, as it demands very little, but in your state I'd rather replace some glass than see you damage yourself further." Slowly, he disengages himself from me. "I'm certain you've had enough of that. Might I ask a question, though?"

"About?" I turn to face him, and the covers are up to his waist. I keep my eyes on his, and luckily golden eyes are easy to stare at.

"Is there some reason you're always in such a hurry to leave at sunset?"

"Well, the zombies?"

He replies with a blink of confusion.

"You know, Cale, the walking dead? They come out at night and roam the streets, eat people, all that?"

"You're worried about *vampyr*? You're Keth, James. They fear those who created them."

"Wait, they were created by..." Okay, I'll ask about that later. "No, not vampires, Cale, zombies. You know, rotting corpses that are still moving around? They eat brains or... Well, I don't know what they eat, but I'm not about to..."

"Zombies?" Cale starts laughing loudly, for several seconds, and it's a deep warm sound. "Oh..." He wipes a tear from his eye. "Oh dear, you worry about *them*? James, those are simply ghosts who still have a functioning body. They wander about, and that is all. They're to be pitied, not feared."

"Pitied for what?"

"Have you ever lost something and not been able to find it? Imagine that, for eternity, or at least until what's left of your body rots away. That is their existence."

"Why doesn't anyone help them find what they're looking for, then?"

Cale stares at me for a second. "James, that question is practically human."

"What, is that bad?"

His lips are pressed against mine and my eyes drift closed. Again, his tongue gently slips into my mouth, just to brush my own before he pulls back, his voice softer, pleased. "Far from it. However, communicating with their ilk requires death magic, which is nothing I'm familiar with, nor do I wish to become so. Even life magic feels off to me. I've only practiced it once, in fact, and under great duress." He grumbles. "Fae can be quite...pushy."

"You kissed me."

He nods once. "I did."

"Why?" My voice is small.

"For reminding me that I'm human as well. Also, I'm not intruding on anything, and you've admitted you prefer men, and perhaps I'm not as perfect a gentleman as I believed. Forgive my breach of etiquette, if you would." His lips brush mine again, and I return the gesture, however meekly. "I just wanted to say thank you, James."

"By kissing me when just saying it would have sufficed?"

"I'm Keth, dear boy. I'm used to doing what I desire without asking permission. It is the prime reason that several gods would love to see me draw my last breath. Someday they will, but not before the Recluse meets his end." He reaches to the night table and inspects a brass windup clock. "Regardless, given the late hour, I would suggest we continue this in the morning. I'd prefer you spend the next few days recovering, studying, and perhaps..."

"What?"

"Well, it's a dull task, honestly. It will be quite an adventure for you, though."

I swallow hard, but I can feel tendrils of excitement wrapping around me. An *adventure.*

"So, what?"

"You'll need an item to focus your will. Perhaps one of the standard phallic symbols—a wand, a staff, a rod. Like it or not, we are men, and our power is driven by..." He blushes slightly. "You get the idea."

"How do I find one?" I chuckle. "A focus, I mean."

"Don't look for something destined for your hand, Fate will play no part of it. Seek something that you *know* to be yours, and make it so."

"How do I do that, though?"

Cale smiles with a touch of indulgence. "James, I can't tell you how. You may be my student, but you will not work my magic, you will work your own. That is something I can't teach you."

"Anything I want, then?"

He nods.

Even though we've done this twice in the last few minutes, I'm nervous. I expect Heath to kick in the door. I still feel like I'm cheating, even though he never did anything to deserve my fidelity. But he's dead. He drowned.

"Cale?"

"Yes, James?"

I press my mouth against his, my teeth bumping his at first, my tongue awkward and clumsy as I'm out of practice, but he seems to welcome the gesture. It continues on, under the gentle glow of the twinkle-lights in the corner. When I pull back, he's smiling.

"I had best get to sleep before I commit a major breach of etiquette, though I wonder what Emily Post would advise about this." He turns away from me, wriggling his legs slightly. I'll admit my pants are slightly...uncomfortable as well, but if I'd gone Cale's route I suspect we'd both be crossing Emily Post.

"Sleep well, Apprentice."

"But..."

"James Black, go to sleep."

I fade into slumber seconds later.

Chapter Nine

I wake to the smell of coffee, which is never unwelcome.

I dreamed about a big oak tree in Oxford that Thom and I pretended was full of elves and fairies when we'd visit Mom. Knowing what I know now, I wouldn't be surprised if it actually was. Strange that I fell asleep so quickly, it usually takes me an hour of tossing and turning, especially on an unfamiliar bed. Maybe it was the "soul-sickness" Cale had spoken of or...

He'd told me to go to sleep, and I did almost immediately.

Suffice it to say, when Cale enters the bedroom carrying a cup smelling of a delicious French roast, I look quite cross.

"Cream and sugar. I didn't know how you took it, but this is the only way I know how to conjure it." Cale is dressed, black slacks and an off-white shirt. He watches me, sets the cup on the night table. "Is something wrong? Didn't you sleep well?"

My voice quivers. "*Never* do that again. Ever."

"I suspect we're not talking about the coffee."

"Don't...*make* me do things."

Concerned now, he kneels before me. "James, it was only because you needed—"

"Just don't. If it takes me an hour to get to sleep, that's on me, all right? I don't give a damn if you're Keth or not, that is the one thing you don't do without asking permission. Just don't..." I look away.

That's something Heath would've probably done.

"James, I'm sorry. Honestly. I have no excuse. Knowing someone's name, the temptation is always there. It is something the Recluse would do, and for that I am truly sorry. Will you forgive me?" He takes my hand and squeezes it.

He seems sincere. For now, I guess.

I look down at his hand that covers mine. "Maybe." I slip my hand free. "Listen, uh..." I take the coffee from the night table and sip it slowly. "I should probably get going. I'll at least need to call my boss and use a personal day or something." I glance around the floor, searching. "You see my shoes anywhere?"

He nods as I take a long gulp. God, that's good coffee.

"So, where are they?"

"I had to dispose of them, they were threadbare and the soles were heavily damaged."

I shouldn't be surprised, considering my jaunts into Tartarus. Apparently that's hell on your footwear. Ha ha. "So you just threw them out?"

He shakes his head. "No, I transmuted them. Waste not, want not."

I stare at my coffee. "Oh." For the first time in my life I don't want a second cup. "Well, I am going to need shoes."

Cale nods again.

"So..."

Cale waits expectantly for me to continue.

"So do you have a spare pair of shoes I can borrow?"

Cale appraises me a few seconds. "Is that all? Are you truly planning on going out like that?"

I blink, as my clothes aren't that bad. Thrift store, sure, but not ratty. At least they don't seem that way to me. "What? This is what I wear."

His eyes widen slightly, his mouth parted. "I simply assumed you were dressing like a vagrant to avoid notice."

"Well, you know what happens when you assume."

Cale nods matter-of-factly. "Of course, you'll always turn out to be right. But, it would appear this time I was mistaken." He looks into my eyes, worried, his hand resting on mine again. "James, are you indigent? It's all right, you can tell me."

"Cale, do you have any idea how much you're insulting me right now?"

"I'm quite serious, James. Please, I want an answer."

I scoff in disgust and get off the bed, leaving him behind as I advance to the doorway. "For God's sake, I'm not homeless!"

Instead, I'm sharing a loft with a dragon who snores like two chainsaws having angry sex.

"James, don't leave."

I stop at the doorway and look back at him. "And if I do, what then? Will you command me to be happy? Order me to dress better?"

Cale gets a bit huffy. "If this is the attitude you plan to cultivate then—"

I step toward him. "What, we consider it off? Good luck finding someone to get you more books. Christ, to think I kissed you last night."

He narrows his eyes. "You won't have to worry about me making any advances in the near future. I suppose we'll keep this professional, yes?"

I set my jaw. "Fine. Those eyes are creepy anyway."

"At least I don't pass for an unhinged vagabond."

A minute passes while we exchange spiteful glares. He folds his arms. "You may go."

I manage to slam the door behind me as I move into the hallway. "Asshole."

Unfortunately a certain part of my body doesn't quite agree. God damn it.

Cale doesn't follow me downstairs to the shop. Just as well, I guess. I do find shoes along the back wall, though they're all Oxfords, which will hardly go with distressed jeans and a faded *++ungood;* T-shirt. I fetch the shoes, since no matter how much they might clash I can't go traipsing about the Benedict in my bare feet.

I'll admit I think about taking some clothes off the racks, but I just don't want Cale to be right. Mom and Dad both had issues with the way I dressed, and I remember the tantrum I threw when they sent me to private school. Uniforms just beg you to get rolled for lunch money by the public school kids.

When I look in the mirrors on the dais, though, I wonder if I should have at least taken a shower, and perhaps washed my clothes. And brushed my teeth. And my hair. Okay, so I look a *little* haggard, but it's not that...

"God damn him."

I'm browsing through the racks when there's a noise behind me. Cale is by the counter, a stack of folded clothes next to him, no jacket.

"I hate being a foregone conclusion."

Cale shrugs. "Consider it a peace offering? I pulled them from the rack while you were still asleep. Besides, I'd prefer my apprentice looked..."

"Employed?"

"Respectable. You have a pleasing appearance, you should accentuate it with the correct attire."

Wordlessly, I take the clothes and walk over behind the dais and mirrors so I can dress. All neutral colors. Black trousers, charcoal socks, black Oxfords, slate gray shirt. I'll admit everything fits nicely, not perfectly, but nicely. There's no tie, so I leave the top button undone. When I step up on the dais I catch the curtest of nods from him, and I do look a lot better, more like someone who finished college than someone scrubbing greasy dishes for an under-the-table wage.

I head for the door, opening it, but stop in the doorway and look back. "Do you want me to pick anything up for you?"

He doesn't answer, so with a shrug, I exit into the midmorning weather. It's already warming up, probably in the low eighties, though I have no idea what time it is, considering Cale doesn't believe in clocks and all of the watches in his display case are set to noon.

The zombies have already receded to their various and sundry resting places, so no checking to see if they really are as innocuous as Cale claims. Instead I get to deal with walking more than twenty blocks in a set of Oxfords that haven't been properly broken in. I swear that my right foot is just one big blister by the time I make it to the 90th and V station to catch the Blue Line back to Beckettsville. The time is shown on the interior of the car: 9:34 a.m. I am so very late for work.

Now I have to wonder if teleportation is a spell I can actually do, though given that it's a higher-level spell I'd have to transmute a chunk of the Blue Line to make it work. The UTA would take issue with that, not to mention I don't want to accidently transmute a bunch of people as well. Just because Hades said my magic is linked to Tartarus, it doesn't mean I'm going to go death-mage and start listening to Bauhaus.

The diner's not far from the 65th and L station, so it's a quick walk. I arrive at the same time as a uniformed officer, who stops and stares at me.

"James? You're looking good." A couple seconds pass, and he chews his lip during it. That means he's feeling awkward. "Still working here?"

"Mostly splitting my time between here and learning a trade. Seriously, I'm an *apprentice*." I puff myself up with faux pride.

He laughs, and I feel a little better. "Dare I ask?"

I shrug. "A tailor, but hey, free clothes, right?" I motion toward the diner. "C'mon, I'll buy you a cup of coffee."

"I thought I didn't have to pay here."

"Well, then you can buy the coffee." I get the door for him and we both head to the counter. I can see Annette in the kitchen, working on dishes while Monica handles the counter, Sharon getting the tables. It looks to be a generally slow morning.

"Jimmy, I thought you were *sick*." Monica darts her gaze at Dave with the last word. She whistles softly, looking me over. "You look hot though, even with that creepy streak in your hair."

Dave pokes his head through, narrowing his eyes at me, a plume of smoke erupting from his nostrils when he snorts. I should mention that employers hate it when you don't call in for your shift. They *especially* hate it when you show up at work later in the day looking fine. It should go without saying that this wouldn't be a good time to ask for my pay.

I smile gently to Monica. "Thank you. May the officer and I have some coffee, please?"

She staggers back, hand over her heart. "Whoa, I may need to sit down. A thank-you *and* a please? From *you*?"

I perk a brow. "What's so weird about that?"

"Well, the last few weeks you've been kind of..."

Sharon passes by her sister, putting an order on the wheel. "An ill-tempered brat who'd spit on an angel's face for asking about the weather." She looks at me before going back to the tables. "I've been praying for you, though."

Thom chuckles softly. "Ouch." Monica gives him coffee first.

Ignoring me, she leans across the counter, reading his tag. "So...Officer Canmore." I try not to twitch at the name. She grins big, looking into his eyes. "Is there a *Mrs.* Canmore?"

Blushing slightly, he gazes into his coffee. "There's going to be one in a few months."

Monica slumps. "Oh."

I look toward him. "Oh?"

"Yeah, we've been living together a little while and..." He shrugs, but still smiles. "It's time, you know? Beth is—"

"Beth? You're marrying her?"

Beth, well, Thom had been dating her, but I saw her at the university a couple months before the bus accident making out with a prof, one of *my* profs. I'd promptly told Thom about it and he called it off. I had thought he was working up the nerve to ask out a girl who worked at the university library. But if Thom doesn't remember me...

And right now, he doesn't appear too happy considering the tone I used. "What's wrong with Beth? Hell, how do you even know about her?"

"Uh..." I now have Monica's undivided attention as well. "Well, you've been dating her since high school, right? You used to complain that she was spending all of her time working as a

TA? Y'know, at the parties? Whenever you'd have a few, you'd go on about everything."

He looks at me suspiciously. "And you were my confidante?"

"Whoever was handy. I was still a pledge, so I had to clean up when someone ralphed near the keg."

"Ugh, I remember when I had to do that. Well, it doesn't mean anything, she wants to be a professor, and Dr. Evans is really helping her out." I try not to bite my knuckles. Oh God, it's even the same guy.

"Are you sure he's not uh...*helping* in another way?"

Thom's face goes stone. "Listen, that's my girlfriend you're talking about, okay?"

"I just—"

"No." He gets up from the counter. "And another thing? I never drank at those parties, so I don't know what angle you're trying to work here, but it ends now. I don't know if you're trying to flip me to the boy's team or just trying to fuck with me, but *stop*."

"Thom..."

"Seriously. Stop. Apologize for what you said about my girl."

He isn't supposed to be with her. I know it. "She's banging Dr. Evans behind your back and has been since her sophomore year." I remember the details from when he called me afterward. "And she did three guys in your frat, including Joey. Wake up, Thom."

He shoves me back against the counter. "That's *Officer* Canmore. You say one more word about Beth, and you and I are going to have problems."

Fuck. What possessed me to say all that? I stand mute, let his fury abate.

He eventually tosses a couple singles on the counter and nods once to Monica. "Thanks for the coffee." My brother then exits the diner, leaving me sitting at the counter, staring at the now-closed door, wondering what just happened.

Monica whistles softly. "Damn. I'd hate to say it, Jimmy, but you kind of had that com..." She leans over the counter to get a better look at me, her face playful, if a bit cruel, but immediately softening. "Oh shit." I'm handed a napkin, which makes me aware that my face is wet. "Did you like him, Jimmy?"

I wipe my eyes, my chest aching, throat tight. "He was my best friend. I wish he could remember that."

Sighing, she comes around the counter and hugs me. I sniffle and sob lightly, wishing I could call Dad, Mom, any of my brothers who would give Thom a call and help me smooth things over. Thom believed me before. He hated me for a few days when I'd told him, but he believed me, though he didn't talk to me again afterward. He'd just needed time, he said.

I have to wonder now why anyone would want the pain that comes with a soul, having felt the effects of a diminished one, but sitting here, feeling Monica's arms around me as she attempts to comfort me despite how I've apparently treated her the last few weeks...

It reminds me why I'm glad I still have one.

Chapter Ten

One of the big changes at the diner over the last few weeks, besides hiring on a new waitress, is that Sharon got promoted. No title change, but a couple of times she's had the distinct honor of doing final count-outs for the register. For Dave, that's a big deal. Also, she'll take over the grill when he needs to step out for a smoke.

"So tell me, Black." Dave flicks ash from his Virginia Slim. "Am I going to need to bring someone else on?"

I shrug, leaning against the wall of the alley. "I'd prefer to keep the job, but Cale might be stepping things up, and I've run myself ragged trying to do both." I glance toward the door leading back into the diner. "Have I been that bad, Dave?"

He snorts, looking up to the sky and muttering. "Last six weeks all you've done is bitch about your studies. Me, I think it's a little funny. That, and we dragons are used to whiny sorcerers." He winks at me and gestures at the diner. "But you have to remember, *they* don't believe in sorcerers or magic or any of that."

"They see me though." I point at my hair.

"They see your *Mark*. They know something's off about you, they just don't know what. All you've been complaining about is magic. They don't hear that. All they hear is complaining." He takes a long drag on his cigarette, exhaling another plume of smoke. "And let me ask you, when humans hear someone they know complaining, what's their first instinct as to what it's about, huh? Themselves. They can't hear what you're really talking about, so what's to keep them from assuming all that *sturm und drang* is about them?"

I arch a brow. "You speak German?"

"*Ja. Du nicht? Und ich dachte, man muss clever sein zum Zaubern.*" He shrugs. "At least my parents think so."

"You never talk about them."

"They're old. They're rich." He flicks his cigarette away. "I'm young. I'm not, but I was on my way. Fucking Coyotes. Thanks for sending that one on his way a few weeks back."

"Wasn't a problem. I could see right through him, he was obvious."

"Of course you could. You're Keth. All their tricks don't work on you. People like me though..."

It's best to change the subject before he starts lamenting his lost fortune. It's a very touchy area with him. "So how do I fix things?" I shuffle my feet slowly, kick away some loose trash. "I mean, with everybody, if they don't hear what I'm really saying?"

"Simple, lay off the shop talk while you're on the clock. Remember when you first started you told me you were thankful for the job because it got your mind off, well..." He trails off. I've told him about the accident, about Heath. After two years it's faded enough to be manageable.

"Studying with Cale isn't anything like that, it's just irritating, and I keep messing up and..." I take a breath. "Better stop before I start ranting again. Plus I need to find a magical focus. Probably gotta be something around here I can use, right?" I chance a smile. "Could you maybe lend me a spatula?"

Dave blinks. "You really have no idea what you're talking about, do you?"

"What?"

Again, he mutters to the sky. "From what I know? When a sorcerer takes a focus, it's not a matter of picking it up. They have to *make it* theirs."

"Cale said that too. What's it mean?"

He shrugs. "I don't know, I'm not a sorcerer. It's not easy, and it attracts a lot of unwanted attention. If you're going to do this, use...what means something to you."

"I don't know what to use, other than my St. Jude medallion. And using a Catholic medallion to practice what's essentially witchcraft will likely punch my ticket for the bullet train to hell."

He steps closer to me. "This is one of their trials." His voice drops low, barely a whisper. "You're Keth, Black. You're a loaded gun pointed at the world. Be sure you want to take this step, okay?"

I nod. "I'll think on it. That and I should probably get Cale some more books. I was a bit of a dick this morning."

He pats my head with a grin. "As long as you can admit it."

I make my way past him and go upstairs, loading up my knapsack for another adventure. I get the shear, seeing as I'm eventually going back out to the Benedict, and despite that I'm supposed to be an intimidating magical badass, the key word is still *supposed*. I could get mugged, and if I'm as drained as I feel, I probably shouldn't hop into Tartarus and run away. I might not make it back out.

The shear.

I take a deep breath and look up through the skylight, remember that night. I held the shear, cut Heath's hand, and then I stabbed the Plexiglas window. It never should've broken, honestly. But I yelled a word as I hit it with the blade.

"*Break.*"

There's a sharp report at my feet, and I step back instinctively, finding a shattered length of board in the hardwood floor, where the shear was pointing.

Oh my God.

I run my finger along the edge. I took it that night, from Heath, because I wanted to protect myself. When he saw I had it, I shattered the window of the bus, even though it meant letting the water in, even if it meant me dying.

I don't get to choose my Keth name, though, Hades told me that. But if I'm going to be the Lightning Rod, then damn it, it's going to be on my terms. It'll be because I choose to be it. I won't let someone make that decision for me. I will *make it* mine.

As I made the shear mine. This is my proof that I won't be Heath's anymore. This is what I used to cut myself free.

Is it my focus though? I need to talk to Cale, I need answers.

I stow the blade in my jacket and leave the building without another word, no goodbyes, and I run to the 65th and L station to catch the Blue Line.

Did I work magic that night? Did I force the water in? I wanted Heath to go away when I was hiding in the bathroom. Oh God, did I make the bus crash? I bury my face in my hands, my fingers cold. Someone mutters near me, but I don't quite catch it. Something about children of man?

The mutterer speaks up. "Hello, Miles."

No.

I lower my hands and see a dead man sitting across the car from me, still wearing that white leather jacket, his face gaunt, pale. I start trembling.

"You're dead." I shake my head violently. "No. You're dead. This is a dream."

"Maybe I'm a ghost. I certainly have plenty of reasons to haunt your ass seeing as you tried to *kill* me." A few seconds pass, and he stomps the floor and makes a sudden move. I cringe, reflexively shielding my face. He laughs in response.

"Go away, just go away." My voice grows smaller, cracking. "You're not real." I reach in my jacket for the shear and my hand is slapped away hard, stinging. I can't stifle the whimper that follows, which only makes him laugh louder. My eyes dart to my left where the other passengers are, all of them focusing attention on their newspapers, out the window, the floor, the adverts, I mean advertisements, anywhere but us. I catch Heath looking too.

"Don't you just love Genovese syndrome? I'll bet I could stab you, right now, and they wouldn't lift a finger." He laughs again, hearing me start to sob. "You think they're going to give a fuck? You're a damned fag, Miles, they can say they've got gay friends or some shit but when your blood starts sliding past their feet they won't do more than lift their shoes."

The old conditioning is still strong. I should cry for help, do something, but if I do anything I know he'll...

"Please, Heath. Leave me alone. Please." I can't work a spell. I try to remember my anger but it fizzles. I only remember him hitting me.

"You never told me how you got that ticket, Miles. You fucking someone? They help you get away from your big bad boyfriend who wasted a year of his life on you?" He grabs my chin, my face stinging with cold as I'm forced to look at him. "We aren't finished, Miles, not until I'm done with you. Not until I've gotten what I want out of you."

"Please, Heath, don't, I'm sorry." I immediately wince. That's always a mistake.

"Sorry? You're *sorry*?" His fist connects with my stomach, chills spreading through my body. I hunch forward, coughing, sobbing uncontrollably now. I reach frantically for the shear, instead my fingers touch something hard, brittle. A scale. I snap it in half before Heath grabs my wrist, yanking my hand free. "What's this, Miles?"

"Please, Heath." My face is wet, streaming with tears. The people in the car aren't even glancing in this direction. "Please stop."

His fingers work the broken scale free from my hand, and he shoves me back against the wall of the car. I finger my medallion, whispering a prayer.

"Christ, Miles, you're always *whining*. Going to pray? To who? Some god too lazy to get off his ass for anything but condemnation? Some bitchy *servant* who's forgotten his fucking place?" His palm connects hard with my face, the left side blossoming with freezing pain. "We don't *need* them anymore, Miles. We're better than them now."

"What do you want?" I'm cowering, I don't know what else to do.

"What do I want? I want the last three years of my life back. I want to be able to have what I want without getting lip from some uppity bitch and her sewing circle. That's why I took it, Miles, I wanted control over my fucking life. You were supposed to give me the power to do that, but you're weak, aren't you?" I nod once, still sobbing. He shuts me up with a slap across my other cheek. "Quit fucking crying. Now. You're going to bring what you stole to me."

He grabs my chin again, his fingers digging into my cheek, the cold seeping into my brain. "This isn't a negotiation, Miles. You're going to do what I tell you." He lets go, pain blurring my vision now. "Copacetic?"

Closing my eyes, I just nod in assent. "Yeah. Yeah, Heath. Copacetic."

"Good. You know where to bring it." He discards the pieces of the scale to the floor and then vanishes in a cloud of crimson mist that quickly disperses. I curl into a ball on the seat, letting the tears flow again, no longer caring if the people on the train hate me. They already do. Why wouldn't they?

I gaze down at the broken scale and gather the halves, slipping them quietly back into my knapsack. I wipe my eyes dry, sit up straight and wait for the train to pull into the 90th and V station. The passengers file off the train before me, not looking my way, talking amongst themselves about the weather, what was on TV last night. I try to remember what Dave told me, that they don't really hear what I'm saying, see what's going on. As far as they're concerned, I was probably having a flashback or a breakdown.

Am I losing it? Dave once joked that I couldn't be crazy because the world wasn't coming to an end, but if Heath really was there, maybe it is. Isn't there some whole bit in the Bible about the dead walking again? Plenty of zombies wandering around to support that idea.

I gently rub my medallions between my fingers. I did take his St. Anthony medal, but would he crawl back out of hell for it? Cale said that the dead are all looking for something, but could it be that simple?

Cale will have to wait. I return to the train to head back to Allora. To the place where Heath died, and I survived.

The North Bridge.

Chapter Eleven

I don't want to be here anymore.

By all rights, it's a lovely day for a stroll. The sun has broken through the clouds, the heat tempered by a cool breeze off the bay. I should get out more, really. I should go for a walk sometime, just to stay grounded.

As long as it's not here.

The North Bridge is named such because the river is the North River. The people who settled this area weren't all that creative, or one of them was named North, or something like that. It's not a fancy bridge, like the Brooklyn or Golden Gate, just a long straight affair with walkways and lanes and notices that the bridge freezes before the highways do.

It's where I almost died. Where Heath died. Where God knows how many people drowned.

You wouldn't know it, though. There's no plaque, no flowers of remembrance, no memorials. I guess the City got it out of its system in the first year and moved on. I can barely tell where the replacement guardrailing is.

It's better that I'm here anyway. Maybe I'll get some closure or catharsis. I'll give him back his medal, and then I won't see him anymore. I'll let go. It'll be over. Simple as that.

I set down my knapsack, leaning it against the guardrail, and start to take off the medallion. The clasp proves a bit difficult, as it's been a while since I've taken it off and I've recently trimmed my fingernails. After half a minute of struggling it comes free, and I dangle it before me, over the railing, the image of St. Anthony of Padua spinning in the breeze that chills my hands. Patron saint of missing things.

And he'd lost it.

I bite my lip, but I let myself laugh, finally.

"What's so funny, Miles?"

My blood runs cold. I don't want to turn around.

"You aren't real, Heath."

"I didn't think you'd actually come back here." His hand runs along my side, and I flinch, which earns a laugh from him. "Back to our special place." His lips brush my neck. "Strange as this sounds, I've missed you."

I shut my eyes tight, let go of the medal, and when I open my eyes, it's in his hand.

"So that's where that got to. Don't need it anymore though, I'm not a child of God." He throws the medal into the river. "*We are children of man.*" A shudder goes through me just before he gently shoves me against the railing, his body pressing to mine. "Y'know, I didn't want to kill you, when we first met. Still don't." I fight off trembles, trying to push back tears as he leans in, his tongue invading my mouth. I return it, but meekly, old habits stirring from fear. He pulls back after a moment. "Never got that part of it, Miles. In the beginning, I thought this was more of a gift. Finally, someone who'd understand, wouldn't judge. I could have everything I wanted." His free hand slips behind the waist of my slacks, and I whimper, cringing, not reacting to his touch. My feet feel like they're encased in lead. Damn it, do something!

"Heath, please, leave me alone."

He kisses along my neck, his hand still massaging my groin, which thankfully doesn't betray me. "You know you don't mean that, Miles. You still love me. Despite all this. I have plenty of reason not to, but..." His lips press to mine again, and I can't keep a sob from getting through.

Heath's eyes narrow on me. "Are you *crying?*" He shoves me hard against the railing. "After I come here and decide to forgive you? To let you give back what you stole so we can be together again?" Spit collides with my face. "*Fine.* Have it your way, Miles, like you always do."

Heath brings his hand back, and half of me wants to brace for the strike. As the cars keep going by behind him, I know that no one will stop to help. If someone calls the police on their mobile, it'll be done by the time they get here, and if I live through it, I can hardly say I was assaulted by the ghost of my dead ex-boyfriend.

I grab my knapsack and swing it at him, expecting it to pass through him.

Instead he doubles over as I slam his kidney, a pained cry emerging from him that makes me stumble back, my feet clanging as I tumble to the walkway. Oh shit, Heath's not a ghost. But how did he get out of the bus? I thought I was the only one who got out? Oh fuck, oh fuck. Wait... Clanging?

The bottom rails of the guardrail have vanished. The missing steel is now wrapped around my legs from the knees down. Enraged, Heath holds his hand aloft, and I'm raised to my feet through no effort of my own, my legs gripped by some force.

"Fucking *useless* shit!" He does a cruel one-sided smile, the kind he'd show just before he'd... "Like your new shoes, Miles?"

Heath's working magic. He transmuted the rails. He's levitating me. Fear permeates my voice. "You're a sorcerer like me?"

"Like you?" He spits, rolling his eyes. "You think I'd be something weak and pathetic? That I'd need magic words and shit? I can do whatever I want." He flicks his hand upward, and I'm lifted up farther and pushed back over the railing, now suspended over the side of the bridge. "I'm more than that."

Oh fuck.

"You're the Recluse."

Heath shrugs once, still smoldering. "Whatever you need to call me. I'm just going to kill you and take your power like I *should've* when we first met."

"Heath, please. Don't do this."

"Has to be done. Both of us got out of that bus and left a lot of angry people behind. They want one of us down there, and I have plans tonight." He *hrms* a second. "Well, I could change my mind. You going to give me back what's mine?"

"I already gave you the medal!"

"Jesus, you think I give a fuck about that church shit *now*? None of it's going to mean anything by the time I'm done. I want the shear, Miles."

Huh?

"Why?"

He flicks his wrist and my left leg no longer feels held. I tumble over, screaming, until I stop inverted, my right leg burning with shocks of pain, my left leg aching as I try to keep the weight on my feet from doing any damage. I don't stop screaming. Cars keep driving by, a pedestrian even walks by the two of us, oblivious, as I would guess the sight of someone held up by an invisible force doesn't even approach the right side of human denial. It doesn't keep me from shouting at the man, though, however fruitlessly.

"He won't hear you, Miles. I cloaked the two of us. We're both currently the easiest people in the world to ignore." He grins darkly. "Children of man. Handy little trick. Keeps people from getting involved in shit that's none of their business."

That's what he was muttering about on the train, the bus, and who knows how many other times when we were living together. Oh my God, no wonder no one paid attention. If I weren't dangling above certain death, I'd apologize to humanity for losing faith in it.

"You've got a pretty easy choice here, Miles. Give me the shear and live, or you don't and you die. I don't care either way. It's not like I need to worry about hell anymore." He glares at me. "Jesus, quit crying! You're the only one making this complicated."

I meet his eyes, feeling a spark inside me. "No."

He visibly blinks. "What?"

"You're doing all this, Heath, not me. This..." I take a breath. "This isn't my fault."

He steps toward the mangled railing, glaring. "There's a couple dozen pissed-off spirits down there who might say otherwise, Miles."

113

"My name is James."

Heath shows teeth. "What did you say?"

I fan the spark inside into a flame. "I said *fuck you*, my name is James. That is *my* shear." The knapsack tears as the shear bursts through the fabric to my hand. "And its name is Sigil."

I point the blade at Heath, Sigil glowing white as it strikes him with a bright blue arc of electricity. Heath screams as his hand is burned, his palm bright red and bleeding. The magic holding me aloft dissipates immediately.

I fall.

Instinctively, I flip myself over, pointing my weighted shoes toward the water, and hug the blade to my chest, sucking in a deep breath as I hit the river. The impact makes me all but certain my legs have probably shattered as the world goes black and I slip into Tartarus. Thankfully, it seems that the North River isn't actually the River Styx, whether Hades keeps his yacht on it or not. I'm submerged to my waist, the water more like concrete. I'm held fast, but alive. I know when I have to breathe I'll sink to the bottom, and I can already see a multitude of dark lights below me, growing in number and intensity as they lessen the distance between us. I can either be torn asunder by angry ghosts who have good reason to hate me, or drown.

How the hell is Heath a sorcerer?

No, no, worry about that if you manage to live through this, James. More important shit going on right now.

Can I transmute the water? It's a simple element, right? Granted, the North River isn't the cleanest in the world. God knows how much other shit I'd have to take into account to come up with the name. And even if I turn it into air, it'll float up away from me, and I have no idea what the name is for scuba gear, not to mention I'd have no idea how to use it even if I could...

Damn it, I need to breathe! I feel the built-up exhalation leaking through my lips, no bubbles eking out. My lungs burn, demanding air. I don't want to die.

The lights from below grow close, and I feel so many hands on my legs, pulling on me, downward, my name, my real name being screamed in rage amidst the howling of an agony that still hasn't stopped after two years. Long-dead fingers have withered into bony claws that shred through my pants, into my skin, ecstatic screeching as my blood starts to flow into the time-frozen water. The pain makes my mouth burst open to scream, the sound weak as the world returns, the bright sunny day vanishing quickly from my eyes as the river claims me, the sun a wispy image on the surface.

The weights pull me quickly downward, the light from above giving little view through the murky water. The wreckage isn't here, long since dredged out, the bodies recovered. My breath is held, but there's no air left in my lungs. I touch bottom, and jab at the metal encasing my legs with the shear, trying to imagine names.

I don't have the breath to shout "*Break!*" and shatter the metal. I'd probably destroy my legs in the process anyway.

I was supposed to be safe.

It was supposed to be over.

I should be washing dishes right now, waiting on my break to start so I can grab an order of French fries with just enough crisp and almost too much salt and...

And my left foot doesn't feel as heavy.

I look down, seeing patches of the metal gone, along with French fries floating up toward the surface. Wait, I didn't need to know the name of the bench on the train when I transmuted it, or the glass of the sconce when I turned it into light, maybe it'll work with the plating.

I focus on the memories, drawing on their power, and repeatedly tap the steel plating with the blade, the water around me filling with the entire side order menu from the diner. Fuck it if it's ridiculous, I want to live.

My feet come free from the weights, and I desperately kick upward, the strength gone from my muscles, but I can't give up, not when there's hope. I know I could move faster without the shear, but it's gotten me this far, so I keep my grip on it as I swim toward the light.

I ache to open my mouth, my will losing its grip over my lungs. I can't even see the reflection of the sun against the surface.

I don't have anything left, do I? I'm going to die because while I can apparently turn solid steel into a fresh batch of onion rings, I can't transmute water into air.

Am I close? I thrust the shear upward, hoping to break the surface, maybe claim one more breath. My fingers grip tightly as my mouth finally betrays me, the river pouring in, my lungs readying to pull.

A great force yanks me upward, clutching my arm painfully tight as I break the surface, the river suddenly under me, moving away. Wait, am I flying?

I promptly cough and purge what water managed to work into my throat. My chest feels cold, but sputters of air manage to make it between my coughing retches. Weakly, I look upward, and see that my arm is held fast by a clawed foot armored with deep-red scales. Above me I hear the beating of huge wings, and below me a terrifying shadow is cast.

My throat is hoarse, but still I vocalize my fear. I've been rescued from drowning by a red dragon that's flying with ease and speed between the buildings of downtown Allora.

"Calm yourself, Keth." Unlike Dave, this dragon does not sound like he could commentate for *Monday Night Football*. He does, however, sound like a shoe-in for narrating the end of all things. "You are protected."

The dragon swoops over the park and with little fanfare drops me in the middle of one of the baseball diamonds. I tumble a few feet, but nothing feels too damaged. The dragon turns and lands in the outfield, and a second later, accompanied by a flash of golden light, is no longer there. A man of willowy build wearing a three-piece suit in the same deep red as the dragon's scales is in his place, shouldering a knapsack that looks out of place on him but familiar. He wastes no time in closing the distance between us before I can even consider a hasty exit, much less attempt one.

"Are you hurt?" Now that he's closer, I can see that he's human, or human-looking at least, six feet flat, his skin ruddy, but flawless otherwise, his hair as red as his suit and slicked back, his eyes a bright gold, his ears definitely pointed. I can tell he's strong, no one to mess with.

"Yes." I slump back to the dirt and concentrate on breathing. "Who are you?"

He bows elegantly. "You may address me as Salondine the Magnanimous."

I cough a few more times through a look of incredulity. "Seriously? You call yourself that?"

Salondine nods with a smile. "It is a title I have rightly earned, my liege."

"Your *what*?"

He sets my knapsack before me. "My apologies for delaying your rescue, but I supposed you would want your various artifacts and components."

"How did you even know where I was or who I am or that I was—"

He raises a hand, still smiling, but warmly. "If I may, my liege." Salondine waits patiently until I shrug, and he opens up my knapsack and retrieves the broken halves of Dave's scale. "Davinicus was most worried when he felt his scale broken, and requested I search for you. I followed the scent of his scale and found you."

"Davinicus?" I arch a brow. "You mean Dave?"

"I suppose it would be untoward for you to refer to him formally." He picks up my knapsack again, shoulders it and offers his hand. "It would be best if we moved out of the open."

With his aid I get to my feet, and he gives me support, helping me walk slowly toward a stand of trees that border the outfield. He's warm, and his face is almost fixed with a smile that's gentle, the sunlight dancing in his eyes. I stop myself from staring both because this is hardly the time to get all googly eyed and because a couple minutes ago this guy was a dragon the size of a crosstown bus.

"So, are you really human right now or…"

He shakes his head once, pushing aside a stray branch from my way as we come to a small clearing not twenty feet from the edge of the field. "This is merely a form, a gift bestowed when the cities grew larger and we could no longer guard our lieges properly. Size may be intimidating, but it does little good when a Keth is deep within a skyscraper." He sets me down against a tree and inspects my various wounds. "A pity a golden isn't close, my clan has never had much skill in healing. I don't see why you wouldn't recover, though, my liege."

"Why do call me that?"

He cocks his head, confusedly. "You are Anu'keth, one of those who may become the Ra'keth." Salondine blinks at my equally confused look. "The Sorcerer King. We have sought the Ra'keth but cannot find him."

"The Recluse?"

He nods once.

"I'm pretty sure he was the one who tossed me in the river."

Salondine stares at me in amazement. "It was my honor to retrieve you, then." He notices the bleeding on my legs from the ghosts in the water, a few of them still open. He places his hand over the wounds, grazing my thigh, the warmth from his skin soothing away the pain.

"Salondine?" I tremble softly, but it's not fear.

He looks up, his eyes meeting mine. "Yes, my liege?"

I practically grab his head and pull him to me, my lips pressing hard to his. I don't know what I'm doing, all I know is that…

God, it's been two years since I've been with anyone, and I've nearly died who knows how many times in the last few days, and he saved me and he's been nice and he's good-looking and…

And I almost fucking *died*, okay?

And, again, it's been two *years*.

And the last person to have kissed me, to have slept with me will not be *Heath*. Sure, Cale's good-looking and everything, but I can't tell if he wants the relationship going that way.

And Salondine's also here and looks human enough for me right now.

After a few seconds I pull back, my face now as red as his. "I'm sorry." I cast my eyes to the side. "Just been a hell of a day." My face feels hot, the weight of the day's events piling on again.

I expect him to get up, walk away. Instead, he leans in, his forehead resting against mine. "It is often customary to ask first, but I feel no regret for it." He smiles again, my eyes filled with the sight of gold flecked with silver. "Might I return the gesture?"

I barely nod, but he takes me in his arms and kisses me—long, deep, passionate—like it was with Heath at the beginning, but not exactly the same. I've never been kissed quite like this, so grandly. The warmth of his body seems to flow into mine, easing the soreness and aching in my muscles, getting the blood flowing.

Salondine breaks the kiss only after I've softly grunted into it, and he stares into my eyes, seeing the growing hunger in them. "May I be with you, Sorcerer?"

"By 'be with', you mean..."

He smirks, sliding a hand down my chest, but hovering over my waist. "I'd prefer not to use a vulgar colloquialism."

"Uh...here? Aren't we a little exposed?"

Salondine smiles indulgently. "You will be lying with a dragon, Sorcerer. I do not believe I could suggest a better means of protection."

Rationally, I'm aware that he'd be a little too occupied to keep an eye out for potential attackers, not to mention I might not really be up for this, no matter how much a certain part of my body rigidly denies that, pardon the pun. Irrationally, well...

I kiss him again, and his body shimmers a moment. When I break the kiss to see what happened, he's no longer clothed, his musculature well-defined despite his willowy build, skin as ruddy as his face. My eyes dart downward, and it appears human enough and apparently as eager as I am.

"Um, if we do this, is anything going to, well, happen?" I swallow hard when he blinks in confusion. "I mean, this isn't going to mean anything big, right? Don't get me wrong, you're really nice, but I just met you and..." He rests his finger gently against my lips.

"Other than sated urges, it will carry no more meaning than you wish to ascribe. I will admit it has been some time since I've lain with a male. It is not my preference, but occasionally I indulge my curiosities." His lips brush against mine again, and he grins. "If I was to be your chosen protector, this would certainly be an unorthodox way of announcing your decision."

"I get to choose a protector?"

He nods once. "Should you become the Ra'keth, yes. For now..." Salondine kisses me again, his fingers running delicately over my skin, drawing tingles that aren't unwelcome. "I've never lain with a Keth, are you all this nervous?" He smirks good-naturedly and lays me gently on the ground, joining me a second later. "You're safe here, with me."

"You can call me James." I manage a weak smile. "Do you really talk like this?"

He grins, a bit more genuine. "I'll admit I speak more formally when around a Keth. My clan wouldn't appreciate a casual tone." Salondine kisses me again, and I return it with more earnestness. "Perhaps you are merely taking solace in my company, but for my kind, I am providing comfort to one who ranks just below our god."

I quirk a brow. "So this is like fucking a celebrity for you?"

His hand runs over my groin, confirming that I haven't lost interest yet. "Or perhaps you are not the only one who is pleased to be alive." His gaze darts down to his roaming hand and back at me. "May I?"

I take a deep breath, then nod.

What follows is...

It was never like this with Heath.

Salondine goes slow, his touch warm and comforting, like being in front of a roaring fire in the dead of winter. He spares no part of me from his caress, his kisses varying in their length and intensity but never losing their passion. I almost feel unworthy, the way he looks at me during it, as if I'm being worshipped rather than coupled. He doesn't speak, not once during it all, only a soft grunt when he straddles my waist and sinks himself downward, but his face tells me that he isn't doing this for my benefit.

My mind races while he moves himself slowly on my body, my thoughts almost panicked. I don't really know this guy, Heath's still alive and nearly succeeded in killing me, not to mention that he's a sorcerer too. I don't know how I'm supposed to protect myself from Heath and God knows what else might be out there.

I should probably find a safe place to think this over. Definitely a safer place than under an oak tree in Tolon Park where I have my shredded pants around my ankles while a dragon in human form is...

Is...

I close my eyes tight, grabbing his hand as my body spasms, my mouth parting as I squeeze his fingers. For a moment all of the tension and weight melts away, hidden under a warm blanket of bliss.

It takes me some time to catch my breath, my eyes fixed upward at the glints of sky through the trees. "Sorry I didn't last that long."

Salondine grunts softly again, and I gasp as I exit, but he joins me on the ground after pulling my pants and boxers back up. His clothes have appeared back on him as well. "I wasn't aware we agreed on a time requirement. I'll instead take it as a compliment that my body could inspire you so quickly." He taps my nose gently. "I wouldn't make a habit of it, though."

He gathers me in his arms and holds me close, and I relish the lingering warmth. "That mean you want to make a habit of it?"

"If you would prefer something like this, I wouldn't argue, and if you're in the Capital, of course. This is Davinicus's city, it would be rude for me to continually visit, especially to see the Keth he's *supposed* to be protecting." His tongue drags slowly along my earlobe. "You could always come to the Capital, though, and stay with me."

I will admit it's tempting. Best to change the subject before I give it too much thought.

"How do you know Dave, again?"

"His mother is clutchmate to mine. In human parlance, I suppose you could call us cousins."

Wait... "You donate to Greenpeace, by any chance?"

He nods, gently stroking my chest. "In addition to other organizations, yes. Does this surprise you?"

"Well, you are a red dragon, you don't really get good PR."

He laughs. "Ah yes. Well, there are quite a few bad eggs in my clan, and they get all of the attention." Salondine turns my head slowly and kisses me softly enough to make me close my eyes and continue it for half a second after he pulls away. "Consider it, at least, my offer?"

Trying not to grin, I nod, and his smile is full of light and life as he helps me to my feet. Once upright I'm met with another barrage of kisses that make me wonder if we can knock out another go before anyone notices that we're over here.

Unfortunately for my resurrected libido, a large group of people are moving toward the baseball field, all wearing caps and carrying bats and gloves. I wouldn't want anyone, sprinting to shag a pop fly to deep center, to stumble on to us. Look at me, making puns. Definitely can put this guy in the "conversational" column as opposed to "scared rabbit".

"We should get going." I pick up my knapsack from under the tree, slinging it over my shoulders. "I should probably rest after all that, and at least get some new pants."

My gait is still unsteady, and I'm rather certain that I'm going to be feeling every minute of today tomorrow. All that I want to do is go home to bed and sleep for a week. I'll figure everything out in the downtime.

Salondine takes my hand as we walk along the border of the outfield toward one of the footpaths, his disposition relaxed, but his eyes are vigilant, taking in everyone he sees. I guess this is what it'd be like to have a bodyguard. "May I ask where you'd like to go, my liege?"

I give him a look, and he blushes slightly, his face going a deeper red.

"My apologies. Where would you like to go, James?"

"Just back to the diner. I can catch the bus to Victory Station and take the Blue Line to Beckettsville." I chuckle slightly. "I hope that everyone's not still pissed at me. I wasn't exactly pleasant, and Dave didn't really want me to go out."

He snorts, and a soft plume of smoke puffs from his nose. "Dragons are not to question the motives of the Keth. We are here to serve and protect you. Perhaps Davinicus needs to be reminded of that."

"No, no, it wasn't like that. He was worried, that's all. After today, I can see he was right to be." He interlocks his fingers with mine. It feels nice.

"As you will. If I might posit my opinion, though, you did stand against another sorcerer and live to tell the tale."

"Only because you fished me out of the water."

He smiles warmly and kisses me on the cheek. "You needn't bother with that minor detail in your retelling. Also, you needn't use public transportation, I can give you a ride home."

I smirk. "Such a gentleman." Looking down the footpath, I hear the soft sounds of distant traffic as we start to cross through another clearing. "So, I guess you've got a car nearby?"

He lets go of my hand. "No."

"How are you driving me home, then?"

"I didn't mean to intimate that I owned a car. Too cramped for my taste." There's a rush of wind with a flash of light, the clearing largely filled now as he assumes his draconic form. He lowers his head to the ground, smiling toothily, his voice returning to its previous depth and power. "I said I'd give you a ride."

Chapter Twelve

Riding a dragon is nothing like it's portrayed in the movies.

I'm sure that given time, training and adequate rigging, it would be a raucous and thrilling affair, and a hell of a way to get from A to B. The first time, though, I'm clutching Salondine's neck so tight I'm amazed he's not choking, or driven deaf by my panicked screeches whenever he banks a ninety-degree turn.

The view of the City's streets sweeping underneath me is breathtaking, but next time, I'll just buy a few UTA tokens, thanks.

The diner is easy to pick out, considering it's the only building in the neighborhood with a skylight, especially one that big. Salondine descends toward it, and I panic when the glass doesn't retract or fall away or arch. Instead, we pass *through* it, and the dragon lands with a muted thump on the floor, straddling the wooden tub in the center carefully. He lowers his head for me to slide off and shakes a back leg, a few things impaled by his footclaws. I move to help him and wince, seeing that he's just killed a stack of Dave's AC/DC albums. Vintage vinyl too.

Once his feet are free, he assumes his human/elven form and dusts off his sleeves, looking about the room with disgust.

"You'd think a *hatchling* was living here." The room hasn't changed much since I moved in, save a futon in the corner, a small rack for my clothes and a general pile of my books.

"C'mon, Dave's not that bad." I want to clean up the mess but I'm exhausted from... I'll have to make a list later. Right now my cheap futon looks like a bed of down.

Considering that he's seen everything there is to see, I don't mind shedding my soggy clothes as I make my way toward the futon and put on a robe before practically flumping onto the mattress. Fingers gently rub my shoulders afterwards.

"I can stay, if you'd like." Salondine kisses the back of my neck gently. "I'm sure given the recent events Davinicus wouldn't mind some assistance."

"He most certainly *would*."

Groggily, I lift my head to see Dave ascending the last few stairs, looking none too happy.

I turn on my side as Salondine stands up straight, bowing elegantly to Dave. "You'll be pleased to know your portal is still functioning, despite its...lack of use of late."

Dave stomps straight to him, snorting smoke into his face. "Thank you for your aid, you may go now."

Salondine folds his arms and looks to me grandly. "I shall take my leave, James. I look forward to our next..." he winks, "...encounter."

Dave snorts again, his eyes narrowing. "Fuck. Off. Sal."

Salondine bows elegantly with great flourish and assumes his greater form, the dragon beating his wings and taking off through the skylight, the glass and framework only shimmering as he passes. Dave grumbles and approaches me.

"All right, I'll be pissed at him later. *Hmph.* Calling you by your *name* like that... Are you okay?" He looks me over to get the answer to his question and lets out a stream of draconic cursing before taking a deep breath, smoke punctuating his exhalation. "What the hell did you do, Black?"

"Can we talk about this later, when I've recovered a little?"

"Better I know exactly what you're recovering from."

I take a deep breath and sit up, and proceed with the debriefing, everything from when I left earlier to seeing Heath until Salondine pulled me out of the river. I figure what happened after isn't really something he'd need or want to know.

"You think you see a ghost on the train that's capable of hitting you, and you *didn't* think this was something to come find me about?" He's been pacing the last few minutes, listening, trying to limit his frustrated noises, and he's on his third cigarette already.

"I thought he wasn't real. I mean, no one else saw—"

"You thought he wasn't *real?*" He stares at me. "Black, you're a sorcerer, working for a dragon, not to mention you buy your smokes from a unicorn after the zombies have gone down for their naps, and you're having trouble believing in *ghosts?*"

"I thought I was losing it, okay?"

Dave points through the skylight at the picturesque weather. "World look like it's ending to you? You *aren't* crazy, Black." He snorts a huge plume of smoke, not all of it from his cigarette, and he drops the now mostly incinerated stick. "I'm just thankful you had the sense to break that scale."

"Yeah. I don't think Heath's really dead. I think he's Keth. I think he's the Recluse, actually."

He blinks at that. "How could he have survived the bus... Wait, if he's the Recluse like you said, then hell, the Ra'keth can do whatever he damned well pleases." Dave sighs, looking down. "I'm sorry I had to send Sal to get you, I should've been able to myself but..." He motions to his comparatively diminutive stature. "I wouldn't have reached you in time."

After a second, I decide to tell him. "Salondine wants to be my protector, maybe..."

Dave throws his arms in the air. "Of *course* he does! You're a damned Anu'keth. Smart money's on you being the next Sorcerer King, so he wants to get in on the ground floor of that."

I settle my gaze on him. "Don't want him moving in on me, Davinicus?"

Dave shows teeth at that. "Tell me, Black, how'd you spend your April this year?"

I shrug. "What does that have to do with any—"

"Tell me." He folds his arms, waiting expectantly.

"I was here. Working. What else?"

"And the September before that? Or the May before that?"

"Uh, working and working? Why does it matt—"

He steps toward me. "So you *weren't* being paraded in front of the Argent Clan or the Crimson Flight—"

"Who are they?"

Dave shows teeth a second, not appreciating the interruption, but he explains. "Clans of dragonkind. Officially I'm Argent Clan, the silver scaled, and generally the family with the largest hoards." He takes a deep breath, pushing down frustration at the h-word. "To continue, have you been spending your time in a tiny room waiting for *me* to clear when it was okay for you to go, oh I don't know, anywhere?"

"No. What, was I supposed to be doing that?"

"Protecting a Keth is the most important thing a dragon can do, and that's still not explaining it right. That's why it seemed odd to me, in the beginning, that Hades would call in my favor by doing me a huge one. I lost my hoard, my status, my title, I've got *that*..." He points up at the skylight. "A Fae-crafted portal that made me the envy of every dragon in the region, that is now nothing more than a freakishly expensive window..." Dave takes a moment to collect himself.

"Dave, what does that have to do with—"

"Hades didn't tell anyone else, so I felt I shouldn't tell anyone about you."

I furrow my brow, trying to work through it. It's a tad unclear what I should do with this information. "Why?"

He sighs. "Doesn't matter anyway. Now that Sal's involved, I'll be getting calls, visitors, you'll likely end up in Europe by the end of the week."

"Wait, what?" I get up off the bed. "I'm not going anywhere."

"You think the Dracon Council is going to let a Keth, much less an Anu'keth stay here under *my* protection, Black? They'll pack you up, give you a list of bodyguards to choose from, and you'll be under their protection until they deem you strong enough to go after the Recluse."

"The *hell* they will!"

He practically glares at me. "You told me what you went through, what that guy did to you. There's enough on your shoulders. Keth are supposed to be free to make their own choices. You deserved the chance to enjoy that a little." He grits his teeth and shakes his head. "But when I felt my scale break, and I knew you were too far away to get to... I had to risk it. I'm sorry. I just didn't want to lose the first real friend I've ever had."

I don't really know what to say. "Thanks, Dave." I mean it, but it feels pitifully small compared to what he just told me. "I don't suppose there's any way to get out of it? I mean, I can't say that you're my choice?"

"They'd reject it. You have to choose from their list. I suspect the politicking is already afoot." He looks upward, cursing softly.

"I'm guessing Salondine will be on that list?"

He snorts loudly, a bit of flame joining the smoke. "No doubt of that. Speaking of which, could you shower or something? You still smell of him."

I freeze. "I...uh...do?"

He shrugs. "Well, he did give you a ride. It's to be expected."

I bite my lip. "Listen, I don't even know what I was thinking when I did that. It'd just been a while and..." Dave looks at me oddly, his head cocked to the side. I look at my feet. "Right, from the flight here."

"Yeah, what'd you think I..." His eyes go wide. "Tell me you didn't, Black. Tell me you didn't."

I sit back on the futon, still focusing on the floor. "It didn't mean anything." Looking up at him meekly, I chuckle. "Right?"

Other than shuddering visibly, his reaction implies no impending doom. "Ugh, I can't believe that. That's revolting!"

"It wasn't that bad..."

He looks back at me. "With a *human*?" He shudders again. "That's just...just *sick*."

My turn to glare. "Why thank you, Dave."

"Ugh, some drakes will do anything to be the protector. You do know that's probably the only reason he did it, right?" He shakes his arms at me. "I mean, it's not an insult against you personally. Your people are all just so soft and squishy, I can't imagine why any self-respecting dragon would..." He makes a face, similar to *bleah.*

I fold my arms. "Dave, stop talking or I give details." I try to change the subject to a more important matter. "So what do I do? I don't want to go to Europe. I mean, it's nice and all, but I suspect I won't be staying at a chalet in the Swiss Alps."

"Likely it'll be a cavern, somewhere the council can keep an eye on you while they make their decisions. You'll have a heavy guard, as well. I think you're the first *known* Anu'keth in a few decades." He shrugs and gets one last shudder out of his system. "Anyway, nothing's going to be moved on for a couple days, so you can at least get some rest while we figure something out."

Nodding, I lie back down on the futon, tugging my blanket over me. "Sounds like a plan. I'm not getting out of this bed until dawn."

"Uh...Black?"

I lift my head up, and Dave sheepishly points toward the bathroom and makes an exaggerated sniffing sound. Grumbling, I trudge toward the shower. "Fine, fine. You know, if you weren't acting so disgusted, I'd swear you were jealous."

Dave's expression implies anything but jealousy, but he starts back toward the stairs to give me my privacy. The bathroom is pretty simple, an addition since I moved in, since dragons don't need to shower and toilets aren't really sized for Dave. I don't know where or how he does his business, he hasn't told me, and I think that's one of the cornerstones of our friendship.

After I start the water running, I drop my robe, inspect myself in the mirror, and realize a shower's a good idea. There are recently closed cuts on my thighs, dirt and grime from the river on my skin, not to mention several marks on my neck and collarbone that I'll do my best to cover for Dave's sake.

I lean against the sink, stare at my reflection, my hair plastered against my forehead in an unflattering fashion, my eyes tired and a bit red. Taking a deep breath, I remember the last time I gazed into a mirror looking like this.

It was a month before I left, and I had a black eye, bruises on my cheek, all courtesy of a C-minus I'd gotten on one of his papers. I spent half an hour rehearsing my speech, knowing that when he came home...

"I..." Jesus, I should be able to do this. "I'm going to be honest with you, Heath: I'm free of you now. I'm not afraid of you. There will never be another night where I get nervous in a dark room or walk away from the sight of a white jacket. I will never sleep in a corner again, nor will I wonder if leaving you was a mistake. And maybe I won't ever be able to forget you..." I meet my reflection's eyes. "But I will not remember you, Heath. It's over."

I get in the shower, leaving my reflection to disappear in the steam.

Chapter Thirteen

The next two days rank among the most boring of my life.

Bed rest, mostly, watching daytime TV and getting up for meals from the diner and to use the bathroom. I feel fine after one day, but Dave's overprotective and wants me to go at least seventy-two hours without suffering mortal peril first. I've had one visitor, uninvited, who takes care to wake me up in the gentlest way possible.

I emerge from my nap with my head in his elven lap, his hand stroking my hair. When I blink a few times to confirm it's really him, he winks and places a finger over his mouth. "Shh."

"So Dave doesn't know you're here." I make no move from his lap, because it feels nice, and despite his sudden appearance, it breaks up the monotony. "You realize this is only going to piss him off."

Salondine shrugs with a smile. "Have you considered my offer?"

"To what, be your fuck buddy?"

He snickers at that. "I wouldn't mind another go, certainly, but I was referring to the rest of it."

"Before I answer that, what's this about it being revolting for a dragon to, well..."

He stops stroking my hair. "To...?"

"Have sex with a human." I work my way out of his lap, because if he starts enjoying the concept I don't want my head getting poked. I cover it by yawning and stretching, and he takes the opportunity to run his fingers over my back.

"There are some who would consider it lowering themselves. Myself included." His lips brush the nape of my neck. "But you are Keth. So I would not be lowering myself. If anything, I am honored that you allow me to touch you so." His hand drifts around my front, slipping inside my robe.

"Salondine, you're only doing this so I'll pick you as my protector."

It's difficult to push him away, his eyes glint as they meet mine. "Sorcerer, there are many reasons I am doing this." He straddles my waist, his legs wrapping around me, and I have flashbacks of the brothel scenes from Dungeons & Dragons that we'd have to pay our gamemaster twenty bucks to run. "For instance, I had never been with a human before you, but I was curious." He pushes my robe open farther.

"Salondine, Dave's right downstairs. We shouldn't do this. Besides, I think he could still smell you on me after you left."

His eyes light up at that. "I know." The dragon slips his hands behind the waistband of my boxers as his clothing shimmers away.

"Wait, wait, wait." I push him back, catching my breath, even while my body marshals itself for what's being teased in front of me. "You need to go. Seriously, you need to go."

Salondine kisses along my neck, the tingles promising distraction. "The council will make you choose, Sorcerer. Wouldn't you rather know your choice?"

I shove him back this time, narrowing my eyes. "That's the thing, Sal, I *don't* know you."

He grins, showing teeth. "But you've *known* me."

"Well here's Human Men 101, Sal: just because I fucked you, it doesn't mean I like you." It takes a little effort to push him off me, but he doesn't resist. I would guess he knows forcing himself on me wouldn't aid his chances. "Now go away, or do I have to command you by name?"

The dragon shrugs as he gets off my bed. "It matters not, Sorcerer, but I will take my leave as requested." He bows deeply, still nude. "Please consider my offer though, James. The Capital is much more enjoyable than where you'll likely end up."

"And here I thought you'd tell me that Switzerland is lovely in the fall." I start toward the bathroom, retying my robe to dissuade roaming eyes. "Now I have to take a shower, so if you'll excuse me."

"So eager to wash my scent off, are you?" He steps toward me and runs his finger along my cheekbone. "I cannot imagine why you would prefer Davinicus. He is a *hatchling* and has spent too much time among humans."

"Sal. I'm not kidding, you have to go."

"Kiss me, and I will."

"You tried, you failed, leave with some dignity, okay?" When he doesn't budge, I grit my teeth. "Salondine the Magnanimous, you will go now."

The dragon laughs. "You don't know my real name, Keth. It cannot even be shaped by a human tongue."

I feel something stir inside me, the same spark I felt on the bridge, my skin tingling as I remember a trick from a book I read when I was young. "I'm sure your draconic form has a name, but did you bother naming this form?" His eyes go wide, but I don't stop. The few lights in the room begin to flicker, the TV crackling loudly with static. "I *name* you, Stuffington Fluffypants the Third, Esquire, from head to toe, from sight through sound to scent and feel, and I *bind* you to this form until you are three hundred miles away from me. Now fuck off."

He trembles, clenches his jaw, eyes filled with rage. He's trying to change forms, but finding himself unable. Strangely enough, I'm not surprised that it worked even though rational thinking would suggest I should be shocked as hell. I just...knew I could do that.

I nudge him backward. "Trust me, I could've done worse. I know people have done worse, and I have no plans on being like them." He's still nude, unable to produce an illusion to preserve his modesty. "You can borrow some of my clothes, but I want you out of here by the time I get out of that bathroom. And you owe Dave some new AC/DC albums after you landed on his last time."

He starts to speak, but I stop him, holding up my hand. "You broke 'em, you bought 'em. And I think it's safe to say I won't be taking you up on your offer. Don't think of it as a rejection, Sal, rather as a misguided one-night stand with a three-hundred-mile walk of shame." I turn away from him and head into the bathroom, closing the door.

Outside, I hear a bit of rummaging while I glance at the mirror, pointing at my reflection. "Okay, I want bonus experience for that." I sit down on the edge of the tub, waiting a few moments before I hear the slow and steady clomp of Dave climbing the stairs.

I've pissed off a dragon. One who, let's face it, probably would have been my best choice for a protector. If there was only a chance that I'd get hauled off to Europe "for my own good", it's probably a certainty now. I peek out the door, seeing Dave emerging from the stairwell. He doesn't look pleased.

"So Salondine just left." He snorts. "Wearing *your* clothes."

"It's not what you think." I walk over to my pile of clothes and start getting dressed. I go with the shirt from Cale's, my old jeans, and my winter boots with flat tread, since apparently Salondine, aka Fluffy, walked off with my Oxfords. "So if the council came here, I couldn't pick you as my protector and stay, right?"

Confused, he crosses over to me. "Uh, probably not considering my standing with them. So what *did* happen with Sal?" He sniffs the air.

"He wanted to. I didn't. He didn't force the issue, don't worry. He also doesn't have a high opinion of you, and I'm not about to let someone trash my friend, whether he saved my life or not. So no, he won't be my protector. He wouldn't leave when I asked him to. *Several* times, in fact."

Dave blinks as I lace up my boots. "But he did leave."

I smile wickedly. "Yes. Yes, he did."

Dave takes a step back, his voice nervous. "What'd you do, Black?"

"Did it seem odd to you that he didn't just fly out of here? I mean, he flew in, your portal still works. Why tromp down the stairs and walk out in front of you wearing clothes that I've been told give an impression of indigence?" I look up at him. "Nothing permanent, don't worry, but I suspect he'll be back here and none too happy with me in a few hours, or however long it takes him to clear three hundred miles."

Dave stares as I stand up and fetch my knapsack.

"Don't worry, Dave, all I did was give him time to think over his methods. I, on the other hand, am chalking him up as a misguided one-afternoon stand and nothing more."

"So, what, you're leaving?"

I nod to him. "When Salondine showed up, I think we both knew I was going to have to get out of here sooner than later."

"Where are you going to go?" He stops, shakes his head. "Don't tell me. They'll ask and I won't be able to say no. It's happening awfully fast."

"Doesn't mean we're not still friends, Dave. We'll figure something out. I figure there's got to be a way to scry or divine or something. I'll look in every now and then, and if it doesn't look too bad, I'll drop by." I try to smile. "Now you have to find someone willing to wash dishes for what you were paying. I don't envy that task."

Dave tics his head toward the stairwell. "You want me to tell them anything?"

"I'll admit I'm tempted to have you tell them the truth just to see how they'd hear it." I take a deep breath. "Tell them I'll miss them, and tell Sharon I wouldn't mind her praying for me."

Shouldering my knapsack, I double-check that the shear is inside, still there, the hole it made covered with duct tape.

"Hey, Black."

I turn to face Dave.

"Anything you want me to tell your brother?"

"Tell him I'm sorry." I cross back to Dave and hug him, trying to stay strong. "This isn't goodbye, okay?"

It probably is.

I head to the stairwell, leaving him there as I descend to the side door. The alley is barren, only bits of scattered trash tossed about by a light breeze. This really is the right decision. I just have no idea how I'm supposed to duck a bunch of dragons who, thanks to Sal, probably know what I smell like.

Cale's a sorcerer and hasn't been bothered by any dragons. But then that's because no one can find him, since the gods themselves show their disapproval the moment he steps out his door.

I admit I'm curious what exactly my predecessors have done to earn all this animosity. Considering that we're talking about humans with magical power, it's not too hard to go with the old adage about power corrupting. And what I did to Sal, I mean, I know I've got a good reason, but there's another adage about where good intentions lead you. I'm hardly pure as the driven snow, no matter the color of that streak in my hair. That lightning I drew from my memories when I faced down a goddess is a good indicator of how I could fall.

When I finally find my way to Cale's, it's midafternoon, and I suspect not a moment too soon, as Sal has likely found a way beyond the three-hundred-mile limit by now and is either reporting in to the council or coming after me.

The shop is dim, none of the sconces alit, and Cale is seated on the dais, looking into the double mirror. He's rocking back and forth, slowly, muttering. "Now don't get up, my Orchid King, the flowers are for your rule. I taught you my heart but you kissed the moon and made me look the fool."

I advance toward him with caution. "Cale?"

He doesn't seem to notice me, still staring into the mirrors. "A silly boy you were, young fox, but you never could trap me. You thought me a prize but never a man, so I sent you 'cross the sea."

Gingerly, I tap his shoulder, and he turns quickly, his eyes fixed on me, his grin a little too wide. "And the boy who thinks me Cheshire, the river in his wake. He'll dance through storms to find my heart, but it's the throne that he will..." Cale trembles, and his eyes brim with tears as his face softens. He

137

looks toward the mirrors, then back to me, his voice firmer, sounding closer to normal. "It doesn't matter."

I motion toward the mirrors. "You going to tell me what that was all about?"

"I suppose you should learn from my mistakes. Never become involved with a god or a trickster, my young apprentice. You are only a means to an end for them and they care little for what damage they do." He smiles. "Unless of course you only involve yourself for a few moments." Cale blushes but regains his seriousness. "Never more than once though."

"Should probably add dragons to that list too, right?" I sit down on the dais. "That's something I need to talk to you about."

Cale peers at me. "Why would I need to add dragons?"

"Well, I guess there's some sort of council?"

He nods once. "The Dracon Council, yes. A fine organization though they were a bit meddling in my day."

"I think they're coming for me." I wince. "I might've bound one of their representatives into a human form."

Cale's jaw drops, and he works through several looks of confusion before gesturing with his hands for me to continue. "More."

"Well, there was a red dragon named—"

He covers my mouth. "Don't say its name. It might not be able to pinpoint where you are, but let's not give it any hints, shall we?"

"They can tell when someone says their name?"

"They can tell when a *sorcerer* says their name. It's how we designed them after all."

"We designed?"

"Of course. A properly trained sorcerer in the ancient worlds could easily create life according to their whims. How else do you believe the mythics came about? In dragons, we created the perfect combination of servant, seneschal and protector. Unbreakable loyalty too. Lots of other little things have been added on as the worlds have come and gone. Without a Ra'keth telling them what to do, I'd imagine they'd leap at a wandering Keth. But you've driven me off on a tangent." He taps my nose. "Shame on you. Continue."

"Anyway, he wanted to be my protector."

"Red dragons are excellent for that, second only to a golden in my opinion. You didn't approve though?" He looks out the window, mutters a string of names, and the top half of a parking meter vanishes, a tea set appearing on the dais behind us with sugar, honey and biscuits. Cale pours both of us tea, leaving me to decide how much sugar and honey I'd prefer. He glances at my knapsack. "Your focus is in there?"

I nod.

He *hmph*s. "The ordeal must not have been too impressive."

"Cale? I nearly drowned to get it."

He shrugs. "As I said, not too impressive." Cale stands up and draws a longsword from thin air, the blade covered in runic markings and glowing with a golden flame. "Tell me, Apprentice, have you ever heard of the Claw of Shoshare?"

I scramble back away from the sword, as it's kind of close and definitely on fire. I hit a clothing rack, which wobbles, dropping a couple pairs of slacks on my head. "No?"

"You haven't? You've never heard the story of a blade tempered in the hearts of storm gods, which cleaved a city in twain with one stroke, that devoured the soul of a cannibal god and drank our second sun dry?" He flourishes the blade with a grin. "Still no?" Cale sheathes the sword back into whatever invisible portable hole he pulled it from. "There's a reason for that. No one remembers it, because its history is gone. It is *mine* now."

I gulp audibly. "My God, Cale, who are you?"

His golden eyes bore into mine. "Who do you think I am?"

I chew my lip and titter nervously. "Money's still on Cheshire cat?"

Cale looks out the window, muttering. "The terrible names that I have been branded with, only to be saddled with an affectation." He walks past me toward the stairs. "Fine, you may stay here, as I know you wished to ask. If the council cannot find me here, the same would extend to you."

I get up from the floor and walk toward the stairway after him. "Thank you."

"Don't just yet. You'll be a proper apprentice, and you can begin by tidying up." Cale starts up the stairs.

"What, the whole build—"

He stops on the landing and shoots me a self-satisfied smile. "If you're going to think me a cat, you should know better than to approach one who's growling." He vanishes up the stairs.

I can't help it and mutter under my breath. "I think you a Cheshire cat, and you call it growling. *I* call it purring."

Part III

Asylum

Chapter Fourteen

December

Cowardice has its advantages.

I shouldn't be surprised staying at Cale's for a few weeks to lay low turned into a few months. I can conjure my own food, there are no clocks, no calendars, and being a sorcerer's apprentice means there's always something to do. Thankfully, no water fetching. I doubt Cale would get the joke anyway.

Unlike Cale, though, I'm not under house arrest. Should I step outside, the sky will not suddenly be filled with dozens of dragons, at least not for a few hours. I haven't seen any sign of Heath either, though I haven't brought him up to Cale. I don't know why, I'm sure a shrink could give an explanation. I don't know. Cale sees me as his apprentice. I guess I don't want him to see me as someone Heath beat on for a year.

Since I can go outside, Cale's added gofer to my job description. Eating the same six foods probably gets to a person after a few decades, so I've been gathering more "modern" cuisine for him to sample. Fast food is always cold by the time I get it back to him, so it's not memorable enough to conjure, and neither of us can cook worth a damn.

After that, he wants books, mostly mysteries. Arthur Conan Doyle, Agatha Christie, Dashiell Hammett, Raymond Chandler. I brought him some James Patterson, but Cale's cultural paradigm is still a few decades behind. Gives me something to read at least.

The downside is that washing dishes under the table paid better than this. When you can conjure anything you need, things like money probably slip your mind. Because of this, I've become a regular patron of a pawnshop on 79th and J, which is just inside Beckettsville.

Considering I'm about fifteen blocks from the edge of urban renewal, it shouldn't surprise me that the shop doesn't have a clever name.

79th Street Gold & Services.

It's the only place in the neighborhood that's not scraping to get by. It's a squat, two-floor brick affair, the alley walls a palimpsest with mottled mixes of ads for Coca-Cola and Burma-Shave. The front windows are whitewashed to complete opacity with plain letters offering check cashing, payday loans, currency exchange, vintage guitars, stun guns and buy/sell/trade.

I'm only interested in one of their services.

It's just after sundown when I enter the shop. Winter is still officially tomorrow, but the weather never seems to mind. Snow has fallen, temperatures spending more of the day below zero (centigrade, not Fahrenheit). So I'm dressed warmly, wearing one of Cale's gray turtlenecks, a charcoal greatcoat, and black BDUs and thick-soled boots I got cheap from a surplus store. Not really a fashion statement, but I'm going for warmth and utility.

The pawnshop's decently sized, a couple clothing racks with leather jackets and military surplus, shelves with DVDs and CDs, decorative swords hung up next to battered musical instruments. The counter runs the width of the building, the glass cases filled with jewelry and firearms. The proprietor, a rat, stands behind the counter on two legs, an inch taller than me, black fur with a streak of white on his forehead (which gives us something in common). He wears an old beige trench coat with a red scarf about his neck. His voice sounds like some cartoon character who spent the last twenty years smoking cigarettes and drinking whiskey.

"You back already?" The rat proceeds to light a cigar, shaking his head. "You have to lay off."

"How's business?" Neither of us is into small talk, but he's one of the few people in the City, mythic or otherwise, that looks at my Mark and honestly doesn't care. He holds up a hand and heads into a small office, closing the door. I wait, patiently, figuring he had to go to the bathroom or something.

He returns a couple of minutes later and snorts. "Every time you come in here, you ask how business is."

I shrug and look behind him at the array of goods hanging from hooks on the wall, then at the cases. "You sell one of those TASER guns?"

"Nope."

I point to an empty spot where I'd seen one the week before. "But there was one there, right?"

"I don't carry TASER guns." He puffs a bit of smoke, thankfully away from my face.

"But..." I point toward the sign painted on the front window, starting to feel lost now.

"I sell TASERs. Not TASER guns. It's an acronym for Tom A. Swift's Electric Rifle. To call it a TASER gun would mean you're saying it's a Tom A. Swift's Electric Rifle gun." He takes another puff on his cigar. "Which would be redundant."

I blink. "Well, after that I guess you'd be an expert on redundancy."

This time I do get smoke in my face. "What have you got for me, smartass?"

"Nothing too big this time, I promise." I reach into my pocket and remove what an hour ago had been five fistfuls of newly fallen snow. It's a memory now, dangling from a golden fob. I don't remember the details about the jewel movement or anything. I don't know if it's actual gold or if the hunter case gives it a little oomph in value. I hand the watch to the rat, who lays it on the mat in front of him.

He clicks his tongue several times, so it's already looking bad. "There's an engraving here."

For my son, who now has all the time in the world.

I'd pawned it three months before I left Heath, to help us make rent, but I guess my memory of it is the only proof it ever existed.

"Can you take it or not?"

The rat looks up from his inspection. "You mind telling me where you're getting these? Weird enough buying shit off a Keth. Weirder still that you're not just bringing me gold bars. This thing hot?"

"No, just like all the other stuff." I don't tell him they're transmuted copies, that'd drive the price down. Besides, that's the only reason I can bring myself to sell my father's watch, my mother's crucifix, the engagement ring that I'd helped Thom pick out for Beth... "I'm not asking for a lot here."

The rat chortles, rests his cigar in an ashtray. "You never do. Never had a customer before you who didn't try to haggle. You don't tell me this shit's antique even though I can tell it is. I offer you a little more than what I'd give a junkie, and you take it no questions asked. You're denying me one of the great joys of being a merchant."

"You want me to know you're ripping me off?"

"I want you to tell me why a sorcerer needs money."

I shrug with a small smile. "Because I haven't figured out how to make it grow on trees yet."

He looks down at the mat and grumbles. "What the hell. I'll give you fifty."

He wants haggling? Fine. "Two hundred. I know where that was bought."

"Ninety. It's engraved."

"One-fifty. That's still gold."

"One-ten. And I won't call the cops."

"Split the difference. One-thirty." I smile beatifically. "It has sentimental value."

"One-fifteen. If it really meant anything to you, you wouldn't be selling it, but I'll kick in five for using a classic."

I meet the rat's eyes. "One-twenty-five, and I don't turn half your inventory into a slab of bacon."

The rat returns the look, but dubiously. "You would honestly threaten me with magic for ten measly dollars?"

I shrug. "A guy's gotta eat."

The rat chuckles, which sounds like an attack of smoker's cough, but he grins and shows dirty yellow teeth all the same. "One-twenty, not a penny more."

"Deal." I extend my hand to seal it, but he waves my hand off while he removes a fat wad of twenties from his pocket.

"You know I don't go for handshakes, 'specially not with sorcerers." He lays out six bills, all of them wrinkled. "Take your money, and I don't want to see you back in here until after New Year's."

"That's two weeks away. I'm supposed to get by in *this* city on a hundred bucks?"

"Nope, on a hundred and twenty." He scoffs, putting the wad of bills away. "Thought you had to be smart to be a sorcerer. Or at least know how to count. You don't like it, find another shop."

I gather up the bills and stuff them in my pocket. "You're the only one that'll deal with me." I point to my hair.

The rat takes a clipboard from behind the counter, marking down the transaction. "Then I suppose you'll be waiting." He motions to the door. "I get more customers around the holidays. You scare them off."

Considering that I just sold a wad of snow for three figures, I take the hint and walk out the front door.

"You do a lot of business here?"

I wince immediately and turn to find the Coyote from months ago. He's dressed warmly, black jacket, dark-colored scarf knotted loosely about his neck, looks like he hasn't shaved in a few days. I'll admit I let my eyes linger a second, mostly on the woolen holiday knit cap complete with reindeer that obscures his hair. Good thing, God only knows what hair color he's trying this time. "You owe me forty-five bucks, Spencer."

"I had a feeling it was going to be you." He grins, rubbing his ungloved hands together for warmth. "I mean, it had to be, you know?"

"What, Fate?" I roll my eyes. "Doesn't work like that with me."

"No, no. You don't get it. You see, you and I met in the diner, right? I was there to trick your boss, you were there to foil me. Now you're hocking trash for top profit to a mobbed-up rat, which is ironic as hell if you think about it, and here I am to pull your ass from the fire before he figures it out."

"That's not destiny, Spencer, that's blind, stupid coincidence."

"Is it?" His grin widens as he steps closer. "Or is it a classic meet cute?"

"Bullshit. Why are you really here?"

The Coyote sags with a sigh. "Yeah, I figured I couldn't sell that." He motions to the pawnshop. "He stopped buying my stuff because he's taking your stuff, okay? I slipped him a Benjamin to give me a call the next time my competition dropped by. When he called I told him to stall you a little."

That would explain the rat slipping away for a minute when I got there, and why today he was interested in haggling.

I point at the shop. "He's mobbed up?"

The Coyote rolls his eyes now. "Of course he is. And eventually he'll find someone who can tell that you're selling, what, mounds of dirt to him?"

"How do you even know the stuff is fake?"

He growls. "Let's just say I've been paid in leaves before."

I blink in confusion. "Leaves?"

He mutters "damn Foxes" under his breath. "Anyway, clearly, we're supposed to be together. If this were the internet, seventeen-year-old girls would be writing slash fiction about us as we speak."

Okay. He's crazy. Cale is sane compared to him. "I'll be going now."

"Hey, c'mon back." Spencer comes up alongside me. "What I mean is that you and I should team up, you know? Fight crime, pull cons, have adventures. Think about it, a trickster and a sorcerer? There's not a mark in the world we couldn't nail, and the differences between us alone could fuel a sitcom for at least five seasons."

"Fine, just go do that on your own, okay?" Maybe if I walk faster... Shit. He's matching pace.

"Nah, I tried the hero thing once and ended up in the hospital and almost didn't graduate high school. I'm comfortable playing second banana. We get the best lines anyway."

Yeah, I don't really see him as a hero type either. If I saw him help a stranger in need, I'd tell said stranger to check his pockets.

He looks thoughtful a few seconds. "Though if this is an action-adventure, I would get kidnapped a lot more. Maybe we shouldn't go the UST route..."

I glance at him. "UST?"

He winks. "Unresolved sexual tension. Well, if you change your mind, I live down in Grunstadt."

"Didn't you tell me to remember your name because you were going to be the one to trick me?"

He stops. "Oh yeah. That. Uh..." He chuckles nervously. "Changed my mind?"

"Goodbye, Spencer." I resume my walking.

"You know I can follow you anywhere, right?"

I give a grin of my own back at him. "Not *everywhere*."

I hold my breath and slip into Tartarus. I run away.

Perhaps it wasn't the best of ideas.

Already I can feel the cold water rushing around me, the screeching of the dead, vaporous shapes flowing through the black toward me, drawn to the magic that glows from me like a beacon now. My power's grown, but I'd rather it wasn't so obvious. I keep running along the darkened shapes of the buildings, loud scratching sounds coming from the pavement as the time-frozen snow tears at my shoes. I round a corner as my lungs overpower my will, the world returning just as a ghostly arm grabs at me, my slacks clawed open along the length of my left leg as I emerge. I stumble into a snowbank, which doesn't help my now-exposed skin. Still, could be worse.

Damn it, I just thought that, didn't I?

A roar barely precedes a split of the clouds as giant wings emerge, the beast easily twice the size of Salondine. I'll admit part of me is satisfied that I'm finally seeing a *proper* dragon. The rest of me panics and runs, but to little avail. I'm on foot and that's a *dragon*. And given the severity of the roar that will likely be taken as a low-flying plane by the general public, I have to guess that I'm spotted.

"Oh *fuck* Murphy's Law."

It likely has my scent now (considering that Salondine tracked me through the scent of one broken scale), and I can't run far enough through the land of the dead to get away before it picks it up again.

"Okay, bitch, you want me? It's not going to be easy." I run down the street, farther away from the pawnshop and find a tight alleyway to duck into. A Dumpster provides a good spot to hide behind while I summon up my will, my memories. I plunge deep, feeling my skin tingle, silver sparks and currents running along my hands, crackling in the air. A rush of wind channels through the alley as the dragon lands at the mouth, the worn brick walls lit by a brilliant flash of crimson light. I peek around the Dumpster, my breathing steady, and see an older woman dressed in vermillion robes, gray-streaked auburn hair draping her shoulders, her eyes a brilliant, shining violet. Her steps are cautious, though she looks directly at me.

"I'm not going anywhere with you." I spit hard at the pavement, static cracking loud in the air around me.

She clasps her hands and bows her head, her eyes closing during it. "I am not so easily dissuaded, Anu'keth."

"Stay back!" I extend my hand toward her, an arc of lightning striking the wall. The brick explodes, though she remains unfazed, even as the shrapnel strikes her. With one brush of her hand, her face is cleared of the debris.

"I am no lowly drake seeking a greater station, Anu'keth." She walks toward me deliberately. "I am curious how you have evaded detection. My finest trackers could only keep your scent a moment before you would vanish again, sometimes for days, sometimes for weeks. If you had not attempted such a major working, you would have eluded even *me*."

Damn it, I keep forgetting that dragons are sensitive to magic. Ducking into Tartarus and coming out again was like sending up a signal flare.

"Just go away, I don't want a protector!" I get to my feet, come out to face her, and hold up my hand, the lightning still sheathing my arm. "Back off."

She nods once, curtly. "As you wish."

I glance at her feet. "That's not backing off."

"I see no reason to. It will take more than a young sorcerer throwing a tantrum to undo me. Also, you do not wish a protector. I am not here to offer my services. I will however pass your wishes to the council." She reaches forward and pushes my hand downward, electricity shooting through her body, her face setting in determination, but I have no greater effect than making some of her hair stand on end. "Calm yourself, Anu'keth, I am not your enemy."

I take a deep breath and step back, my hands going to my sides, but still glowing with silver sparks. "What do you want, then?"

"I want many things, Sorcerer, but I make no demands. I could easily demand retribution for what you have done to a member of my brood, as the bond between dragons and the Keth has been sacrosanct since your kind created us. We are to choose our own names, Anu'keth, our service grown from honor and duty, not from obedience." I catch a small smile on her face. "No matter how humorous the moniker."

"I take it Salondine is still pissed?"

"We have long memories, Anu'keth. I feel he should count himself fortunate, as your treatment was minor, and you brought a glaring issue to the council's attention." The smile is definite now. "We have all taken names for our lesser forms now as a result."

I let the energy fade from my hands, my body getting a little wobbly, as I wasn't drawing on anything other than myself. Best to watch my behavior over the next few days. "So what happens now?"

"There is a trickster." She inhales through her nose. "He is still close. Shall I dispose of him?"

I blink. "No!"

"Tricksters are threats, *irritating* threats, it would be best to—"

I shake my head. "No, he's just annoying. Leave him alone."

She clasps her hands and bows again. "As you wish."

"Thank you."

She perks a brow at that, but regains her composure. "If I may, Anu'keth, might I address why the council has sought you for these past few months?"

"Yeah, sure, go ahead."

"We ask that you, as the sole Keth who will have dealings with us, perform a minor task that is sorely needed."

"That task being?"

Her violet eyes meet mine with deadly seriousness. "We humbly request that you end the world."

Chapter Fifteen

"You want me to do *what*?" I stagger back from her, both from fatigue and the "humble request".

"This is a world that has gone on too long, become damaged. It must be ended, Anu'keth." She hasn't moved, but she hasn't lost any seriousness either. I keep hoping that the humor she's displayed extends to this. She tilts her head, watching me back away. "Surely you can feel it, can you not?"

"Lady, I don't care what your opinion of the world is, I'm not ending it. I've made a lot of mistakes as a sorcerer but I'm not going to be evil."

"You..." Her face scrunches up in thought and confusion. "I do not understand. Sorcerers end the—"

I hold up a hand.

"Yeah, lady, you might want to explain that bit. I'm not killing off billions of people, even if I *could*."

"You do not understand. This should have been expected. You are not killing anyone, per se." Her brow furrows as she searches for words. "It is...like a car that has broken down." She looks to me hopefully. "You are following, so far?"

I look at her oddly. "I know what a car is, yes. But when a car breaks down, you fix it."

"What if it cannot be fixed?"

I shrug. "You buy a new one if you can afford it, I guess."

"And the people who drive the car, do you throw them away with the old one? Of course not, they simply use the new one." Her fingers gently click against her teeth. "It is an awkward metaphor, but simple enough. You understand? As a sorcerer, it is your duty to—"

"Junk the old car and buy a new one. And it has to be *me*?"

"The world is ended by a sorcerer, by a Ra'keth, specifically."

"A Ra'keth? I've always heard him referred to as *the* Ra'keth."

She nods. "Yes. The number of Ra'keth has dwindled to one, but that is due to the law of the Usurper, who slew the Widow for her throne, and promptly ended the world she watched over. In the world he created from her blood, he decreed that the throne may not be inherited, only usurped."

"That sounds more like a fairy tale."

She smiles. "So does the idea of a sorcerer addressing the Broodmother of the Crimson Flight in an alleyway."

"Touché. He created this world from her blood? That's a little..." I shudder.

"He created *a* world, one that is long since gone, but every world after, including this one, is descended from that world, and bound to its law, as well as the laws before and after it. A sorcerer creates a world from whatever he or she wishes, anything that carries power for them." She steps closer to me. "But this world, it has gone on too long, Fate's tapestry is growing frayed, and she must begin anew."

"Go back to the car analogy?"

She exhales forcefully. "We were speaking of a car that has broken down, yes? Little danger to the driver."

"I'm following."

"And if the problems with the car grow severe enough to cause an accident?"

I think I get it. "The driver gets hurt. So what you're saying is that if I don't junk the car, err, end the world, then a whole lot of people are going to die."

She nods. "I know this all matters little to you, the lives of others, but..."

I glare at her, my body covering with dancing sparks in spite of myself. How fucking *dare* she... "Why would you think that?"

She gestures with her hands, trying to find the words. "You are Keth."

"So you *assume* I don't give a damn about other people?"

The dragon goes through the same motions, and once again only finds, "You are Keth."

I whistle softly. Okay, it's not a personal reflection on me, then. "Wow. I guess sorcerers hang out on the chaotic side of the alignment table."

She perks a brow. "I do not understand. You require a table in the metaphor now?"

I shake my head. "Forget it. Not important. I'm not like that. I want to make sure that everything you're saying is true, okay? You can understand where I might have a bit of trouble trusting what you say."

She sets her jaw, a plume of smoke leaving her nose. "You believe I would *lie*? To a *Keth*?"

"Okay, sorry. But do you understand that I would at least want some confirmation?"

The dragon takes a moment to collect herself, and nods. "I understand. But when you see that the damage is irreparable, you will do what must be done?"

"I don't even know how to do what you're asking."

"It is simple, Anu'keth. You know what your purpose is. Once you fulfill it, you can accomplish your task." She can see that I'm still confused. "You must usurp the throne. You must slay the Ra'keth."

Kill Heath.

"I don't know if I can."

She tilts her head to the side. "You are an odd man. However did you come to be Keth?"

"I don't know. I think I looked into a mirror and didn't want to see what I saw anymore." I meet her eyes. "So what happens now, with the council, I mean?"

"You do not require a protector unless you become a Ra'keth, simple as that. To protect lesser sorcerers would betray our king, but he is...difficult. As a result, we have not approached him."

"So, what do I call you?"

She smiles. "Normally the Keth decides that. I have been called many names, the majority of them can no longer be pronounced."

"Well, tell me one that can be pronounced."

She nods curtly. "You may call me Jutte, if you like." Yoo-teh...

Wait a minute... "Is that German?"

She grins knowingly, showing teeth. *"Ja, natürlich spreche ich Deutsch. Du nicht?"*

I point at her. "So you're..."

"I will leave you to your task. We cannot render you any aid further than advice, but should you need it, you need merely call." She bows deeply and turns, leaving the alley, ignoring my questions and assumptions. A flash of light soon follows, as well as the heavy beating of wings.

Well, shit.

Kill Heath? I'll admit in my darker moments I've entertained the thought, but there's a big difference between thinking about it and really doing it. Plus, it'd be murder, and I'd rather see him powerless and passed around a cellblock for packs of cigarettes.

Honestly, I'd rather regain a semblance of normalcy, as normal as buying groceries from a unicorn and used books from a werewolf can be, that is. Since today's sale brought in double what I was expecting, I splurge on used vinyl records as well, and throw the rest on my UTA pass.

Getting back to Cale's isn't the hassle it used to be. Maybe I've lived there long enough that the enchantment or warding that keeps it hidden has me on the approved-guest list. I just know that it only takes me a minute to remember the intersection, but it's still a frustrating minute.

Cale is behind the counter when I return to the shop, running his fingers over the pages of a book that looks a little too big to be a hard-boiled crime novel. When he sees me, he closes it and glances to the bags I'm carrying. "Anything of note happen?"

I take a second to consider my options. "Nothing world-shattering." I try not to chuckle at my choice of words.

He murmurs a few words as his golden eyes scan me and then narrow. "You've been casting. And drawing on yourself again. You were attacked?"

"Not really. Almost ended up with a Coyote sidekick, but I'm okay, no one's hurt or dead, and I don't really want to talk about it. What are you reading?"

He pushes the book behind the register, out of view, and looks at me smugly. "Nothing world-shattering."

I return the look. "Fine."

He sets in a harder stare. "Fine."

I drop the bag of groceries on the counter unceremoniously. "I'm taking a bath." I head up the stairs, carrying the other bag.

Cale rummages through the groceries and calls after me. "These are all canned goods."

I don't break stride, rounding the landing and heading to the second floor. "You can't work a pull tab? I thought you had to be smart to be a sorcerer."

Five months of this.

I now understand why I never role-played my elven mage's downtime with his mentor. If it was anything like this, they would've killed each other. Every now and then Cale and I have a moment where we aren't prickly, but I'm well aware that casting puts me in a bitchy mood, so he gives me distance and we both don't say anything we'll regret.

Considering the time of year, I'm starting to wish we hadn't agreed to keep things professional. Not saying I want something heavy, just... It's a shitty time to be alone.

While the water runs for my bath, I drape my pants over the sink, hang my sweater from the doorknob. The bath fills as high as I'm comfortable with, and I relax before settling my attention on my dirty clothes. I've moved on from basic transmutation and conjuration to beginner's abjuration. Turns out getting rid of things is a lot easier than making them appear.

And a good way to practice is banishing unsightly dirt and grime so your clothes can be April fresh without spending an hour at a Laundromat.

The simplest spells, which I can't help but call cantrips, are only a syllable.

I draw the energy for the spell from the water, extending my hand toward the pants, particularly the soaked and slushed-up cuffs. I utter the word, and the water grows colder, the heat from it carried on my breath toward the BDUs...

Which promptly light on fire.

"Fuck!" I scramble out of the tub, grabbing the pants by the waist, and throw them into the water, dousing the flames. I lean against the door and bang it with my fist. "Damn it."

It's still a complex syllable.

"Is everything all right in there?" Oh bloody hell.

"Everything's fine."

"I sensed magic." He's right outside the door now. "And smelled smoke."

I pull on my underwear for modesty's sake and crack the door, finding him there, his arms folded. "It's fine. It was just a little fire. It's out. Nothing's damaged except my pants." I sigh, looking down. "Say it and get it over with."

"Whatever do you mean?"

I roll my eyes. "Just say it. 'You flubbed a cantrip? I thought you had to be smart to be a sorcerer.' Get it over with."

He blinks several times, his arms falling to his sides. "James, you have been my apprentice less than a year and practicing magic less than five. That St. Benedict is still intact is more surprising. It takes some time for a Keth to learn control over their power." He smiles slightly. "In other words, do not be discouraged. You are progressing as well as any apprentice."

"I thought you'd never had one before."

He shrugs, keeping that smile. "I was one once. The sorcerers of old would likely still consider me one, in fact." He glances to my bare legs. "I'll fetch you some trousers." Cale vanishes from my view, but I hear him descending the stairs a second later.

Well, don't I feel like shit. "Thank you."

I didn't have much time to bathe, but I dry myself off regardless and slip into the bedroom to put on a clean shirt, at least. Cale moved out of his bedroom a couple of days after I "moved in". He stays up on the third floor, which I still haven't seen. If I had to guess, it's where his sanctum is, considering that I don't see any doors or stairs or hatches leading up there, even though anyone can plainly see from outside there's a third floor with windows.

I go with a T-shirt I picked up a couple months ago, fashionably worn, but clean. Cale cracks open the bedroom door, holding the trousers, which clash with the shirt, but it's not like I'm going anywhere. I put them on, but I don't hear him moving down the hallway. Sighing, I open the door, find him standing there. "What?"

He picks up the second bag, filled with vinyl albums, and presents it to me. "You left this in the loo." I take it, his expression having a curious bent. "Were you hoping to play them on the Victrola?"

I leaf through the albums, all still there. "Did you go through these?" That came out sterner than I wanted, because he exhales forcefully and starts down the hall.

"I ask a simple question..."

He's almost to the stairs. Fuck. "Wait."

He stops at the foot of the stairs, not turning his head.

"Before I answer, please just answer my question. Did you look through them?"

He glances over his shoulder. "Perhaps I did."

"God damn it." Again, probably sterner than I intended. Cale starts down the stairs. I stop him at the landing. "It was supposed to be a surprise."

He looks to me, cautiously. "What *kind* of surprise?"

I descend the stairs to him, offer him the bag. "Happy Christmas." Gingerly, he takes the bag while I cast my eyes away, awkwardly. "I figured since you can only conjure what you've read, it probably explains your lackluster vinyl collection."

It's largely classical, all two albums of it. And no matter how pretty it is, one can only listen to *Pachelbel's Canon* so many times. I motion to the albums in the bag. "So I got you some stuff." Etta James, Dinah Washington, Billie Holiday... Outside of jazz, this is mostly what my father listens to.

"I..." He looks down at the bag, then at me. "I don't know what to say."

"You don't have to say anything. Like I said, Happy Christmas. Though it's a few days early."

He nods, though I don't know if it's to me or himself. "You'll have to forgive me, few holidays give me concern anymore."

I smirk. "Is that your way of saying you didn't get me anything? Besides, don't thank me yet. I don't even know if those will play on your Victrola or if you'll like them at all."

He gives a Cheshire cat smile. "Oh, I can *make* them play." Cale takes a breath, bites his lip a second. "Would you..."

"What?"

"Tonight will be another year for me. I mark it with the beginning of winter." Right, the solstice starts at midnight.

"Isn't that kind of depressing?"

Cale shrugs. "Perhaps, but the City does little to mark the beginning of spring. Winter, however..."

Right. The tree-lighting in Victory Square. It's a lot like the tree-lightings in other big cities, with a media presence and thousands of people crowding together to see someone hit a switch.

Dad used to take me every year. The first time, though, I've never forgotten it.

I thought it had to be a magic tree of some sort, with little doors and windows speckled about the bark for the Fair Folk, a canopy that would block out the sun. Instead, it was a tall triangle of deep green, fading to black at the core where the lights of the Square couldn't reach.

And then the tree lit.

The lights were all white, not like the one at home we'd spent hours decorating until it was a mass of garland and tinsel and antique ornaments that I wasn't allowed to touch. Nothing like that tree.

It was a fountain of light crowned by a shining jewel, yet through it you could see the branches, as if we'd all been waiting for its leaves to bloom and glow like a bared soul.

How'd they make the tree do that, Daddy?

Magic, Miles. Magic.

I come out of my reverie, Cale looking at me. "So you're going to watch the tree-lighting?"

"I'll use the mirrors downstairs to scry and show the event." Cale shifts his weight from foot to foot. "Would you care to join me?"

"Given that it's likely the only way I'll see it, sure." My turn to feel awkward. "Listen, afterward, could I talk to you about something? Some stuff did happen today, but I'm still working out how to ask."

He perks a brow. "So it *was* something world-shattering."

I smile weakly. "Let's not ruin this nice moment, okay?"

Cale nods in assent. "For once we are in agreement." He peeks in the bag, fingering through the dozen albums. "Any suggestions where I should begin?"

I shrug, follow him down to the shop. "Can't go wrong with Nina Simone."

Chapter Sixteen

The rest of the day is spent cleaning. During the first two weeks here I hated every minute of it, but now I can see why Cale keeps the shop going even though he never gets any customers. I can go outside occasionally but if I didn't have something to do, I'd likely end up as cracked as Cale was when I first met him. It's dull and mind-numbing, and that's exactly why I do it.

No thinking about Heath being out there, alive.

No having to worry about dragons. Despite what Jutte told me, I'm certain her attitude doesn't extend to every other dragon in the world.

No having to think about anything, really.

Dinner's on me, Cale hasn't made anything other than tea since the Great Depression. I wish I could make something elaborate, but mostly I got canned pasta because it's cheap and doesn't taste too bad when you heat it up. Conjured and transmuted foods, I've found, are just empty calories, even when you conjure a salad. I'm curious how Cale hasn't died of malnutrition, actually, but then again he's over a hundred and only looks thirty, so he must be doing something right.

I, on the other hand, have to pop a multivitamin every day.

Not a lot of experience cooking (I washed dishes at the diner, Dave never let me near the grill), but it doesn't take a genius to heat up Chef Boyardee.

"What *is* that smell?" I don't need to turn around to know Cale's poked his head in the doorway.

I chuckle to myself. "What is it about cats always seeming to show up around dinnertime?"

"It's not my fault I was marked so. And I am not nearly so contrary." He enters, looks over my shoulder. "What is this?"

"Well, you can only eat SpaghettiOs and Beefaroni so many times before you need variety, so I got a couple cans of ravioli. It's pasta stuffed with meat in a tomato-like sauce."

"What kind of meat?"

I chew my lip. "Probably best if you don't ask. I didn't get anything to drink. You have anything stashed away?"

"Step back a moment."

"Ugh, Cale, don't transmute my dinner." I'm gently pushed aside as Cale steps in front of the stove and gives me a smug look. He reaches into the cabinet above and retrieves a very dusty wine bottle. He appraises it a moment, wiping the dust off on his sleeve, inspects the cork.

"Good. Wine goes well with pasta, or so I've heard."

"Cale, I wouldn't really call this pasta. How many bottles do you have?"

He moves away from the stove so I can continue stirring. "Just the one."

"Wouldn't you rather save it for a special occasion?"

"Tonight will be the first solstice in several decades that I won't be alone, Apprentice. That, in and of itself, makes it a unique occasion." He sets the bottle on the counter. "There should be a corkscrew in the drawer, though I would suggest cleaning it. I need to fetch something upstairs."

I stop him at the door. "Am I ever going to see what's up there?"

"Perhaps." He smirks. "I'll meet you downstairs."

Cale lingers a moment, leans toward me a few inches, but then stops, smiles awkwardly and leaves the kitchen. I watch him go, letting my mind linger on his smile and...

Oh God, this is a date.

Now I'm a little pissed at myself for cleaning all day when I could've been preparing for this. We're supposed to keep things professional. Right?

Right?

For God's sake, it's *Cale*. Sure, he's kissed me and we slept in the same bed once and, yeah, he's handsome and there *have* been a couple of dreams here and there that it wouldn't be proper to discuss. Sure, he's been good to me, patient, caring when we aren't having a row, and even then he's kind of...

"Fuck!" I yank the pot of ravioli off the burner and feel like a bigger moron because I somehow managed to burn a can of Chef Boyardee. "Damn it."

Shit, I've got it bad.

Deciding to make the best of it, I call on a memory of a fancy dinner, where I had to wear an itchy suit with a bow tie and eat on the good china and our water glasses were replaced with champagne flutes that Mom had lectured me endlessly on the proper handling of. I whisper the name, and the pot with the burned ravioli vanishes, replaced by six identical flutes with floral etchings in the glass.

I turn off the stove, put four of the flutes in the cabinet, and search for the corkscrew which does need a bit of cleaning. Luckily the plumbing still works here, so no having to conjure water. Once I'm satisfied, I pick up the corkscrew, the bottle and the two flutes, and carry them carefully downstairs.

Cale is seated in the chair on the dais, his face set in concentration as he murmurs words, his hand outstretched toward the mirrors. I stop to watch, and after a few seconds he sags in his chair, breathing heavily. "That gets harder every year." He beckons me over. "I see the wine's not opened."

"Not much experience with popping corks."

He inspects the twin flutes in my other hand. "And those are for champagne, not wine."

I smile. "Technically, champagne is sparkling white wine."

Cale narrows his eyes, playfully. "A pity then that we're drinking red." He takes the bottle and glasses from me, and then the corkscrew to start on the bottle. "Did you want me to open this, while you fetch dinner?"

"Yeah, uh, we're going to be drinking our dinner." I look at my feet. "I got a little distracted and..." I shake my head. "It's not important. I figured it was more important to see the tree-lighting. I can always make dinner after."

He nods. "Fair enough." The cork pops out, and he sets the bottle and glasses on the dais. "Best to let that breathe." He motions to the mirror. "What do you think?"

The reflection is replaced on both mirrors with the image of Victory Square, the tree at the center, people already crowding toward the main stage. It's like looking through a window. Experimentally, I tap the glass, half-expecting my hand to pass through, but the image only ripples slightly, nothing more. "I can't hear anything."

"You're not supposed to, mirrors are for seeing, not hearing." A moment passes. "Shall...shall I put on some music then?"

I nod. "I didn't pick up any Christmas music. Don't suppose you have any?"

He shakes his head. "It's difficult to be religious *and* Keth, James. Magic functions on the belief that we have a better way of doing things than gods. Another reason they resent us." Cale goes to the Victrola and starts it up. Dinah Washington fills the air soon after.

"So you're an atheist?"

"Atheists believe there are no gods. Seeing as I've had encounters with divine beings, that would be unlikely for me. I simply don't follow any."

"What about morality?"

He smiles warmly. "My Nan raised me on plenty of stories about what happens to the wicked, no gods were necessary."

I walk toward him. "You were raised by your grandmother, then?"

He nods. "She was Keth. A good woman, but strict. No one to trifle with. When I was born she saw the power in me, took me in. It was a dangerous time to work magic, after all. Even then folk had little issue laying their problems at the feet of a stranger. She was..." He looks away. "I've made you something." He hurries behind the two mirrors and takes out a large thin package, square, wrapped in linen. "You'll have to excuse the shoddy work."

I start to unwrap it.

"It's just been a while since I've done portraits and..."

The linen falls away, and I see my family.

I can only stare at it.

There's a photo like this, above the mantel at my mother's maisonette.

"Cale... How did you...?"

I remember when it was taken, all of us dressed in our Sunday best, another return to the itchy suit and bow tie for me. I was only eight, and I was squirmy. Thom kept making faces. Mom and Dad were just into the bickering that would precede another long separation.

Where I would be in this photo, there's no one.

"You mentioned your mother teaches at Oxford. I'm familiar with the area, so I scried, found her, and found a photograph similar to this in her home. You've mentioned your family several times, I thought I could..."

Instead, I'm in the portrait inserted next to my father, painted in as an adult, as I am now. My lower lip trembles, my eyes feel wet.

He reaches for it. "You don't like it."

I don't know who's more surprised when I slap his hand away. "Sorry. It's just..." I swallow hard. "I didn't think I could ever see them again. I mean, I know this is a lie now, but it's..." I set the painting next to the counter and face him as Cale rubs his hand. "Why?"

He gives a small shrug. "Happy Christmas."

I hug him tightly, my face buries in his shoulder, tears flowing freely as his arms encircle me, his hand stroking my hair. "Thank you." I pull back to meet his eyes. "This means... Cale, thank you."

He smiles, and we remain there, the moment stretching on. And then it happens. My lips are pressed to his, our eyes closed as our mouths open. Several seconds later we part, no fear between us.

Cale glances toward the chair, the mirrors, and I can see the ambient light from the image of Victory Square flickering. "We should probably go over there."

I nod.

His lips brush mine. "I don't really want to let go, though. I feel as if I've captured a dream."

I smile in return. "You're not alone in that."

Cale squeezes me. "That's what I have to thank you for. All this time, I've felt alone, not just here in this building, but my whole life. I have always been seen as Keth, never as anything else."

I smirk. "Well, now you're seen as a Cheshire cat."

He kisses me quickly. "Indeed. But there's more than that. This time with you, I'm beginning to wonder if I've ever been alone. Time, space—both are illusions invented to make everything make sense, or so I've heard. And if that is true..." He looks away awkwardly, nervously, summoning up the words. "If that is true, then I have never been alone at all, for you have always been here, beside me."

On the other side of the City, Victory Square is now illuminated, but I barely notice. Despite the darkness in the world, I feel the spark inside me flicker into a gentle silver light, warm and soothing.

"Cale?"

His fingers brush the lock of white hair from my face. "Yes, James."

I blush. "Do...do you want to..." Why am I so afraid to ask? I had no problem getting Salondine to hop in my lap. Heath wouldn't even give me a choice in the matter. After so long it's just a stupid mechanical thing, a safety valve for stress. Why can't I ask him?

Cale holds me closer to him. "Yes, James."

"It's just, we were fighting this morning and now..." I rest my head on his shoulder. "I'm afraid, okay?"

"Of what?" He rubs my back, his breath on my neck.

"That this is going to pass. Right now, I..." I need to say this. "I think I could..." Is that what I'm feeling? I mean, it's *Cale*. But I don't want to leave. I don't want him to let me go.

"If you have misgivings, James, we don't have to."

"Miles." The name slips out before I realize it.

"Pardon?" He leans back so he can look me in the eye. "What was that?"

"My name is Miles." I close my eyes, break his gaze. "James Black is just a name on a fake ID someone gave me."

His fingers stroke my cheek. "No, it's not. You are Keth, and you have taken that name, made it yours, just as I am no longer who I once was. That is the nature of the Keth, to know, to name and to stand. As we will it." Cale kisses me again, holding my face in his hands. "You are James Black of the Argent City, the Lightning Rod." It's an old name for the City, back when the five cities of Allora, Destry Bay, Grunstadt, Beckettsville and St. Benedict flirted with the idea of unification. "You have fought for and claimed your names, and though you may be struck, you will *never* fall. And that..." His eyes moisten, fear tingeing his voice, no, it's apprehension. He takes a breath, steels himself. "And that is why I love you."

Seconds pass as his words settle in. I know what he wants to hear, what he aches to hear, what his eyes plead me for. But I can't tell him that because he wants to hear it back. I can't tell him that because it might be what he's pinning his hopes on, a bulwark he'll set against madness. I can't tell him that because Heath could never get a guy like him. I can't tell him that because I don't want him to be alone, or because I don't want to be alone. I can't tell him that because of a million stupid reasons that he would eventually see through, and resent me for. I can't lie to him.

"I love you, Cale."

I tell him because I mean it.

A tight embrace holds me for the next minute, soft sobs muffled by my shoulder. I kiss his neck, and I wipe a tear from his eye when he looks at me again, his face wet. He bites his lip, a small smile on his face. "Shall we go upstairs, my love?"

Through the soothing warmth a fiercer heat begins to spread, our kisses more insistent as we awkwardly make our way up to the bedroom, avoiding any chance we might break contact. I'm pushed onto the bed, and I roll him onto his back, straddling his waist, our kisses only broken long enough to pull our shirts off. The Victrola downstairs plays on, the music wafting up the stairs, echoing down the hall, present but not distracting.

His touch is careful as he undoes my pants, his eyes never leaving mine. "Do you... Or shall I?" He blushes, trying not to laugh at himself. "No matter how much I want this, it still feels so improper to just *say...*"

I smirk. "Who you want on top?"

He manages a look of faux-indignation as he shimmies off his trousers. "I'll have you know I lived through an era where it was uncouth to admit that a *table* had legs. Do you believe it is easy to ask you to take my phallus?"

I chuckle. "I'm more surprised you call it a..." I look down at his groin and see a well-sized manhood there. I'd seen it before, when we'd shared the bed, but he wasn't excited then, and even then he was... "Table leg. Wow. Uh... That's going to hurt."

He glances downward. "Ah yes. I forgot the last man I was with was Fae." Cale holds my waist and rolls me on my back, atop me now, and maneuvers to get a better position as he pulls my boxers downward. "You, on the other hand..." His fingers run along my length, which is average in size, maybe a little thick. Cale leans down and kisses me. "I care not for how it is done, what matters is that I am with you. I'll feel bliss all the same." He blushes again, deeper. "And I perhaps...prefer..."

I grin. "Taking phalluses?"

He sighs. "James, this is our first time making love—"

"And I doubt it will be the last. Lighten up, okay? Yes, we love each other. It can be fun too, you know? Hell, I'd like it to be fun, it rarely is with me." I reach up, trace some of the tattoos on his chest. He shudders, but doesn't stop me, instead exploring my body.

"This is a new experience for me as well, you know. I don't believe I've ever actually been with a man before. Males, yes, but not a man."

I perk a brow and say, "You'll have to explain that," while I squeeze his thigh.

"I lost my innocence to a satyr, who showed me that I preferred a male's company to a woman's. After that was a trickster, but..." He takes a breath, his fingers running circles around my nipples. "It didn't end well with him. I've lain with a Fae, but it was relieving tension for the two of us, never anything more. As Keth, we tend to attract those types. As much as we repulse the mythics, we fascinate them as well." He wriggles forward, letting my length rest against his backside. Cale's face reddens again. "Unfortunately, there were long stretches of time between bedmates, and I am still a man, with certain urges. So I had to be...inventive with my magic."

His fingers grip me, and I feel a warm slick substance spreading over my shaft, my eyes threatening to roll to the back of my head. "Oh God, what *is* that?"

"A little conjuration of mine, made from some of my more carnal memories." His fingers get acquainted with my groin, and he observes my reactions, mostly moans and writhing. I manage to say his name a couple of times, which he retorts with soft chuckles. "I suspect this will be different than what we're expecting."

I shrug but let my fingers run along his shaft, eliciting a soft but sharp gasp. "Maybe for you, Cale, but I have been with a guy before. And a dragon. Not really all that different other than the dragon being oddly warmer."

Cale shakes his head and lifts himself slowly, taking hold of me, aiming before he sinks downward, both of us going silent as we feel our bodies join. "I..." His eyes close as he descends farther. "I more meant that we're Keth. My Nan told me to never couple with a Keth, as it can be a terrifying experience."

I shrug. "Not scared yet." My hips push up, and he muffles a sudden grunt. "Sorry."

He catches his breath. "Warn me before you do that, love." Cale furrows his brow in concentration, and a contented sigh escapes the two of us as my hips press flush to him. "You cannot imagine how this feels."

Glancing at his erect length, I chuckle. "Likely no. You'll take a lot longer."

Cale looks around the room and curses softly. "This isn't right, we should have the music up here, perhaps candles. I should've paid more attention to you before I just..."

"Cale, it doesn't have to be perfect. What matters is that we're with each other, right?" I wriggle myself back and forth inside him. "And really, I'm not complaining. At all."

He looks down at me, pensively. "I'm going to spill too quickly."

"Spill?" I notice his hand straying to his manhood, giving it a slow and even rhythm as he starts to rock his body against mine. "Ah, that kind of spill. How long has it been for you, Cale?"

"Since I last shared my bed, or since I last..." He breaks eye contact. "Spilled?"

I try to keep focus as my hips join his rhythm in counterpoint. I earn a sudden moan for my effort when I hilt at a good angle. "Let's go with both."

"At least a week since my virtue failed me." He looks at me crossly. "Honestly, I was practically ready to throw you into the street if it meant I'd get an hour to myself. As for my last partner, that was the Fae, and I do not know how long it was, but he was the one who recommended *The Maltese Falcon*."

That would make it...

"Oh my God... No wonder you were almost crazy. Wait, you were waiting for me to leave? Why didn't you just do it upstairs?"

"I will not debase my sanctum with onanism." He shivers, his free hand taking mine, our fingers interlocking. "May we please concentrate on more important matters?"

We move on in silence, save the occasional impassioned noise. He abandons himself early on, taking my other hand, my stomach getting wet with his leakage. Cale's eyes remain closed, it's strange to watch. He's so different right now, almost younger. Vulnerable, I think. I could almost say there's a desperation to his movements, like I could change my mind and call it off at any moment.

"Cale?" I squeeze his hands.

His eyes open slightly. "Yes?" His breathing is growing more ragged, and I can feel my body charging toward the summit.

"Cale, I'm right here. I'm not going anywhere."

Cale sniffles, but smiles. "How did you know I needed to hear that?" His eyes open wide. "James, are you about to?"

I don't know how he could tell that, but I'm *certain* that he's just as close and...

And...

I can feel the name of what's happening, what Cale is feeling, what I'm feeling, our bliss combining to become greater than the sum of its parts. I *know* the name. Cale can feel it too. I say it aloud, or Cale does, maybe we both do, I don't know, but it's the most beautiful name I could ever imagine.

My eyes roll back, my body goes numb in a heartbeat.

There is a presence beside me, then inside me, or am I inside it? Then there is no presence, just a feeling of...rightness. I was so empty before, how could I have never known that? But I'm not alone. I'm...

Complete.

My mind floods with so many memories, so many names, all of them meshing together, condensing. I know everything. I can name anything. My will is law. I open my...perception? Eyes seem so...limited.

There's a room about me, two names made of flesh below me... James, Cale, those are the names. They tempt me with their shared bliss, but I can resist their call for now. I expand my perception outward, and I'm aware of an immense tangle of names, woven in the shape of towers and roads that are forged with steel and pain and joy. So many names made of flesh here, with blood red and silver and purple and blue.

I push out further, find names that shine with power and purpose. The gods. I could stop here, speak their names, make them my servants, finally know freedom, but no...

Something holds me back.

Memories come to the forefront. I remember being controlled, my will shackled, drained, being treated more as a pet than a man. A fate I would wish on no one, not even gods.

It wouldn't be...right.

So I push out further.

The names become a blur, the number immense, almost blinding. I don't know how I could know them all, use them. They're tangled, knotted, tied, interlocked, woven together and pulled apart, it's too much, too much...

But I can't stop. I have to see. I've come too far. I can still hear the siren's call from the two names of flesh, from James and Cale, so far away, but I must resist. Even as their bliss clouds the edge of my perception, I push out one last time.

I cannot see the names anymore. There is only the tapestry of them, three bright and shining names buzzing around the weaving madly, battling against a seemingly endless fray.

Fate. This is the very tapestry of Fate. The complete destiny of the world itself, and the three names are the goddesses who tend it. There is desperation in their movements, they fight a losing battle, a war of attrition, spinning and weaving and cutting to preserve one thing, one name.

The very Name of the world itself.

But the name is nearly unpronounceable now. So much has been added to it, it must be simplified. I could give the world a new name, keep it intact, as it is, but...

But I can call that name. So much power would be mine. It's a right, *the* right of the throne, and I *am* the—

No. No. No.

It would be wrong. I can be better than that. I will be. I *want* to be.

In my moment of indecision, though, I'm caught unaware. My being floods with ecstasy, as the tapestry races toward my perception, the name losing itself in the din of billions of smaller names. I scream at my lost opportunity as I'm ripped in twain, split into two simple names again, torn into just being James and...

"Cale, what the hell was that?"

I open my eyes suddenly, seeing Cale still seated on me, our bodies soaked in sweat. But I was expecting another sight. I *wanted* to say that, but I didn't say it.

Cale did, and his hair has a white streak now.

Scared rabbit. Scared rabbit. Scared rabbit.

I swallow hard, try to concentrate, open my mouth. "Cale, why did you say what I wanted to say? How did you know that?" I blink, and my tongue moves on its own. "James, be calm. I believe I know..."

Cale continues, my eyes wide. "What is going on? But we mustn't speak." I'm scared, so scared, and he speaks again. "Cale, I'm freaking out here." Cale sets his jaw, and I know what he's going to say before it emerges from him, and it comes from my throat instead.

"James. *Don't* talk."

Everything's a mess in my head. I start crying, terrified that I've well and truly fucked up everything. Cale's thinking the same thing. Oh God, how do I know that? I'm having memories that aren't mine. When he places his hand on the bed, my own fingers experience it. What do I do, what do I do?

He pulls himself off me, another surge of fear taking us, locking us in a hard, tight embrace.

Only one thing is clear: We need to stay together, as close together as possible. He kisses me, rushed, panicked, and I give in, my breathing steadying as the tension seems to ease. Slowly, ever so slowly, I become aware of simple things. This is my hand, this is my foot, my leg. After that, my mind sifts through the endless memories and names and places, outside of my control, finding me, disengaging it from Cale. Memories that were so clear to me are now on the tip of my tongue. Names that held such terrible power now seem unpronounceable.

When we finally pull away from each other our lips are raw, our bodies slick with sweat. Cale's hair is back to its previous auburn, his breathing as ragged as mine. I've never felt so exhausted but I'm afraid to sleep.

I close my eyes. "Cale, what happened?" I'm relieved when the words come out of my own mouth.

We're still holding each other, but not with the same urgency as before. "I believe that was love, James." I open my eyes to look at him dubiously, and he smiles. "Nice to see your eyes are back to normal. For a while there we matched."

"That wasn't love, Cale, that was... I don't know *what* the hell that was but—"

"The love you and I largely know was interpreted by poets and bohemians in the late eighteen hundreds. Romantic love. The love you and I just experienced was love between Keth." He rolls onto his back but continues to hold my hand. I'm still a little nervous about letting go of him. "Granted, my Nan didn't go into the details of how such a love is achieved, nor how truly awe-inspiring it is."

"You knew that would happen?" He'd suspected, but never anything to that degree. Wait, how do I know that? "Cale, what number am I thinking of?"

"You aren't thinking of a number, you're wondering why I don't just tell you what my Nan told me." He looks toward the ceiling. "I find this as worrisome as you do, my love. But at least we aren't finishing each other's sentences."

"Or starting them," we say in unison.

"What we did forged a connection, however brief, between us. At least, that's what I suspect. It seems to be fading, thankfully." Cale takes a deep breath. "My Nan told me that once there were many Ra'keth, countless numbers, in fact, and as we are human with a predisposal to selfishness, a Ra'keth sought to change that. He ended the world and decreed that in the new one, all but a few of the mighty Ra'keth would be split in twain, weakened, half-souls wandering the earth. Thus, the Keth were created. Still sorcerers, but below those who sat on their thrones of power."

"I get the feeling that doesn't end well."

Cale pulls me to him, squeezing me tight, kisses me carefully, our lips needing time to heal. "This will fade to something more manageable, but at the moment, my love, I need you close to me. May I sleep here with you?"

"I was going to ask you to, but what happened next in the story?" I'll admit the idea of Cale going up to his sanctum, being away from me, even so short a distance, rattles me to the core. I know that's strange, but the fear refuses to be rationalized.

"According to the legends, the Keth would occasionally find the one who possessed the other half of their soul. Together, the two Keth could rejoin and know their original power."

"That's kind of romantic." I rest my head on his chest, his heartbeat steady in my ear. "Is that what happened with us? Am I your other half?"

"I doubt it. Please don't take that as an insult, but as I understand it, we've all had complete souls for many worlds now. Two Keth who found each other ended the world and decreed in the new one that Keth could find each other, rejoin. Many worlds followed quickly in its wake, some lasting less than a day. The gods were created to mitigate the growing tangle of Fate, until Keth were cut free of the tapestry altogether." He strokes my hair. "As frightening as this is for me, I've never felt more at peace than I do right now."

"Same here." Outside of the subconscious disengaging from Cale, everything seems a million miles away or not worth worrying about anymore. "So what happened with us?"

"There are vestiges of the past worlds, little things that were never cleared up that managed to slip through the cracks. What began as a means to revolt against the Sorcerer King became something else entirely. I believe..." He gathers his thoughts, which are becoming harder to discern. "I believe you and I ceased to be."

I blink. "*What* happened to us?"

"That is the point, precisely. For a moment, there was no you, nor was there a me, nor even an us. We ascended from our bodies and there was only an *I*. One being of remarkable and terrible power, a Ra'keth of old." His voice starts to crack. "And if you hadn't been... I would've..." I lift my head up to look at him, tears streaming down his face. "To have fallen so far... I thought myself better, but you..." He smiles and kisses me again. "You felt it, yes? The want for power, to know the name of the world and control it and I, I mean we... *It* didn't. That thing we became. It stopped at the brink."

I remember it perfectly.

I also understand why the world has to end.

He holds me tightly, and I can feel him growing ready again. "My apologies, this must be confusing. James, I know what you are. You are my Anu'keth." He smiles widely, and I feel a weight of dread in my chest. "I don't know if you've heard the term, but it means—"

"Usurper to the Throne." I look away, but his hand nudges my chin back toward him.

He laughs. He actually laughs. "Who filled your head with that rubbish, Apprentice?"

Wait, what? "It doesn't mean that?" I was so sure, I was *certain* it meant that.

"That's not its original meaning. Anu'keth means *heir* to the throne. Sometimes the heir would not get his or her throne as quickly as liked, so a usurpation was often the result but..." He smiles warmly, and it's infectious. "For my heir to be the man I love. I would almost believe Fate had welcomed me back to her fold."

Hold on. "*Your* heir?"

He nods as the dread returns. "Of course, my love, I am the Ra'keth. Finally, *finally* I can step down, and the reign of the Recluse will die."

Chapter Seventeen

"Wait." I push Cale backward, starting to feel sick. "Wait, wait, wait. *You're* the Recluse?"

Cale simply nods, and my heart sinks, rage bubbling up to claim it.

"It was hardly accurate at first. I was thought crafty, manipulative, venomous, like a spider, and so the title was whispered. Suddenly I was named and little could be done about it." He studies my face, showing concern. "Is something the matter?"

The spark returns within me, the air around me starting to pop and crackle with static. "Why didn't you tell me?"

"James, there is no need to attack me. I have told you I will step down when you are ready to take the throne. I know being the Ra'keth—"

"I don't care about that!" Silver sparks dance along my body as I get off the bed. There are shivers of power, memories of names from our joining. My God, the things I could do to him right now... "Tell me why. Why did you make that horrible decree? Why did you make me lose my family?" My hand extends toward him, electricity jumping between my spread fingers.

Cale's face sets as he stands. "I made that decree before you were even a thought, likely before your grandparents were even thoughts." He swats my hand aside, his eyes boring into mine. "At least you have the comfort of knowing your family is *still alive.*"

I don't back down. "Was that a threat?"

"Do you know what I would give for what you have? Nan took me before I could even know my parents, my brother, my sisters..."

I shove him back. "So because you never got to know your family the rest of us—"

"They were put to the torch!" Cale turns away from me, seething. "It mattered not that none of them were Keth. All the village cared about were vineyards lost to a drought. They could not find me or Nan, so they..." He takes a deep breath, looks at me over his shoulder. "All of our vaunted progress, our enlightenment that we so eagerly trot out, and we still give in to violence at the barest suggestion. Gladly, even. If the world had not remembered my connection to my family, they would have lived and died at peace. That is why I made my decree, James." He faces me now. "And I will never regret it."

I just look at my feet.

"James, imagine what could be done to your mother, your father, your brothers? Imagine them being punished simply because your enemies are unable to harm you directly. This way is painful, yes, but it is far superior to the alternative." He places his hand on my shoulder, the sparks dying. "Regardless, I have caused you pain, and I offer my apologies."

"I can't just forgive you for this, Cale." I go to the bedroom door, open it. "Please go."

He stares at me. "James, do you still..."

"I need to be alone right now."

Cale stands resolute. "James, please. Please, do not tell me I have come so far only to..." He gathers his clothes, gets dressed while muttering. "I have bound a god with flowers, taken the prized treasure of the Dracon Council with my wits alone, and slain a demon prince in single combat using naught but a *bread knife*, only to be evicted from my own bedroom simply because *you* cannot be pragmatic."

I shrug helplessly. "Can't you just lift the rule?"

He laughs. "Oh yes, as if changing the laws of reality itself were as simple as that. I made a *decree*, Apprentice, not a suggestion. It is immutable. Even if the world were ended, the decree could not be changed. Every new world is built on the shoulders of the old."

I tighten my grip on the doorknob. "Do you even care?"

Cale looks at me plainly. "I'd rather you learned to let go of things you cannot change. Yes, I wish I could have known them, learned if my mother sang me to sleep or what trade my father practiced, but dwelling on such thoughts only brings me pain. And this will only hurt you, James. But yes, I do care." He sighs, starts for the door. "And with that, I shall take my leave. Please remember though, no matter what occurs..." He runs his fingers along my cheek. "You are still my apprentice." Cale exits into the hallway.

I take a breath, the words coming out softly. "And you're still my Cheshire cat." I shut the door and go to bed.

I wish this could be easier. I wish I could just switch everything off and not love him. When I take a step back, all of this was decided long before he and I ever met. Cale made his decree. If I end the world, I'll have to make mine. How many decrees have been made? How many have been reactions to those that preceded them?

I dream of Cale that night. Despite my anger and frustration, my body is all too happy to review our lovemaking. Even with it getting weird at the end, up until that point it was what I'd wanted it to be. If I hadn't melded into an omnipotent magical badass in the seconds before I climaxed, I likely would've wanted to ask Cale afterward if he was liking those Agatha Christie novels I'd picked up for him.

I wake up with arms around me, warm and comforting.

"Cale?" I find him there, his face somber. "Cale, I told you I needed to be alone."

"I know."

"So why are you here?" I bite my lip. "And if you give me a line about sorcerers doing what they want..."

"No." We're face to face, but he doesn't make any moves. "I went to my sanctum and... I'm used to being alone, you understand. But I was lonely." He squeezes me tightly. "I apologize for intruding."

"Part of you doesn't seem all that apologetic."

This only causes him to blush hard, breaking eye contact. "Well, the fault for *that* lies with you. And the hour."

"I don't know where to go from here, Cale." He brushes a lock of hair from my face while I try to continue. "There's so much wrong. You could fix everything if you wanted to, and you don't. Instead you want to give this up."

"James, eventually you will learn that our life is a curse. It is an endlessly complicated game against the whole of existence, and every move we make only moves us further into checkmate. I don't want to make things worse, but I am the Ra'keth, there is no one else. I've wanted to step down since I took the throne, but I don't want to die either."

I shrug. "Surprised you haven't already died of malnutrition, really, if all you've been eating is conjured and transmuted food."

"Hm? Ah yes. That. I'm more surprised you haven't asked how I could be as old as I claim and still appear on the cusp of middle age. To answer, though, I am the Ra'keth. I am the *only* Ra'keth left, in fact. I cannot die."

"Huh?" I maneuver to sit up, my back against the headboard. "Then why were you worried about me killing you?"

He joins me, yawns while stretching. "I cannot die, but I can be killed. Should a usurper catch me unaware, I suppose I would lose the throne. When I step down, I will begin aging again, though I doubt the gods will allow me to stroll in the sun. They have long memories, but I could always contract a dragon for protection, should you allow them to. I'll still be Keth, after all."

I blink. "So, when you step down and give the throne to me…"

"You will live until you're killed, yes. I won't abdicate for some time though. You are still an apprentice. I suspect you'll be prepared in ten years, perhaps fifteen." He looks away a moment. "You do want the throne, yes? I feel foolish for asking a fellow Keth that, but one never knows."

"I don't know, really. Are you going to end the world, Cale?"

He looks into my eyes. "Why would you ask me that?"

"Because you know it needs to be done. You saw it. You saw how messed up that name was. I know you felt it." I take his hand.

"I'd be asking the gods to finish me in a heartbeat. And the ritual... It is not as easy as simply swapping one name for another. The death of a world, it is a dark and violent thing, and it grows more difficult every time, and a sorcerer is at his most vulnerable. During the last ritual, the previous Ra'keth cracked open the world to the void hidden within." Cale sighs. "For all I know he is still there, raging at me for shoving him in, but I took the throne, made my decree. And despite its complications, the name of the world is still the name *I* gave it, and to stand before it, I do not know if I could resist the temptation to use it."

"But you did." I nudge him. "Remember?"

"The Ra'keth that turned away from the name was not me."

"What if I did it with you?"

Cale closes his eyes, smiles weakly. "That's what I told the last Ra'keth."

I blink. "What?"

"I had good reason. He was a vile man, truly cracked in the head. He believed that he was an evolution, that all other humans were insects to stand in awe of him. Killing him was a pleasure, the same went for his damned dragon." Cale shrugs. "At least I hope I killed them. It matters not, they're in a world that's dead and buried."

"Cale, do I want to know if you were a bad person before we met?"

"I acted out. Like all new Ra'keth, I was drunk on power and thought I could do whatever I cared. Old rules and restrictions were for humans, after all, and lesser Keth. I cannot have trysts with a god?" He chuckles, and motions to his numerous tattoos. "One more of these markings and I would've been his property. I thought myself able to love a trickster, and he was everything I wanted at first, but then I learned that *all* tricksters want nothing more than to make us the fool." Cale grins wickedly. "So I told him the true names of the wind and the snow, and then I cursed him, so that they would remain forever on the tip of his tongue until he drew his final breath."

"Wow. That's..."

"Nothing compared to what my predecessors would have done. I pray the Dracon Council has forgotten about my theft of the Claw, it was their most prized possession, after all. They lost their most honored elder to it, and I claimed it as my focus. It had an ancient and terrible name..." He draws the blade from thin air and inspects it a moment before placing it back wherever it came from. "And now it's simply known as Lorus. When I am killed, it will likely fall to dust."

"Why haven't you ever told me any of this?"

"Because my reign was once an interminable sentence. Now that you are here, there will finally be an end to it, and that is a relief. I hope you will not make the same mistakes that I made, but the only way I can help accomplish that is to tell you of mine and pray you don't think less of me." He appears lost in thought a moment.

"Cale?"

"People will die, James, if we end the world. Such is the nature of the process. I would not ask you to do such a thing, but I fear if you didn't take part I would fall to temptation."

I sag against the headboard. Jutte didn't mention anything about having to kill people to do this. "What happens if we don't do it?"

He shrugs. "It is difficult to foresee. The tapestry is fraying, but still holds. Perhaps it will continue on until my reign is over, until even your reign is over. I cannot say. Fate and I have an antagonistic relationship."

"What if it doesn't hold on?"

Cale's eyes take a solemn cast. "The tapestry tears itself apart. The world dies. Nothing takes its place."

"So we either kill some people or kill *all* the people?"

He nods with a finality. "You understand why we are so hated now. It was once the job of a god, but that responsibility was taken away some time ago in a decree. As selfish an action as it was, it made us necessary. It also hardens us to some unpleasant realities. Idealistic fantasies are quickly dashed when you find blood on your hands."

I feel a weight of dread pressing on my shoulders. "There's no other way?"

"In order for the world to end, a large number of people must believe that is what is happening. As the world has grown, it has taken far grander acts of destruction to convince them." He caresses my cheek. "It need not be done now. I suspect the tapestry has a few more years left in it. Until it is necessary, we will simply continue your instruction."

I look downward and hear a creak on the mattress as Cale maneuvers over to straddle my waist. He takes my face in his hands and presses his lips to mine, soft and tender. "I love you, Apprentice."

I smile in return. "Love you too, Cheshire cat." He wraps me in a tight embrace soon after, our bodies yearning, a remnant of our joining. I should be angry still or ask more questions, but being with him, in his arms, nothing else seems to matter. No him, no me, only us.

"I ache to be with you again, James, but until we can be certain it's for the right reasons..."

"And not for power. Yeah, we should hold off." I furrow my brow, concentrating. "Damn it, I know what you're thinking again."

"Truly?" He beams at that. "What am I thinking now?"

"You're wondering if we'll join if we just use our hands." I narrow my eyes at him. "You're also wondering if we had the same dream."

He *hmph*s and breaks eye contact, but doesn't move his hand from just above my waist. "I simply thought that it mattered not which paths we took as they were bound to lead somewhere." Reluctantly, he gets off the bed, still nude, and goes to his dresser to seek clean clothes. "I need to give you an errand of some sort, lest I spend the remainder of my day acting improperly."

I shrug. "It's been a few months since I've seen Dave, and if the Dracon Council really isn't out to get me, maybe I could drop by. Should get me out of here for a few hours. Let us both recover." I chew my lip. "Cale, is that going to happen every time we make love? What if we end up too entangled?"

He looks at me, conflicted. "It was *amazing*, James."

"It was scary, Cale."

Cale sighs and starts toward the door. "I don't want this to turn into an argument. Perhaps you will see it for what it was in time. Until then, we will be careful. I will leave you to your errand." He steps into the hallway.

"What are you going to do, Cale?"

I hear him grumble as he opens a door. "Since you'll be out for the day? Allow my virtue to fail me."

Chapter Eighteen

The loft hasn't changed since I left. My futon is still here, clothes in a pile that's grown musty, compared to the suit and overcoat from Cale's I have on now.

"Look at you."

I find Dave at the mouth of the stairwell, and I smile, walking toward him. "Hey, Dave."

"Five months, Black." He holds up a hand. "Five months."

"Sorry it's been so long. Been hiding out, you understand." I shrug. "Only found out yesterday there's not much to worry about as far as the council's concerned." I look at my feet. "I don't suppose my brother's been in here?"

"A few times, he's asked about you. The girls are convinced you're a criminal now. I hear tell a sorcerer's been hocking his family jewels. Any truth to that?"

"Transmuted copies. Keep that on the DL." I chance another smile. "I met the Broodmother of the Crimson Flight."

Dave freezes at that. I had a suspicion. "You said you had cousins who are reds. Plus she's just as condescending when she's speaking German as you are, so I figured... She's your mom, isn't she?"

"I take after my father." He exhales hard, smoke escaping his snout. "You didn't mention me, did you?"

"Not that I remember. She seemed okay, more personable than Sal. She didn't treat me like someone she could to ride to the top. Even had a sense of humor about it." I take a tentative step toward him. "Are we okay, Dave?"

"This a visit, or you back?"

I glance away.

"Thought so." He makes his way toward the stereo, slower than I remember.

"You all right, Dave?"

"Damned winter. You already forget?"

Right. Cold-blooded. Everything gets slower for him in the winter months. One time the heat went out in the loft, so the diner went twenty-four/seven until it was fixed. The stove was the only thing keeping Dave alive without setting the building on fire.

"There anything I can do? I know a couple of enchantments." Said enchantments mostly involve turning random objects into flashlights until the spell consumes them. The denser the material, the longer it lasts.

The other enchantment is a simple beacon. I learned that early in my time at Cale's while running errands. If I saw wings in the sky, I needed to get home quickly, and I couldn't afford the roundabout way of getting through Cale's wards. Instead, I'd leave a beacon in the shop and make a beeline for it in an emergency.

I don't really see how either of them could help Dave, but I should at least offer.

"Are you okay, Black? You seem, I don't know, different." He narrows his eyes. "You're not messing around with demons, right?"

My eyes go wide. "Why would you think that?" I rush to the bathroom, stare into the mirror. My reflection looks the same as this morning. I need to shave. Hair's the same, no snakes entwined in there, eyes are human, no change in hue.

"Black, a corrupted Keth never looks any different on the outside." A chill runs down my spine, Dave stands in the doorway now. "Not that you seem corrupted. Just...different. The feel about you, well, before you left there always seemed to be static around you. It's still there, but it feels cold too."

"Like, heartless? Emotionally dead?"

"Like *cold*. The opposite of warm." He steps back from me. "You're going to be tough to be around, at least until spring. What kind of magic has that guy been teaching you?"

"Just simple stuff, nothing involving..." I trail off, because Cale's never taught me anything about it, but I swear I remember lessons, learning names, variations on pronunciation in an older woman's voice, all of it in a French accent, strangely enough. I turn on the sink and place my hand under the warming water.

"Involving...what, Black?"

I extend my other hand toward the tub, imagine the air above it, the heat from the water, the energy flowing over my fingers. The syllables come easily, joining in tandem in a steady cadence, but only one word emerges from my lips.

"*Ice.*"

A perfect foot-by-foot-by-foot cube of clear ice appears above the tub, and it falls in, crashing, shattering into large sharp shards. I stagger back into Dave, my hand covered in snow.

"Holy shit, Black."

"I never learned that." I trip over Dave's tail but still scramble away from the bathroom. "I swear to God I never learned that. How did I do that?"

Dave stares at me in shock. "I think the better question is *why* did you do that?"

"I...I don't know. I just knew the name, like it'd been drilled into my head a thousand times."

The dragon snorts a plume of smoke, rubbing his head. Right, he's sensitive to magic. "So you cast because you knew you could? That's never good, Black. That's what—"

"I'm sorry, okay? I didn't even know it would work. The word was there and it came out perfectly, in..." I'm confused. It was the language of names, of magic itself, but is it called Lorus? Sigil? The latter seems more me. Hell, that's what I named my focus, but the former is more familiar. "Sigil, I think it's called. Or Lorus." I look at Dave. "Do you know which?"

"Yeah, it's..." He seems confused as well. "I...I don't know, they both sound right. That's strange." Dave gapes at me. "You found the Recluse. Wait, but you already saw Heath, and this only just started."

"Heath's not the Recluse, turns out. Cale is."

He takes a moment to process. "Well, that makes more sense."

I chew my lip. "What makes you say that?"

"Because magic doesn't have a clear name right now, Black, probably because you two are all chummy. You named magic Sigil, same with your little scissor there. The Recluse named it Lorus, and it's supposed to be called that until he's usurped."

"Or steps down." I shrug off his dubiousness. "It's a throne, he can do that if he wants to, right?"

"Never heard of that happening, and my kind are experts on those that sit on the throne. Ra'keth don't give up their power. You know how bad this is?"

"What's the big deal? So people are a little confused on the name for a while."

Dave looks up toward the sky, muttering a long string of draconic expletives. "Magic is about *certainty*, Black. A Keth doesn't do his stuff because he *guesses* he's right. He knows and wills it to happen. Now you have a language of names that functions on that certainty, and the *name* of that language isn't clear-cut."

"Could that end the world?"

"For Keth, for dragons, for the Fae, all of the blue and silver blooded. Magic's weak enough in this world, Black, and this is giving it a sucker punch. The council's probably already aware, and that's not good for you. You have to fix this."

"How?"

Dave looks at me solemnly. "The name has to be certain again. Simple as that. And there's only one way to do that. Either Lorus or Sigil has to go."

I step back, dread creeping over me. "You don't mean..."

"One of you has to die, Black."

I shake my head quickly. "No, that's just stupid! Every language in the world has at least a dozen names but because magic doesn't have one that's ironclad..."

Dave shrugs, not making eye contact. "Don't look at me. I think it's bullshit too, but it was a decree. Blame the Ra'keth for it."

I slump against the wall, rub my face. "What am I going to do? I'm starting to see why Cale never leaves his building. Every time I go out everything gets messed up even more. I guess I can't ever have a normal day in reality, huh?"

Dave puts his hand on my shoulder. "You're a sorcerer, Black, so probably not." He helps me up soon after. "But you need to deal with this. You don't have time to mope."

I glare at him crossly. "Mope?"

"Sorcerers by and large are either cracked in the head or broody as hell." He adds on a toothy smirk. "Or both. Wonder why that is..."

I try to smile. "Easy. No one bothers a crazy person and brooding gets you laid. I should get back to Cale's though, let him know what's going on."

"You're going to..." He takes a few seconds, awkward silence filling the air before he drags his claw gently across his throat.

"No. But he should know about this. Maybe he knows how to fix this without anyone getting killed."

"So you're leaving? Now?"

"You're the one telling me that this is urgent. I wouldn't mind sticking around for a burger and fries, though. I am so sick of conjured food. How anyone can eat the same memory over and over and over again..." Exhaling, I start toward the stairs and then stop, looking back at Dave. "Everything okay here? You get in any trouble with the council?"

"Not so far, but then again it takes them years to reach a decision on anything not involving sorcerers. So it's not a problem until it's a problem." He motions to the futon. "Might as well take a seat. I'll bring up some food. Could be a little while, though. You got time?"

"You tell me."

He shrugs. "Well, I'm pretty sure the name of magic is Lorus, so we've got a few days, at least. Going to be a shitty new year if you don't handle this, though. You still take your burgers the same way?"

"Rarely legal? Yep." I sit down on the futon and toss my jacket off to the side. "Thanks, Dave."

"Not a problem. Been lonely here. I almost started reading those game books of yours."

"There is a module that lets you play as a dragon."

He quirks a brow before starting down the stairs. "Why would I want to play what I am?" He winks. "That'd just be pathetic."

I avert my eyes from my character sheet, still sitting on top of the pile. I couldn't stand up against Radcliffe, my elven sorcerer.

Radcliffe, comparatively speaking, wears robes woven with moonsilk and golden thread, wields a staff wrought from silverwood with enchanted steel inlay, and has several magical rings and necklaces that can produce devastating effects with naught but a simple spoken command. Should he need anything better, he'll likely only have to walk about fifty feet to stumble over the latest omnipotent magical doodad.

I, on the other hand, wear an off-the-rack suit that doesn't compliment my skin tone, wield a broken scissor, and my magical powers are limited to lightning bolts that nearly kill me and failed attempts at conjuring shoes that, according to Dave, look and taste like pomegranate Jell-O.

I tear the character sheet in two.

Then I immediately begin searching for Scotch tape.

I rub my hands together while rummaging. No wonder Dave's moving slowly, it's cold up here. No luck. I'll have to redo the whole sheet. Damn it.

About ten minutes pass before I hear someone ascending the stairs. I set down my rulebook, dog-earing the page, and lean against the wall, stretching my legs and back. "That was fast. Guess it's running slow down there?"

And arm slips around my waist, lips pressing against my neck.

"Shit, Sal, I told you I wasn't interested—" My head then gets knocked against the wall, everything blurry and bleary and nothing focused other than pain.

"So there *is* another guy."

No. No, no, no.

"How did you get in here, Heath?" I try to shove him back, but I feel a sharp jab against my side. When I look back, I see his hand holding my shear in a stabbing position. I shouldn't have left it in my coat.

"Through the door. And up the stairs. I told you I can find you." He chuckles as I tremble. "All out of bravery, huh?"

"Heath, for God's sake, just leave, please." The blade cuts through my shirt and glides against my skin, just above my kidney. Fear claims my words.

"Shhhh." He kisses my neck again, his tongue warm against the nape. "This doesn't have to be hard, Miles." Heath snickers, pressing himself firmly against me, so I can feel that something else is firm. His free hand slides over my waist, fingers running along the fly of my slacks. "And when I finish, I promise I'll go away."

I try to fight back the tears. "You're going to kill me, aren't you?" My eyes go to the stairway. "There's a fucking *dragon* downstairs, all I have to do is—"

The point of the shear slips up my side, a light twinge of pain followed by warmth. "I could carve you in ten pieces before he makes it to the second step."

"Heath, stop this."

His teeth graze along my ear. "No. It looks like you've still got some power in you, so I can take it the fun way..." His free hand rubs my groin. "Or the quick way." The blade presses softly against my skin.

Keep calm. Keep him talking. "What are you on about? How the hell are you even a sorcerer?"

"My dad was one." His hand slips behind my waistband.

"You said your dad was a minister."

He chuckles darkly. "Yeah. He *was*. 'Do not suffer a witch to live' and all that shit. As far as he was concerned he was just getting his prayers through to God. Fucking idiot, begging favors off some lazy son of a bitch who couldn't get off his ass to stop *one fucking thing*." The blade presses harder against my skin, and I suck in my chest, trying not to whimper and really set him off. *Please, Dave, move faster.*

"What does that have to do with me?"

"Easy. You ever heard of the Usurper's Decree?" He laughs. "Of course you haven't, you're an idiot. If I take the life of a sorcerer, any sorcerer, I can take his power." His fingers graze against my balls. "And it turns out, 'taking the life' can apply to other things too. Doesn't even matter who's on top."

That might explain why I suddenly know how to sling ice spells.

"That's why you were with me?" I can't believe I'm offended by that.

"I could tell you had potential, and you had a tight ass, so why not take what I needed? Wasn't like you were using it. You could've given me more though, then maybe we wouldn't have been living in a slum."

Keep him talking, just keep him talking. "Why not transmute some shit and pawn it off?"

"Do what? You talking about that stupid game of yours? One of your dumb books about wizards and shit? You think I'm going to beg favors off some god like my old man? Fuck that." My God, he's untrained.

"How do you know about the Usurper's Decree, then?"

"Didn't know it was called that until a couple years ago." He kisses along my neck, and I steel myself. Dave should be on his way soon. "Just know that's how Dad got his power."

Wait, according to Heath, the decree can be interpreted that you can get your power through sex... And if his father...

"Oh Christ, no wonder you're so fucked up." The blade presses into my skin, cutting anew. My face scrunches in pain, but I won't cry. I refuse to. Damn it, I am *not* letting him take my power. I can't. I find the spark within me, feel it crackle and fork. "You might want to let go of me, Heathcliff Case."

He snickers in my ear. "What are you going to do to make me?"

I turn my head slowly to meet his gaze, then glance upward at the skylight, at the clouds overhead that are burgeoning with snow. "I'll call the lightning."

Heath grins widely. "Bullshit, you'd be struck too."

I match his smile and raise my hand toward the sky and call the name. "I know."

The result is nearly instant, my soul finding the energy pulsing through the skies, snatching it, yanking it forcefully from the clouds, down through the skylight which shimmers with a myriad of colors, down into my body, my muscles locking in place from the shock, the electricity arcing quickly to Heath from his contact, the shear doubling as a conductor. My wounds singe shut as we're thrown apart, opposing brick walls catching us, but I find my feet. If Heath has taught me anything, it's how to take a beating. I pick up the smoking shear and stride slowly toward him, the energy of the lightning still racing through my body.

I look into Heath's eyes as he watches me approach, and I see fear.

And it feels *good.*

I point the shear at him. "Tell me, how did you get out of the bus that night?"

The fear vanishes as he glares at me. "I traded. A life for a life. Figured it didn't matter. The bitch was going to drown in a few minutes anyway, but those few minutes were all I needed to get to the surface."

"Remember on the bridge? How you told me those drowned people wanted one of us? Ever wonder where you sent that woman?"

He laughs. The bastard laughs. "What, you going to kill me, Miles?"

I step closer to him. "No. That'd be too far." Grabbing his shoulder, I pull him to his feet. He's mostly dead weight, still weak from the lightning strike. "I'm going to show you something, Heath."

I take a deep breath and fade into Tartarus, pulling him through the rift along with me. The light off me is dim now, my soul drained from casting, the lightning expended from bringing Heath over. Heath is frantic, panicking before he looks at me. He swings at me, but I avoid it, his motions slow, sluggish, sending reverberations through the dark water. When he draws breath, he doesn't pass back into the real world.

"What is this place?"

I conserve my breath as I exhale the words. "This is the frozen river, Heath. Those people on the bus? This is where you sent them. And now?" I let go of his shoulder and shove him away. "I'm going to leave you here."

Before he can scream for me, I take a deep breath, the waters rushing into my lungs, only to vanish as I return to the world.

I promptly head into the bathroom and dry heave for several seconds before noticing blood dripping into the bowl from my nose. I grab a hand towel to dab my face clean and look in the mirror. My face is gaunt, eyes bloodshot, my skin has a ghostly pallor that's only fading slowly. I look like absolute shit, but that's nothing compared to how I feel.

And how do I feel?

I flash a bloody smile at my reflection.

"Copacetic."

Chapter Nineteen

"Good, you're still here." The dragon takes the last few steps, holding a large plate with a burger and fries on it. "Were you casting up here? I've got a bitch of a headache."

"Yeah, uh..." I sit down on the futon. I really don't want to explain what just happened. "Just got bored."

Dave stares at me in concern. "Bored? That's how it starts, Black."

I chuckle, folding my arms, smirking. "How *what* starts?"

"How Keth get a bad reputation."

"Don't worry, I'm not going to turn into some power-mad evil overlord. Though if I go that route I've got an excellent list of what not to do." I let the moment hang a little bit before saying, "Kidding, Dave. Kidding."

Dave sets down the plate on a milk crate near the futon. I poke gently at the hamburger bun a couple times, the room feeling colder now. I should be careful, I might've just drained my soul down to a mote. Still felt good though.

"You okay, Black?" The dragon points to the food. "Usually you're all over French fries."

I keep my eyes on the plate. "What would you think of me if I'd killed Heath?"

"You didn't though."

"But what if I did? What if I'd killed Heath? Wouldn't it be justified, after what he did to me? Wouldn't it be okay to have him be the one suffering for a change?"

"Why are you even thinking about this?"

"Just...wondering. What if I'd become a sorcerer sooner, decided to kill him rather than run. I could've ended it and instead I was a coward."

"Hey." A claw lifts my chin up to meet the dragon's gaze. "You told me all about that night. You weren't a coward, you took control of your own life. You could've killed him, but you were *better* than that. You still are. That's why you'll never be him."

Deep within, the dim light of my soul flickers with guilt, regret, but it's not strong enough to shake me. "It wasn't virtue, Dave, it was fear. I can dress it up however I want to make it inspiring but..."

"None of that. Now get yourself out of this funk and eat your fries. And be careful if you're heading out, think there's a bitch of a storm on the way, given I heard thunder real damned close. Unless that was you?"

Forgive me, Dave.

"No, I'm not capable of that."

"Good." Dave starts for the stairs. "Want me to say hello, or you coming down later?"

I shake my head. "Give them my regards, I need to get back to Cale's. I'm kind of out of it and it's a good place to lie low."

He looks back at me, waiting for me to say something, but no words come. With a smoky sigh, he starts down the stairs.

I make slow work of the meal, everything having a bitter aftertaste.

This is how it starts.

Fuck.

I don't want to be here anymore.

I make my way downstairs, not stopping to say hello or goodbye, going out the side door and to the street, making my way east toward the Benedict. A few people glance at me, my Mark drawing all of their attention as I part the ragged passing crowd like the Red Sea. Heath had a fix for that. I remember the incantation. It'll be nice for it to be used for this instead of forcing Genovese Syndrome on everyone, covering up his...

My anger flares a moment, providing the power to work my will.

"*I am a child of man.*" The words flow out, the energy of my exhaled breath forming a small cloak. Attention is drawn elsewhere, to more interesting things. As far as the world is concerned right now, I might as well be invisible. I slump against a building at the intersection of 69th and K. I need to calm down, I feel capable of too many things I'll regret.

"You look out of sorts." I know that voice...

An older woman in an expensive black pantsuit is standing in front of a town car, parked in the red zone, the passenger door open, a black leather interior inside. I pat my jacket, confirming the presence of the shear.

She makes her way toward me, wearing a shark's smile. The Fate with the abhorred shears. Now I know who she is.

"Atropos, right?" I shimmy away from her, my breathing quickening.

She easily covers the distance between us in a flash of movement. "I've half a mind to demand retribution for your stunt."

"How did you find me?"

She motions to the sky where clouds have started to gather. "Lightning on a relatively calm day? A storm that wasn't fated? I *know* when someone meddles with my daughter's tapestry, Keth. After that, it's not difficult to follow a man with a Mark."

The cloud cover increases, and I can feel it flowing through the air far above. I did that. I forced a storm into creation.

The cold seizes my muscles, my lungs unable to draw in air as she draws close to me, her face inches from mine, hand on my shoulder. "I want the blood of the Recluse, Keth." She takes her hand away, and I clutch my chest, sucking in the winter air. "I want his thread."

"Why the fuck do you care anyway? Can't you find someone else? Hell, I practically left someone in Tartarus for you not fifteen minutes ago." I snort softly. "I'm not going to kill the Recluse for you. It shouldn't matter anyway. He's going to step down, he won't be the Ra'keth anymore. That's what you want, right?"

"I care little for his throne." She drags a bony finger along my cheek. "He has slipped the cut for too long. That you will take his throne is simply a perk. It will be good to have a sorcerer who knows his place."

"Excuse me? I don't have a destiny anymore, lady. What are you going to do to me?"

She laughs, her smile turning cruel. "Did I ever suggest retribution would be taken upon *you*? You are correct, your thread is beyond my reach, Keth, but what of the threads you were once tied to?" Her hand pulls away from my face. "My daughter is quite familiar with the thread of your father, your mother... Your brother."

I narrow my eyes. "You stay the fuck away from my family or..." Memories are already answering my call, around me I can feel vibrations of power: electricity, gas mains, trickles of mystical energy and the gathering of the elements far above...

"Or what? You are but a Keth. A human with a whisper of power. We are a *god*."

"We?" My hand slips inside my coat to grip the shear.

She steps back, but not much, and she motions to the town car, where two women exit—one middle-aged, frumpy, brown-haired, dressed like a cab driver, the other young, early twenties, long black hair, pale skin, dressed couture.

The young woman proceeds over, smiling, but it doesn't put me at ease. "So troubled, this one. I remember spinning him."

The middle-aged woman comes to the young woman's side, standing between her and Atropos. "Indeed. A stubborn thread. Never went where I wanted it. Why some cannot accept that they are meant to be cautionary tales..."

I draw the shear in their direction. They only laugh.

Atropos steps toward me. "You truly believed you could claim *my* shear as your focus? That that would save you from the cut? We are *Fate*, Keth." She produces a set of heavy foot-long bronze shears from thin air. "We are not so easily outrun."

Oh shit. No wonder Heath was so pissed I ran off with it.

Fear is at the wheel as I continue my retreat. "Stay away."

The middle-aged one, Lachesis, I think, chuckles. "You will return to my loom. It will be all right, child. Submit to our service, help our tapestry be beautiful once again. There is so much I can give you, you need only accept it."

The young woman, Clotho, smiles as well, drawing a long thread from the air. "Indeed. We've missed you. You will see, our servants are grateful for our oversight, as you will be. We have even led our prized servant to you. We can lead you to anything you will need."

Lachesis continues her advance. "I can reweave you to your family, Miles. Isn't that what you want? I can give you purpose, direction, I can lead you to a fulfilling life, to a man who will love you with no conditions, whom you will love effortlessly in return."

Atropos matches the grin of her descendants. "The Ra'keth will finally rejoin our tapestry, be woven as they should, *cut* as they should."

I point the shear at them now, but that doesn't halt their advance.

Clotho. "You are no threat to us."

Lachesis. "You lack certainty."

Atropos. "You are weak, Sorcerer. But you think to stand against Fate? Against the goddess herself? Then tell me." Her grin widens into a rictus. "Will the world remember your name?"

Through the fear, I feel a spark that dances with a swirl of ice. I remember the joining with Cale, where I gazed upon three lights buzzing about a complex weavework, about the world itself. Where I learned three names.

"Maybe it won't." The air about me darkens as I reach out my will to the electricity running through the wires above the street, to the lines of power deep in the earth. Fear and anger bolster my certainty as I make a smile that once terrified me. A smile that would precede... "But I remember yours."

The syllables come in quick succession, but I repeat them, faster and faster, my eyes closing as the three names become a blur in my mind. I hear panicked screams that grow in volume and terror, but I don't stop. God, I should stop, I need to stop, but the words won't stop cycling.

Damn it! Stop! Stop, James! Stop it now! This is too much!

But I can't. I want to say this will keep them from hurting Mom, Dad, Thom, my brothers, that it will get them to leave me alone, but I can't. All I know is that it's horrible and terrible and it feels *good.*

God, please stop me.

The shear grows hot in my hand, focusing whatever it is that I'm doing. Through the growing din in my mind, an idea worms through.

If you're the goddess, you shouldn't be three people.

The shrieks begin to meld into a singular sound, and when I open my eyes, only one woman remains, her face a war of ages. Her eyes open wide and squint, producing crow's feet while her face smooths, then covers in rouge. Her hands are young and liver-spotted, holding thread and shears, desperately searching for a loom. Through it all she screams, her voice varying in pitch and intensity, but the fear is gone. Only rage remains.

Fate rushes at me as I'm cut by the winter wind, but I am a sorcerer.

I will not be helpless anymore.

I raise the shear high and call forth memories of my youth, storms that sent me running to my parents in fear, lightning that split the heavens and thunder that rattled the world, cold that sliced through the thickest clothes, and snow thick enough to hide your hand from your gaze. The power flows through the air around me, down from the sky, striking me again and again but I refuse to fall. I channel it all into the memories, the power too great for just one. I give it to all of them, the gentle greeting-card-worthy snowfall intensifying, the wind sharpening with a chill that I funnel in front of me, the goddess leaning hard and forward, still advancing.

I demand the storm to grow, take more of my memory. Far above clouds sprout dark veins, thunder rumbles through the sky, cars slide slowly on the now-frozen streets, sickly creaks and groans fill the gaps left in the sound of the raging gale. Still she comes, her body changing by the moment, slipping between the three faces. The power I've taken is nearly exhausted. I can't keep the storm under control anymore.

I stagger backward, the wind shoves me toward her. I burn through memories, my will devouring images of storms, blizzards, my desperation pushing through the sudden pain to fuel the spell. There will be a price for this, I know it, but I can't back down. Not now.

I call the name of lightning, the flash instantaneous, the thunder nigh deafening, windows shattering around the intersection, shards raining to the pavement as I'm struck down. I can't hold on to this. My God, it's too much. Oh God, there's so much pain, please make it stop make it stop make it—

Cackling, Fate renews her efforts, closing the distance to stand over me. She raises the bronze shears high, preparing to take her vengeance. "Last words, Sorcerer?"

I weakly nod, expending the last of my strength to press my hands to her chest, and I grin.

"Clear."

I release the lightning.

The goddess is knocked back, the air filled with a loud and sudden slapping sound, my muscles locking down, feeling like I've run for hours. I can't feel the storm anymore, but it rages on around me regardless. Blinking slowly, I can't get up. A silhouette in the whiteout vanishes to my right, and I become aware of how cold it is.

I taste blood, and the wind cuts into my skin...

What? I reach my numbing hand to my chest and find the truth: my clothes are gone, transmuted for the final burst of lightning.

I get to my feet, finding the shear in the snow after some digging. The visibility clears, the weather looking less like the ninth circle of hell and more like a nasty blizzard now. Tracks lead away from me, down 69th Street, though the wind is obscuring them quickly. When I make out the street signs, I sigh with relief, as I'm two blocks from the diner, where it'll be warm. The key will be getting there without freezing to death.

I try to conjure memories of warmer clothes, but my head is fuzzy. I can't really remember a damned thing from winter. I'm too exhausted to draw on my soul without probably killing myself in the process. I need to get somewhere else.

My crossing of 69th to continue on K Street is interrupted by a car horn, and I turn to face a distressed sedan sliding to a halt. Panicking, I stumble back, landing in the snowy street, the bumper stopping just short of me.

"Thanks a bunch, Fate. Make me hit a guy. You never minded me borrowing a car before!" I think he's looking at me now. "Holy shit, are you okay?" He's wearing a winter jacket and a thick wool hat. I envy him right now. "Jesus, what happened to you?" The voice is familiar...

It's so damned cold, maybe I could just rest here for a little before getting up and...

I'm yanked to my feet, pushed into the backseat of the car, where the heat is going full blast, or I think it is. I can hear the fans going, at least. He gets in with me, opens his coat and pulls me to him, his body warm.

"You're lucky, usually I have to let a guy buy me a couple drinks before I'll let him do this. Roads were fucking fine a few minutes ago." His voice is fast, nervous. "Stay with me, okay? You still with me? Hey!"

"Huh?" So cold, so fucking cold...

"Stay with me. You gotta stay awake. Uh...I think I gotta keep you talking, ask you questions, that's what they do on TV. Did you hear the one about the blonde Coyote?" He hugs me tighter to him, his head on my shoulder, rubbing my back quickly with his hands. I can't really feel it. "Think we can call that debt even, huh?"

"Spencer?" I hug myself closer to him, weakly. If I'm going to die, at least it's with someone who knows me.

"Yeah, I noticed you haven't been around the diner so I figured I'd try talking to your boss and... That doesn't matter. What the fuck were you doing naked in the snow, James?" He chuckles, fear edging it. "Don't suppose you're being chased by a crazy chick with bondage gear and a .45?"

"Huh?" I concentrate on my breathing.

"Just a story I read once. C'mon, man, you gotta give me more than one-word answers."

"I'm so cold..." My voice is barely above a whisper. I'm tired too. I just want to sleep.

He takes his coat off, putting my arms through the sleeves before climbing into the driver's seat. "I'm going to get you someplace warm, okay? Don't fall asleep, James. Stay with me." He puts the car in drive, and the car lurches forward, his hands working the wheel frantically as the wheels spin, trying to find traction. "Damn it, move!"

The car weaves slowly forward, the engine roaring as we move into the intersection. "K Street. Diner on 69th." I just want to get home and go to bed. I want Cale to hold me and tell me I'll be okay. I want Cale here.

I try to say his name, the syllables carried on a whisper drowned out by the heater.

"I don't know if she's gonna make it two blocks, these roads are *shit*." He punches the steering wheel, the horn blaring his aggravation. "Damn it. Jesus, I can barely see the buildings."

The spark feels so dim, a crackle in the dark. I can do this though. He's using the gas too much, the tires can't grip, but I can't summon the strength to form the words. The storm above ripples with power, but it's so far beyond my reach, its name incomprehensible. I don't know what to do.

I lean forward, I want to thank him for trying. I catch my reflection in the rearview and jump back. Spencer doesn't notice, still trying to get the car moving, but that isn't my reflection.

It's Cale's.

Tensely, I touch my nose, testing to see if the face in the mirror does the same. But it doesn't. Instead, the reflection looks worried and mouths words I can't make out. I shake my head slowly, trying to let him know that I don't understand. I'm so tired. Please, I just want to sleep.

I see fingers press against the other side of the rearview's reflection, Cale's brow furrowing, jaw set. His lips are moving again, and I can almost hear him.

Abjure.

I'm so tired, Cale.

Ice. Abjure.

Ice isn't snow though. No, wait, isn't it? Snowflakes are just tiny bits of ice, right?

"Damn it, move!" Spencer glances over the seat at me, worried. "Shit, okay, I'm going to try to push us out of this rut. Okay? Stay right here. Stay awake." He keeps the car in drive, the idling engine not making any headway as he gets out, frantically shoving against the trunk of the car.

"I don't know what to do, Cale."

I can see his mouth moving again, his face just as concerned as my would-be rescuer.

Abjure the ice? I don't know the name of this kind of ice.

His fingers press the mirror again, growing terror in his gaze.

Cleanse.

Why would he want me to...

I stare through the windshield, the wipers clacking loudly as they keep the view clear, only about ten feet visible in front of the car. Shakily, I aim my hand forward, focusing on the snow-covered street, remembering the string of syllables I used when trying to practice my cantrips.

I draw on the heat flowing freely from the vents, take in its energy, my body warming for a moment before I push it through the glass.

"*Cleanse.*"

The street before me suddenly bursts in an explosion of silver flame, only lasting a second, the snow refusing to defy physics any longer than my will demands, and my will is drained. The car starts rolling on the now-bare asphalt, and Spencer quickly gets back in, using the traction to gun the engine and gain momentum.

I collapse in the backseat, the air frigid now, the car's tiny heater having to start its work all over again.

"My lucky day..." He grins back at me. I think we're still moving forward. I don't have the strength to shiver anymore. I don't have the will to see the point in it. I close my eyes.

When I open them again I'm in water, and I thrash in panic. I died. I'm in hell, at the bottom of the North River where I belong. Hands keep me steady, the water vaguely warm.

"Easy! Easy! You're okay."

I'm in a hot tub, a pretty small one, a giant skylight above me assuring me that I'm not underwater. To my left is a silver-scaled dragon, to my right is a man with warm, golden-brown eyes and a scraggly goatee and a knit cap obscuring his hair.

"You okay, Black?"

"Am I dead?" God I sound awful.

"Nearly were." Spencer hands me a washcloth and I grab it to retake my modesty. "I'm curious how you knew there was a Jacuzzi here."

Dave looks over at him. "He lived here for a little while. Thanks for getting him here, if there's anything I can do..."

He grins, easy and comforting, in reply. "Well, you could give me, say, ten free meals here and we'll call it even."

Dave nods readily. "Fine."

"Great, nine free lunches for me."

Dave arches an eyeridge. "You said ten."

"Yeah, I had to dine and dash once." The Coyote appraises me. "You should probably stay in there a while longer, just stay warm. Don't know what the hell is up with that storm. It's like the end of the world out there. I should probably get home. At this rate they'll probably halt the UTA in an hour or so."

Dave moves around the tub toward him. "Should probably move your car, then, if you're leaving it here. Plow might take it out."

Spencer chuckles. "Don't worry about that."

I push myself back, sitting closer to upright as I become aware of the warmth of the water. I glimpse his eyes again. "Thank you."

"You stay warm, okay? I guess I'll be back later for my free lunch." He starts toward the stairwell, and I lean over the lip of the tub, a bit of water splashing to the hardwood.

"Hey, you never told me your last name."

He looks over his shoulder and smiles that easy smile. "Spencer Crain, but just call me Spence." He vanishes down the stairs, and Dave snorts loudly.

"Fucking Coyotes."

I nudge the hot water back on, the feeling starting to return in my extremities, which I take as a good sign. The events of the last hour play through my head in a blur, the images hazy. I try to go further back, because I remember thinking I walked in on Dad with my nanny, but I could swear that never happened. I can't remember it now, either, nor my parents fighting, or much about my brothers, really, save Thom.

I know Mom and Dad broke up because Dad was supposedly cheating, but I don't remember anything like that happening. Why can't I remember anything about my older brothers...

Like...all of their names. Oh fuck...

My memories. I thought I was calling on them to fuel the storm, but... I was burning them, sacrificing them for power. Oh God, what kind of person would do...

"Dave? I think I might be crazy."

The dragon looks up through the skylight at the thickening snow, and a rumble of thunder echoes far above, the blizzard sky suddenly alit, impossibly, by a flash of lightning.

Dave stares at me, realizing what I've done.

"Black? I think you're right."

Chapter Twenty

"*My mind is focused, my heart is steady.*"

Already the exhaustion fades away, the weight off my eyes, my brain evening out. I don't think I can cast much more than this. Even transmutation needs a bit of will to kick-start the process. I need to get back to Cale, but with the storm above looking worse with each passing hour, I don't think I could make it out to the 65th and L station, much less to the Benedict.

Dave already retreated to the kitchen, the stove running in anticipation that the heat will eventually give out. I join him shortly after getting dressed, start washing dishes because I want to do *something*. Dave cleans the rest of the kitchen. We both work in silence, listen to the radio, the broadcast frequently interrupted by updates on the storm.

I need to stop this before it gets worse.

I duck into the alley for a minute to check on the storm. I can sense the name of it, the syllables dancing through the clouds on arcs of lightning, but never coming together. The wind cuts through the narrow space, robbing my body of the heat I'd reclaimed, and I hurry back inside. Being outside so soon after nearly freezing to death probably isn't the best idea.

"You feeling any better?" Dave is right next to the stove, and he lights a fresh cigarette on the flame.

I shake my head in reply and lean against the counter. "You think any dragons would give me a ride out to the Benedict?"

He snorts in retort. "Doubt it. Suicide to go out there now. Reds would freeze fast as humans. Only the golds have fire in the blood, and there hasn't been one here in decades."

"Where'd that one go?"

"In order to 'get on it', I need to get to Cale's, and as you succinctly pointed out, the world is ending. How am I supposed to get there?"

He blinks. "You're a sorcerer, the impossible is your job. You're a smart kid, are you telling me you managed to combine a blizzard and a thunderstorm, not to mention getting here naked, and you can't think up a way to get across town?"

"The last bit wasn't all me. Spencer found me through blind, stupid luck, and even then Cale helped me out, he contacted me through..." Could it be that simple? "I've got an idea."

I dash to the hallway and up the stairs to the bathroom, to the mirror. Staring hard into it, I concentrate on Cale...

And nothing happens.

"Fuck." Well, Cale has had a few decades to work on his crying. I've never even tried it myself. "Please, I need you right now." I rest my forehead against the mirror. I call his name, the name I gave him at least. "Please, Cheshire cat."

I can almost feel his touch as I close my eyes, his arms pulling me to him, holding me in a tight protective embrace, maybe some Nina Simone playing on the Victrola while he whispers in my ear that I'm safe now, that everything will be all right even as his breath is ragged.

I'd swear I can almost hear the music too, the second verse of "Ne Me Quitte Pas" weaving through the air and...

I open my eyes to see golden eyes looking back into mine. His face is pale, a drip of blood having slid from his nose. He's shaking but still smiling.

I'm standing on the dais in the shop, and when I look over my shoulder, I can see bathroom at the loft replacing our reflection, the surface still rippling gently. Cale sinks to the floor, and I follow him down, holding him up now.

"Didn't think I could still do that," he says, sounding drunk, drained.

"Died with the last Ra'keth." He glances at da
moving slowly outside the front windows. "Zombos
Probably going to be a bunch more. End times tenc
them awake."

God damn it. "Dave, what's going to happen?"

He shrugs. "We stay here, stay warm, and
damnedest to ride this out until the Recluse ends this
a new world. Weird though, everything feels kind of off.

"I think that'd be expected during the end of t]
Dave."

He shakes his head quickly. "No, no. Usually the:
sort of order to it. End of the world gets kicked off,
takes the reins. This doesn't feel anything like that
magic everywhere right now, can't you feel it?"

I honestly don't, but considering how much I fuck(
over to bring about that storm, and that I'm still able
Maybe my recovery isn't entirely my own grit and gui
I'm sucking up the free magical energy outside
osmosis.

"That's not supposed to happen, Black.
just...chaos."

Dread creeps up my spine. I remember somethi
Fate, chanting names faster and faster until they beca
Oh God, what did I do?

"I need to get home." I head into the diner proper a
toward the front door. My fingers brush my St. Jude m
out of old habit. If there was ever a time to pray for hel
impossible cause, this would be it.

Dave glances upward, muttering an expletive.
outside, these are the *end times*. I don't mean to sound
but you picked one shitty way of kicking this off, so wo
mind getting the Recluse on it before the heat gives ou
lot of people like me freeze?" A second passes, and he :
"No disrespect meant, of course."

The reflection fades in the mirror, the two of us taking its place. I kiss him, wipe the blood from his face with my sleeve. "God, Cale, what did you do?"

He needs several breaths before he responds. "I found you, and I pulled you through. There are very few who still believe mirrors can be portals, you know. Reality was not happy with me for my audacity." He swallows hard and smiles, puffing up his chest in mock pride. "But I am the Ra'keth and reality submits to *my* will, not vice versa." He touches his face, where his nose is still bleeding, and inspects his reddened fingers. "Granted, it does not submit so easily."

"Cale, I think I screwed things up out there." I maneuver behind him, resting his head in my lap, and I stroke his hair gently. "Like, I might've started the end of the world."

"Truly?" He looks through the window, where the snow is progressing back toward a whiteout, and the dark gray suddenly alights in a brilliant flash. "I hadn't noticed." Chuckling, he looks up at me. "You really want the throne sooner rather than later, don't you?"

"Cale, this isn't funny, people are going to die. We have to stop this."

"I am aware. I just am trying to not be reminded of the last time this happened. The end began, I wanted to stop it to save lives, and it ended with a blade in my predecessor's heart. I always suspected I'd meet my end the same way, honestly." He stretches, luxuriating a moment. "As much as I believe you incapable of such a thing, especially considering our bond now..."

I nod. "Cale, I wouldn't kill you. I don't even want the stupid throne."

He smiles and leans his head up. Taking the hint, I kiss him, and it lasts for a few seconds before he returns his head to my lap. Grunting, he rolls off me and gets into a kneeling position. "Help me up, would you?"

I stand and give him my hand, and he takes it, getting up to lean on me. He leads me over to the display case set in the counter. "Cale, c'mon, we've got to get started on this."

"Apprentice, I will require at least a few hours before I am feeling up to conjuring biscuits, much less finishing this world and beginning a new one. In the meantime, there are other matters to attend to." Using the counter to support himself, he moves to the brass cash register. The drawer opens with several dings, and I move to his side, curiosity getting the better of me. Slowly, he drags his fingers over the empty velvet-lined drawer, wobbling visibly as the material vanishes, revealing the wood underneath and a slot in the center partition. He works it open and pulls out a silver chain, a large clear stone serving as a pendant, faceted and cylindrical in shape, each side etched with a symbol.

After inspecting it a few seconds, he offers it to me. "I want you to wear this."

I blink and take it, the stone warm in my hand. "Why? What is this?"

"All that remains."

Confused, I run my fingers over the etching, feeling a shiver run through my body. "I don't get it."

"My Nan gave this to me before she died. It belonged to her mother, who gained it from another Keth, who took it from..." He smirks. "Suffice it to say, it has a long and bloody history. But for me, it is simply a memento of the only family I knew."

I start to give it back. "I can't take this, Cale, not if it means that much to you."

He pushes my hand away. "That is precisely why you will take it. I love you, yes, but there is more. We *joined*, Apprentice, and in that moment, I was complete, my faults and flaws no longer seemed insurmountable, and I wanted to be better than I am." His hand closes around mine, my fingers still holding the stone. "Didn't you feel it too?"

I have to agree. As terrifying as it was, at the core there was something...right about it.

"That is why I can give this to you, because I know it will mean as much to you as it does me."

I free my hand from his and place the stone on the counter. For a second, he shows concern, but I slowly remove my medallion. "My father gave me this, for my First Communion. St. Jude, patron saint of lost causes. After the accident, and I became Keth... This is all there is to show there was a Miles Canmore. And I've never taken it off. I'm surprised it's held together, actually. But when you gave me that portrait, I knew you appreciated how much they mean to me. It's like you gave them back. And then I burned away some of those memories, but maybe if we start a new world, maybe in that one I can get them back."

I lean forward, putting the medallion around his neck. "So even though this still means a lot to me, it means more that you know how important you are to me."

Seconds later, he does the same for me, though the chain is much longer, the stone resting against my sternum. Cale wraps his arms about me after. "I accept, gladly."

"Same here."

"And should we both survive this...I am hoping you will continue to stay with me?"

"Formally asking me to move in, huh?"

He smirks. "I would prefer to have my bedroom back, yes." He takes my hand, still needing my support as we start toward the stairs. "Nonetheless, we should start our lives together in a world that *isn't* falling apart, so it would be best for us to begin our preparations while my will gathers itself."

"Is there anything special we have to do?" We make our way up the stairs, resting at the landing before finishing the trek down the hallway.

"Normally, I suspect it would require hours, perhaps days, of rites, spells, cajoling spirits, corralling mythics... I don't see a need, though." Cale pushes me away, gently, draws Lorus from the air, and taps the wall, chanting. Slowly, the faded floral pattern of the wallpaper rearranges, dancing across the wall to form the outline of a door in a string of white flowers. The door opens in, revealing a set of stairs that lead upward, a bit of cold air blowing down into the hallway.

"Wow..." I step toward the stairs, and Cale quickly bars my way with his arm. "What?"

Grinning, Cale reaches into his pocket and picks through some coins until he finds one to his standards. He tosses it casually into the stairwell, where it suddenly becomes encased in a block of ice and clatters to the stairs. Cale waves his hand before the doorway. "*Open.*"

I glance at him. "You take your security seriously."

"We are entering my sanctum, Apprentice, a place of power where reality works as I dictate. I do not wish it to be sullied by interlopers." He takes my hand and squeezes it, reassuring. "Someday, you will have your own, but while you are learning, my sanctum will be available to you, although under my *strict* supervision."

I remember another concern, besides the impending doom outside. "Cale? Before we go up there, there's something I need to ask you."

He perks a brow but waits patiently for me to continue.

"What's the name of magic?"

Cale chuckles and starts up the stairs. "A rather silly question, but I'll humor it. It's currently called..." He stops dead on the fourth step and remains silent for a moment. "Oh dear."

"You can't decide between Lorus or Sigil, right?"

Sighing, he tightens his hands into fists, his tone losing all joviality. "You have Sigil with you?"

My turn to stop. "Shit." I know I had the shear when Spencer got me into the car, but then I passed out and...

Fuck.

I doubt my savior took it with him when he drove me to Dave's, given that getting me warm was likely his first priority. "Do we need it?"

He turns slowly, facing me on the stairs. "Yes, Apprentice, the world cannot end if magic is uncertain, so we must have the two symbols that it is certain of. You will retrieve it, immediately. I will set to the preparations. You will have some hours, but do not dally. I sense the storm outside is only beginning to flex its muscle."

I laugh, nervously. "Uh...I don't really have it. And it might be in the back of someone's car, and I don't know where he is..."

I expect him to rage, to yell, to rant, but he shrugs simply. "Do you know this person's name?"

Spencer Crain. I nod readily. "Not his whole name though. He lives in Grunstadt, but that doesn't really narrow it down."

He descends the stairs and fingers the stone about my neck. "This will be enough to track him. Concentrate on the name, and it will lead you in the right direction."

"But I'll freeze to death out there before I make it three blocks."

Again, he shrugs. "Transmute the snow about you into heat in a continuous cycle. You'll stay warm and clear your way as well. A storm such as this has no shortage of power to draw on."

I blink. "You never thought to teach me this before?"

"And have you setting my home ablaze whilst practicing in the dead of summer?"

I narrow my eyes. "You really think I'm that incompetent?"

"*I* was your age once. That is the point in being a mentor, isn't it? To have one's dreadful and embarrassing mistakes serve a purpose?" He shoos me off. "Now go on and fetch your focus, I have work to do."

"Okay. Wish me luck."

He scoffs, ascending the stairs. "You're retrieving a focus dedicated to you from someone you know the name of. Hardly an adventure, Apprentice. I suspect this will be a rather dull task."

I begin my trip down to the shop, grabbing a gray overcoat and scarf to be safe, and proceed outside. The cold bites hard through the wool, my hair pulled and yanked by the wind. I close my fingers around the stone, working through my memories, trying frantically to find one of warmth. All that comes to mind is Victory Square, seated on my father's shoulders and dressed in a hand-me-down yellow snowsuit that had elephants on it (though I have no idea what elephants have to do with winter). The cold and snow buffets my face as I reach into the storm with my will, feeding the power around me into the memory, the name of it crystallizing.

Suddenly, the air about me clears, the chill vanishing in a heartbeat, the wind calm, and I feel warm, safe and loved. I stand there in the snow that melts slowly around my feet, luxuriating in the feeling, the thick impenetrable white at least ten feet away on all sides, like being in a reverse snow globe. I step forward, and the orb of warmth follows along, the stone around my neck glowing softly now, one of the etchings especially bright and lighting the way.

I take a deep breath and run my fingers along the stone again. "Spencer Crain."

Quickly, the stone lifts and points off toward Grunstadt, another etching pulsing now with a gentle light.

Grinning now, I start the journey. Cale was right, there shouldn't be too much to this. Certainly won't be as bad as when I claimed Sigil as mine.

Then again, *that* was supposed to be a "dull task".

"Fuck."

Chapter Twenty-One

Despite the increased number of zombies wandering the streets, they're as easy to avoid as Dave said they would be. They don't even notice that the snow suddenly vanishes when I pass by; they just plod along. There's no logic either, no general direction they're heading in, no speech or sounds, just congestion. It's more like navigating the halls of a high school than a wet dream of George Romero.

I don't get down to Grunstadt often, but despite its German name, the German population is relatively small, the vast majority of ethnic neighborhoods taken up by the Irish, Caribbean and Japanese, with plenty others packed in the spaces between. The stone leads me to the Irish neighborhood, which is barely recognizable as Irish, save the names of the restaurants and bars.

The apartment building is upper class with its own underground parking garage, gargoyles at various points on the eaves and overhangs, and probably costs more in rent than I'd make in a year at the diner. The front door opens to a small glass room with another door and an electronic lock, a long list of tenants behind thick glass along with a call box. A scan of the list doesn't reveal the name Crain.

According to the stone, though, the guy lives here, but I remember him mentioning a roommate. Too bad I didn't get that name. I hold the stone in my hand, the etchings still glowing, and wave it slowly over the list, murmuring his name, hoping I'll get some sort of sign.

When the thick glass cracks suddenly, spiderwebbing over the name *Rourke*, I decide that's all the sign I need. Though it'd be nice if I could've found that out *without* property damage. I'd fix it with a cantrip, but given my track record with them, I'd accidentally detonate the first floor. I dial the apartment number into the call box, and it rings several times, no answer. Shit.

Well, I could always go into the garage and look for his car, if he made it back here. But the stone wouldn't lead me here if he wasn't home, right?

Damn it, what if he's in trouble?

I don't want to try using the stone on the electronic lock. If *that* glass breaks, I get the feeling alarms will go off, and given how I left things with Thom, I shouldn't involve the police. They likely have their hands full anyway, what with Armageddon and all.

No fond memories of doors just clicking open, not outside of the game that is. Hell, that spell could crack open anything. Shrugging, and with no other recourse, I gently rap my knuckles against the glass, drawing on myself to fuel the memory of seeing the spell in the *Player's Handbook* the first time.

"*Knock.*"

The door makes a sharp thunking sound and opens freely, no alarms blaring, the lights not even flickering, so I enter the lobby proper.

Note to self: pick up game books should I survive.

A sitting area is off to the left, a couple of comfy-looking chairs on opposite sides of a small coffee table that has a vase of fake flowers on it. The rest of the lobby is comprised of a bank of mailboxes and a pair of elevators, the carpet deep red and plush, the walls a muted green occasionally interrupted with portraits of flowers.

The elevator takes me up to the correct floor, the ride smooth, but I need to steady my breathing regardless. I should've taken the stairs, honestly. The hallway is done in the same manner as the lobby, the doors evenly spaced. When I reach the right apartment, I knock on the door, and when no answer comes, I push the doorbell several times.

It takes a minute, but I see a shadow in the peephole, and seconds later, the door opens to reveal Spencer.

And he is, uh, without attire.

For the sake of his modesty and the health of my eyes, I keep my gaze above the waist. He keeps himself fit, some definition in his muscles, a light dusting of dark hair accenting his chest and arms, though his right wrist is inked with a playing card, the Ace of Clubs to be exact. His eyes are lighter than I remember, closer to golden, but still in the realm of brown, and his hair, which is no longer obscured by a wool cap or a treatment of Just For Men, is a mishmash of brown, black, blond, a little gray, like...

Like a dye job gone horrifically awry.

Oh my God, it's him.

"Uh..." He looks at me, confused, then smiles. "You feeling better..." Spencer's face furrows in concern. "Hold on, how do you know where I..." He glances down at himself. "There a reason you're staring?"

How could I not have seen this?

"Why are you naked?"

Well, his hair was really the only memorable thing about him, but still, I should've remembered his voice at least, the easy way he explained ripping people off with Three Card Monte before giving me his bus ticket.

"I'm not..." He grumbles and leaves my view, the door left open. Taking it as an invite, I step in, finding a definite bachelor apartment. The walls are lined with bookshelves, the floor having mismatched furniture of varying ages and retail pedigrees, as well as a pricey-looking flat-screen TV. Spencer emerges from an adjacent room to the right, now wearing jeans and a large Harley Davidson T-shirt. "Okay, there a reason you're here?"

I swallow hard. "I know you. At least, I think I used to, you probably don't remember me, that's how it works." It's been two years, I only knew him for five minutes, maybe, but he was my hero, the man who saved me from Heath and...

His face scrunches up in confusion, mouth parted. "All right, you're going to have to run that by me again." He heads into a small kitchen and fetches a bottle of whiskey from a cupboard, pouring it into a pair of tumblers. "Of course you know me, we've met a few times. You were naked and freezing, I gave you a lift home, I earned a free lunch or nine, and I left you in a hot tub that was very oddly placed under a big skylight." He takes a sip of his whiskey. "Kind of weird, really. Seemed like the sort of thing that would end up as a crime scene on a procedural show."

"But you don't remember me from anytime before that? Before we met at the diner?" Would he remember me? Did I become a sorcerer when I cast that spell on the bus, after I met Spencer, or before, when I saw my reflection and decided to leave Heath?

He shrugs and nudges the half-filled glass across the counter. "Don't know if you drink, but I figure I should offer. It's not the good stuff, if you're curious. I'd catch hell if I even thought about it." Spencer stares hard at me a moment and shrugs again. "Other than when we played the shell game, not really, no. Never met a guy with a white streak in his hair before you, and you've got one of those faces."

"Guess I've got the wrong guy. I just knew someone with hair like yours, met him a little over a couple years ago. He helped me. I never got his name."

"Sorry, man, I don't remember you before..." He chews his lip and exhales before pointing at me. "James, right?"

"Yeah, James Black."

His tumbler hits the floor, shattering. Spencer takes a deep breath, his eyes serious, his tone measured. "Is that your real name?"

I shake my head, a glimmer of hope visible. "No, the guy gave me his fake ID at Victory Station before I got on the bus. He just told me to consider him a coyote, since he was smuggling me north, only..."

"Without the extortion and shit." Spencer just stands there a moment, then smiles. "Sorry I didn't recognize you, I mean, I only met you for a few minutes and you were kinda...well...beat to hell, you know? I mean, black eyes, your face was swollen, bruised, you were dressed pretty ratty... I mean, like I told you when I gave you my ID, you didn't really, uh..." He shrugs awkwardly.

"Look like anybody, yeah."

He pulls me into a friendly hug, his hand patting my back a couple of times before he pulls away. "You clean up pretty good, though. Always wondered what happened to you. I thought you were back in the Capital."

"Didn't make it that far. The bus..."

"Damn, they didn't let you on? Shit, I would've stuck around to help but I ended up having a pretty messed-up night myself after that." He smiles, and it's a warm, easy smile. "So what's with the hair, you see dead people?"

I want to tell him I saw plenty walking around on the way over, but I'm here for a reason, and I'm short on time. "Actually, I need to talk to you about something. When you found me in the snow, I was holding a broken scissor."

"Okay...?"

"I really need to find it. I think I left it in your car, so if you could show me where it is in your garage, I'd seriously appreciate it."

"Car? What car?"

"The one you drove me back to the diner in? You told Dave not to be worried about the plow getting it?"

He grins. "Well, yeah, I figured it wasn't a good place to ditch it. Some questions might end up getting asked, and I wanted to save your friend the hassle."

Huh? "Why would questions be asked about where you parked the car? There's a damned blizzard out there. I think you'd be forgiven for not seeing where the red zone is."

And he laughs. "Oh no, it's not that. I had to ditch it somewhere out of the way. It wasn't really my car."

I gape. "You *stole* it?"

Offended, he folds his arms. "I didn't *steal* it, I took it for a joyride. There's a big difference."

Blinking, it takes me a few attempts to start my retort. "No! There's no big difference, there's not even a little difference. Oh God, I'm an accessory to grand theft auto, that's all my brother needs to hear." I rub my forehead. "Okay, I can worry about that later. Where did you leave it?"

"Firstly, you're not an accessory because you didn't help steal it and you had no idea you were in a stolen car. Secondly, you were freezing to death. I doubt any cop would bring you in for more than a statement. Thirdly, why does a broken scissor matter?" He points out the window at the falling snow. "Because I would be more concerned about that."

"I *am*. That's why I need to find it."

"What does it have to do with the storm? Your brain not finished thawing?" He plops down on a couch, sitting in front of an expensive-looking TV, and flips on the screen. "Besides, the car's out in the storm. I ditched it a few blocks from the 65th and L station. It's probably buried by now."

I move in front of the screen, blocking the latest set of weather advisories. "Where *exactly* did you leave it?"

Spence folds his arms again. "Why *exactly* do you need it?"

"I'm a sorcerer, and the shear is a sacred artifact that I'll use to lower the difficulty of enacting a ritual that will stop the storm and save the world."

He blinks once, and slight disgust crosses his face. "Oh God, you sound like a LARPer."

"I don't LARP, I play Dungeons & Dragons."

"Ugh, that's even worse." He gets off the couch. "Guess I did you a favor pulling you out of the snow. No one should die a virgin." Spence starts pulling off his shirt. "I've got some time, don't worry, and hey, it'll be a fun way to keep warm."

I start toward the door. "Put your shirt back on and just tell me where to find the car, okay?"

Grumbling, he holds up a finger (not that one) and heads into the adjoining room. A couple of minutes later he emerges dressed in a hoodie, a light jacket over the hoodie, and a heavier black coat over that, as well as work boots and his wool cap. "It's better if I show you. Plus I can't have you dying if you owe me your life."

Just what I need, another life debt.

We exit the apartment and move wordlessly to the elevator, which rattles a bit as it descends, but Spence seems unaffected. I sigh at him. "You could just tell me the intersection, you know."

"And then have your frozen corpse on my conscience? No way." A second passes. "So...did you finally get away from that guy? Y'know, the one who was..."

The elevator dings as the doors slide open.

"Not really, no." I walk into the lobby with Spencer in tow. "I left him, but I don't think I'll ever get away from him." I turn to him and try to smile. "I do want to thank you though, for what you did that night."

He smiles back. "I thought you were going to bolt any second. Guess I'm lucky I came across so charming."

I look at him plainly. "Honestly? I thought you were a drug mule."

Without missing a beat, his grin widens. "Nah, I could never be a mule. My ass ain't that spacious." He stops in front of the door, the snow being whipped about by the wind. "You sure you don't want to go back upstairs? My housemate and I have a pretty open thing going."

Rolling my eyes, I step around him. "I'm sure you do, but I'm involved."

"Boyfriend?"

I meet his golden eyes. "The Ra'keth."

He chuckles. "No wonder the storm doesn't scare you." Spencer glances out the window again. "So it's not an open relationship?"

I glower.

"Not trying to offend you, James, just putting off going out in the cold."

I nudge him aside and push the door open, the wind hitting me hard, the door meeting plenty of resistance. The cold is about as bad as I'd expect. The gale surges, and I take the opportunity to murmur the spell of warmth, drawing on the snow and gust of wind. The visibility clears, and I beckon Spence to follow. Gingerly, he steps outside, confused.

"Huh. Guess it's not as bad as I thought." He tics his head to the left. "UTA station is this way. With the snow this bad, it's probably a good idea to follow the tracks since the train's shut down."

"Sounds like a plan, just stick close to me. Don't want to lose you in the whiteout."

He draws close, almost to the point of awkwardness, but we proceed on, the wind slipping around the orb of warmth I've created. I tuck the stone farther inside my jacket.

"So you never told me your name." Spence needs to speak up, but not too much.

"I told you, it's James."

We pass a few parked cars, all of them large white mounds now. "No, not the name you took off my ID."

I smirk at him. "You told me that until I got off the bus in the Capital, if anyone asks, my name is James Black."

"So?"

I shrug. "So I never got off the bus in the Capital."

"What happened?"

I stop walking, take a moment to weigh the choice. "Do we have to get into this now? It's hardly important."

"Just passing the time. This is going to be a long..." He stares off ahead, and I follow his eyes to a silhouette in the falling white, moving slowly, deliberately. "Jesus, someone else is out in this?"

During a break in the wind, a low guttural moan echoes through the air from the dark shape's direction. Great, another one of the shambling undead. It'll be easy enough to step around. "Don't know, but let's give a wide berth."

Pushing Spencer toward the street, I follow, the snow not any more shallow here, the plows not out here yet. Allora and Destry Bay will get preferential treatment, given the money living there. I can't imagine how shitty the roads must be out in the Benedict by now.

The walking dead man passes on our left, his skin bluish-green, movements stiff. I have no idea where he could be trying to get to—

"Shit! Shit! Shit!" Spencer is on his ass, scrambling away from it, his eyes wide with terror. I'm about to tell him there's nothing to worry about when the creature's head snaps in Spence's direction, a louder groan issuing from it as it advances toward us. The Coyote descends into panicked profanity, still scrabbling backward, reaching into the snow as if he could find weapons there.

As the thing enters the orb, Spencer screams. I've practically bumped into these things before and they've never...

It hisses, a green bile dripping from sharp and broken teeth as it lunges toward me, screeching.

I can't call the lightning, it would likely jump to Spence and cook him. But I have other memories of storms and what accompanies lightning. Accessing the memory, the name comes to me as I raise my hand, my palm pressing into rotting flesh.

"*Thunder.*"

My ears feel like I've just borne witness to the world being torn in half. The palm of my hand is throbbing, and in front of me, there's only a wobbling set of legs which quickly topple over into the snow to join the splatter of gore. A few seconds pass before my ears stop ringing. I shake off the debris, wiping the rest off on my coat before extending my hand to Spencer, who still cowers in the snow.

"God, get up, you wuss." I chortle. "It was only a zombie."

Trembling, he takes my offered hand and pulls himself up, dusting off the snow that clings to him. "Only a zombie? Are you listening to yourself?"

"Jesus, don't tell me you're one of those geeks with an irrational fear of the zombie apocalypse." I gently pat his shoulder, trying to calm him down. I can't have him freaking out, though I'm more surprised he's not commenting on my de-torso-ing of said undead.

Behind us, I hear a screech, then another, more and more joining until it's a dissonant cacophony, but growing closer. Spencer points off to a distant, spreading multitude of silhouettes and dark shapes moving through the snow.

Toward us.

The Coyote practically squeaks, "It's not irrational."

Chapter Twenty-Two

Spencer is ten feet in front of me, on the edge of the orb, his movements frantic as he charges forward, muttering something about a shotgun. I'm following behind, keeping pace, the keening cries of the horde behind us growing in volume. Apparently zombies can run if properly motivated, and I plan to have a long talk with Cale about this if I make it home alive. Right now I'm thankful for the storm, because at least there's no one else on the street.

The snow is halfway up my shins, my legs starting to burn, my lungs aching, but I doubt the zombies are going to run out of breath. I consider crossing into Tartarus where I could run on top of the fallen snow for a few meters, but I'd leave Spence behind.

Besides, hell hardly seems like a sensible escape route from the undead.

Ahead, Spencer cuts hard to the left to scramble up the stairs to a rail platform, the station an offshoot of the Blue Line. The train has stopped here, vacant, the UTA shut down.

I follow, reaching the top just in time to see him start banging on the door to the token booth, which is dark. I reach him and touch his shoulder because no one's going to open up for him.

He screams at my contact, swinging his fist wildly. I barely dodge, his knuckles grazing my coat. When he recognizes me, he returns to his muttering panic. Screeching follows from below. They heard him. Fuck.

Spencer kicks at the door to the booth, screaming, swearing, but it doesn't budge.

"We have to find somewhere else, Spence." I pull him away from the door, and my eyes fall on the train, which is dark, vacant. "Over here!"

I yank him toward the closed doors of the train. I pull at them, but they don't move. I bang on the windows, but they're Plexiglas and care little for my blows.

Shit, what do I do?

The windows are smudged, dirty, no reflection, so I can't hope that Cale will give me a hint. Spencer is no help, gibbering in panic. I want to be angry at him, but I can't. I know that kind of fear. We can't die here, not like this. We can't die here.

I will not die here.

I don't want to be here anymore.

I feel the spark inside me, and I take hold of it. My fingers press to the cold metal of the doors.

"*Knock.*"

Nothing.

"Damn it, *knock*!"

The first zombie comes into view on the stairs. The sparks dance in my being, and I fan them with my will.

I grit my teeth. "I am the fucking Lightning Rod and I command you to open." My body feels hot, the stone's etchings a blazing silver-white as it tumbles out from inside my coat. "*Open!*"

The doors slide quickly, and Spencer and I leap in. I extend my hand toward the open doors as we land, a pair of zombies lunging at us. "*Close.*"

The doors slam shut with a loud snap, a severed head dropping to the floor. The zombies begin to gather outside, amassing against the side of the train.

"Oh God, oh God, they're gonna get in." Spencer is sitting on a bench on the far side, his back pressed against the window, his face wet as he continues to tremble. "Do something."

"What do you want me to do, get out and push?"

He cowers, sobbing while a horde of two-hit die monsters continue to pound on the glass. He's right, we can't stay in here forever. I have to get this train moving, but I have no idea how.

"Spencer." I shake him by the shoulders, which gets his attention after a few seconds. "I need your help, okay?"

He whimpers but nods.

I take the stone off, holding it in my hand, the etchings still glowing. "If I'm going to start up the train, I need to know what the name of it is."

The Coyote starts to regain his composure. "It's the Blue Line."

I shake my head quickly. "There are three trains that run the Blue Line. I need the name of this one specifically. Can you do that for me?"

I don't know if that's true, but I have to assume it for two reasons. One, it cuts through Spencer's panic and makes him useful. Two, magic is likely sadistic and literal minded. I remember a game once where someone wished for enough gold to buy a castle. Unfortunately, he didn't specify he wanted gold *coins* and was subsequently crushed by an avalanche of gold *ore*. I don't want to imagine the consequences with several hundred-ton commuter trains.

So I draw a circle in the floor, the edge of the stone sharp like a diamond. Any occultist out there will extol the virtues of a well-made circle. If anything, it's at least a symbol that humanity hasn't forgotten yet, a last vestige of belief wedging open the door of denial that I can slip my magic through.

Besides, circles are a material component for a lot of higher-level spells in Dungeons & Dragons. Everyone knows that.

Drawing the circle is easy enough, knowing what to fill it with, that's another thing altogether. "Any luck on finding that name?"

Spencer is standing in the middle of the aisle, his attention constantly being drawn by the creatures banging on the windows, groaning. It appears that they don't have superstrength, which I'm thankful for.

"Spence!"

He looks back at me, still trembling, but I meet his eyes and push my will onto him, into his name.

"Spencer Crain, we're safe for now, but I need you to find that name. Just calm down, okay?" The Coyote visibly settles as the command wraps around him like a warm blanket, and he nods in assent as he searches the wall.

"How about the registration number? That's got to be unique, right?"

I smile, relieved. "Yeah, that'd be perfect."

He reads off the long string of numbers and letters, which I carve into the center of the circle. With the final number inscribed in the floor...

Nothing happens.

Maybe I should've done more than just a regular, unadorned circle.

"Fuck." I look up at Spence. "We're okay, I just need a little more to make this work, be more specific about what I want it to do. Okay..."

I grin nervously at him, chuckling. "I don't suppose you know any words in Lorus or Sigil or whatever you think it's called?" It's the same language, but I'm still uncertain about the name. "Something to put the lights on, make it run?"

The Coyote impossibly speaks a long string of syllables that I recognize as Sigil, or Lorus. Damn it, Cale and I really need to fix that. Instead of quickly inscribing the words, though, I just stare. "Spence? What the fuck?"

"My housemate's Fae. They all use that language for their oaths, and their bards tell their stories in it. You just pick it up after a while, I guess."

Christ, I've been busting my ass for six months to possess the equivalent vocabulary of a three-year-old, and he can manage story time in Sigil?

"Okay..." I glance toward the window, the zombies still at bay, but there are at least thirty of them now banging at the doors and windows, the car starting to rock ever so slightly. "Let's go a little slower, all right?"

It takes a few attempts. I need to be sure the pronunciation's right before inscribing it. I've lost enough characters to badly drawn circles to not take any chances. Plus the groaning and screeching of the undead horde is hardly conducive to my concentration. In the end, I inscribe the Sigil into the border of the circle, putting down the words to turn on the lights, keep the car warm, to extend a heat ahead of the train to melt the snow, and most importantly, to respond to simple commands since I doubt either of us knows how to operate a commuter train.

"That should do it." I place my fingers on the edge of the circle and concentrate.

"James?" The thumping outside is growing louder.

"Spencer, I've never done anything like this before, so I need you to be quiet." I can feel the electricity coursing through the rail below. Its name calls to me, to power the working, but warns one thing.

It will hurt.

"James?" An odd crunching sound now. I can control that power. I need to focus on that certainty or I might kill us both.

I shouldn't be able to withstand it though. It's so much voltage, amperage, it'll fry me in mere seconds and...

No.

"James!" A crashing sound now, the screeching deafening.

I am the Lightning Rod. I do not fall.

"*Lightning.*" My body seizes as it jumps into me in an instant, the spark inside possessing the ferocity of a thunderhead. It's too much, too much... I see the silver current racing up and down my arms, my chest. Oh God, I can't hold on anymore, I can't...

No. No. Damn it, I am the Lightning Rod.

I will not fall.

Screaming, I force my hand into the center of the circle, the inscribed Sigil suddenly ablaze in an argent conflagration. The fire spreads through the car, over me, over Spencer, over the creatures outside which howl in agony at its contact. I funnel the power into the circle, my will starting to crumble as the ordeal grows more Sisyphean.

Just a little longer...

I can see Spencer out of the corner of my eye, swinging a fire extinguisher at a mass of arms that have broken through the window.

Just a little longer...

I can't feel anything anymore.

Just a little...

I'm thrown back as the connection between me and the circle breaks, my back slamming into the door to the cab, and I slump against it, my eyes heavy, my arms literally smoking as the lights come on. "Go! Go! Go!"

The train goes into motion, pulling away from the platform.

Spencer smashes the extinguisher down on the arms of the zombies dragged along, the force and the broken window completing the rough amputations. Once the train is clear of the platform, the horde of undead recedes into the distance. The Coyote drops the extinguisher to the floor and staggers back to one of the seats, laughing, relieved.

I sob in agony in the meantime, my arms burned with jagged bloody lines that run from my shoulders to my wrists. Clenching my eyes tight does little to abate the pain. It's all I can do to keep from screaming.

"James? Are you...oh shit..." I'm aware of Spence moving around the car, and he returns carrying a green case with a white cross he retrieves from under a seat. I fade out from the pain for a few seconds, or maybe a minute or two, but when I become aware again he's wrapping my left arm in gauze, the right thoroughly bandaged, my chest bare, my shirt off to the left, the sleeves scorched and bloody. I'm also on my back, his coat under my head as the train continues along.

The Coyote smiles reassuringly. "So, is this par for the course with sorcerers or something? I thought you guys would be more like the ones in the movies, you know?"

I return the smile, weakly, though my arms still sting like a bitch. "Competent?"

"Nah, older. Thought you guys had three-foot beards or some shit, or at least wore black leather dusters, you know?"

Ugh, I feel like I ran a marathon uphill. "I'd prefer a gray London Fog, personally. Thanks for coming through at the end."

Spencer looks away, closing his eyes a second. "I want to apologize for that, yeah. I don't know what happened. I mean, I thought I could handle something like that. I've certainly seen my share of Romero movies, read the comics. You'd think I'd know that zombies are attracted to loud noises so screaming your head off isn't a wise decision but..."

I nod to him. "But knowing's a lot different than *knowing*."

"Plus I usually don't make it that far into the movies before shutting my eyes for the scary parts. Still have nightmares, but I figure you gotta toughen up that psyche, right?" He chuckles softly. "Listen to me going on while you're lying here with burns all over your arms. How's the pain?"

"Did you give me something? *I* should be screaming my head off right now." I try to lift my arms and wince, shivers of pain reverberating up and down my skin. "Fuck."

"I think it's more like shock. Or maybe sorcerers have a high threshold of pain." Spencer checks the view out the window. "World's really ending, isn't it? I always thought that was just a joke."

"What is my purpose, master?"

Spence and I both look at each other, and then around the car. In unison, we both say, "Was that you?"

"What is my purpose, master?" The voice comes from the speakers, in the same automated voice that tells people not to smoke or bother pregnant women and that their stops are coming up.

I strain to lean forward, and Spencer helps me into a sitting position. "Who's there?"

"I do not have a name, master. Would you give me one? What is my purpose?" Again from the speakers, the tone cheery and polite, a hint of British in the accent.

"Oh fuck." I point at the circle, gritting my teeth. "Help me over there, would you?"

Spencer nods, still looking around the car to discern the identity of the voice, as well as double-check the zombie debris that remain on the train, though the head and arms appear dead and immobile. I'm dragged to the circle, which glows brightly, and I study the Sigil. I mean, it couldn't be... I couldn't have screwed up *that* badly...

"Fuck fuck fuckity-fuck."

Spencer appraises the circle, shading his eyes. "What? What's wrong?"

I gently tap one of the marks. "See this? This is supposed to say 'give light to the machine'. There's just a minor problem."

The Coyote perks a brow, inspecting it. "What?"

"I *might've* accidentally miswritten a word. Like, *light*."

His jaw drops softly, and he stares at the circle, then back at the speaker. "So instead of light you wrote..."

"What is my purpose, master?" The voice is still just as sunny, but there's an edge of impatience there.

I shrug at Spence with a nervous smile. *"Life."*

Chapter Twenty-Three

"Dull task, my ass." I wave off a look from Spencer. "I'll explain later." With a great deal of wincing and sucking breath through clenched teeth, I get to my feet. "So are we talking to the *train*?"

"Yes, master!" The voice is eager now. "What is my purpose?"

I lean toward Spence. "We have to pick our words *very* carefully."

Spence whispers, "This happen a lot around you?"

I remember playing my mage, and a few encounters with summoned creatures that ended badly. "In a way..."

I speak up to the train. "Uh, you're a train. You go along the rails and take people where they need to go according to the schedule."

"I understand." The voice resumes its polite and cheery tone. "Where do you need to go, master?"

"For starters, you don't need to call me master."

Spence mutters, "Could be worse. Could be calling you *Daddy*."

I glare at him, not wanting to give the train any ideas. "We need to get to 65th and L." Outside the snow has progressed to a near whiteout, the rumble of thunder growing more frequent. "I just hope we get there fast enough."

The voice sounds hurt. "I don't go fast enough?" The train accelerates, already beginning to rattle from the speed, the spells I'd worked into the circle not melting the ice and snow on the rails as quickly as needed. This is going to end very badly.

"What'd you do?" Spence starts banging on the door to the cab. "Hey! Slow down."

Shit. "No, you're plenty fast, we're just on a tight schedule, that's all."

"My master doesn't think I can keep to the schedule? You're going to leave, aren't you? You're going to take another train. I'm not good enough to take people where they need to go." Over the speaker we hear sniffles and soft sobs.

Spence stares at me. "For Christ's sake, is the train *crying*?" The stare becomes a glare. "Fix it."

"No, that's not true." I force the fear out of my voice, make it soothing, calm, but parental. "You're a very good train, we just need to stop at 65ᵗʰ and L so we can pick something up."

"You're just saying that." It sounds extra hurt now. If I don't do something I'm going to find out what happens when a hundred-ton commuter train throws a temper tantrum. "You won't even give me a name, master."

The train goes faster, the vibrations becoming more turbulent until a sudden jostle sends me flat on my ass.

"Fine, I'll give you a name. Just slow down."

Its words barely come through choked sobs. "I'll slow down when you give me a name."

Spencer checks the windows. "There's a curve coming up. If we don't stop, this thing's gonna derail and send us into a building." He braces himself against the seats. "Just give him a name!"

Unfortunately coming up with names isn't my strong suit. It'd take me four hours to name one character back in Dungeons & Dragons (seriously, an *elf* named Radcliffe?), and when I was six I missed out on having a puppy because after three weeks I was still calling it "Here, boy!"

Zippy? God, that's just lame.

Uh… Trainy? Just move on.

Shadowfax? Dear God, you're not Gandalf.

I panic. "I don't know."

The Coyote blinks at me. "Just shout a name, *any* name."

"It's not that easy!"

"James, are you telling me I'm gonna die because you can't think up one name?"

I glower at him as the train shakes violently. "Well what the fuck do you name an intelligent machine that's emotionally unstable?"

Spencer immediately shouts toward the speaker. "Marvin! Your name is Marvin. Now slow down."

The car rattles, quakes, and Spencer grabs me, pulling me to him. We huddle against the seat, heads buried in each other's shoulders. I shut my eyes tight, a Hail Mary slipping past my lips, because a loud impending death has that effect on people. When the train begins to slow down, resuming the gentle rock and rumble of normal transit as it takes the curve, it still takes a few seconds before I let myself believe we're safe.

"Station's coming up soon." Spencer pulls back, smiling in relief, his eyes looking into mine. "You know..." He waggles his eyebrows.

I roll my eyes and nudge him aside, and call out to Marvin. "Next station's our stop."

"Are you going to leave me, master?" The train sounds hurt again.

"We just need to pick something up, then you can give us a ride back to Grunstadt, and then out to 90th and V." I curse as there are a few fresh red blotches on my bandages, all the moving around not having helped much.

"That doesn't sound very safe, master."

Spencer speaks softly, "He's talking about safety after nearly killing us?"

I groan, getting back up. "You don't have to call me master, Marvin."

"Yes, ma— Er, yes." There's a pause as the train pulls into the station, at least over a foot of snow on the platform. "What do I call you then?"

"You can call me James."

"Do you promise to come back, James?" The train sounds younger. Childlike.

I expect the Coyote to shake his head, but instead he just watches me, appraising.

Like it or not, I gave Marvin life and intelligence. I can hardly run off and leave him. Maybe other sorcerers could, I don't know, but I couldn't live with the guilt.

Plus, I don't want to add abandonment issues to his low self-esteem.

Look at me, already calling Marvin a him.

"I promise." The doors slide open, and we both step onto the platform, the cold slicing through the bandages on my arms, into my skin. I reinvoke the heat spell, needing a second to warm back up as I'm not wearing a shirt now. "Marvin? We shouldn't be more than a half-hour. Lie low until we get back. Turn off your lights, we don't need any new passengers."

The train goes dark a second later, and Spencer hands me his outer coat before he and I trudge through the snow toward the stairs. I glance at him, putting the coat on as we start our descent. "Thank you."

"I figure we can take it out in trade." He grins. "Kidding. Unless of course..."

"Jesus, you don't ever turn it off, do you?" I take the first step with care. "So...Marvin."

He helps me down a couple more stairs, as my arms hurt too much to use the railing. "It's perfect, what are you talking about? I mean, you get the reference, right?"

I shrug, taking a couple more stairs.

"C'mon. Douglas Adams? Marvin?" Spence chuckles incredulously. "*Hitchhiker's?*"

I make it to the bottom. "That supposed to mean something?" I look back at him and he's staring in shock.

"Seriously, James, there is likely an army of nerds coming to kick your ass right now." He joins me and tries to see through the snow. "Ugh...I think it's that way," he says, pointing to the north. "But I don't know how accurate I'll be in this—"

I take the stone around my neck in my hand and reach out to the edge of the orb of warmth. It worked finding Spence, why not with something else I know the name of? "*Sigil.*"

I feel a weak pulse, and I wobble, Spence needing to support me. "It's that way, to the right."

"You dragged me through a frozen hellscape, complete with a zombie horde, and you could've just done *that* from the get-go?"

I shake my head. "It's an object, not a person. Plus you've had your name all your life, I've only had my focus a couple years." Laughing lightly, I lean into him. "I'm going to sleep for a week when this night's over. Let's get going."

And off we go, following the pulse of the stone which grows stronger with every few yards we proceed. The hard part, it would appear, is over, all that's left is the retrieval.

Thankfully, it doesn't take too long to find a large mound of snow parked in a vacant lot. Good thing too, my hands are freezing. Spence leans me against the car, the orb helping him brush the snow off the passenger door. I start to nod off, the pain and exhaustion having long since taxed my reserves.

Wait...my hands shouldn't be cold, not with the spell.

"There we go!" Spence yanks open the door with a grin and peeks into the cabin. "Yep! Ended up on the floor!"

The last time they were cold like that was just before...

"Thank God, 'cause if I ended up leaving it some—"

Oh shit. Right before Heath—

I'm face-first in the snow, my vision blurry, the back of my head feeling wet, heavy, wonky. With some effort I roll onto my back, seeing a pair of blurry male-shaped figures standing by the car. I try to warn Spence, but I can't form the words.

"So you must be my replacement." No. No no no...

My vision clears just in time to see Heath smack Spencer's head against the roof of the car. The Coyote crumples into the snow as Heath quickly retrieves Sigil and points it at me.

"Heath, how did you—"

"Get out of your prison? There's a very pissed-off goddess who did me a solid, you've met her. And her, and uh...her. But I guess they're just uh...her now." He grins wickedly. "Gotta admit, Miles, that was inspired, you fucked her right up. Good work." Now I feel sick.

Heath points the blade at Spencer. "Get up."

Spencer sits up with some effort. "Fuck, James, your boyfriend's the jealous type, huh?" He glances at me, and with some strain I shake my head.

Heath kicks the Coyote in the stomach, a low hard grunt of pain issuing from Spencer as he rolls onto his side. Heath glares at me. "This, Miles? You seriously picked a *Coyote* over me?"

Spencer groans and looks at Heath, blinking. "What can I say?" He motions to the distressed sedan. "I drive this piece of shit to compensate for my huge dick." He curls into the fetal position to shield himself as Heath kicks him hard in the side.

"Funny guy, aren't ya?" The Coyote's face is splashed with spit. "You think you'll get him in bed with that shit? Ain't happening."

I try to form words, call my magic, call Sigil to me, something to stop Heath, help Spencer, but I can't feel it, not even the storm above.

Spence looks up at him, grinning. "Yeah, you wouldn't want that, would you? If I fuck him he might find out what he was faking the whole time with you."

Heath shows teeth, bringing his leg back for another kick, but Spencer stares beyond him, terrified. The Coyote scrabbles backward, his eyes filled with terror.

"Fuck. Fuck! How'd you find us? Shotgun! *Get a damned shotgun.*"

Both Heath and I look away from Spencer, into the deep of the falling white beyond the buried car, but there's nothing there, no dark silhouettes, no distant groans or roars or voices. No noise at all, save the howling of the gale outside of the orb. When we return our attention to Spencer, he's gone.

"Coward." Heath snorts, but grins and begins advancing toward me, his back to the car. "You've got pretty bad taste in men, Miles."

I weakly point at Heath. "Exhibit A. Why did I ever date you?"

"You're weak, I'm strong. It's the way of the world." He twirls the shear in his hand with a flourish and raises it toward the sky. "Time to get back on track. The storm should push the world into endgame easily enough." The blade begins to glow brightly, the metal a dark blue. "The rest, well... You won't be around to see it."

The shear is pointed at me and sparks of azure leap out, showering over me, forcing me to curl up to protect my face, my bandaged arms racked with pain as the electricity burns through the gauze, aggravating the wounds.

"Fuck!"

Heath staggers to the side, his left leg shaking violently, his thigh bloody as a canine head pulls away, its teeth reddened from its attack. The creature attacks Heath again, biting quickly at his forearm, causing the blade to fall into the snow. The dog-thing quickly fetches the shear and dashes off behind the snow-covered car. What the hell was that? It looked like a...

Coyote.

Spencer emerges from behind the car, holding my shear. Heath swears under his breath, the wind howling to a deafening roar, matching his rage as he screams words I can't make out. But I see the wounds on his arm and leg close. I work myself into a kneeling position, but I can't manage much more. The orb of warmth is starting to drain on me, unable to keep in balance with the surrounding storm, but I can hardly release it without killing all of us.

Heath narrows his eyes at Spencer, beckoning. "Hand that over, and perhaps I'll let your kind stay in my new world."

The Coyote chuckles dubiously. "I practically bit your arm off getting this from you, and you think I'll hand it over because you *asked*? Hell, you didn't say please."

Heath steps toward him. "You're a trickster. Trash. Your kind aren't even servants, just misguided attempts at *entertainment*." He extends his hand, sparks dancing between his fingers.

"Back off, or I back you off." Trembling now, Spencer waves the blade at Heath.

Heath senses the break in Spencer's resolve and steps toward him again. "You think you can intimidate me? I'm *Keth*, Coyote. You wouldn't even know how to use a sorcerer's—"

Spencer's leg sweeps upward in a flash between Heath's legs, connecting soundly and solidly with his groin, causing him to double over with the explosion of agony. The Coyote follows quickly, bringing another hard kick against the sorcerer's lowered head. Heath goes down in a heap, unconscious but still breathing.

"Maybe not, but I know my way around a pair of steel-toed boots." Spencer smirks and rushes to my side, handing me Sigil, the metal warm and reassuring in my hands, the power within it bolstering my will, the orb allowing me to catch my breath and stand, though I need to lean on him.

"Help me get him into the car, James." He hooks his arms under Heath's, dragging him toward the still-open car door.

"You kidding? Let's just leave him here."

Spencer sighs as he pulls Heath's dead weight into the car on his own. "I don't kill people, James."

I quirk a brow at him. "That wasn't you screaming for a shotgun a minute ago?"

"Zombies aren't people."

"They *were* people."

He shuts the car door and returns to my side. "Well, they aren't *now*!" Spencer puts my arm around his shoulders to hold me up. "Can we get back to Marvin so I can get home? I know you've got a world to save, but I think I've hit my sidekick quota for the next year."

We return to the 65th and L platform a few minutes later. Marvin slides open the doors and turns on the lights once we reach the top of the stairs, and starts us back to Grunstadt once we're safely aboard. Spencer prattles on while he changes my bandages with the first aid kit, but I largely tune him out, just resting, letting strength return to my body. My arms still sting, but I figure Cale and I can figure something out.

Sigil has lost most of its glow by the time we reach the station in Grunstadt, but I'm feeling much more up to walking now. The platform is empty of zombies as we approach, but Marvin keeps the doors shut regardless. Either they dispersed after we escaped, or the mob is shambling toward Beckettsville in single-minded pursuit.

"You can open the doors, Marvin. I'll be back in a little while, and then you can take me out to 90th and V." I motion for Spence to follow me as I exit, and he gently pats the door to the cab before doing so.

"Thanks for the ride, Marvin. You did good." The lights brighten a moment, but once Spencer joins me outside, the doors shut and the train goes dark. We warily descend the stairs to the street, where the snow is past our knees. "Christ, it's going to take forever to get back at this rate. Can't you freeze the snow together so we can walk on top of it?"

I blink at him. "Any reason you didn't suggest that before?"

"I was seconds away from becoming a movie cliché before."

I shrug in reply. "Fair enough."

Raising Sigil upward, I point my hand out in front of us, into the snow-filled street. The name of ice returns to my mind quickly, needing little encouragement from my will given the weather. A shimmer extends outward in front of me, five feet wide and continuing on. I nudge my foot forward, only to find a hard block of ice inches in front of us. "Think that worked."

Spencer climbs up and gives me a hand to join him. I take the lead, keeping my hand extended, the shimmer continuing about twenty feet ahead. Our steps need to be more careful, but our pace is still greatly increased, letting us return to the Little Dublin section of Grunstadt faster than expected.

Once his building is in sight, I dismiss the ice, the shimmer fading into the storm, the two of us dropped into the snow without warning. I brace to steady myself, but Spencer isn't as lucky, tumbling face-first into a snowdrift. He digs himself out, cursing softly. "Warn me next time, okay?"

"Of course. Next time I'll know that'll happen."

He fishes his keys out and opens the door into the lobby, where the emergency lights are on. "Shit. Looks like I'll be taking the stairs." He looks back at me. "You're going to fix this, right?"

"Going to try. Should all be taken care of by morning."

Spencer nods and stretches. "Well, I had a lovely evening, we should do this again sometime." He leans toward me, lips parted, and I step back, but he smiles at me, a nice, easy smile. "C'mon, a night like that and I don't even get a good-night kiss? You're a terrible first date."

"That was hardly a date, and I told you, I'm with someone."

"Wasn't the psycho I stuffed in that sedan, was it?"

I shake my head. "No, that was the guy you helped me leave."

He blinks. "What's up with that, then?"

"A long story I don't have time to get into. All I'll say is that he terrorized me for months before I left, and he still won't leave me alone."

"Shit. Maybe I should've hit him harder in the junk." Spencer looks at the door to the stairwell and then back at me. "You sure you don't want to come up?"

"We're not sleeping together."

"Yeah, but we should, if only just to get it out of the way and kill the curiosity. And why shouldn't we anyway? I'm hot, you're hot, and sex is awesome." He shrugs, grinning big. "Even if you're not that good at it, as long as I'm on top we'll have a great time, so why not?"

I understandably roll my eyes. "Good night, Spencer." I turn toward the door and start to open it.

"Hey." Before I can react, he turns me around quickly and wraps me in his arms, squeezing tight. "You stay out of the cold, okay?"

I smile in spite of myself and hug him back. "Don't worry, I shouldn't have trouble keeping warm."

He pulls back, meeting my eyes. "Do that too. Now go save the world so I'll have someone to flirt with at the diner tomorrow."

I nod once and disengage from his embrace, opening the door and calling the name of ice to speed my way back to the platform. The wind sounds weaker than before, but the snow hasn't decreased in intensity, nor has the rumble of thunder ceased in the skies. Determined, I climb on top of the frozen path and start on my way, the Coyote still in the lobby, watching after me as I disappear into the storm.

Chapter Twenty-Four

"I never want to hear the words *dull task* ever again, okay?"

Despite the orb of warmth and having walked on a platform of ice for the last twenty blocks, my clothes are still wet and clingy and cold once I dismiss the various spells around me. The shop is dimly lit by the sconces, and I suspect Cale is still upstairs.

I needed the beacon spell to guide me, which I'd enchanted into a silk tie Cale keeps in the shop's window. It's difficult to use street signs when you can't even see where they are.

After shrugging off Spence's coat and doffing my shoes, I help myself to fresh clothes from the racks, going with new slacks and a gray sweater a couple sizes too big that won't catch on my bandages. Once I'm satisfied with my appearance, I pick up Sigil and head upstairs. "Cale?"

No answer.

I check the bathroom, the bedroom and the kitchen, where I find a teakettle just starting to whistle on the stove. "Cale? Your water's boiling, did you want me to pour you some tea?"

No response.

Chuckling, I make a loud show of getting a teacup from the cupboards. "All right then, so I guess I should serve it *iced* instead?"

Nothing.

Okay, now I'm starting to get worried. No self-respecting Briton would ever allow iced tea in his home, even if he hasn't been to England for decades.

I move the kettle to an adjacent burner and shut off the stove, not wanting any accidents. Taking up Sigil, I return to the hallway and gently rap on the wall where the passage to the third floor opens up, my throat tight, a chill running the course of my spine.

Nothing.

Taking a breath, I tap the wall again, summoning up my will, remembering the word that got us on the train before I turned it into Marvin. The syllables flow, but only one word emerges. "*Open.*"

The flowered pattern of the wallpaper shimmers and then violently arranges into a jagged pattern resembling a doorway, going dark, some soft light from deeper in revealing the stairs. I'm about to head in, when I remember the wards and murmur "*open*" one more time. Pursing my lips, I try to keep my steps light, afraid of what I'm going to find. What if I took too long, what if...

When I reach the top, hundreds of candles illuminate the room, the ceiling dark, a massive bay window showing the rage of the storm outside, but no cold finds its way through. Suddenly music begins playing, Dinah Washington I think, the light growing to reveal a large circle drawn in the center of the room, bordered by a small bookshelf, a work table with various bottles and tools atop it.

The circle draws my attention, inscribed directly into the floor with polished brass, the symbols and etchings emanating strength, will, certainty. There is no question what the name of magic is here. I step toward it, careful not to cross the edge, and I swear I'm in Cale's presence, everything—the circle, the window, the floor, the table, the books, even the air—it all feels of *him*. Even the music... I don't know if I'll ever hear "What a Diff'rence a Day Made" the same way again.

I practically jump out of my skin when an arm slides around my waist and lips brush my ear. "You're overdressed, Apprentice."

I turn quickly to find Cale, and before I can chide him for scaring me, his mouth is pressed hard to mine, my body going slack with the sudden passion, Sigil clattering to the floor. Cale is nude, which my roaming hands readily confirm, as well as confirming something else. When we finally break our kiss, I smile. "I really hope the reason you're excited is because of me, and not because we're ending the world."

He doesn't waste time in pulling off my sweater, revealing the bandages, the pain in my arms subdued now. "Some trouble retrieving your focus?"

I shrug, tracing his tattoos with my fingers. "Just another dull task."

He appraises the wounds and gestures with his hand. "More."

I'm about to tell him. But once my pants are around my ankles and I step out of them, I don't want to postpone the moment. "Long story, I'll tell you later." I glance at the circle. "We aren't doing it in there, are we?"

Cale cocks his head to the side. "Of course, where else? It's the center of my sanctum, my place of power." He leans in, kissing me again. "Though afterward it will more be *our* place of power. I never thought I would wish to share it, much less be eager to do so, but..." Cale pulls me close, our bodies starting to gain a sheen of sweat despite the cold outside. "But I find I adore you more every time I hold you. Perhaps we were two souls split apart at some point, perhaps you and I have never been alone, because we have always been here, in this moment, waiting to arrive."

We hold each other for a minute more, relishing the warmth, the contact, the closeness, even if our union will become more physical than spiritual in the next few minutes. I take a deep breath and look at the circle. "Okay, let's do this."

Cale laughs. "It will hardly be a difficult matter. We will join and find our way back to the name of the world. Since we're both in agreement this time, there should be little problem in giving it a new name. After that the storm should lift, and you and I can..." He grins. "Celebrate?"

I snicker in response, but nod. "Definitely. So this is the method for ending the world, huh?"

"There are many methods, this is simply one of the peaceful means. Making love is symbolic of life from death, after all. The body has its *petite mort* whilst giving the essence of life. We end the world and begin it anew in a heartbeat, in a pulse. A damned sight better than impaling a man and singing a new world from his heart's blood, don't you think?"

I understandably blink. "Is that what you..."

"When I ended the world before?" He shakes his head. "Of course not, though I'd rather not discuss the details as it would ruin the mood."

I look around at the candles, glance at the Victrola that still plays on through Dinah Washington. "Yeah, is this all for the ritual?"

"Candles can be an elementary focus for beginning sorcerers, music is a powerful weaving of chaos and order and emotion, hence why one can sing up power, even to create a new world, but all of this..." He motions to the room. "This is not for the ritual, it is only for you and me."

Cale walks over to the pile of clothes where the shear, Sigil, still lies.

He brings it over to me. "You must draw your blood."

I want to step away, but I keep steady. "...why?"

He points at the circle with the shear. "Because that will not let you within its boundaries unless you do. It is my circle at the moment, but we will make it ours for a short time. The ritual should make it permanent." Cale motions to the circle. "Go on. Try to cross the edge."

Gingerly, I obey, inching up to the brass inlay of the circle which has a soft luminescence. If this were a game, I'd expect a shock, or burn, or for my character to be instantly transported to the fifth ring of hell or maybe New Jersey. Not wanting to appear too trepid, I nudge my foot toward the finely etched brass...

And it's like pushing against a brick wall.

Cale easily crosses the barrier and stands in front of me, smiling while I look to all the world like a confused mime. His grin grows wider when I shove against the barrier, the wall having no give, a thought starting to pulse through my mind that I am *not* the Recluse.

Grumbling, I shrug. "Okay, I give. So how does this work?"

"Normally I'd rather watch and enjoy the show, seeing as you're pushing and straining and working up a sweat without any attire."

I glower at him. "C'mon, Cheshire cat."

Cale narrows his eyes playfully. "Fine, fine. Spoil my fun. I'd rather you worked up a sweat in here anyway." He offers the shear, and I take it, looking at him expectantly.

"Suddenly magic doesn't seem as fun as it does in the books."

He points to the shear. "Best if you do that now. I'm certain the denizens of the city would appreciate an end to the storm."

"How much blood are we talking about here?" I extend my left hand, holding the shear over the skin of my palm. Before I can drag the blade, Cale pulls me gently toward the circle, right to the edge.

"Not too much, but there is a bit to it." He takes the shear from me and holds my left hand before taking a deep breath, and the air begins to shimmer about us, the circle's light more definite now. Cale's eyes take on a golden glow, his voice reverberating with power, his words emerging in the magical language which he named Lorus. *"I am the earth. I am the Throne. I am the Recluse, the Sorcerer King, and my word is law."*

The blade nicks my thumb, the blood dark against the brightening light. The room is filled with Cale, it seems, his will a terrible weight that threatens to drown me. If he commanded me, I fear for my ability to resist.

His eyes bore into mine, and it takes everything not to break down in tears, but I can feel words, and despite his fearful gaze, I catch the slightest of nods from him. He relinquishes the shear, and I take his left hand as well.

Sigil throbs in my grasp, but I can feel its strength bolstering me, electricity starting to race along my arms. I don't know what to say. He's right, if I screw this up I could kill us both.

And he can see my uncertainty, but I suspect he can't tell me what to say. His lips move, but no words come. Cale mouths words again, and I make it out.

Who are you?

I reach my hand to the stone around my neck and rub it gently, the blood from my cut thumb smearing an etching. My eyes flick to the St. Jude medallion he now wears. I have to trust it. I have to trust me. I respond in the same language of magic, the language that I named Sigil.

"*I am the storm. I am the Heir to the Throne. I am the Lightning Rod, and my will is reality.*" I cut his thumb and press my bleeding finger to his wound, a searing heat rushing through my body, causing the shear to drop from my hand, clattering to the floor outside the circle. When I look at Cale, he's smiling.

"Our blood is one. My circle is open to you."

I feel a hard wind buffet my face, and I stagger back. But I don't feel tired or drained. I feel amazing, actually. All around me I'm conscious of every plank of wood, every bit of brass in the circle, even the energy moving through the air, and I could command it all, if I so desired. Cale's right, ending the world and beginning it again will be a trivial matter.

Here, I could do *anything*.

"Is this how you feel all the time?" I lean into him, kissing along the nape of his neck, the rush of power having an effect on me. "God, I don't know why you'd ever leave."

"Because in this room, my love, it is very difficult to remember that I am human. And now that my sanctum is aware of your blood and will accept you..." He pulls me into the circle, and I nearly collapse from the sudden surge, every cell of my body feeling alive and exultant. He picks me up and carries me to the center of the circle where Lorus is already planted, the blade aflame with the light of many suns, but somehow not blinding or burning.

Once I'm on my back in the innermost circle, Cale kneels next to me and kisses me for the space of a breath before straddling my waist. "I never believed I would have to end the world again. I certainly wouldn't have dreamed it would happen in this way. But then I never expected my solitude to end, or that I could find love in my gilded cage." His fingers trail gently along my chest. "Thank you for proving me wrong."

I inhale sharply when his hand slips about my length, and he whispers the spell to ease my way into him.

The circle's intensity grows, shards of ice and sparks of lightning beginning to arc between the etched symbols in the brass as Cale lowers himself onto me.

It comes quickly now, my thoughts muddling with his, the name of our love racing to our lips with ease, the syllables dancing through the air, I can feel us joining, we can feel everything, we can... We are...

I am complete.

And I know my purpose now.

I expand my perception outward, an immense tangle of names in the shape of towers and roads, a great and terrible thing hovering overhead, a storm, a disturbing mesh of fearful names, shattered memories. Strange, it seems oddly familiar, but it matters not. I will leave this world behind, and this storm can rage to exhaustion in an empty reality.

I push out further, find the names of the gods, names that shine with power and purpose. I can feel their anger, and a name that burns with dark light charges from a tower to the east, toward me, but I care little for a god's quest.

So I push out further.

There is only the tapestry now, the three bright and shining names now a single distorted moniker. The storm is wreaking havoc on the weaving, a rapid fraying of threads.

The name in the tapestry, the name of the world, it is nearly lost now. The power is immeasurable, but I could claim it, assert my will...

And use it for what? The storm will eventually tear the threads asunder, leaving nothing to weave anew. I can see that now.

But I will change that.

I reach for the name. I am the Ra'keth. The tools to discard the many additions, strip it to the core are mine, innate to my being, to my throne. It will be a trivial matter.

Far beneath, the bodies of James and Cale call to me. Their love will drag me back, split me again, but not before I accomplish my purpose. Not before I give the name of their...my...love to the world.

I feel the word reach me, and I open my mouth, smiling as I prepare to push aside the old world and give life to the new, to name it *Qa'ne*—

No.

Something is wrong. No.

No!

Cale gurgles softly as I open my eyes, my body aching, head pounding as we're forced back into ourselves, the Ra'keth we were torn violently asunder. His face is shocked, confused, a grimace of pain as he falls forward, pinning me to the floor. His breath is weak, slow.

Oh God, what happened?

"Cale?"

I wrap my arms about him, try to roll him onto his side, but my body freezes when my fingers brush against something on his back.

Something sticking out of his back.

My shear. My Sigil.

And my hand returns to my gaze, red with his blood.

"The king is dead." Heath steps into the center of the ring and yanks Lorus free from the floor. He smiles cruelly down at me, the blade lighting with fire in his grasp, his words emerging in perfect Sigil. "*Long live the king.*"

Chapter Twenty-Five

"What, you gonna cry?" Heath's face creases in a one-sided smirk.

I shake Cale. His eyes are still open, his mouth trying to form words. My mind races. I try to find words that will seal the wound in him, stop the bleeding. God, so much blood...

"Tell me the word, Heath. Please, I saw you use it. I'll do anything you want. Please, God, Heath, just let him live."

"No." My face is slapped by the flat of the sword, the fire lancing pain through my cheek. "I followed the Usurper's Decree in its original intent for a change. End of story. That I did it while you were fucking him was just gravy."

I get Cale onto his side, and he stares at Heath dumbfounded, his eyes darting between him and me. "What..."

"Nothing you need to worry about." Heath kicks Cale in the stomach hard. "You should thank me, you'll never have to find out what a lousy lay he is."

This is still our circle. Our place of power. Where my will is reality. And I'll burn every memory in my head for this.

I extend my hand at Heath. *"Lightning."*

The room dims slightly as the bolt arcs from my outstretched fingers...

And is claimed by the sword.

"Please, Miles, you're embarrassing yourself." Heath chuckles as he exits into an outer circle. "You already made this so easy for me. You had me dead to rights and you leave me locked in a *car*? I'm the *Frozen River*, Miles. I've seen *hell* thanks to you. You think a snowstorm's going to matter? I thought it was going to be hard to find you..." He produces the silk tie that had been in the shop's window. "But you left me a beacon to

follow. I didn't even have to worry about that wall he put up."
He flourishes the shear, still wet with blood from Cale and me.
"You left this within reach for easy access through the barrier."
His chuckle grows to a laugh. "Honestly, Miles, I think you
wanted me to kill him."

I pull Cale close to me, whisper to him, comfort him. "Cale,
tell me how to fix it, how do I heal you?"

"You don't." A woman is standing at the top of the stairs,
long red hair, a shark's smile and a pair of blades in her hands,
wearing a chauffeur's uniform. Kerry, Hades's driver. She
shivers in anticipation as she moves toward the circle, but stops
just at the border, a force keeping her out. "He was stabbed
with a god's blade. There is no healing from that." She licks her
lips, eyeing Cale hungrily.

Heath lowers the blade, steps toward her and points at her
with a flirty smile. "Death goddess, right?"

While his attention is diverted, I hold Cale's face in my
hands. "Hold still, you'll just make it worse."

A sudden choking sound draws me back to Heath, and I
find him still holding that flirting smile, the one he wore the day
we met, the smile that got me in bed with him. Kerry isn't
smiling. She's not doing much of anything, but that changes
quickly when Heath yanks the sword backward, and the woman
collapses in a heap, becoming a pile of ash.

"One down." Heath glances back at me. "I know what you
and the Recluse were doing. Ending the world, and I agree with
you. That's some shit that needs to be done, but I doubt you'd
address the real problems."

I glare at him, my face wet. "Why, damn it, *why*?"

"Why what..." He points at Cale. "What, him?" He sucks in
a deep breath. "Fuck, Miles, you can't imagine how certain I am
of *everything* right now. He was the one on the throne, so I took
it. And you?" Heath grins the same one-sided smirk. "There is
no you, Miles. There is only me."

"Fuck you. If you're going to kill me, just get it over with." I
squeeze Cale's hand, and he weakly squeezes back. Cale shakes
his head, dark veins starting to spread across his face.

"You're the one who wants to live without me, Miles. So I'll let you. And you can die alone." He spits hard into the circle. "Because I'm going to leave you here, in this world, and make a new one."

I hold my breath, cross the veil in the midst of a flash of crimson mist.

The sanctum is no longer dark, the circle instead ablaze with silver light. Heath is gone.

I'll deal with him later.

I run to the table where I saw papers and books. One of them will have a spell.

I tear through them, nothing frozen in place here, my will still law. My lungs ache and burn as I read poetry and notes on ritual by the light of the circle. My breath bursts out in a hail of heavy coughs, the room going dark, but I fight it off.

I hold my breath again.

I feel weaker now. I shouldn't have done it so soon, but I'll gladly pay for it later. I am a sorcerer, damn it. I am beyond the grasp of Fate. I will not let Cale die.

Spells to make fire, to repair clothing, to summon insects, to conjure water and food, to keep the edge on a blade, to make a tree grow, to birth dreams and slay nightmares. Nothing to turn back time. Nothing to heal a cut. Nothing to raise the dead.

Another explosion of coughing brings back time to me again.

"James." Cale's voice is getting softer.

I hold my breath.

My body is trembling, crashing. I lean heavily on the table, flip through the pages slowly, my eyes need to focus hard on the words to make them legible. The light of the circle grows dimmer. I pick up the fattest book and return to Cale. When I find the spell I need, I don't want to wait. Not if. When.

Another hard cough, my lungs burning as I return from the other side. I read the spell on the page before me.

"I'm not cursed, James." He reaches for my hand, and I quickly take it. "James, it's all right."

"I can fix this. Just—"

"Kiss me, James." The words were almost slurred, spaced apart.

"I know I'll find it, Cale."

His eyes meet mine, the feline Mark gone. My God, his eyes are like looking at Destry Bay just after dawn. There's light in them that I know is there even as it fade—

No.

"Please."

Cale shivers, his skin pale.

"Don't make me say goodbye, Cale."

If I cry, I'll be admitting it. I can't. Not yet.

I lean close. His breathing is shallow.

"Remember me. Please." His expression is pained, but I can tell he is trying to smile. Make it easier. "Don't forget me."

"Never."

"Everything I am, everything I know, Apprentice, I grant to you."

Please, God. Please don't let it happen. Just give me the miracle right now.

Please.

I hold my breath.

I only want a few more seconds. Another shade of a minute where Cale's eyes still have a light, where his skin holds warmth, where he can hold me and chide me for bad pronunciation, straighten my tie, touch my face. I want him to be with me just a little longer before...

Before he'll be a body.

I stay in the dark waters of Tartarus, surrounded by silver light that wavers softly, for as long as my will allows me.

"I love you, Apprentice."

I press my lips to his. He returns it for a second and exhales long as his body goes still, my body warmed a moment by his final breath.

"I love you, Cheshire cat."

I hold him close until I finally stop crying. I can't tell how long.

Around me the room goes dark, the power and certainty of the sanctum draining away from it, from me. The only light is the gentle glow of the stone, the illumination not carrying very far. The room is growing cold.

"I'm sorry, kid." Hades steps into the small area of light, the bleakness of the room only darkening the perceived color of his suit. "You're going to have to let me take him."

I hold Cale tighter to me. "No."

"James, he's dead." The god doesn't sound at all concerned, more like a parent dealing with a stubborn child. Fine.

"Fuck you." I fight back a fresh bout of tears. "You can't have him. Why are you here anyway?"

"For starters, one of my employees was brutally murdered while trying to retrieve an errant Keth." He motions to Cale. "And when the Ra'keth dies, I collect the soul personally." Hades narrows his eyes at Cale. "Especially *this* one. And you're not going to stand in my way, kid."

"What did he ever do to you?" I drag Cale away, or try, as he's heavy.

"You've heard of Zeus, no doubt? My younger brother, who ruled over us all, the god of lightning?" He doesn't wait for me to answer. "This world we're in now was grown from his blood, extracted by one swing of the Claw of Shoshare, which killed him. The Recluse did that. You can understand I might want to savor this moment."

My lip trembles as the rage rises within me, sparks of silver dancing along my hands. "You killed..."

"Before we start pointing fingers..." He produces a bag from the air and tosses it next to me. "We can at least discuss this civilly, so I figure you could dress as such. I don't care to negotiate with those who literally have nothing to hide." Hades turns his back to me, the room is growing colder. Already I'm shivering, and I can't think straight enough to do a simple warmth spell without overblowing it and setting the building ablaze. So I concede the point and dress myself with the clothes from the bag—a tailored suit, all deep gray, a woolen overcoat, and black wing tips.

"Happy?"

"Not in my nature, I'm afraid. Now, I would like to state for the record that I don't kill people. I'm not the god of death, I'm the god of the underworld. I run a bureaucracy that humanity makes more complicated for me with each passing century. That is my job. That is my *purpose*. And no matter how much enjoyment I'll take in collecting the soul of the sorcerer who murdered my brother, I would be here if he were a living saint. Collecting dead Ra'keth and delivering them for judgment is one of my *many* responsibilities, and you are not going to prevent me from carrying it out."

I extend my lightning-sheathed hand toward him. "Watch me."

He turns to face me and flashes his million-dollar smile. "I hereby call in your debt to me, Anu'keth." The god shrugs. "Considering you didn't end up the Ra'keth, there's little point in hanging on to the marker."

I blink and feel a strong compulsion to pull away from Cale, the feeling buttressed by magic...my magic. "Would any of this have happened if you hadn't pulled me out of that river?"

Hades snickers and produces a cigarette, lighting it on the electricity still arcing between my fingers. "No clue, kid. I'll admit you caught me by surprise. To think one of my golf buddies would have a kid who's a sorcerer."

"Wait, you know my dad? Why didn't you ever say anything?"

"Why would I need to? I pulled you out of the river, didn't I? Put you with the dragon? But that's as far as I'll go looking out for you." He rolls his eyes. "Miles Coltrane Clapton Canmore. I told your dad he was begging to get you beaten up with a name like that. But the man loves his jazz and your mom loves *Slowhand*, so what can you do." He shrugs. "To be honest, I should've seen this coming, but I've been busy with other things."

"Seen what coming?"

"You've got six older brothers, so does your old man. That makes you the seventh son of a seventh son, untimely ripped instead of born on a day where the veil between worlds is thinnest..." The god *hmmm*s. "Actually, scratch that, you were born the day after, but still good enough for government work. Throw in a few interesting folks here and there back a ways in the family tree, and you get a born Anu'keth. And they tend to have dark destinies that take out half the world before they end it." He motions to the storm outside.

I don't remark regarding the weather. I feel bad enough as it is. Besides, while he's talking, he's not taking Cale.

"Sorcerers don't have destinies, you were the one who told me that."

The god nods in agreement. "Indeed, but you only leave the loom of Fate once you awaken to your power. Would you like an analogy?" Again, he doesn't wait for me to answer. "Imagine you're walking a fenced-in path. You can only follow it, right? You spend years of your life walking along the path, not knowing any other way. Now imagine the fences vanish. You're free to explore, but the path still stretches out before you. Chances are, you'll follow the path because it's what you know, and you're confident it'll lead somewhere. Put simply, just because you aren't tied to your fate anymore doesn't mean you won't choose to follow it."

I grit my teeth. "You didn't think to tell me this when we first met?"

"You think I'm going to tell a half-drowned abuse survivor that I'd just pulled out of the North River that he'll likely cause the deaths of nine million people? You'd kill yourself in a week, and there's no way I'm letting a wrecking ball like you end up the personal property of hell for committing a mortal sin." He folds his arms. "Now if you wouldn't mind, I need to take Cale for processing. You might be mourning, but right now his soul is still in his body and impaled on a Shear of Atropos. I guarantee that he is suffering, and as much as I personally enjoy that, even I have my limits. If he's to be punished, he'll work it off in Tartarus."

"He's really in pain?"

Hades steps closer. "Excruciating." He kneels by Cale and produces a clipboard from within his coat, the bottom already signed in...

"Hades? What's the name of magic?"

He glances at me for a second. "Sigil, what else would it be called?"

It has the name I gave it. Heath didn't think to rename magic when he killed Cale. Can I use that?

Hades taps the clipboard. "I'll need you to sign that, it requires a witness."

I sniff back tears again, signing next to the red tag. "I hate you."

He puts the signed form back inside his coat. "I know you do, kid. But I'm confident you'll get past it." The god of the underworld brushes his fingers over Cale's eyes, closing them. "And that's it. Now that we're even, would you mind doing me a favor?"

I steel myself, my eyes boring into his. "The man I love was just murdered, you took his soul, and you have the gall to ask me a favor?"

He butts out his cigarette on the deadened brass of the circle. "Technically since I'm not human, I don't have any gall. And given the situation, that is why what I ask will be considered a favor."

"How do I know you'll pay me back?"

He shrugs gently. "I'll swear it on Styx."

I perk a brow. "The river or the band?"

"The one that means more to me."

The god pulls the shear cleanly from the body.

"What do you want me to do with that?"

"Your ex-lover is going to end the world tonight, kid, and take every living soul in the City with him, which means a truly

Sisyphean amount of paperwork I'd like to avoid, and trust me when I say I know the meaning of Sisyphean. I want you to return this to Heath."

Hades puts the blade in my hand. "Preferably in his heart."

Part IV

Uprising

.

Chapter Twenty-Six

Hades vanished seconds after I accepted the shear. He took Cale with him. I'm alone.

The sanctum is dark, cold. Lorus is gone, claimed by Heath. It was supposed to die with Cale. I guess Heath broke that rule, but then, he's the Ra'keth now. He sets the rules.

Only the stone remains as a beacon of certainty. I use its light to lead me downstairs, averting my eyes from the books, the rugs, the paintings on the walls as I descend to the shop. All of it is just a reminder of what happened not fifteen minutes ago.

I don't want to be here anymore.

The urges war inside me, devouring each other, a cold slipping in, savage and soothing as the storm outside. I glance at the shear in my hand, wet with blood as I lean against the counter.

The windows and door are glowing faintly, the frames laced with Sigil, Heath's work, no doubt, to delay me so he can go through with his plan, and I doubt he'd be willing to step down. The Usurper's Decree will apply.

One of us has to die.

And it will not be me.

The door refuses to budge, and the knob stings coldly when I touch it. I hold the stone toward it, focusing my will, and I aim it toward the door. *"Knock."*

The runes on the frame glow brightly before a force throws me back into a rack of coats, a torrent of words flooding my mind, all smug in tone, Heath's voice. *By decree of the Ra'keth, these portals are sealed to all, save the Sorcerer King.*

So no way out, unless I want to go back up to the sanctum and try jumping out the window there. No chance of that, I'm not a fan of heights.

"Same fucking trick he did at the old apartment and I still can't beat it. Christ, you'd think I could figure this out considering how much I played..." I stop and grin.

I wag my finger at the windows and door. "You only sealed the portals. Not the building. It's okay, Heath. Rookie mistake." Summoning my will, I lift the stone and direct my hand toward a vacant stretch of wall. "*Open.*"

There's an explosion of force, a four-foot-wide jagged hole appearing in the brick, debris showering into the snow outside. As I step through it into the storm, I check the still-sealed portals from the front of the shop. "Don't worry, Heath, but keep that in mind when you roll up your next character."

After slipping the shear in my inside coat pocket, I pour my will into the stone, its warmth flowing freer now, but it won't push outward into an orb and hold back the snow, or allow me to see where I'm going. I reach my will far above into the storm. I created it, God help me, but it's still mine, those are *my* memories up there, damn it.

I'm struck to the ground by a sudden force, Heath's laughter and a decree echoing on the wind. He closed it off from me. All I have to draw on is myself, and I need that to keep myself alive. I'm too far from 90th and V to get back to Marvin, even if he could go along the tracks with the storm this intense.

He's probably scared too. Alone.

To think I was going to name him Shadowfax, I am hardly the Gray Wizard. Hell, I'm not even my mage Radcliffe, and I can't even play *him* as competent. Dave had to have him saved from certain death by...

Wait.

I'm still Keth, and dragons serve the Keth.

I proceed into the center of the intersection and hold the stone aloft. I need to give this some juice to make sure I can be found. The warmth cuts out and the wind cuts in, pounding into my back as I force the words into being, the air reverberating with power as I call to the only dragon I know with some pull.

"Broodmother of the Crimson Flight, I beseech your aid and advice. The Lightning Rod requests your presence." The stone glows brightly despite the snow, forcing me to avert my eyes as I struggle to keep myself standing in the driving wind.

There's no guarantee that she's around, but I have to believe. I have to be *certain* that my words broke through the gale and found her. I have to *will* my light to shine.

I crumple into the snow, still weakly holding the stone aloft, the glow strong but dimming, the ever-rising blanket of white starting to claim me.

"Jutte!"

I can't...

I fall back into the snow, only to be snapped up suddenly, the street receding quickly into a vast field of white as the sound of thunder and wind grows all around me, though the beating of massive wings accompanies it all. Above me I see only crimson scales as we climb and climb and climb, the air growing cold against me.

Below I see vague shadows of gray, buildings that we pass over. I would guess we're into Beckettsville by now. I funnel my will back into the memory of warmth, taking solace in my renewed ability to breathe and retain heat.

The dragon descends suddenly, nearly into a dive as the roof of a four-story parking garage comes into view. She pulls up quickly, releasing me into a corner mound of plowed snow, which softens the impact but still hurts like hell. A sudden roar fills the air, the roof strafed by fire, and I burrow back into the drift as the flames melt the snow off the cars and bathe them in the conflagration on the following pass. Deafening explosions punch through the air as three cars are set ablaze, still burning despite the storm as the dragon lands beside them, assuming a human form, staying close to the heat while she beckons me forth from my impromptu hidey-hole.

"You called, Sorcerer?"

I brush the snow from my coat as I make my way toward her, the flaming wrecks providing enough warmth for me to drop my spell and form a wall of ice to act as a windbreak and keep the fires from going out, as well as let us speak without having to yell. She appraises the barrier and nods in approval. "I see you have been endeavoring to improve yourself."

Not really, I just knew the words, words that Cale knew.

"Jutte, I need your help."

The dragon smiles curtly. "So it would seem. It is rare that a Keth shows such manners when summoning one of the Dracon Council. I am curious why you request my help. Our seers tell us that the Recluse has been usurped."

I blink. "How could you know that already?"

She doesn't lose that smile. "We are dragons, Keth. It is our purpose to know the ways of your kind and when the order of things is shaken. The Frozen River has taken the throne." Her courteousness cracks a moment. "He has...unorthodox plans for the new world."

"Sorcerers don't have fates or destinies. How can you know what we're going to do?"

"We don't. The seers tell us what you are doing, not what you will do. There was not always one Ra'keth, Sorcerer. Dragons were used as spies as well as protectors."

"Why didn't you tell me any of this before?"

She furrows her brow, confused. "You are not our king."

"So what's the council going to do about Heath?"

"The council has decided to wait and see. The Frozen River will end the world, as needed, but it is difficult to say if the world he will create will be any better off. That is why I am able to speak with you, why this action is simply unethical rather than treasonous."

"Wait, they already decided, in the last half-hour? Isn't the council in Europe, how could you all have already decided?"

She taps her head. "We are always in constant communication." Her smile returns. "We were designed *quite* well, Sorcerer."

"So you'll help me find him? Put him down?" I brandish the shear to make my point.

"Even if I could render aid, would you ever trust me or the council afterward? Advice is all I can give, I apologize." She bows deeply.

"Jutte, you know if I succeed then I'll be your king. Wouldn't you rather have me on the throne?"

She smiles curtly. "It would be treasonous to give you aid." The dragon glances to her left, gazing at the solid wall of ice. "But should you succeed in your usurpation, the council will ask one thing of you."

"That being?"

"Our name, Sorcerer." She steps toward me. "We crave certainty. Stability. The Frozen River plots to remake all magic in his own image. Make all of the silver blood his devoted servants. That..." a plume of smoke escapes her nose, quickly claimed by the wind, "...*child* wants to take our name from us."

"And what name is that?"

She leans closely to me, her lips nearly brushing my ear as she whispers the syllables, nine of them.

I nod. "It stays the same."

"And you will take a protector."

I shake my head at her as I pull away. "No, I told you I don't want one."

She folds her arms. "You wish to know where the Frozen River is?"

Fuck.

"Fine." I fight back the grumbles of frustration. "I'll take a damned protector."

"It is agreed, then. While I cannot tell you the Ra'keth's exact location..." Her gaze alters focus, off behind me. When I turn I see that the storm is beginning to calm, snowwise at least, the cold and wind remaining. The sky is filled with oppressive clouds, all of them seeming to pull toward the west, spiraling over a single point, several flashes of lightning striking the highest point in the City, Victory Tower. Far above the sky is turning red, veins of crimson reaching outward from the center of the spiral, moving farther with each moment. The dragon finishes her statement. "He should not be difficult to find."

Behind me as I gape, I hear the sudden beating of wings, and I turn quickly enough to see Jutte as she climbs high into the clouds, presumably above the storm.

I call for ice to create a curving ramp from the roof of the parking structure down to the street. The slide down is fast, terrifying, but I only end up in another snowbank for my efforts, uninjured, and safe at ground level. I pick myself up, dust myself off, reinvoke the spell of warmth and start walking toward the 90th and V station.

And so began the last night of the world.

Chapter Twenty-Seven

"What the hell do you mean, I need to get out of here?"

It took...a while to get Marvin going to the 65th and L station, but I'm not about to let my only friend freeze to death. I've lost enough tonight. I went in through the side door to find Dave huddled in the kitchen of the diner, the grill running at full strength, which isn't that strong given how cold the room is. His movements are sluggish, voice drunk sounding, but at least he's still alive.

"Are you okay?" The radio is on, but it's a static-filled repetition of the Emergency Broadcast System's warnings about the storm. Seek immediate and adequate shelter. No travel except for dire emergencies. Conserve power, warmth and food.

"Damned sorcerers made us cold-blooded. Do I look like a reptile to you?" He manages a half-hearted glare. "Don't answer that."

"Dave, haven't you noticed the crimson spiral of death hovering over Victory Tower?"

"Yeah, so? World's ending. Figured you'd be helping the Recluse with that, seeing as you two are chummy." When I don't respond, he turns slowly, mostly from the cold but also apprehension, and faces me. I can't bring myself to say the words, but he can read me well enough. "Oh...I mean...I felt something an hour ago but... The Recluse is really dead?"

I close my eyes. "Heath killed him. And now he's on the throne and preparing to end the world."

The dragon blinks at me. "So what the fuck are you doing here? Go!"

"Dave, I can't leave you to freeze to death." But what can I do... Wait. "Hold on."

I take off the stone and push my will upon it, the etchings glowing brightly with silver light, and I motion for Dave to lean his head forward. "You're going to do me a favor and watch over this for me, okay? On the off chance I die a brutal death, I don't want our new Sorcerer King to get his hands on this. It's all I have left of Cale, and I'll be damned if it ends up a trophy for the guy who killed him."

I hang the stone about his neck, and he visibly sighs in relief. "What'd you do, Black? Feels like I'm wearing a space heater."

"You pretty much are. I'm going to get some gloves and a hat from upstairs. It's a long walk to Victory Square."

Before I can leave the kitchen, though, a voice comes from the diner proper. "You're going back out in that?"

I find Spencer, his clothing caked with snow and ice, his skin pale from the cold.

"Jesus, Spencer, what the fuck are you doing here?"

He's shivering heavily, and I pull him to me to share warmth, draw on myself slightly to create some heat and prevent hypothermia. He hugs me tightly, desperately. "He wasn't home, my roommate. It was cold and dark in there..." The Coyote manages a weak, forced smile. "I couldn't think of anywhere else to go. My family would let me freeze, I'm not in good enough with the Fae, the Kitsune don't think that highly of me since the noodle incident..." Spencer meets my eyes. "I didn't want to die alone."

I hold his face in my hands, the conjured warmth flowing off my exposed fingers. "And now you think a half-frozen Coyote is just what I need?"

Weakly, he nods. "You're still a sorcerer. Safest place in this city is right behind you."

"It's better if you stay here with Dave. That stone around his neck should keep the two of you warm as long as he keeps the stove running."

Almost on cue, a whirring and grinding sound comes from the kitchen. Dave pokes his head through. "Generator's out.

Thank the gods you got here, Black." He taps the stone. "I'd have been dead in a few minutes."

I look out toward the sky. "Well har-de-har and fuck you too, Murphy."

Spencer gives me a dubious look. "Well, you *did* sort of invoke it. You might as well have asked what else could possibly—"

My hand quickly covers his mouth. "Finish that sentence and I'll transmute your prostate into a pound of butter. I'm a sorcerer, I can make it happen. This is by far the worst night of my life, and the only way I can think to cap it off on a high note is making sure it's not the worst night of *everyone's* lives." I take my hand back. "Stay here with Dave. I've lost enough people tonight."

Spencer quirks a brow. "What do you mean by..." He reads my expression. "Shit... By *lost* you mean your boyfriend..." He closes his eyes after I nod. "Fuck, man, I'm sorry."

"I have to go, okay? Time's a wasting, and I need to kill his killer." I start toward the door, feeling the power surging through the air.

"No." Spencer blocks the doorway, folding his arms. "No way you're going out there like this."

I narrow my eyes. "Spencer, move. God only knows how much time we have, okay?"

"James, your boyfriend was just murdered—"

"And you want me to what... Cry? Did that. Do the five stages? Can't do denial as he was stabbed to death *on top of me.* Bargaining? You want me contacting entities that *could* bring him back?" I don't give him time to respond. "No? Then what, depression? Great, I'll get drunk and listen to jazz while the whole goddamned world ends. What's next, acceptance? Move on? It just happened tonight so *fuck that.*"

I get right in his face, my lips trembling. "All that leaves me is anger, Spencer, and I'll be damned if you're going to take that away from me."

"He's the damned Ra'keth, James. Look at you. You're half-dead already, he'll kill you or you'll kill yourself taking him out. Just…" He grits his teeth. "Do you really want to end up standing over Heath's broken body with a knife in your hand asking yourself 'My God, what have I done?' Please, just…*think*."

"He took Cale's life. I'm taking his. Fair trade. Now move, Spencer. I will invoke your name if I have to."

He sets his jaw. "No."

I summon up what power I can. "*Spencer—*"

He covers my mouth. "No. You're not going out there alone. You need someone to keep you grounded." The Coyote matches my gaze as he drops his hand, his voice edged with fearful determination. "I'm coming with you."

"The hell you are."

"I'll just follow you if you leave. And you don't know my whole name, so no, you can't command me. You're not going to face this alone, James."

"Black." Dave pokes his head through the pass-through. "Please. Take him along."

Damn it. "Fine. It's going to be a bitch keeping both of us warm, you know that, right?" Grumbling, I push past him and out into the night, the Coyote in tow.

I can't draw on myself to power the spell or we'll be long dead before we reach 65th and L, much less able to get Marvin going to Victory Station. Only one thing I can think of.

The cold is biting, the wind cutting at my skin as I stride into the center of the street.

Holy fuck, this is going to hurt so much…

"James? What are you doing?" I barely hear Spencer through the wind, but I don't respond.

Heath tried to close off the storm from me, but it is *my* storm, and I am the Lightning Rod. He will not take anything further from me.

I raise my hand to the sky.

"*Lightning!*"

The first bolt brings me to my knees. The second bolt brings agony, my chest heavy. The third bolt hits like a shower of nails, my mind unable to form thought, the spark within me crackling and forking and pulsating with the same four words again and again...

I do not fall.

With the fourth bolt my vision goes white. The fifth, it goes black.

Through the void that has become my senses, I feel something in the darkness, a comfort...

Everything I am, love, I grant to you.

You will never fall.

...never fall...

Never fall.

Something touches me, some time later. I don't really feel much, just the sensation of movement as I'm nudged again. It takes a second to regain some semblance of vision, for the loud ringing to dissipate and to make out that words are being spoken. Smoke rises off me and is quickly claimed by the winds.

I wave my hand weakly, but confidently. "*Warmth.*"

The orb leaps out from me, the visibility clearing as the air calms within. Spencer has knelt before me, inspecting but clearly afraid to touch me, the reason for which becomes apparent as electricity continues to jump along my body. Staggering to my feet, I take a moment to catch my breath, my pulse racing from the energy, the spark within having grown to a tempest. I need to expel some of it, and I've got the perfect place to start.

"Follow me." I don't turn to see if he's behind me. I dash for the station, the power flowing through my being fueling my pace despite my exhaustion. The snow melts as I move, creating a wide and watery path, but thankfully the lightning caged within me doesn't use it as an easy way out.

Getting up the stairs at the station proves more difficult than I expected. Every few seconds my muscles start seizing, bringing me to my knees again.

"You okay? You're not looking too good, James."

"I'll be fine..." But to hear my voice... It reverberates, distorts in the wind.

"James, your face is *cracking*. You need to stop whatever you're doing!"

"Just..." The sparks are starting to jump off me now, my will fading. "Just get me on the train."

Arms hook under my shoulders, the power wanting to jump into the adjacent body, surge through it, consume it, and I do my best to hold back, focusing all my concentration on keeping it in check. Someone shouts, screaming in pain before I'm practically thrown onto metallic floor.

In front of me is a circle, but I can't reach it, if I try to move I'll lose control. The energy will release and kill both of us, destroy Marvin. Oh God, just let me reach the circle...

I hear screaming as someone takes my hand, the power sending shocks through the connection just before my palm is yanked forward and slapped down into the circle. The energy jumps from me into the enchantment, sending lances of electricity through the rails to melt the ice, the lights in the train coming to life as the car goes into motion. The energy expels, drains, heat drawing lines in my skin, closing wounds. Slowly, I return to myself, my face warm and wet, my hand smearing the circle with my blood.

"Are you well, master?" Marvin's voice is decidedly not all that cheery.

I answer with a series of hacking coughs just before I dry heave.

Spencer is slumped against the door to the cabin, eyes half-lidded, his right hand burned and bloody. He whimpers softly as the shock begins to fade. I manage to crawl over to him, and he shrinks away from my touch at first, before seeing no sparks dance between my fingers. Half-chuckling, half-sobbing from pain, he works a small smile. "Told you that you needed a sidekick."

"You gonna live?"

"I'd cut my hand off if I thought it'd hurt less, but that'd really fuck up my monte." He grimaces as he flexes his fingers. "Oh fuck, I hope you sorcerers know how to heal people."

I shake my head. "If I did this night would've gone a lot different." I look up toward the speakers. "We're okay, Marvin. We need to get to Victory Station, all right?"

There's no response, but the train continues moving. Maybe he just doesn't know what to say.

"So how did...you know..." Spencer looks away a second. "I mean, if you're up to talking about it."

"How'd my boyfriend die?"

Spencer nods.

"We were ending the world, starting a new one. And then... Heath stabbed him to death." The words leave my lips before I can stop them. "Cale is dead because you left Heath alive." I motion to the reddening sky. "All of this is because you left that motherfucker alive."

His eyes bore into mine. "I am not a killer. And I didn't kill your boyfriend, that guy did. We could play indirect what-if scenarios all fucking night, but at the end of the day, it wasn't me holding the knife." Spencer shoves me lightly with his good hand. "So back the fuck off." He motions out at the storm as well. "Because no matter whose damned fault it is, *that* needs to be stopped."

We match glares for a few more seconds. I'm the first one to break.

"You're right. We have bigger worries."

Spencer nods. "Like, for starters, you looking like a comic-book villain. At least wipe the blood off your face."

My sleeves are wet and dirty already, so I don't see the harm in staining them further. Marvin continues along through the awkward silence as Beckettsville gives way to Allora in the passing cityscape. Spencer uses the last of the gauze from the first aid kit under the seats to bandage his hand and shuffles a few cards to pass the time, four aces and a joker, though his moves are slow and uneasy due to his wound.

"Thank you for coming along." I glance at him. "Sorry about your hand."

"Still works. I know a guy who can fix it, but it'll end up tattooed. No idea why. Any suggestion on what kind of ink I should get?"

"Nothing tribal, no barbed wire. You'll look like an idiot. Or a criminal."

He shrugs. "It'll be scarred regardless. Might as well get something flashy so people notice it on my terms."

I take out the shear, look at it a few seconds. "I have to kill him, Spencer. It's the Usurper's Decree: the only way to dethrone a Ra'keth is to kill him."

"Well, I don't know anything about that, James. What I do know is that's not the reason you're killing him." He chews his lip. "If there's any other way, just promise me you'll try."

"Spence..."

He looks at me, pleading. *"Promise."*

"All right. I'll try." Besides, Heath will likely let me off the hook for that one.

When we finally reach Victory Station, we're beneath the tower. The station is lit, but deserted, some residual warmth remaining in the air. My gait is slowed, more of a limp. Spence offers his shoulder, keeping his cards fanned out in his good hand.

"Why on earth would you have those here? I doubt Heath wants to play the shell game for the fate of the world."

The Coyote manages a knowing smile. "It's Three Card Monte, and that's not it. I stole a fox's tail, and God, did I ever pay for it, but it's a handy trick."

"You stole a what?"

Spencer makes his way to the bank of elevators, mashing buttons for the ones assigned to the upper floors.

"A fox's tail. Not...literally. It means I lifted a trick off a Kitsune." He flashes a coyote smile as the elevator opens. "Amazed this is still running."

We both enter and I punch the button for the top floor. The tower is, according to the building directory, 1,622 feet from the south entrance to the tip of the antenna on the roof, so I don't even want to consider how many stairs that will be.

On cue to Spencer's comment, though, the lights flicker within, the Muzak version of "Can't Help Falling in Love" slurring back and forth across the appropriate speed. Still, we're on the way to the 106th floor, observation deck. Exhaling hard, I press my palm to the panel, let the remaining power ebb from my body into the car, the doors shutting smoothly as the Muzak shifts to "Don't Stop Believin'". The elevator goes into motion shortly after, the numbers on the display climbing. It's probably a waste of power, but we're running short on time, and the prospect of getting stuck or plummeting sixty-three floors is not my cup of tea.

"How did you do that?"

I shrug, leaning against the wall. "When I was little my dad took me up to the observation deck. Terrified of heights ever since, but the elevator ride, he picked me up to push the button for the top floor. All I did, really, was invoke that memory, and fueled it with my will."

"It still doesn't explain the Journey."

"Oh." I try to grin. "Wizard did it?"

To that, he laughs. "Try to hold on to that sense of humor for me, okay?"

I don't feel much strength left in me magicwise, but as the elevator grows closer to the observation floor, I feel something else that's growing closer.

Lorus. Cale's sword, his focus. That Heath stole.

The observation deck is near dark when the doors open to an array of benches, informational signs about the tower itself, its construction, the few lights outside the window providing weak illumination.

I keep myself vigilant, motioning for Spencer to follow silently, as this is the perfect place to lay traps. After a moment we continue toward the far side, the door hanging off its hinges, flickering fluorescents within revealing stairs going up, the ambient light from the doorway just enough to make the sign above legible: *Roof Access.*

We climb the final flight of stairs, and I push my way through the door onto the roof of Victory Tower.

I enter another world.

The railings of the roof's edge are replaced with a stonework wall about five feet high, tall parapets at the corners. The antenna is gone, the roof as a whole relatively barren save a massive circle etched into the surface, which has been altered into a smooth deep-gray stone. The runes etched in Sigil inside the circle glow a sickly red, several rings making up the circle proper, a bastardization of Cale's sanctum. Above, the sky looks close enough to touch. Lightning arcs across the gaping eye of the storm. There's no wind, even as I hear a deathly howl rising and falling in a strange but steady rhythm.

Heath stands just outside the innermost ring, dressed in white, his clothes adorned with Sigil runes that dance in a vibrant crimson to match the sky. He holds Lorus toward the eye of the storm, coaxing down a blood-red funnel that pulses with veins of black every few seconds. His gaze falls from his work to me, and he smiles.

"*Silence.*" The word echoes through the heavens, a visible force that thankfully shoves me against the doorframe instead of down the stairs. My throat feels numb, my lungs still able to draw breath, but when I open my mouth no words emerge.

Heath plants Lorus beside the swirling funnel, the force kept in place and in check as he advances toward me.

"Best way to shut down a sorcerer, Miles: shut them the hell up. Wish I'd known about this word earlier. Would've made living with you so much easier." He waves a hand at me. "*Stay.*" A force pulls down on my feet. I'm frozen in place.

Spencer emerges from the stairwell, glancing at me before looking at Heath, the funnel, the circle, the storm, the power glowing with vile energy.

"Huh."

Heath smirks at the Coyote, then at me. "*This* is your protector? A *comedian?*"

"Fuck you, I've learned from a grandmaster magician." Spencer brandishes one of the cards, an ace, the wind whipping his face as he shouts. "*Kaze!*"

In an instant the wind on the roof reverts to a dead calm, save the funnel, which continues to revolve with power. Without missing a beat he brandishes another ace and snaps it through the air, the card falling impotently at Heath's feet. Spencer cries out quickly. "*Tsuchi!*"

In a second the Ra'keth's legs are encased in rough stone. While Heath glances, surprised, at the result, the Coyote throws another ace, the card striking Heath square in the chest as Spencer shouts, "*Ka!*"

A burst of flame envelops Heath in that moment, and I expect to hear screaming, but there's no sound from Heath. Spencer grins, pocketing his cards as the Ra'keth burns. "I learned from Ricky Jay, *bitch.*"

And Heath steps out of the stone, the fire, like it's not even there. "And I learned real magic." He points at Spencer. "*Force.*"

The Coyote is thrown hard into the door and slumps against it, dazed as he feebly reaches for his final cards. Heath doesn't move from his position as Spencer throws another ace. "*Mizu.*" Water explodes at Heath into a rain of razor-sharp ice. Heath holds up his hand, and they all stop dead in the air and slowly turn their blades in the Coyote's direction.

"This is why tricksters shouldn't play sorcerer." Heath smiles. "*Bitch.*"

The ice flies at Spencer, and he weakly pulls his final card, saying, "*Sora,*" just before the shards impact, impaling him again and again, blood seeping from the wounds, an unbelieving stare frozen on his face.

The son of a bitch laughs and waves a hand at me, the magic holding me fading, and beckons me over.

He doesn't cease his laughter even when I point the shear at him, rush at him. Fuck the promise, he dies.

Heath simply waves his hand, and I'm suspended suddenly a foot above the ground.

"Now what were you planning on doing with this, Miles?" He wrenches the shear from me.

"You thought you could beat *me*? The fuckup? The subby bitch I had to take care of? The *mistake*? You think you're going to take *my* throne?" The shear is put cleanly into my thigh, and though I'm still silenced, my body voices its agony well enough.

"What'd you think was going to happen, Miles? You were going to come up here, stop the evil wizard and save the world? This ain't your fucking game or one of those stupid books you read."

Heath punches me, the impact sending me floating back toward the stone wall, Spencer's body still in plain view. "*I'm* the strong one, Miles. And you think you have the balls to kill *me*?" He kicks me, and I slam against the wall, held aloft, pain flooding my body, but I strain to keep focused.

He grits his teeth. "And I'm *still* doing this for you!" Heath points to the funnel. "I'm ending the damned world, Miles. The world that hurt us, that caged us, that fucked us up just because some idiot gods said so. Gods who don't do a damned thing when they see something wrong, who don't give a shit about what happens to a scared kid. Well, fuck 'em." He leans in close. "I'm going to kill them all tonight, Miles. For you and me and everyone out there. I'm going to make a world without gods."

Heath pulls my head against his. "That's why I had to kill him, Miles. You were going to keep them all around, keep everything as it is. I couldn't let that happen." His lips press mine, I struggle, but he doesn't relent. "There's still time, we can still be together. I'm the Ra'keth, I can make that happen. I'm going to fix everything so you and I can be together. How about it?"

I stare hard into his eyes, hate filling my gaze, but he either doesn't notice or doesn't care. So I rear my head back and slam it hard into his face, my forehead stinging as I hear a crunch, his nose breaking. He staggers backward as I smugly grin and spit on his bloodied face.

He murmurs syllables I don't make out, but immediately his nose shifts and resets itself, the blood seeping back into his skin. "So it's going to be like that, huh? Still think you're going to pull this off, that you can win the game? Wanna play wizard?" He lifts his mouth in a one-sided grin. "Fine. How's it go in that book you wouldn't shut up about? Wasn't there a wizard named Goldorf?"

That's Gandalf, you ass.

"He was on a tower once, right?" He waves his hand, and I'm lifted up suddenly, the wall passing underneath, nothing under me now but sixteen hundred feet of air. "How'd that turn out for him?"

Oh fuck.

"What, no help from the audience?"

Oh God, please Heath, don't do this.

"Oh yeah..."

The magic holding me aloft releases.

"He fell."

Chapter Twenty-Eight

If I could offer one piece of advice—as I fall past the eighty-fourth floor of Victory Tower, with the sky above me the swirling eye of a crimson hurricane, the Shear of Atropos stuck in my thigh, my newly acquired sidekick sliced to death by ice, and a man I used to love preparing to end the world—it would be this: Magic is not the answer to your problems.

But right now, it's the only answer I have.

I hold my breath.

The world stops, and strangely so do I, in midair. Above, the sky is ablaze in a sickly green flame, wispy figures caught in the spiral which spins at a terrifying speed. Victory Tower itself is a solid onyx obelisk, no windows, the surface covered in miniscule text that I can't make out. I reach forward to touch it, a cold shock racing up my arm. I gasp, but the world doesn't start up again. On the upside, the silence spell seems to have worn off.

"Fantastic. The world's ending and I'm trapped in hell."

"Beg to differ."

I scream, because I wasn't really expecting a response.

There's a man wearing a black suit, black shirt with a black tie, kind of short. I'm staring at his wing tips because that's where my head is and he's upside down, or I am. Also, because he's not standing on anything. "Oh, I'm sorry. Is this a bad time?" Hades.

I crane my head to confirm his identity. "How'd you know I was—"

"I know everything." One of those wing tips nudges my shoulder, setting me spinning until I come upright, face to face with the god of the underworld. "And as I was saying, this isn't hell, it's Hades, *my* domain. And while we're on the subject, must you constantly be traipsing in and out of here? You're setting a terrible example for the residents."

"Mind telling me why I'm breathing here?"

He shrugs. "My best guess? You have a pair of functional lungs. I'll be nice and not even charge my hourly rate for that."

"No, I mean, I can't just phase out of here. Not that I'd want to, considering..." I motion to the long drop beneath me. "Come to think of it, why aren't I falling here?"

"Again, this is Hades. My domain. One more foolish question and I contact Minos in Billing." The god glances nonchalantly toward the sky. "I should probably panic at that."

"Heath says he wants to make a world without gods."

Hades grumbles, producing a cigarette and lighting it. "Atheism too hard for him?" He offers one, and I wave it off, but he offers again. "That rule only applies to the food and drink of the dead, and I see little point in trying to smoke a pomegranate. It doesn't even apply anymore. Seph had it repealed in the divorce settlement. Besides, it's common to offer a condemned man a last cigarette."

"Condemned?"

He motions to the vacant air below me. "Can't stay here forever, kid. If it's any consolation, it probably won't hurt that much, and given that you'll be hitting the pavement in front of my branch office, it won't take long to collect you." Hades looks to the sky again. "Even during the damned apocalypse my work is never done. But as long as I have you here..."

He produces a paper from his coat pocket. "Last will and testament."

I give my best dubious look. "What, you want me to leave you everything?"

"No, seeing as he had no surviving family, I am required to act as executor for the estate of Cale William Andrew Roberts."

"That was his name?"

"The one he took, yes. You think you're the only sorcerer to ever take a new name?" Hades removes a set of thin horn-rimmed glasses from his shirt pocket and puts them on. "In the matter of..."

"Wait, how could Cale have a will? He wasn't planning on dying."

"Kid, nobody plans on dying, but everyone does. And when they do, they know how they'd like their worldly possessions actually settled. Sometimes it meshes with an existing will, sometimes this is all there is, but everyone has one. In the case of the Recluse, he wanted his personal effects left to his apprentice, which would be you." He presents the will. "Sign, initial and date at the bottom, please."

"I'm about to die, Hades, who cares?" When he glares sternly at me, I grumble in reply. "Give me a pen." I sign, then sign, then sign again, and initial, date and hand it back to him. He produces a stamp from a pocket and presses a symbol into the parchment before rolling it up and tucking it back into his coat. Hades takes out a digital recorder, holding it close to his lips.

"Let it be known that the estate of the Recluse, Cale William Andrew Roberts, Sorcerer King, has been processed, and his heir has accepted his inheritance. Final recommendation is assignment to the Asphodel Fields for a period of no less than five decades and no more than three centuries." He clicks off the recorder and smirks at me. "You'll of course keep that secret. Lawyer/client confidentiality and all." The god takes a long puff on his cigarette. "So you're giving up, then?"

"I don't see a lot of options. Heath dropped me off a building, and I don't really know how to fly."

"Don't you have a screaming diamond?"

I perk a brow. "Huh? What, that a hair metal band?"

Hades rolls his eyes. "A screaming diamond. A relic of a past world that contains the very *essence* of magic. Normally I'd be terrified of a sorcerer having one in this day and age, but I'd much rather have you wielding one than your counterpart." He blinks at my confusion. "The stone the Recluse gave you."

Shit.

He folds his arms. "Don't tell me you left it up there."

I shake my head. "I left it with someone for safekeeping. My friend Dave—"

"The *Impecunious*? You gave a screaming diamond to a *dragon*? Those relics are priceless. Literally. By Styx, kid, what were you trying to get him to do?"

"He was freezing to death, I had to help him somehow."

Hades throws his hands up in frustration. "Fine. Fine! But if it were me, that's a clusterfuck so monumental that I'd look into changing my name. It's like going to a duel and leaving your sword at home." He checks his watch. "And with that I'll be going. I have some important calls to make. Pay the last alimony check to the ex. Maybe check on the kid. If you ever need my legal services, just let me know." He flashes a winning smile. "See you in a few minutes."

Hades winks at me and walks into the onyx tower.

"Dick."

And then the world returns, the fall resumes.

Wind shears at my face, the ground getting bigger every second. This is it. No time for a shaken fist at the sky and swearing revenge. So much for never falling. Hades is right, I should change my name.

Wait...

If I can change the name of a parking meter to the name of a tray of edible biscuits, why not change *my* name? From that of a human to a...

Fuck, the ground's getting closer.

No! Focus. Change the name to what? I don't know the name of the Lord of the Eagles. Hell, I don't even know the name of...

Dragons.

Jutte told me the name of dragons. And there's a chance Heath hasn't changed it yet.

Now or never.

I yank the shear clean from my leg, pouring my panicked will and my memories of facing down the signature challenge of Dungeons & Dragons to fuel the working.

A bright flash of light... I scream, the sound growing in volume and intensity until the light fades and instinct flexes muscles I'm not really aware of. The wind slams against me, and I lean back, or try to, the angle of my descent lessening as my speed remains constant.

I aim myself down Tolon Avenue as the street grows closer, the snow-covered cars looming in my sight, my vision sharpened to the point of disorientation. As impact approaches, I curl into the fetal position and shut my eyes. I roll as I hit the ground, hear crashing and crunching sounds, all of it unbearably loud, but oddly, I don't feel any pain.

When I finally come to a stop, I uncurl myself to view the trail of destruction, a long path of wrecked cars, impacted pavement, knocked-over streetlamps and stoplights, and a sideswiped Starbucks that won't be making four-dollar brownies anytime soon.

"Fuck." Holy shit, was that me? That's a voice I'd half-expect to be demanding tribute in the form of gold coins or firstborn children.

Inspection of myself (with a now extra-long and disturbingly flexible neck) reveals thick milky-hued scaly plates covering my body, which is now quadrupedal, though I can handle that. It's easy to think of the front legs as arms. The wings and the tail however...

Okay. Okay. I need to get back to the tower. I have to avenge Cale, Spencer, everyone who's died tonight, stop Heath from destroying everything, I need to...

I need to fly. This body has some sort of instinct to it, so I might as well try to use it. I stomp and clomp my way down Tolon Avenue, wincing when I feel myself brush against yet another car and likely totaling it. I get enough distance to face the wind and let whatever strange new muscles there are in my back do their job.

The wind rushes under me, my body feeling lighter. With a bit of faith, I jump into the air, let my wings continue beating...

Shit!

Well, uh...if I succeed tonight, that department store will be good as new in the next world. If not...

"All right, listen up, body. We're going to need to work together, and you likely know more about flying than I do, so how about I worry about Heath and leave the flying to you?" I'm sure I look ridiculous, a listed fifteen hit-die creature that skews toward the chaotic-evil end of the alignment table talking to himself in front of a Bloomingdale's that's now ripe for a demo crew.

Once again, I let my wings start beating, and slowly but surely (and rather awkwardly) I lift off the ground. As I gain altitude, I tilt this way and that to keep between the buildings. To think Salondine was able to fly through the urban canyons so expertly, while I'm wobbling like a toddler just trying to climb upward.

Once I'm clear of the shorter buildings, I instinctually turn into the wind currents to aid my ascent, my flight a bit more confident as I circle Victory Tower, gaining altitude with every pass. After what seems like forever, I'm finally high enough to see the summit.

The circle is intact, Heath standing within, holding Lorus high above his head, his body sheathed in a fierce blue glow, the eye of the storm splitting open to a void from which terrible sounds emerge.

I fly toward the circle.

I fly toward the end of the world.

Chapter Twenty-Nine

Heath looks surprised to see me return, considering he dropped me off Victory Tower, and in a fashion befitting an evil wizard assumed everything went according to plan, even getting in a Gandalf dig at me. After all, it's not like I actually know the Lord of the Eagles.

Though he's probably more surprised that I'm a dragon.

My claws dig deep into the stone floor, making large furrows while I skid to a stop. It's not the most graceful landing, but considering I don't topple over the side, I'll call it a win.

A sudden vibration starts through the building, and in the distance I can hear what sounds like glass shattering, steel groaning in the night as the cracks spread through the sky, the air filling with the maddening screams coming through the opening void. The Ra'keth smirks in my direction and points Lorus at me.

I leap toward him, releasing the draconic form and retaking my name, retaking the name *James Black* as Heath speaks a single word in Sigil.

"*Crush.*"

In a flash of light, I feel his magic coalesce above my head, the air compressed with massive and sudden severity, the sound not unlike thunder.

The word escapes his lips as I collide with him, tackling him to the floor. His elbow catches me in the face as I brandish the shear. I summon everything I have, every memory, every strike, every lie he told and that I had to tell for him, every time I felt helpless, worthless. I owe him pain.

I am settling debts.

Heath kicks me off him and gets up, flourishing his blade. We circle each other even as darkness begins to spill down from the hole in the sky. "What do you think you're going to do, Miles?"

There are tears, but fuck it, I let them flow. "You killed my friend. You killed the man I loved. Now I'm going to kill you."

And he laughs. "And why do you think you can do that? 'Cause you're the Lightning Rod?" The sorcerer scoffs and punches Lorus at the air between us, a wave of flame erupting and rushing toward me.

Calmly, I wave my shear, my Sigil, the word coming as if Cale were whispering it in my ear. A frozen wall appears, melting quickly but bearing the brunt of the attack, naught but cinders reaching me. "No, Heath, because I am no longer afraid of you."

Heath staggers back. "You shouldn't have been able to... How did you..." He grits his teeth. "*Silence.*"

I hold Sigil in front of me. Cale's words in my mind again. "*Deny.*"

The words come quickly, and I can't help but grin a Cheshire smile, gesturing to the remains of my frozen wall. "Did you enjoy that, Heath? That was but a syllable." I glance at Sigil, the frozen metal crackling in my grasp. "Ice can be a wonderful teaching tool..." My will funnels through the shear, the focus magnifying it into a sharp cone of cryonic energy. "Would you care for a lesson?"

The spell releases, the air freezing as it races toward Heath, the Ra'keth calling a fierce retort, dark water surging into the oncoming wave, sapping it of its energy, leaving shards of ebon ice littering the floor between us.

Heath swiftly plants Lorus in the stone, green sparks splashing from the impact before the air starts shimmering between us. "Why are you fighting for them, Miles? Gods are servants, nothing but tools. We made them in *our* image, and now we're expected to bow and scrape? You want that?"

I walk to the shimmering air, tap it with Sigil, the shear bouncing back with the same speed it hit. "A wall of force..." I smirk at Heath. "These commonly can't be dispelled, you know. A wise choice, for a beginner."

"What the hell are you talking about?"

I wave Sigil at the wall. "My character was trapped in one of these once, evil wizard taunting on the other side. But my guy had an ace up his sleeve. He would've died if I hadn't been so lucky with the dice. I remember everything about it, a spell called..."

I recall the name of the world, rein it in with my will and funnel its power into the working. Victory Tower shakes violently as I gather the magic in the area, shape it...

"*Disjunction.*"

And kill it.

The spark within me, my magic, flickers out with the shimmering wall, the sword, Lorus, rusting into the stone. Heath's eyes are wide as I walk to him, ball up my fist and solidly connect with his face. My knuckles sting, my fingers ache, but it's the greatest feeling of my life.

The surprise is short-lived, though. Heath has always been stronger than me.

I'm tackled to the floor, shielding my face from his blows while he screams at me. "What did you do? I can't *control* it now!" His hands start to close around my throat, but I knee him hard in the groin and roll away as the roof rattles hard, the circle cracking in the floor which is starting to angle down.

"Maybe Dungeons & Dragons is just some geek shit, Heath, but at least it gives me a better paradigm to work in than your fucked-up daddy issues. I obliterated all the magic in this area. All circles, all enchantments, all magic items, all spells. Gone. Cast a ninth-level spell and you get your money's worth." Wincing, I falter back a few steps both from the sudden tilt of the building and the wound in my leg that is still spilling blood into the snow.

Up above the storm has returned to its previous violence, the arm of darkness thrashing, spilling over the walls and creeping down the sides of the tower. This has to stop, or there's not going to be a world to save. We can't continue this dance forever; it has to end.

I have to kill him.

I raise the shear, Sigil alighting with silver flame. Heath stares at the argent light.

He smirks. "Thought you could bluff me, huh?" Heath snaps his fingers at the sword. "*Lorus, to me.*"

But the blade remains in place.

"The sword's still in the stone. Looks like someone doesn't get to be King of the Britons." I limp toward him, careful to keep my footing. "And I did kill all of the magic items on the roof, Heath." My grin grows wide. "But this is an *artifact.*"

"You're right, Miles, it is. I'm the one who stole it, who broke it, which would make it...*my* artifact." He doesn't lose his smile. "*Shear of Atropos, to me!*" The blade jumps from my hand and flies to his, the edge now burning with a blue-green flame.

Fuck, fuck, fuckity fuck. I hadn't thought of that.

"Seriously, Miles?" He advances toward me, I stagger back.

"My name's not Miles. Miles Canmore is dead, we *both* killed him." The building is starting to tip. "Damn it, Heath, if you're going to end the world just fucking do it before you kill us both. Before you kill *everyone!*"

But he doesn't stop. He's not going to, not until I'm dead, stabbed to death with his artifact...

He draws near, able to cover the distance while I try to limp away.

But is it truly his?

Heath raises the blade like the killer in a slasher movie.

Heath took the Shear of Atropos, but it's not *his* artifact...

He lunges.

The night I left him, I took it from him. And it's not the Shear of Atropos anymore.

It's mine. And neither I nor it will respond to his call ever again.

"*Sigil, to me!*" The scissor leaps from his grasp, into my hand.

Heath knocks me onto my back, my hand pressed against his chest as we go down, both of us sliding to the wall now as the angle of the building has grown too steep. I pull my hand away from Heath, the skin soaked red.

The handle of the shear sticks out from between his ribs.

I really just...

My God, what have I done?

Heath looks down at me, shock in his eyes, tears welling up as he sees the shear and reality hits him. "You... You... I... What..."

I roll him onto his back, see the blood stain his clothes. He tries to summon his magic, whisper the words that will heal him, but he coughs up blood instead. I really did it. Heath is going to die. Because of me.

His hand reaches upward, and I take it, squeezing it gently. "Why are you..." Heath coughs hard again, and I tilt his head forward, let the blood dribble out.

"Because no one should have to die alone." I exhale and look down at him. "I'm glad you're dying. I guess it makes me not all that enlightened, but I'm glad you're dying, Heath. I'll stay with you to the end, but I'm going to be honest with you: I'm happy. I'm free of you now. There won't be another night where I get nervous in a dark room, or walk away from the sight of a white jacket. I won't ever wonder if leaving you was a mistake. It's over."

His hand tightly grips mine, and he strains to get closer to me. "You're nothing...nothing but mistakes." He coughs again, blood spattering into the snow. "You will not forget me."

"You're right, Heath. I won't forget you..." I lean in close to meet his eyes. "But I will not remember you." He shivers, the blood loss and the temperature helping him into the final seconds.

"You..." He hacks weakly, the blood flow slowing from his mouth. "Won't make it..." He's trembling now, his body giving out, once so filled with magic but starving without blood. "You need..."

"You?" I smile softly. "There is no you, Heath."

Heath trembles, a slow, croaking exhale leaking from his mouth. I close his eyes for the last time.

The Ra'keth dies, and the world goes dark.

"There is only me."

Chapter Thirty

"The king is dead…"

When I look up, Hades is standing over me, his face placid. "Long live the king."

"Some king I turned out to be." I motion to the endless black that surrounds us. "Couldn't even save the world."

"Sorcerers don't save the world, kid, they end it. And that's what this is, the end of a world." He kneels down by Heath and pulls the shear from his chest, blood dripping off the blade and pooling slowly. "A new world sang from heart's blood. Haven't seen one of those in ages."

"How are you here? Where is this, what is this?"

Hades still carries the shear and walks through the black, which seems ankle-deep. "This is a dead world, James." He points off into the abyss. "You can't see it, but there are billions of lives hanging in the balance right now, and trillions of souls…"

The god of the underworld takes out a cigarette and then pats down his coat a moment. He leans toward me. "Would you mind?"

The word comes so quickly, so easily. "*Fire.*" An orb of silver flame appears in the palm of my hand, and he lights his cigarette on it, taking a puff. "How did I do that?"

"Simple. You're the Lightning Rod, Slayer of the Frozen River, James Black of the Argent City, our Sorcerer King." Into the air he blows smoke which quickly vanishes. "Now I owe a Ra'keth. Splendid. And how am I here?" He points to Heath. "No matter how long the reign, I collect the Ra'keth."

"You didn't really answer my question. I killed all the magic so I could…" I motion to Heath.

Hades shakes his head with a chuckle. "Don't get it yet, do you? You are the Ra'keth, your will is law. What happened to the magic, you ask?" His finger points at me.

"What?"

"Right now, kid, you are magic. How else could a human being end a world and start a new one? And we should probably get on that." He bows slightly and flashes his million-dollar smile. "I'd be happy to write up the paperwork, of course. I'd rather not be here too long. This is a depressing place, and I've created plenty of depressing places."

"So what do I do?"

"Creating a new world... It's like making a Xerox of the old one. Generally, it's the exact same as the old one, but...different. Lesser. The world has to be diminished in some way, something has to be taken out of it that can never be again. Just the way it works, kid."

"The Usurper's Decree." I look toward Heath's body. "The law that Ra'keth have to be murdered to be dethroned, I want to get rid of that."

Hades sighs dismissively. "Doesn't work like that. Decrees are decrees, you can't just—"

I stand, the spark within me now a silver inferno. "I'm sorry, are *you* the Ra'keth? Decrees are laws, and when a law doesn't work, you repeal it. I am hereby repealing that law. If the Usurper doesn't like it he can drag his homicidal ass out of the abyss and discuss it with me." I pause for effect, even glance around at the surroundings. "Huh. I guess he's not coming." I stare at the god of the underworld. "Write it up."

Hades smirks, and with a curt nod produces a legal pad from inside his coat. "Okay, we'll see if it sticks. You know, that law isn't the reason that..." The god catches my stern gaze. "It isn't the reason that Cale is dead, and quit glaring at me, kid, I've faced down Titans. The throne changed hands twice in one night, that's three Ra'keth in one city."

"Fine, there can only be one then." If anything, it'll keep competing sorcerers out of the City for a while so I can figure this all out. Hades perks a brow, but writes it all down.

"Anything else? I'd be happy to make suggestions."

"You said it yourself, I'm a human being. I'll just stick with what I've got concerning the Keth. I'm hardly the person to make decisions about gods or the rest of humanity."

This gets Hades's attention. "You're not diminishing the gods? Or..." He drags a finger across his throat. "Dismissing us?"

"Why would I do that?"

"Heath was going to." He smiles, stopping me before I can respond. "But then, you're not Heath."

"How'd you know I was going to say—"

"I know everything."

A few seconds pass in the dark before I ask. "Hades? In the new world, could Cale be there? Or Spencer?"

The god shrugs, flicking his spent cigarette into the void. "I don't even see how you could bring the Coyote back to life. And Cale... Sorry, kid. That's something even sorcerers can't do anymore."

"I'm never going to feel this way about anyone again."

"You're right."

I stare at him in disbelief.

"What, James, you wanted sympathy? Maybe a pat on the shoulder? You're right. You will never feel that way about anyone again. Ever. Instead, you'll feel something else, and I'll lay even money it'll feel just as good."

The god waves his legal pad at the abyss. "Now, are we going to do this or not?"

The pool of blood, Heath's blood, is barely visible now. "How do you sing up a world?"

"You're the Ra'keth. Just sing, I don't know, something that has meaning to you." He grins. "And failing that, I can make a few suggestions."

"I am *not* singing Styx. The new world is not going to be crafted from the chorus of 'Come Sail Away'."

Hades snorts. "Doesn't *have* to be that. 'Show Me the Way' is good too."

I close my eyes. Singing has never been my thing. I'm not on key, and puberty really did a number on me. My voice still cracks occasionally when I try to warble a few bars in the shower. But for Cale, I'll try.

I go through a verse of "Feeling Good".

Can't go wrong with Nina Simone.

I find myself flat on my ass on a snowy rooftop, my leg screaming in pain, my body aching and tired and cold. A tall antenna towers above me, the air a bit thin to breathe. In the sky the clouds are breaking up, giving way to a fuzzy field of stars and a gibbous moon.

Welcome to the new world.

I tear my coat, wrapping it tightly around my leg wound and hobble toward the mound of snow where I know I'll find Spencer's body. I begin the process of clearing away the snow, using my hands instead of magic, considering magic's what killed him.

"God, I'm sorry, Spence, I'm so sorry." I take a deep breath, my fingers starting to go numb. I could work a spell, but I don't want to feel warm and loved and safe right now. This right here, digging out the body, this is the price of becoming the Ra'keth.

The snow continues to be cleared away until I hit something hard. "Oh God, he froze solid..." I dig farther in, picking with my fingers, punching at the ice that coats him, the ice that killed him, the form beneath dark. Shit, shit, shit...

"God damn it, why did you try to take him on alone? Damn it, why?" In my anger, I smash the ice with the point of the shear, the ice suddenly cracking and falling away like shattered glass, revealing the...

The log under the ice.

The log...

The log?

I gape a few seconds. "...the fuck?"

Held against the wood I find, still impaled on a shard of ice, a playing card. The joker.

Wait a minute...

"That son of a bitch." I stand up, my weight on my good leg and turn to find the Coyote standing there.

"You know, if you hadn't killed that guy I would've pulled an Emerald in the Snow. I mean, you figured it out, but he fell for it and…"

He's brought to silence when I hug him. "I am going to kick your ass."

Spencer leans away after a second. "Hey, none of that. I'm just sorry I was out for most of it. I mean, one second the tower's about to fall and the next…" He takes in the clearing sky, the surrounding buildings where the power is coming back on. "Well, if *Star Trek* is anything to go by, that's a clear sign of victory. Everything's always okay when the lights come back." The Coyote looks back at me. "You wanna get out of here?"

"Absolutely. Hospital would be nice."

Spencer puts my arm around his shoulder to help me down the stairs, and I slip the shear in my pocket. "Could we have one night where you're not getting patched up by the end of it?"

"No argument from me." I take the steps slow and easy.

"So…you mean what you said?"

I glance at him before we take another stair. "About what?"

"When you thought I was dead—"

I interject. "And I called you a son of a bitch?"

"No, you said Heath killed your friend. I'm your friend?"

I sigh, then grumble, which only draws a chuckle from him.

"I see you're not refuting it. I gotta admit I'm going to get a hell of a lot of good stories hanging around you, and if there's one thing a bard needs, it's stories."

We make it to the observation deck, where the lights are on and some heat is getting pumped through the vents. "Bard? You're calling yourself a bard? And you ride *my* ass for being a geek?"

Spencer laughs. "I haven't ridden your ass for being a geek. Believe me, you'd remember if I rode—"

"*Silence.*" I grin at him a few seconds while he tries to speak and then flashes a famous hand gesture at me. I wave my hand to dismiss the spell. "Going to have to dog-ear that one."

"Asshole. And you wonder why sorcerers are hated."

We finish crossing the floor to the bank of elevators, and I reach for the panel to summon the next car, but the up arrow is already lit. Someone's on their way, and since the power's back on, I would have to guess that the security cameras are working just fine now.

Despite being the newly crowned Ra'keth, I'm not feeling so hot, physically or magically. Besides, I don't want to blast some security guard who's only doing his job.

The doors slide open to reveal my brother, his eyes tired, face haggard, like he's been working nonstop. It doesn't surprise me that he'd throw himself into a crisis. He quickly brings up his gun, training it on me. "Police! Freeze!"

I nod quickly. "Okay. No problem."

I show my hands in a slow and nonthreatening fashion. Thom eyes me a moment. "Jesus, James? What are you doing up here?" His tone suggests he's not all that happy to see me. Considering there's no wedding band on his finger, I'm pretty sure he figured out what was going on with Beth.

I have no idea what to say. Spencer bumps into me gently and raises his hands as well, like he's done this before.

"Officer? Could you put your gun down, please? He's fragile enough as it is right now. His boyfriend died earlier, his abusive ex-boyfriend came back around to smack him... I don't even know how he got up here, I practically had to break in and..." He looks at me, his face apologetic, then at Thom, his expression getting caring, sincere, responsible. "He came up here to..." The Coyote motions with his eyes to the door leading back to the roof.

Thom's jaw drops slightly.

Wait a minute, if Spencer is implying that I was going to—

"You thinking about jumping, James?" Thom stares at me in shock.

"I…"

Spencer steps in before I can tell my brother that no, I'm not suicidal. "I know how bad it seems. Both of us are looking at trespassing, B&E, maybe some property damage but, Officer, you gotta consider the circumstances. I mean, I couldn't let my friend just…end it." Spencer looks at me. "It's not that bad. It's really shit now, I get it, but we're going to get through it, remember? That's why you came down the stairs. It's a brand-new day, brand-new world, right?" He nods gently at me. "Right?"

I glance at Thom, at Spence. Damn it, he's right. I don't see any other way out of this. We are likely getting arrested here, no matter how civil it is, and unless I want to work magic on my brother, which I don't, I have to face the music. I just wish that the way out was something better than my brother thinking I want to end it all. It hasn't even crossed my mind, really. Cale wouldn't want that. He'd want me to live.

"Right." I offer my wrists to my brother. "Will you help me, Thom?"

He nods in reply, and Spencer and I are taken into custody. It's a depressing start, but as the elevator doors close, one thought slips into my head that draws a smile: Holy shit, I saved the world.

Chapter Thirty-One

In the end, I guess James Black gets to be a real person, at least in the eyes of the Unified City Police Department. I'm booked, photographed, printed and made to sit on a hard wooden bench that's impossible to sleep on while I wait for the more violent criminals to be attended to. At least my leg got looked at and wrapped in bandages at the station. I was told several times by the EMT that I'd been "awful lucky" the stabbing hadn't nicked anything important. Normally I'd be taken to a hospital but given the storm...

Trespassing, something about damage to private property, mostly misdemeanors. There's no room in the holding cell, as that's packed with the looters who could be rounded up.

Also, despite the hustle and bustle of the almost-apocalypse's aftermath, it's still really fucking boring.

Around seven in the morning I'm nudged awake by Thom, who still looks tired as he undoes my cuffs.

"I can go?"

Thom shakes his head, "Your lawyer's here."

Huh? What the hell is he talking about? I don't have a—

"Mr. Black." Hades is standing in front of me, complete with tailored suit, power tie, and a briefcase that looks to cost more than two months of Thom's pay. "So glad to see you haven't been mistreated."

"How'd you know I was—"

"I know everything." He helps me to my feet and glances at Thom. "Might I be directed somewhere I can confer with my client?"

My brother grumbles but motions to a currently empty office. "You've got five minutes."

With that, I'm led into a rather cramped space filled with file cabinets and a desk and little room to move, and instructed to take a seat while Hades sits behind the desk.

"Okay, enough bullshit, why do they think you're my lawyer?"

"You remember a few months ago when you blasted Atropos in the face with lightning in *my* realm? The day you became the Lightning Rod?"

"Yeah, that's not an easy thing to forget. What about it?"

"Remember afterward when you sat on the Blue Line feeling sorry for yourself despite my excellent advice?"

I blink. "I remember you being a dick about it, if that's what you're saying. You gave me a quarter and told me to call someone who gave a shit."

The god flashes a winning smile. "And I told you if you ever needed legal assistance, to just let me know." He produces a quarter from his vest pocket. "And you said sure. And then you gave me this as a retainer for my services."

"I threw the quarter at you out of spite."

He shrugs. "To-may-to, to-mah-to. Luckily, attorney-client privilege prevents me from revealing what might have allegedly been your intent when you paid me the retainer. In the meantime, I remain your legal counsel and have since arranged a plea deal to walk you out of here."

"You're kidding. I broke into an office building and practically destroyed the roof, not to mention how much I fucked up Tolon Avenue, and I get to walk out of here?"

The god smiles. "You nearly destroyed the building in the old world. The Victory Tower in this new world is perfectly fine, as is everything else. You're not getting off scot-free though. The building's owner wants to make an example of you. Community service, two hundred hours."

I blink. "For *trespassing*?"

"There are many companies in that building, Mr. Black, that don't take kindly to the access you can gain. In order to quell their concerns, I offered the deal, and the work you will be doing."

Leaning back in the chair, I mutter under my breath for a moment. "And what kind of work would that be?"

"One of my employees was killed recently. Kerry, you met her. It will take time to find a suitable replacement." He removes a cigarette from his jacket pocket and lights it. "In the meantime, you will perform her duties."

"What, chauffeuring you?"

He exhales a plume of smoke in my face. "Collecting the souls of the dead."

I roll my eyes. "Fuck that."

Hades isn't fazed. "It's that, or the various organizations in that building considering you an enemy. I might add your reign is fairly new, and your predecessor's didn't last long either, and these are *not* people you want to antagonize, Mr. Black. That's not a threat, just a statement of fact. The work is simple, and you will only be called on when you are truly needed, and it's not forever. Just two hundred hours, that's all. Five weeks worth of work, and you're square."

I level my gaze on him. "You owe me, you admitted that."

He matches it with equal intensity. "If you cash in that favor *now*, even though I cannot see a Ra'keth's destiny, I am certain you will regret it for the rest of your life." He stubs out the cigarette on the desk blotter. "Take the deal."

I narrow my eyes at him. "Before I answer, one question."

"Hm?" He sits back in his chair, slightly amused, arms folded, expectant.

"You own the building, don't you?"

To that, I get a million-dollar smile. "I *am* the god of wealth as well."

"So you set this all up so I'd have no choice but to work for you."

"For two hundred hours."

"Or burn my favor and get us even."

He smirks. "Indeed."

Dick.

I extend my left hand. "Fine. Deal."

Hades chuckles. "A handshake." He clasps his hand with mine. "How quaint."

A surge goes up my left arm, my wrist coloring in strange Sigil that I can't make out. My left hand feels numb, but my fingers still respond to my commands, make a fist.

"So glad that's all done and over with."

"What the hell did you do to me?" I inspect the Sigil, but I can't quite pronounce the words.

"Just the terms of your plea deal, that's all." Hades gets up from the chair and opens the door for me as the numbness fades from my hand. "This way, please."

When I exit the office, the hustle and bustle is still there, but the police are gone. There seems an endless array of desks, computers of varying ages, the clatter of typewriters in the distance, everyone moving to and fro, this way and that, but no voices, no talking.

"Where are we?"

Hades shrugs slightly. "Just making a quick stop before you're processed and released." I'm led through the maze of desks and cubicles, every person I pass engrossed in their work, filling out forms and requests and entering data from tapes, compact discs, sheaves of paper and even rolls of parchment.

"What is this, Hades?" I poke one of the workers, but she doesn't seem to notice me at all, continuing to transcribe a recording of some unidentifiable language.

"Welcome to the Asphodel Fields, kid. Get a lot of assignments here these days, and since I couldn't have them all picking flowers for eternity, I put them to work." We continue on through the bureaucracy, Hades playing tour guide. "Humans aren't the only things that die, you see. Death happens all over the world, and it's my job to process it. Granted, when I started this place, there weren't literally billions of you stomping about, so I have to delegate a bit now, work with the other regions, network, all that. Still requires an enormous amount of paperwork though." He claps a few of the drones on the shoulders. "So I figured, why not use them for it? Better than having them wander about in a haze."

"But why am I here?"

He cups a hand over his ear. "What?"

I get close to him and speak up. "Why am I here?"

"Oh, I figured after the night you've had..." We reach a wall, and he pushes gently on it, a door opening to a dimly lit hallway with an array of doors on either side, a caged light bulb above each door. He stops in front of one where the light is lit and knocks on it. "I thought you could use a conjugal visit."

I blink at him. "Huh? I hardly even spent the night in jail. I wasn't even technically in jail, just handcuffed to a bench. How would I get a conjugal visit?"

The god grins slightly. "It's not *your* conjugal visit."

Oh my God.

He pushes open the door. "Once a season, on the solstices and equinoxes. That's four a year." I can see a man inside the room. I start to enter, and Hades bars my way.

"We even, kid?"

I nod quickly. "Yes, yes, we're even."

He flashes his winning smile and pulls his arm away. "You get one hour."

The god steps aside, and I gingerly walk into the room, the lights coming up to reveal a small room with cheap carpeting, two old-looking high-back chairs and a bed tucked in the corner.

The man looks at me in shock. "Are you...did you... Are you dead?"

I shake my head quickly, my eyes brimming with tears.

"Then how are you—"

I keep my face dry a moment longer, breath sputtering as I try to smile. "It doesn't matter."

I'm in his arms a second later, the tears flowing freely now. He pulls away long enough to meet my eyes, his like Destry Bay after a storm. His smile is calming, hopeful. "Hello, Apprentice."

I return the smile and tighten my embrace. "Hey, Cheshire cat."

About the Author

Writer, Scorpio, and self-professed waffle addict, Vaughn R. Demont received his Bachelor of Arts from Oswego State University, and his Master of Fine Arts from Goddard College, where he studied creative writing and being poor. He has published several works, including *House of Stone*, *Coyote's Creed*, and *Lightning Rod*.

Find Vaughn at:

Homepage: www.vaughndemont.com

Facebook: www.facebook.com/VaughnRDemont

Twitter: @vaughndemont

E-mail: vaughndemont@yahoo.com

Always have an ace up your sleeve.

Coyote's Creed
© *2011 Vaughn R. Demont*
Broken Mirrors, Book 1

If con games were taught in high school, Spencer Crain would be on the honor roll. As it is, he'll be riding the edge of failure to graduation next month. Then Spence gets the news that his long-gone father is not only dead, but was a Coyote, one of three clans of tricksters in the City.

With a near-catatonic mother on his hands, Spence couldn't care less about the Coyotes' ongoing feud with the Phouka and the Kitsune—until it lands on his doorstep. Suddenly he's thrown headfirst into a dangerous world he knows next-to-nothing about. His only guide is Rourke, dashing King of the Phouka, plus a growing pack of half-siblings, a god, and Fate herself.

As Spence embarks on a journey to learn the Coyote's creed, the truth about his heritage, and how to handle his growing attraction to Rourke, he wonders when his life turned from TV sitcom to real-life danger zone. And what price must he pay to survive the next roll of the dice...

Warning: Contains PG-13 rated violence, R-rated language and X-rated hotel scenes. Meta-humor, pop-culture humor, utter disregard for the 4th wall abound.

Available now in ebook and print from Samhain Publishing.

The faeries at the bottom of the garden are coming back—with an army.

Bomber's Moon
© *2012 Alex Beecroft*
Under the Hill, Book 1

When Ben Chaudhry is attacked in his own home by elves, they disappear as quickly as they came. He reaches for the phone book, but what kind of exterminator gets rid of the Fae? Maybe the Paranormal Defense Agency will ride to his rescue.

Sadly, they turn out to be another rare breed: a bunch of UFO hunters led by Chris Gatrell, who—while distractingly hot—was forcibly retired from the RAF on grounds of insanity.

Shot down in WWII—and shot forward seventy years in time, stranded far from his wartime sweetheart—Chris has been a victim of the elves himself. He fears they could destroy Ben's life as thoroughly as they destroyed his. Chris is more than willing to protect Ben with his body. He never bargained for his heart getting involved.

Just when they think there's a chance to build a life together, a ghostly voice from Chris's past warns that the danger is greater than they can imagine. And it may take more than a team of rank amateurs to keep Ben—and the world—out of the elf queen's snatching hands...

Warning: Brace yourself for mystery, suspense, sexual tension, elves in space and a nail-biting cliffhanger ending.

Available now in ebook and print from Samhain Publishing.

It's all about the story...

Romance

HORROR

www.samhainpublishing.com

CPSIA information can be obtained at www.ICGtesting.com
Printed in the USA
LVOW12s0303261113

362850LV00003B/119/P